Remembered Dreams

Remembered Dreams

EMMA DALLY

LITTLE, BROWN AND COMPANY

A *Little, Brown* Book

First published in Great Britain in 1999
by Little, Brown and Company

A CIP catalogue record for this book
is available from the British Library.

ISBN 0 316 64832 9

Typeset by Palimpsest Book Production Limited,
Polmont, Stirlingshire
Printed and bound in Great Britain by
Creative Print and Design, Ebbw Vale, Wales

Little, Brown and Company (UK)
Brettenham House
Lancaster Place
London WC2E 7EN

For my mother,
who passed on to me
her love of history and family stories

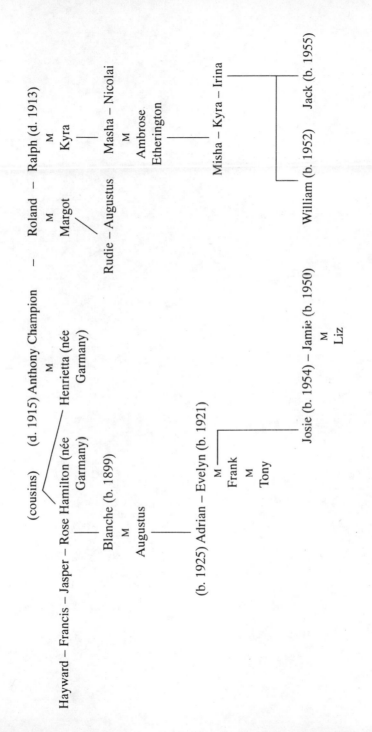

(cousins)   (d. 1915) Anthony Champion   —   Roland   —   Ralph (d. 1913)
                                              M   M
Hayward – Francis – Jasper – Rose Hamilton (née   Henrietta (née   Margot   Kyra
                                      Garmany)   Garmany)
                                                                                    Rudie – Augustus   Masha – Nicolai
                          Blanche (b. 1899)   M
                                      M   Ambrose
                                Augustus   Etherington

(b. 1925) Adrian – Evelyn (b. 1921)   Misha – Kyra – Irina

                          M
                        Frank
                          M
                        Tony   Josie (b. 1954) – Jamie (b. 1950)   William (b. 1952)   Jack (b. 1955)
                                                                      M
                                                                    Liz

JOSIE

CHAPTER 1

London, 1990

The house was quiet. The letters on the doormat made the front door difficult to open as Josie pushed her way into the dark hall. There was a chill in the air as she switched on the light and leaned down to pick up the envelopes from the floor. Most of them were bills. One was a letter from a mail order company informing her mother that the cardigan she had ordered was temporarily out of stock but would be posted to her within the month. Her account, the letter added helpfully, would not be debited until the order was fulfilled.

Josie made a mental note to write to the catalogue company telling them not to bother now. The cardigan was no longer needed.

So much has to be done when someone dies. Letters to be written to the bank, the building societies, and all the shops where her mother had accounts. Josie still felt as if she were in a dream, as if her mother was alive and merely away on holiday somewhere, about to return next week. She had to keep telling herself that she was never going to see her mother again, never talk to her, never hug her or touch her. Her mother had gone.

At the same time, it was a relief, after those draining days at the hospice, watching the life slip away from her. No more visiting. No more of the frightened expressions or the panic about dying. No more worrying, no more anxious ringing up of the hospice first thing in the morning, expecting to be told that she had died in the night. Her poor mother. It was a sad end to what essentially had been a sad life.

The period between her mother's death and the funeral still seemed surreal. Josie had been aware of behaving as normal but feeling blanketed by some close film of quiet shock.

She had taken a couple of days off work to sort out the essentials – collecting her mother's belongings from the hospice, picking up the death certificate from the doctor and registering the death at the register office. She had felt dazed as she answered all the questions asked by the registrar to confirm that the deceased was indeed the person she was supposed to be – her maiden name, her two married names, her divorced status, then widowhood, her age, her address at the time of death. As Josie spoke the words, giving the information, she was aware of how these private details of her mother were becoming part of the public domain. It was the law, it was for history. This death certificate joined her mother's birth certificate in the vast archive of the history of the British people for any stranger to look up. She felt for a moment that she was losing her mother twice over. She no longer belonged to her. But then, over the years, she had actually lost her mother many more times than that.

The funeral had been a horrible event, a sombre cremation in East Finchley, attended by Jamie and Liz but not their children, the grandchildren. (Liz thought it would upset them.) Andy's mother, Helen, had turned up, which was considerate. Josie had been touched by this gesture from the woman she once thought would be her mother-in-law.

Helen had been fond of Josie, and of Evelyn. She had visited Evelyn several times during those bleak last weeks in the hospice. Whenever they met in the corridor, Helen had looked concerned and kind. Josie was pleased to see her but she did not make a pretence of being interested in Andy. She did not bother to ask how he was, and in return Helen kept a tactful silence about her son. It seemed that she had at last accepted that the relationship was truly over. But apart from that small group at the funeral there was nobody else, except the undertaker. Tony was dead and her mother had no other friends to say goodbye.

Now it was over, Josie had collected the ashes and scattered them over Hampstead Heath as her mother had stipulated in the will. She had been surprised by how heavy the ashes were and then surprised by her surprise that her mother could be reduced to two pounds of grey ash and bone, and still seem heavy.

There had been an upsetting moment on the Heath when a large dog, a cheerful panting black labrador, had run over to her as she scattered the ashes over the ground, and begun to gobble them up. Josie had to throw a stone and shout at it before it loped off, licking its chops as it headed in the direction of Parliament Hill.

Now Josie had to sort out the house. The real work was just beginning.

She was early. She had arranged to meet Jamie there at seven o'clock but she wanted to have a bit of time by herself before he arrived. She hoped that he would not bring Liz; with any luck she would be putting the children to bed.

She shivered. The house was cold, and there was a mildewy smell in the air. Josie wandered around through the musty rooms, thinking of what had gone on there, imagining her mother slumped in the chair in the sitting-room, her nose stuck in a book, as it always was as she escaped from the world, or just sitting in the rocking-chair, rocking backwards and forwards, staring, staring at the wall, at the packed and warped shelves of books.

In spite of its mustiness the place was clean and tidy because Debby, the cleaner, had come in earlier in the week. The kitchen surfaces were clean and the furniture dusted and neatly arranged.

Josie began to walk through the rooms of the house, trying to see the place through the eyes of a prospective buyer. It was in a good position, of course, in Dartmouth Park, close to Parliament Hill, a Victorian terraced house built in the mid-1800s. It had a pleasant garden, even if it was overgrown. The place had been painted and decorated throughout when Evelyn first moved in in the 1960s (organised by Josie's grandmother, of course, because Evelyn had been incapable of doing such things), but nothing had been done since, apart from the occasional patching up of wallpaper and the repair of a leaking roof. Tony had done a bit of DIY but it was not really one of his great strengths.

Josie walked around the house, thinking back to her life there as a teenager. The kitchen was at the back; the dining-room, where she did her homework, in front. Halfway up the stairs, there was a lavatory on the landing (with a rickety antiquated overhead cistern operated by a chain). On the first floor was the sitting-room, with the old walnut wireless and Grundig gramophone, and book shelves stretching from floor to ceiling, packed with books mainly of art history and French and Italian literature. They would probably fetch a good price from the serious young book dealer in Camden Town, she thought. And she'd like them to go to someone who knew something about books.

Standing now by the door of the sitting-room, Josie was suddenly aware of how shabby the place looked, with the worn Persian carpet, threadbare sofa and chairs and rickety lampshades. All good quality but very old, all given to her by Evelyn's mother, Blanche, when she first moved in. Josie liked them all, they were like old friends, part of the family, particularly the upholstered mahogany rocking-chair brought by her grandmother from Savannah, Georgia, when she first came to Europe to escape the scandal. Josie gave the chair a gentle push and watched it rock backwards and forwards with elegant balance, thinking of all the people who had rocked themselves in it before now.

Next door was her mother's bedroom. The bed had been stripped by Debby and the blankets and eiderdown neatly folded on top. Josie had a brief look in the wardrobe and chest of drawers. There were no clothes she wanted. Her mother had never cared about her appearance, even when she was not depressed. The clothes were all clean and in good condition; they could all go to the charity shops.

Upstairs there were two more bedrooms, Josie's and Jamie's old rooms, though Jamie, away at boarding school and then university, had hardly ever lived there. Both rooms were now packed with boxes and trunks and furniture, all from Josie's grandmother's house, Avery Hall, in Sussex. After that big house had been sold, what was left of the furniture and other unsold belongings had been sent up to Evelyn's house in London, where it had all stayed – unpacked, uncared for, and ignored – cluttering up the two bedrooms. There were tennis rackets, glass cabinets of birds' eggs, trunks full of silver cutlery engraved with her grandparents' initials. There were leather boxes of jewellery and the less valuable objects that had not been auctioned with the family heirlooms after the grandmother's death

– walking sticks, boxes of letters and old photographs, half-empty bottles of expensive Parisian scent and ancient Parker pens in which the ink had dried up long ago.

Josie sighed as she thought gloomily about the task ahead of her. They were going to sell the house but she had to clear out all this stuff first.

The doorbell rang.

Jamie had lost his door keys years ago and never bothered to get another set cut. As Josie walked downstairs the voices on the doorstep told her that Liz had come along, too. This annoyed her. Surely this was private business between Josie and Jamie, the two children. After all, she would not have dreamed of bringing Andy along, even if she and Andy were still together.

'Jesus, this place is cold!' Jamie's voice boomed down the hall as he strode in, pulling his cashmere scarf closer around his neck. 'Can't you put on some fires?'

Josie stepped back to let her brother and sister-in-law march past.

'I can't believe your mother never had central heating installed,' said Liz, hugging her arms around herself dramatically. She had clearly come straight from the office and was wearing an expensive-looking grey wool suit and pale pink silk blouse.

Josie shrugged. 'Mother always said she didn't like central heating. She preferred to keep the windows open and wear pullovers.'

'It'll make the place harder to sell, I suppose,' said Jamie as he walked around inspecting it.

Liz shrugged. 'Not necessarily. Someone might like the idea of being able to rip everything out and start from scratch, especially if the original features are still here, as they are in this case. That's my idea of bliss.'

'The man from the probate office is coming round tomorrow,' said Jamie. 'It should be pretty straightforward. I don't think there's anything much of value here, though the trustees say that Mother's assets are considerable. The house has to be valued but I can't believe it's worth much in this state.'

'I wouldn't be so sure,' said Liz. 'This is prime location, you know. Close to Hampstead Heath and good private schools. It could be a lovely family house.'

'It was,' murmured Josie under her breath but no one heard her.

'Anyway,' Jamie looked around with some satisfaction, 'we should get a tidy sum by the end of it.' He smiled. 'It'll come in handy, especially now.'

Liz smiled up at him coyly and glanced at Josie, who looked quizzically at her brother.

'We're having another baby,' Liz said, '*and* we're buying a weekend cottage in Wiltshire. We need all the dosh we can get our hands on.'

Jamie and Liz were both investment bankers and between them probably earned more than £300,000 a year. They had a massive, heavily mortgaged house in Chiswick and an army of staff to look after them and their brood of four, soon to be five, children.

Josie forced a smile. 'Congratulations. I didn't know you were planning another one.' As she said it she knew it was a stupid thing to say. Why should she know how many children they planned to have?

Liz laughed. 'Well, I just love having babies. It makes me feel . . .' She hesitated, searching for the word. 'It makes me feel so creative, so fecund. Yes, fecund, what a good word that is!'

'Will you take maternity leave?'

When Liz had her last baby she gave up her six weeks of maternity leave in exchange for a parking space in the company car park.

Liz shrugged. 'I expect I'll take some. We'll just see what's happening at the time. The trouble is, my company offers bonuses if you come back early, and they're very hard to resist.' She looked at Josie. 'Anyway, it's about time you and Andy started thinking about having a baby. You shouldn't leave it too late, you know, or you'll find yourself having trouble. A lot of my friends are having one form of fertility treatment or another.'

Josie ignored her sister-in-law's remark and decided at that moment not to say anything about splitting up with Andy. They would not be interested anyway. They were not interested in any aspect of her life. She beckoned them upstairs to the sitting-room.

Liz walked around the room, running her fingertips over the furniture and pictures on the wall. 'Oh, I like this,' she said, examining a small water-colour. It was of a woodland scene depicted in warm autumnal tones of brown and orange. Whale-backed hills reached across the horizon.

Jamie peered at it. 'That belonged to our grandmother. She always claimed that she was given it by a lover but I never believed a word of it. She was a perfectly respectable little old lady who led a perfectly respectable life as the wife of a banker. There's no way that she ever had it off on the side.' He laughed in a rather nasty tone. 'People invent things like that to make their boring little lives seem more interesting than they really are.' He sat down heavily on the sofa. Now forty, the effects of his affluent and sedentary lifestyle were beginning to show.

Josie was annoyed at her brother's sneering tone. 'Actually, that was painted by Ivo Barnard, who was a very successful painter. I remember him as an old man. He used to come to tea with Grandma, and they were very good friends. He painted several portraits of Grandma over the years but I think Mother sold them off when the Sussex house was sold.'

Josie had spent much more time with her grandmother than Jamie had, and she knew the truth of Blanche's feelings for Ivo. 'That water-colour is probably quite valuable. The view is from the wood near Grandma's house. Those are the South Downs in the distant horizon.'

'If it's valuable, then we should sell it,' replied Jamie quickly.

'But I like it,' protested Josie. 'It reminds me of Sussex. Grandma used to have it hanging in her bedroom. It reminds me of her a lot, too.'

Jamie scoffed. 'God, you are sentimental!' He made a dismissive face and ran his fingers through his thinning hair.

'I just knew Grandma better than you,' Josie said quietly, lowering her eyes. 'After all, I lived with her for several years when Mother was ill and you were sent away to school.'

His sister's words had no obvious effect on Jamie. 'Well, the old bird was always very generous when it came to Christmas and birthdays, I'll give her that. She had quite a lot of money, but what galls me now is the way the family fortunes have been lost or squandered. *My* birthright. Our great-grandfather was a very rich man, a multi-millionaire by today's standards. He and his brothers were merchant bankers, and they were rolling in it.'

Liz looked interested. 'So what happened to it all?'

'Oh, the usual story. They insisted on keeping the business in the family and the following generations weren't nearly as astute or talented. The bank was bought out in the thirties but our grandfather still had a job for life there. He had plenty of money but nothing like what it might have been.'

Josie shrugged. 'And then our father managed to squander much of what was left, or at least what he could get his hands on. He gambled away most of Mother's inheritance.'

Jamie's expression was one of annoyance. 'Yes, Dad was worse than anyone.'

'Well, the money-making genes are still there, Jamie,' Liz said with a laugh. 'Now you're building up your own fortune,' she said teasingly. 'Your descendants will be grateful to you.'

Jamie sniffed. 'Hmm, you seem pretty good at spending it. We're always short of ready cash when we need it.'

Josie listened to the exchange between her brother and his wife and wished they would go away. She always felt tense in their presence.

They had started to walk around the room again.

'There's a lot of clearing out to be done,' said Josie. 'It's a big job.'

Jamie shook his head. 'It's not that big. You could probably get some chap to take it all away. There are firms that clear out whole houses. They take everything away and flog the lot. Then you can sell the place.' He waved his hand around the room. 'The furniture's not bad. Most of it came from the grandparents' house and is good quality. I might like a few pieces, but not a lot. I had a look around a few weeks before Mother died, actually.'

'I rather like this rocking-chair,' said Liz, running her hands over the smooth shining frame of the low rocker. 'It'd go well in our bedroom. It's got a revolting cover on it but if we got it re-upholstered with some bright modern fabric, it'd be charming.' She picked at the blue cord material on the chair.

'That's mine!' Josie was quick to make her claim. 'Grandma said I could have that, years ago when I was living with her. She brought it over on the ship with her from Savannah when she got married. It belonged to her mother, and she always said I could have it.' Her heart was beating fast as she blurted out the words. Surely they were not going to try to take this.

Jamie scowled impatiently at her for a moment. Liz watched him, waiting for him to back her up. But, to Josie's relief, her brother shrugged suddenly. 'All right, if that's what Grandma said, I'm not going to argue. But I don't see why you haven't taken it before, if she gave it to you.'

Josie smiled, trying not to look satisfied at the petulant expression of annoyance on Liz's face. 'Well, Mother liked to sit in it. She always said it was the most comfortable chair she had ever sat in, so I thought it would be cruel to deprive her of it.' She felt a satisfying ripple of triumph. At least Jamie recognised some filial bond.

But at a price.

'I thought we would divide up the work to be done,' he said. 'If you sort out the house and arrange for its sale, I'll do all the probate. Does that seem fair?'

Josie was so relieved to have saved her rocking-chair from the clutches of her sister-in-law without a fight that she was happy to agree to anything at that moment. 'Of course,' she said. 'I suppose that's okay.'

Jamie nodded. 'Well, especially since you live so close by and you don't work the hours I have to.'

Josie ignored the put-down and agreed. 'Do you want to have a look around the house, to see if there's anything you want to take?'

Liz was clearly annoyed not to have got her way. 'I doubt

it,' she sniffed. 'Your mother gave us most of the good pieces when we moved into our last house. And frankly, I generally prefer modern furniture to this Edwardian and Victorian stuff, though I suppose it'd be okay for our country place when we get it.'

Jamie got to his feet and clasped his hands as though he had just closed a deal. 'Right, that's sorted, then. It would be good if you could get the house sold as soon as possible, even if it means taking a lower price. We're desperate for the cash.'

After her brother and his wife had left, Josie stared at the rocking-chair and pulled off the dirty blue cover. Underneath was a very worn but pretty Edwardian chintz cotton.

The chair looked transformed. Her grandmother must have covered it at some point, perhaps during the war, and never had it redone. Now the chair looked as it must have done when it first arrived in England. Josie lowered herself into the soft seat and rocked backwards and forwards for a few moments. She remembered her beloved grandmother rocking like this in a far grander room in the big house in Sussex many years ago, with the imposing view of the Sussex Downs from the large south-facing French windows.

The rhythm of the rocking sent her into a trance-like state and her thoughts seem to spin in the air above her. How dare Jamie talk about getting some 'chap' to clear out all the belongings! What was stored in this house, in boxes and crates and trunks, were artefacts that told the history of the family. Josie could not throw anything out without going through it all, to keep what was essential and precious for preserving the family memories.

For this was a house of women, three generations of women – filled with the belongings of three completely different people – her remarkable grandmother, Blanche, her sad, ill mother, Evelyn, and herself, Josie, who did not really know who she was. She did not know how to describe herself even though she was thirty-five years old. She was a grown-up with a flat in Kentish Town and a job as an editor in a book publishing company. She liked her job but she felt a little unstimulated by it as she had been doing it for so long now. Perhaps, sensing her restlessness, her boss had recently offered her the opportunity to take a kind of sabbatical and work in the New York office for six months. 'So many people have been taking maternity leave,' he said, 'I think you deserve a change for a few months, too. You would learn a lot about the American side of the business, and that would benefit us, I think.'

Josie found the idea of working in New York for half a year rather appealing. Even though she had all those American connections, she had never been across the Atlantic, and it would be good to shake herself up a bit. She was in a rut. At the same time, she felt a little embarrassed by Brian's offer. She knew he meant well but she also felt it was being done more out of charity or pity for her than anything. It was as if it made up for the fact that her life was a mess, or rather non-existent, unlike many of her colleagues who were getting married and starting families and embarking on new stages of their lives. She did not like being regarded as a sad person, so she resisted jumping at this opportunity. If only she could make up her mind. She had a few friends and an unkind ex-boyfriend. Her mother had recently died, rather suddenly, of cancer, her father she had not seen since she was nine, and she had nothing in common with her brother. How could she know who she was, let alone what sort of person she was?

As she sat rocking gently backwards and forwards, she

felt her throat tighten. Tears welled up and began to trickle down her cheeks. She did not know why she suddenly felt so sad. Was it for her mother, Evelyn, she sobbed? Her poor depressed mother who only had a brief period of happiness in her life. Or was it the thought of Blanche, her beloved grandmother, who had died ten years before? Josie had felt a sudden emptiness in her heart. She missed her grandmother terribly. She had adored her. A woman who had loved her, loved life and who, Josie had always thought, represented the sort of courageous woman Josie wanted to be.

The tears, she realised, were also for herself, tears of self-pity for not being something or someone else. She was a sad person, there was no denying it.

Her fingers fiddled with the seat of the rocking-chair. The stuffing was so old, it was beginning to escape from under the fabric. It was soft, like gossamer, and seemed to dissolve in her hands. Liz was right, the chair did need to be completely re-upholstered to restore it to its former glory. However, the frame was still strong and solid, made out of beautiful smooth mahogany, skilfully carved.

Her fingers slipped through a hole in the frayed cover. She could feel something unusual, something lumpy at the back of the chair. Pushing her hand further down between the seat and the back of the chair, she pulled out a crumpled envelope, foxed and yellow with age. Inside was a pair of tiny white cotton mittens with ties of pale blue satin ribbon. Josie turned it over, feeling awed by a sense of the past. On the envelope there was a name written in faded black ink. It meant nothing to her. But it excited her to think that this little treasure, whatever it was, had probably been sitting in the crevice of the rocking-chair for over seventy years. It had come over the ocean, hidden in its secret place, a silent witness to Josie's own family history.

She looked carefully at the mittens. They were stitched with delicate white cotton, and embroidered in white silk on each mitten was the name 'Cooper'.

Josie sighed and stared out of the window. What a shame she had found this now and not years ago when her grandmother was alive. Blanche would have been able to tell her what it meant. She could have told her things about her life and past that were now gone for ever. Nobody was alive to tell her. People take their histories and secrets with them when they die.

She clutched the little package to her chest. This was part of her grandmother's past. It meant nothing to Josie but had probably meant a great deal to Blanche, or at least someone in her life. They were probably just mittens Blanche had made for the baby of a friend but had forgotten to send. But perhaps they had something to do with the scandal that everyone assumed had taken place in the years before Blanche came to Europe but which nobody knew anything about. And now nobody ever would.

HENRIETTA

CHAPTER 2

London, 1920

Henrietta Champion settled into her high-backed armchair and picked up the book lying on the table beside her. It was *Women in Love*, the latest work from the pen of D.H. Lawrence. Opening the book where the leather bookmark lay, Henrietta's eyes scanned the words and locked on to the paragraph where she had left off earlier in the day. She let out a little sigh as she found her mind wandering. Reading could usually take her thoughts off distressing matters. The Russian situation was so awful and seemed to grow worse every day. She was so glad that Masha was now safe in England, and Nicolai was safe from the Bolsheviks somewhere else. But poor Kyra, she had not survived.

Henrietta took her role as matriarch of the family very seriously. Perhaps because she was a foreigner herself, she was always concerned about the welfare of all the foreign cousins. The Russians were her late husband's family, of course, but she had grown to know them all and feel responsible for them as though her own blood flowed through their veins. The two children, after all, had often been to stay when they were little, happily playing with their English cousins whenever they met. Henrietta loved the way the young cousins greeted each other as best friends and slipped instantly into strong friendships even when they had not seen each other for months or years. Such was the strength of family ties, and they made Henrietta feel safe, she who had cut off direct links with her own family in America.

These Russian cousins were the children of Henrietta's brother-in-law, Ralph, who had been a diplomat in St Petersburg. He married a Russian aristocrat named Kyra, and remained out there where he took over his father-in-law's lumber company. They lived in St Petersburg and also had a large rambling estate in Sevastopol on the Black Sea where the family spent every summer. Ralph and Kyra made yearly trips to visit the family in England with their two children, Masha and Nicolai, who grew up speaking fluent English and Russian, in addition to the French that is the first language of the Russian aristocracy.

Ralph had died from a weak heart several years ago but the family had still remained in close contact, visiting and writing regularly until the Great War and then the Bolshevik Revolution had changed everything. Then they went into hiding, and their homes were taken over. Henrietta did not hear anything for a long time and feared that they had all perished.

That had been such an anxious time, not knowing what was happening, if people were dead or alive. And then suddenly there was news – wonderful news that Masha had come out with the British fleet and Nicolai had escaped to Finland. Kyra, sadly, had not made the journey, having given out during one of the long treks they had to make to reach the border. Kyra had always been delicate; she could not stand up to the hardship of being on the run.

So at least the younger Russians were safe, which was a relief.

Henrietta looked back at her book and tried to focus on the

words on the page but again her mind was active, thinking of matters other than the intense sexuality of Mr Lawrence's new novel. Now the Americans were here.

Henrietta's cousin, Rose, had arrived in London with her daughter Blanche. Henrietta and Rose were first cousins; they had shared a childhood in Savannah, Georgia, a set of grandparents, and a deep knowledge of the family tree and who was related to whom, and how.

The Americans were currently sleeping off their long train journey from Florence. Henrietta had not seen Rose for several years – at least fifteen, which was the last time she herself had gone back home. Blanche must have been about five then. She remembered the child clinging to her mother's skirts at cousin Jasper's summer house on Long Island. A pretty child she was, too, who had grown into a beautiful woman. But then Rose was also good-looking, with that willowy frame and fine features. They all were in that family. Henrietta was happy to allow people to call her handsome or imposing, but she knew that her beaky nose and sharp piercing eyes could never have been described as pretty.

'Ah, there you are!'

Henrietta rose to her feet, drawing herself to her full six feet, and held out her arms to embrace her cousin.

Rose Hamilton entered the room with an uncertain smile on her lips. 'I feel so much better now that I've had that sleep and a bath. I feel as though I've washed just layers and layers of dust off me.'

Rose sat on the sofa where Henrietta had pointed. 'Cousin Henrietta, it is so good of you to have Blanche and me to stay. We've had a fascinating tour of Europe but it's good to be able to spend some weeks with our own people.' She smiled warmly as she said 'people'.

Henrietta nodded, amused by Rose's use of the word

'people'. In Savannah it was clearly still considered vulgar to talk about 'family' rather than 'people'.

'I'm afraid you'll find England in a sorry state after this appalling war,' said Henrietta. 'It's going to take many years to recover.'

Rose nodded. 'I couldn't help noticing in the cab coming from Victoria Station the number of gentlemen – ex-servicemen, I guess – standing on the street corners rattling money boxes at anyone passing by. It's a tragic sight.'

Henrietta nodded. 'The young men are pouring out of the services and need work of any kind – to restore their spirits as much as anything else. They have been deeply shocked by this war. Many of them have returned very nervy and tense. We have to help them in every way. A good friend of mine has decided to employ only servicemen as his staff – and I'm afraid the more limbless and disabled the better. He even insists that they wear their service medals, which to my mind is going a bit far.

'He's fortunate to be able to afford a full staff at all. Many of my friends and acquaintances have lost a good part of their fortunes and have to make do with one general servant who does everything. They clean the house, cook the meals and wait at table, changing from a print dress in the kitchen to their best black uniform with a white lace cap and frilly apron.' She waved her arm around the room. 'And that's pretty hard, when you think these houses were built for people who had huge numbers of servants and thought nothing of it.'

She turned her gaze towards the sky outside the tall French windows hung with their expensive Genoese velvet curtains. 'That, of course, is a minor problem. There can't be a house in Britain that hasn't suffered a bereavement in the war. I lost one of my nephews, and he wasn't even fighting. He was killed in a flying accident during training. It was completely unnecessary.' She let out an impatient snort. 'But then most of the war was unnecessary, too. My nephews joined the Army in nineteen-fourteen because they thought, like most young men in the country, that they would be fighting for civilisation in a war to end all wars. But what happened was that all civilised values disappeared and the object of the war in the end seemed reduced to punishing the Germans. It was quite absurd!' Henrietta looked quite heated. 'All those men lost their lives – millions of them! A whole generation! And the truth is that war can never lead to peace. It can only lead to another war.'

Rose Hamilton nodded meekly. She did not have a strong view about the war herself but what Henrietta said sounded sensible. 'Well, we can thank the good Lord that it's all over and we can look forward to the future now,' she said brightly. 'Ah, here's Blanche, at last,' she exclaimed, relieved to change the subject. In Savannah, such serious conversations usually took place between the men at any gathering. But then Henrietta had always been different, which was why, Rose believed, she had fitted so easily into European society.

Blanche Hamilton walked into the room with a broad smile on her pretty face. She was beautiful, thought Henrietta, with an elegant figure. The girl was simply a joy to behold as she craned her neck to look at the oil paintings hanging on the wall.

'Oh, cousin Henrietta, you have the loveliest objects imaginable in your house,' she said. 'Everywhere I look there is something of great beauty – the paintings, the tapestries and pots. And everything is so well displayed.'

Henrietta smiled and bowed her head. 'Thank you, my dear, that has always been my intention, to have beauty around me.' She was impressed by the girl's spontaneous appreciation and enthusiasm. She immediately liked her. Not only did she have those striking good looks, with her rich copper hair, large brown eyes, clear white skin and dark pink lips, but she seemed not to be in the slightest bit self-conscious. It made her all the more attractive.

'I always collect things on my travels, objects that remind me of people and places. So just a glance at something can take me back to another country or into someone's company, and I can recall it as if I had experienced it yesterday. The smallest, tiniest object conjures up a different world, a different time. And now that I'm too old to travel far, I use these reminders to help me travel in my mind.' Her eyes fixed on the jewellery Blanche was wearing.

'Ah, the Wedgwood jewels! How sweet of you to put them on for me.' Henrietta reached towards the earrings Blanche was wearing, and the brooch pinned on her breast.

Blanche bowed her head. 'Well, I have always loved them. They're so pretty and elegant. You sent them to me for my sixteenth birthday. That was the first time that I was given a present suitable for an adult, not a child, and I never forgot it. Also, you were this mysterious cousin who lived in Europe, known to me only through letters. It was just so wonderful to be given a piece of historic Europe, as this jewellery seemed to be.' She fiddled with the earrings thoughtfully.

Henrietta looked pleased, happy that her gift had made such an impression and that Blanche had been so thoughtful to put them on for her. 'But there was a ring too, wasn't there? It was a complete set.'

She thought she detected a momentary blush on Blanche's cheeks as the young woman lifted her face and looked her directly in the eyes. 'Yes, there is a ring,' she said, 'but it's a little too large for my finger and I'm afraid of losing it.'

'Well, then you must get your jeweller to adjust the size of it,' replied Henrietta. 'It's a shame to have jewels that you can't wear. There's no point in that at all.'

'Yes, you're quite right,' murmured Blanche. 'I must do that, I keep meaning to. I left it at home but perhaps I'll have it altered when I get back.'

In the short but uncomfortable silence which followed, Henrietta concluded that Blanche had lost the Wedgwood ring but probably did not dare own up to it. Well, she did not want to embarrass her. If that was true, it was a shame the ring was lost, but not the end of the world. Losing one earring would be worse, since you cannot wear just the remaining one. A ring lost is a ring forgotten.

'So you like my mementoes, do you?' She smiled kindly at her young cousin and moved away from the Wedgwood jewels. For a while they talked about travelling, for Henrietta had for many years been an intrepid traveller. She and her husband had been all over the world.

A maid brought in the tea-trolley and the women settled down to salmon sandwiches, ginger snaps filled with cream, and sponge cake, accompanied by China tea and lemon served in fine white china teacups.

They talked about the cities the Americans had just visited – Paris, Florence and Venice, and all the art treasures they had seen. Blanche was full of enthusiasm for everything.

Rose and Blanche talked briefly about events in America – the good news that American women had the vote at last (though Rose was not entirely sure that they needed it), and the bad news that Prohibition was now properly in effect throughout the United States. But Rose was not comfortable discussing politics or social matters. Family talk was what she liked and what she felt easy with, so she began to fill Henrietta in with the family news from America – who was working where, who was married to whom, which sons and daughters were at college and what their plans were. 'My brothers are all well,' she said. 'Jasper and Francis are now very successful in New York.'

Henrietta nodded with some interest. 'And what about your youngest brother, Hayward? How's that young man getting on?'

Rose smiled quickly. 'He's still not settled down, I'm afraid, neither in his work nor family life,' she said. She thrust up her chin and smiled again. 'I keep hoping that he'll find the right path for him.'

Henrietta looked intently at her cousin. 'He was always an interesting boy, I thought. Very original and independent minded.'

Rose nodded and smiled at her daughter, who had sat in the low bucket chair and was looking down and fiddling with the floral upholstery. 'Yes, he was always Blanche's favourite uncle, wasn't he, Blanche? But he won't stick at anything for long enough.'

Henrietta frowned. 'I'm sorry to hear that. I always thought he'd do great things. I always thought he'd do something special with his life. How old is he now?'

'Why, he's just turned thirty-eight.'

'Well, there's still time for him yet.' Then she added, 'Perhaps.'

'I just wish he would get married,' said Rose. 'If he had a solid home life, had domestic responsibilities, he would have a good base from which to find a profession . . .' Her voice tailed off, and then she added, 'But until he has prospects he is not going to be seen as much of a catch.'

Henrietta nodded. 'Ah, marriage.' Her gaze moved to Blanche, still in the low chair, now studying her hands as her mother spoke.

'Blanche, my dear, is there a young man, a beau in your life?'

Blanche tilted her head as a soft pink blush crept across her face. 'No, I have no young man.'

'But she has always had plenty of admirers,' her mother hurriedly added.

Henrietta laughed. 'I'm afraid eligible young men are in short supply at the moment. Finding a husband in England is not as easy as it was six years ago. And I'm afraid you may even find many other women here being suspicious of you, my dear. They will regard you as a potential enemy – and certainly a rival. They say that there is a surplus of two million women. All those men dead.'

She leaned forward. 'But I do know a few . . . I have an unmarried nephew. In fact, I have two. I did have three, but one died during the war, as I said, and only one is in town at the moment. I'd like you to meet them. Charming boys they are, too, and I'm sure they'll be delighted to meet their American cousin. I have an open house every Sunday afternoon. Rudie is away in France at the moment but Augustus will be coming, and there will also be my young Russian niece, Masha, who has only just escaped from the Bolsheviks. She and her relations have had the most frightful time, all of them. They're my brother-in-law's family. They're very cosmopolitan, these Champions, and of course, you're part of it, too. As kissing cousins, you will be as welcome as can be.

'Now, I suggest you take a stroll around Regent's Park while the weather is still warm.'

Henrietta rose from her chair and moved over to the window. 'It looks as though the rain will oblige you by staying away. And you must visit the rose garden – it's so lovely at this time of year.'

Blanche smiled. 'Yes, I'd like that. I've been so impressed by how green everything is here – it's so lush and fertile. I keep wanting to caress the grass and the leaves on the trees.

It's all so different from Savannah, which is just hot and steamy.'

Henrietta smiled. 'Yes, so steamy, so horribly sticky and humid. I haven't missed the place one bit after all these years.'

Rose straightened her hat and looked at her cousin. 'How long ago did you leave America? How many years is it now?'

'Twenty-four,' replied Henrietta without hesitation. 'Twenty-four years and five months – three days after marrying Anthony, my fine Englishman, in Savannah.'

She smiled and her pale blue eyes turned dreamy at the memory of the dashing young banker who had brought her across the ocean.

Blanche raised her brows with interest. 'And you've never been back since?'

Henrietta gave an emphatic little shake of the head. 'I went home for a few weeks after my mother died fifteen years ago, but that was the only time. I enjoyed seeing your mother, then, but otherwise the trip left me cold. I have not been back since, and I don't intend going back, either. Europe is the only place to be. Europe,' she repeated, lifting her chin in the air, 'is full of civilised and cultured people, even if they do think that it's the highest form of compliment to tell me that I don't seem like an American.' She chuckled and her eyes twinkled.

'My only sadness in life is that Anthony is no longer here to share everything with me as he always did. He died five years ago and at such a young age. But the Champion men do have a tendency to die young. Ralph died of a heart-attack two years before Anthony, and Gussie's father, Roland, is not in good health, either – in fact, I think he's pretty much gaga nowadays.' Her voice tailed off as a sad shadow crossed her face.

Then she collected herself. 'Now, off you go,' she said, ushering them to the door of the drawing-room. 'Take some air while the weather's still fine.'

From the French window, Henrietta stood and watched her cousins walking towards Regent's Park, two elegant female figures walking with the poise and gracefulness of any well-brought-up Southern belle. Henrietta smiled. She herself had been brought up to be like that. What a world away that was!

She had a feeling about Blanche, though. She could empathise with her. She did not strike Henrietta as a typical empty-headed Savannah girl; there was more to her than that. There was something about her that interested Henrietta. She certainly liked her. She had a pleasing and sympathetic manner. She seemed alert and interested in the world around her, and receptive to foreign idiosyncrasies. Henrietta approved of that. So many young people, particularly Americans, were inward-looking and cautious.

Staring out of the window, Henrietta's thoughts drifted as she wondered why Rose had brought Blanche over to Europe at this time. She had noted that her cousin's face had brightened at the news that Henrietta had eligible nephews. Perhaps Rose was indeed looking for a husband for her daughter. But why in England? If Blanche found a husband here, Rose would probably lose her only daughter to Europe. It seemed extraordinarily selfless of her to be ready to accept that possibility. Henrietta liked puzzles, and she thought there was one here behind her cousin's appearance.

Henrietta moved back to her chair and settled into the seat. She was tired; she was beginning to feel her years. But her mind was working hard.

Perhaps something had prompted Rose to take Blanche away. Perhaps there had been a scandal.

She sniffed out loud. Savannah does love a scandal, she thought contemptuously. She, of all people, should know that!

Her thoughts drifted back to those years. Yes, she knew about scandal and what it could do to people! How she was treated! Yet by today's standards what she did was risible. It was so unimportant in the scheme of things, but she had been treated by everyone – friends and society – as though she had committed the worst sin imaginable. It was ridiculous.

It still made her angry to think about it. And that was only the beginning. It had just been a bit of fun – she had to go that bit further than everyone else, it was just the way she had been. It was true that she had never thought it through, never imagined the consequences or what the future could hold. But what actually happened could never have been imagined or anticipated by anyone. It was so absurd, and yet so hurtful, so cruel. She was left in such a humiliating and intolerable position that she had to escape. The anger still burned in her chest. She still shuddered when those memories caused mischief.

But then her knight had arrived to rescue her, much to her and her mother's relief. Dear Anthony swept her away from all the gossip and speculation that had made her life so unbearable. She had been thinking of moving to a place by herself, where she knew no one, to San Francisco, or Santa Fe, even. But fortunately Anthony had taken her away from Savannah and brought her to the safe shores of England, leaving those gossip-mongers behind. In England no one knew what had happened, and having thought that her life was ruined and over, Henrietta found that it had only just begun.

Was that what Rose was hoping for her daughter by bringing her here? Was Blanche in need of a fresh start in Europe, far away from the land of her birth? Henrietta's eyelids drooped as sleep overcame her. She could ask, she thought, but it would be unkind. People are entitled to keep their secrets to themselves, she decided as she drifted towards sleep. And if others chose to speculate, they could do that as much as they liked.

BLANCHE

CHAPTER 3

London, 1920

Henrietta Champion's 'at-homes' were famous for being informal and fun. Anyone interesting or interested in the arts was welcome and Henrietta encouraged her friends to bring any of their friends who were likely to enjoy it.

Intermingled with the writers, artists, musicians and playwrights were members of Henrietta's family. Whether interested in the arts or not, members of the Champions' extended family were always made welcome by the formidable and engaging Henrietta, who held court with sparkling energy, welcoming her guests with open warmth, enquiring about their latest book, exhibition or concert with a genuine interest and knowledge, and debating with gusto any topical issue, from the suffragists and votes for women to the attractions of free love and vegetarianism.

The guests varied in age from early twenties to creeping old age. And with those who were not actually creators of art themselves, she would seek out their opinions.

The first time Blanche Hamilton attended one of these soirées, she felt an intellectual excitement that she had never experienced before. She had seen some plays, read some of the books, and she found it so stimulating to sit down next to a perfect stranger and engage in conversation about things they had an interest in, cared for and had a clear opinion on. Above all, underlying all these dialogues was essentially an exchange of ideas about life. She had never known anything like it.

For all her short life, Blanche had been bored by the social gatherings she had been to in Savannah, where very little was discussed except the social to-ings and fro-ings of the assembled guests and their absent friends. Blanche had never met people who wanted to discuss a newly published book, or who had such strong views about a current play or an actor's interpretation of a part that they were prepared to argue about it.

She was aware of her mother being a little left out of most of the conversation, contenting herself with sitting next to Henrietta's young friends and talking about how she and Henrietta were related. 'Henrietta and I were both Garmanys. Our fathers were brothers, so Henrietta and I share a set of grandparents,' she explained. 'They were Emily and Caleb Garmany of Savannah, Georgia, where we were all born and raised. Henrietta and I are first cousins, while Henrietta and my daughter Blanche are first cousins once removed.' Like most Southern ladies, Rose Hamilton was deeply fascinated by family trees.

Blanche had been discussing Edith Wharton's novels with a nervous, quietly spoken young man called Lennox, who, he told her, worked in a publishing house in Bloomsbury. He also wrote poems in his spare time, he confided, some of which had been published in literary journals.

Blanche was relieved to have heard of Mrs Wharton and, indeed, to have read some of her work and she was able to talk with a confidence that surprised her about *Ethan Frome* and *The House of Mirth*.

'I believe she is about to have another big novel published next year,' said Lennox. 'I shall look forward to that enormously. I admire her writing so much for its irony and observation. Now, have you read Katherine Mansfield's new collection of short stories . . . ?'

Henrietta was moving around the room making sure that everyone was happy and talking to people they wanted to talk to.

She was pleased to see her young American cousin so engaged in conversation with Lennox. Lennox was a bright young man, but probably, Henrietta thought, not a strong enough personality for Blanche once she had gained the confidence of adulthood. Poor Lennox had been deeply affected by his experience in the war and she felt that he was always on the verge of panic.

Blanche really was an enchanting young woman. It was so refreshing to come across an American eager to experience the new and unfamiliar, so thirsty for all the good things life had to offer. It seemed positively unpatriotic of her to want to integrate herself into European life. Why, the child craved intellectual pleasures of all sorts. Henrietta had been enchanted by the look of delighted surprise on Blanche's face when she had told her that in London, in this company at least, it was not considered immoral to read a novel before luncheon, and that women were not only allowed to have opinions about matters of the world but *expected* to.

Henrietta was also impressed by Blanche's facility with languages. She appeared to speak French and Italian with an enviable ease. She must have had good language teachers at the young ladies' seminary she attended. Every day it seemed, she walked down to the National Gallery or the British Museum to familiarise herself with the works of the great European artists, and in the evening she took herself and her mother off to the theatre. Hungry for culture, she devoured the novels of H.G. Wells and Arnold Bennett, Rebecca West and Rose Macaulay, picked off the shelves in Henrietta's library with youthful excitement. She also appeared to have a fondness for poetry – the sign of a sensitive person.

That afternoon was a particularly crowded one at Henrietta's Regent's Park house and, for Henrietta, exciting. Her husband's young Russian niece, Masha, was about to arrive from Norfolk, where she had been meeting her new husband's family. Henrietta had not seen Masha since 1914, when she had been over to England to visit with all her cousins. At that time, she had just become engaged to a Russian officer and was so full of life and excitement with her black hair and large, shiny gimlet eyes and naturally red lips. She was the sort of woman who attracted the attention of both men and women when her tall figure entered a room. Like all Russian aristocrats, she had been impeccably brought up, speaking several languages and becoming extraordinarily knowledgeable about European culture.

Then, poor Masha's life had changed completely. Her family had lost everything in the Revolution. Her brother at the age of sixteen had fought the Bolsheviks, was captured and sent to prison. Then Masha's fiancé had been imprisoned too, freed when Deniken's army had arrived, but then died in circumstances too ghastly for anyone to relate. It was always considered too upsetting and delicate a subject for anyone even to mention.

After this tragedy, Masha met and married a British naval officer who was stationed in Sevastopol. She came out with him and the British fleet.

When Masha finally arrived at four o'clock, Henrietta was shocked to see what the last few years had done to her niece. Masha's once vigorous and rounded figure had become straight and angular. The black eyes that had once sparkled so brightly with mischief were steady and serious. Her face was gaunt. Her hair was pulled back off her face in an unfashionable style.

Henrietta held out her arms. 'Masha, my dearest girl!' Walking up to her, she hugged her tight. 'I'm so glad you're safe and here. We've been so worried about you for such a long time.'

Masha smiled. 'Yes, but oh, it's so good to be back here in London, in these familiar houses with my family. All that time, during the war, and knowing that we were likely to have to escape and leave everything behind and become refugees, I kept myself going by thinking that I had homes abroad in England. Homes where I would be welcomed and not spat upon, where there were people I knew and loved. So many people had nothing. My poor Aunt Olga, who we all used to mock because she sat up so straight in her chair, ended up washing corpses in a morgue. She was in her seventies and had never worked before in her life. I always had my dream, my hopes.'

Henrietta placed her arm around Masha's long, slim waist. 'Well, you must tell me all about it when we have a quiet moment to ourselves. Today is not the time.'

Masha bowed her head. 'I don't know if any time will be the right time,' she murmured. 'I don't think I will ever be able to talk about some things.'

Henrietta started to usher her across the room. 'We must be positive,' she said brusquely. 'The Great War is over. You have escaped from a Russia we no longer know, a new Russia. You must not let life trample on you, or it will destroy you. The most important thing is that you are safe, you have your life, and, indeed, a new husband . . .' She looked around her. 'Did you bring him, your naval officer?'

Masha smiled again and shook her head. 'Not this time. I wanted to come on my own, to introduce him slowly.'

Henrietta nodded. 'Of course. Now there's someone else I am introducing to everyone, and not so slowly. She's another cousin, my first cousin once removed who has just arrived in Europe from the United States, from Savannah – my part of the world. Or what used to be. She's one of my compatriots.' She smiled conspiratorially. 'I think you'll like her. She's unusual for an American. She appears to have a genuine interest in European culture, and she has not commented on "hygiene" once!'

Masha looked sideways at her, coyly and prettily. 'You mean she's like you.'

'Ha!' Henrietta tweaked Masha's nose. 'I know you'll like her. She's young – about five years younger than you, I should think.'

Henrietta led Masha through the throng of men and women standing with their cups and saucers or plates of cucumber sandwiches, to find the young American.

Blanche was sitting on the sofa watching the scene before her. It was an amazing sight of men and women of all ages (though few young men, of course), talking earnestly and passionately about subjects that fired them. As she sat quietly on the sofa, she heard snatches of conversation about spiritualism, the decline of religion, night-clubs, women's education, sexual freedom and votes for women.

She felt so naïve and ignorant, without information or opinions about these matters. When people asked her about American women getting the vote, she realised that she had never really thought about it, what it meant or whether it was a good thing. She was ashamed of her inability to have a view. She longed to be like these people, so confident, so knowledgeable, so opinionated. How could she, a young person and only a woman at that, get to talk like that? Everything about London was different from the world she knew back home.

More guests were arriving. The drawing-room with its high, moulded Adam ceiling had filled up. As it was a pleasant day, guests were making their way downstairs to spill out into the little courtyard, where they gathered in groups, lounging in the teak chairs or simply sitting on the York-stone steps as they talked. And they talked and talked, bright-eyed and earnest, laughing and gesticulating, revelling in the exchange of ideas.

Blanche watched Henrietta come towards her with a tall dark woman of about twenty-five. She looked exotic and friendly.

'Blanche, my dear, I must introduce you to your Russian cousin, Masha Petrovska Champion. Masha, this is my cousin Blanche Hamilton, from Savannah, Georgia. Blanche is here visiting Europe with her mama.'

Blanche jumped to her feet and shook hands with the woman smiling at her.

'The last time I saw Masha, she was about your age,' continued Henrietta. 'She has just arrived in England with a new husband, who is unfortunately not here today.'

She smiled with fondness at the young Russian woman. 'It is so good to see you safe and well. It's been a worrying time for all of us.'

Masha bowed her head and smiled. 'I am enchanted to meet you, Blanche.'

Lennox, who had been standing next to Blanche, greeted Masha, too. But Henrietta made it clear that she wanted the two young women to have a chance to be on their own. 'Lennox, my dear,' she said, slipping her hand under his elbow, gently pulling him aside. 'Come and tell me what you're working on now. I did so enjoy your last collection. Have you brought some more poems to show me?'

As Henrietta steered Lennox to the other side of the room, Masha seated herself next to Blanche. With a pleasing friendliness, she told Blanche her story, of how she had escaped from Russia after her fiancé had died. 'But now I am happy,' she said. 'I have married a kind and cultured man who has a fine career ahead of him in the King's Navy.' She hesitated and looked around the room. 'How good it is to be here again. Aunt Henrietta is my favourite relation. I used to see her every year when I came to visit the family here in England. The last time was 1914, just before war began and travel became too difficult or dangerous.'

Blanche was confused. 'But how are you, a Russian, related to Henrietta, an American?'

Masha let out a deep husky chuckle. 'It must seem strange to you, I can see that. But I am half English. My father was a diplomat at the British embassy before he met my mother, and then he went into my grandfather's firm. Before the war we used to come to England every summer for wonderful holidays. We always stayed with either Aunt Henrietta or Aunt Margot.'

'Who's Margot?'

'Margot is Henrietta's sister-in-law. Henrietta's husband, Margot's husband and my father were all brothers.' She looked quickly around the room. 'I've always preferred Henrietta to Margot,' she whispered. 'Henrietta's more relaxed, and much more fun!'

Masha looked around the room. 'Oh, I do believe Gussie's just arrived. He's another cousin, one of Margot's sons.' She stared at the figure in the doorway. 'My, how he's changed! He was about to celebrate his twenty-fifth birthday when I last saw him. I wonder if Rudie is coming . . .' She turned to explain. 'Rudie is Gussie's younger brother.' Then she added with a laugh, 'Now, Rudie is also fun . . .'

Masha suddenly clasped her hand over her mouth. 'I'm sorry. I have talked much too much about myself. It's so rude of me. But you see how excited I am to be here, to meet my family after everything that's happened. I thought I would never see them again, It seems like a miracle to be here. My father died just before the war started and my poor mama died in the Revolution trying to escape to Finland with my brother. Then my fiancé had that terrible . . .' She looked away and her voice tailed off. 'Here in England I feel safe and with people who love me. It is here I feel real love and warmth. Much of it, I must say, does come from Henrietta, who has done her best to hold the family together. But I'm fond of Margot, too. In her way, she's good-hearted.'

Blanche smiled. 'Why, please don't apologise. I'm finding everything so interesting. It's wonderful to be surrounded by all these fascinating people who care about art and politics and everything. And so different! Where I come from, society is so limited, and you don't get anything like this kind of mix of people.'

Masha nodded. 'I'm sure it can be dull here in England, too, as it can be in Russia. There are boring people everywhere. But Henrietta has always ignored convention. She's a free spirit, she makes her own life. She has always gathered interesting people around her, people of all ages. I think this is partly because she never had any children of her own, but it's also, I think, to ensure that she keeps in touch with the world and knows what young people are thinking. She likes to know the latest ideas and ways of thinking. And there's no one better read than Henrietta!'

Blanche's head was spinning. Masha was so open. She

did not seem to hold back on anything, so unlike the way women were supposed to behave in Savannah. It made her quite disarming.

Masha was looking round the room. 'Now, let's go and find some tea. I'm very thirsty. Henrietta always has the most special kinds of tea here – almost as good as fine wines, when you're in the mood.'

The two women crossed the room together. 'Well, look at you two – you could be winter and autumn!' a voice boomed out from the doorway.

Masha turned and let out a squeal of pleasure. 'Ivo!' She was looking at a man of about forty-five, leaning against the wall. He had long, thick grey hair pulled off his handsome craggy face. His eyes were a startling blue and his red lips surprisingly sensuous for a man.

Masha had Blanche by the hand and pulled her over. 'Come,' she whispered, 'I must introduce you to a wonderful man . . .'

Masha and Ivo hugged each other tight. 'I was so happy to hear that you were safe, my dear. I know that you've had quite an ordeal over the past few years, to say the least. I can see it in your dark sad beautiful eyes. But your lovely camellia complexion is the same. How I would like to paint you!'

Masha smiled modestly as Ivo turned to Blanche and scrutinised her keenly. 'And who is your pretty friend?'

'May I introduce you to Blanche Hamilton, Henrietta's cousin from America. Blanche, this is Ivo Barnard, a friend of the family and a great artist.'

They shook hands. Blanche noticed that his fingers were beautifully shaped and elegant, but rough and well-used.

'Pleased to make your acquaintance, sir,' she said, holding out a soft, limp hand for him to shake.

Ivo laughed. 'You Americans are so polite to us individually, even if you have contempt for us as a nation. Now the war's over and we're an impoverished country, the place is swarming with Americans taking advantage of the strong dollar and a weak pound. You're buying up all our art treasures. Our poor old aristocrats – not that I have much sympathy – are having to sell their family silver, they're so poor nowadays. Their estates are being sold, their London houses converted into flats.' Ivo laughed again and peered down at Blanche. 'You don't look like a carpet-bagger, though. And did I detect a Southern accent in that charming voice of yours?'

'Indeed you do, sir,' replied Blanche, blushing hard. 'I come from Savannah, Georgia, though I have a lot of people up in New York.'

Ivo nodded. 'Like Henrietta, all those years ago.'

Blanche nodded. 'That's right, just like Henrietta.'

'Very nice, very nice,' muttered Ivo. 'Well, I hope you're enjoying Europe. Most Americans seem to spend their time comparing notes about the dirt and the stuffiness of European cities. They don't see all the treasures before their eyes, though they are intent on buying them up to take home as souvenirs!'

Blanche looked serious. 'I am quite taken with Europe, sir. I could never have imagined such a place.'

Ivo smiled and turned to Masha. 'And you, my dear, have escaped the Bolsheviks and found refuge with the guardians of capitalism. What a terrible drama it has been for you. Henrietta has been telling me all about it. I'm so sorry about your mother. I can't say anything that will make things better for you, but you are safe and welcome here. And,' he added with a kind twinkle in his eye, 'you have had experiences unique to you. Keep them in your head, write about them,

paint them, record what has happened. Most of all, create
with them!'

Masha laughed. 'You always say that, Ivo, and you are of
course both right and wrong. In my darkest moments I used
to remember your life lesson – everything, however bad, is an
experience. Remember it and use it in the future.' She giggled.
'The trouble is, we're not all writers or painters.'

Ivo kissed the top of her head. 'We can all be creative in
ways other than writing or painting, my dear. That was my
point. Did you know that I have married again since I last saw
you? And that I am to become a father at this advanced
age? Now, that must be the greatest act of creation!'

Masha grasped his arm and hugged it. 'Yes, Aunt
Henrietta told me all about it. It's wonderful, and I'm very
happy for you. But where is your wife today? Is she here?'

Ivo shook his head. 'No, Dora cannot abide large gatherings, being a shy creature. And she was planning to fire
some pots this afternoon. It'll be the last firing before the
baby arrives.'

Masha smiled warmly. 'I'm very happy for you. I understand life was not easy for you for a while.'

Ivo threw back his big head and laughed. 'That's an
understatement if ever I heard one! I hate to think what
Henrietta has been telling you! Now, I'm going to sit down
and play some music. I've just finished a painting and have
come up to London to celebrate.'

There was a grand piano in the corner of the library, off the
drawing-room. Ivo disappeared through the doors, and soon
the sound of a Schubert sonata could be heard from that part
of the house.

Somebody descended suddenly on Masha with a cry of
delight and scooped her off, leaving Blanche on her own in
the middle of the room. She watched the groups of guests

conversing with each other, all so animated and intense, and it made her feel good. Ivo played the piano beautifully. Blanche could almost feel the music on her skin. Suddenly she had a belief that perhaps life was good after all. Perhaps she could believe that yet again and the veneer she presented to the outside world would truly reflect what she felt inside.

There was a painting on the opposite wall. She looked carefully at it. It was a woodland scene, with bold brush strokes in the warm colours of autumn, sandy paths and broadleaf trees.

Henrietta was approaching with a man at her side. 'I see that you're admiring Ivo's painting. Isn't it vivid? That's a painting of the Downs near my brother-in-law's house in Sussex. Aren't the colours marvellous? Not green, not brown, not gold. Yet all of those colours, too. Few artists have succeeded in capturing the colours, those wonderful elusive colours. But Ivo does.' She looked around the room. 'Ivo's here, he's playing the piano now. He's a truly fine painter, who is only just beginning to be recognised as the genius he is.'

'Yes, I've met him,' said Blanche. 'He seems very interesting.'

'Now.' Henrietta's tone of voice turned serious. 'I want to introduce you to my nephew Augustus Champion. I was telling him all about you and he wanted to see you for himself.'

Blanche held out her hand to a tall thin man in his early thirties, with deep-set brown eyes and straight black hair slicked back off his face and over his head. 'Pleased to make your acquaintance,' she said.

Augustus took her hand and bowed his head. 'How do you do?'

Henrietta passed her hand over her forehead dramatically.

'Gussie, I think it's getting rather warm in here. Why don't you take your cousin out into the courtyard and get some air?'

Augustus bowed his head again. 'I'd be delighted, Aunt Henrietta.'

Augustus gave Blanche his arm as they descended the wide stairs to the ground floor of the house.

'Are you enjoying your visit, Miss Hamilton?' asked Augustus.

Blanche nodded, somewhat awed. Compared with everyone else, he seemed stiff and formal.

'Oh, very much, thank you. I have seen so many interesting things since I've been in Europe. It's almost like fairyland to me. Do you like the theatre?'

Augustus raised his eyebrows. 'Occasionally I go, but only to the big plays. My work leaves me with little time for luxuries like the theatre.'

Blanche laughed. 'I would never describe the theatre as a luxury. We have a good little theatre in Savannah, where I come from, so it is a luxury of a sort. But here in London, the theatres are all putting on the most wonderful plays imaginable every night. And people here seem to regard them as part of everyday life. It's marvellous, to my eyes.'

Augustus nodded. 'Well, you're talking about Henrietta's friends, perhaps. Not everyone regards the theatre as an essential part of their lives, though I do enjoy seeing Shakespeare.'

'Well, more fool them, that's what I say,' replied Blanche gaily. 'Now, tell me, sir, what is your line of business?'

'I work in the bank. It was originally founded by my grandfather but it was bought up by another bank when my father retired. Shall we sit on that bench over there?'

'And does your brother also work at the bank?'

Augustus shook his head dismissively. 'Rudie prefers to work with books. He is a publisher.'

Blanche did not find Augustus the most exciting company but he was attentive and pleasant enough. Perhaps he was just shy, a little ill at case among artistic people. After a while, the air cooled, causing Blanche to shiver. Augustus noticed and immediately got to his feet. 'Come on inside. You'll catch cold. Let's go into the house.'

When they arrived back, Ivo was still at the piano and the doors to the library had been opened up. Ivo was playing music on request – and was now performing jazz tunes.

'Oh my,' exclaimed Blanche, 'it makes my feet want to dance.' She laughed gaily as she started to move her feet around in a few jazzy dance steps. Suddenly, Ivo burst into the Charleston, and Blanche found herself leaping to her feet and dancing in the centre of the room. A circle of people surrounded her, clapping and cheering her on.

'That's the way to do it!' someone shouted. 'It takes an American to show us how to do the Charleston properly.'

Gradually, the other young (and not so young) people in the room joined in until the room shook with the sound of the latest dance music from America.

Blanche looked up. In such a party in Savannah, they would be frowning. Here everyone, young and old, looked delighted.

Masha marched on to the floor and began to dance next to her, copying her movements. 'Look at them!' shouted Ivo. 'Like nymphs in the forest!'

Blanche danced on, her body fired with energy. She felt a great happiness inside her, filling the space that had been void for so long. She could be happy again. Here she was, laughing and smiling, her hair now flying out behind her. In a fleeting moment she knew that she had to stay in England and she felt overcome by a fierce determination to get what she wanted. Suddenly, she could see how to do it. It was a little calculating but it would be worth it. Henrietta had shown her the way.

Then Ivo stopped playing, and Blanche stopped dancing. A great cheer went up as she stood in the middle of the room, breathless and panting. She was sweating in a most unladylike manner, but no one seemed to care. They were all clapping and smiling at her with admiration.

Henrietta took her by the hand. 'Well done, my dear, that was a marvellous performance. Now, come and sit down and rest. It's nearly time for cocktails, another of the few good things we Americans have exported to Europe. We're going to try some Manhattans this evening, Manhattans and White Ladies.'

As Henrietta led Blanche across the room, she was aware of Augustus staring at her with a mixture of admiration and longing in his dark eyes. She lowered her eyelids and smiled back at him shyly.

CHAPTER 4

Sussex, 1920

Margot Champion sat on the terrace of Avery Hall and admired the view of the South Downs as she nibbled her toast and lime mamalade and took sips of her morning coffee. It was a glorious day. Although still low in the sky, the sun was hot, and the horses in the paddock beyond the ha-ha in front of the house were already seeking out the shade of the oak trees in the southern corner by the stream. She could hear the sound of bumble-bees busily collecting pollen from the purple clumps of marjoram on the rockery, and a little grey-brown dunnock splashing lightly in the bird-bath on the edge of the terrace.

Beyond the paddock were the woods where Margot used to walk every day as the mistress of this elegant Georgian house. Beyond those were the fields of the farm which ran along the bottom of the Downs. The Downs in the distance were like a massive grey cloud. Soon, as the mist rose, the colours would be clearer. Greens, blues, yellows and browns would appear along the smudgy horizon line and greens and purples in the deep hollows.

She felt the now familiar tug of sadness. Never again would she be able to clamber up those chalky escarpments, never again gallop her horse over Bignor Hill to look at the blue-grey sea and the hazy outline of East Head in the distance. Her arthritis had put a stop to all that long ago. Now she was trapped in a crippled, cracking body, every movement a nightmare of pain. Some days, of course, were better than others, and certainly the summer months were kinder to her joints than the cold winter.

Well, she could take pleasure in her garden, at least, which was looking particularly good. The roses were in bloom and the white spiraea was a mass of creamy blossom over by the rockery. The copper beech, which she had planted soon after her marriage thirty-eight years ago, was spreading its regular dark shape against the blue sky.

As she looked over the smooth green lawn, Margot saw her husband Roland with his nurse, walking slowly and unsteadily towards the house. They had been on their daily perambulation to the end of the drive and back. That was all he was capable of nowadays.

Watching him from afar, she could still see the blank look on his face, the lack of any meaningful expression. He had been completely gaga for six months now. He did not recognise anyone or know where he was at all. He was like a child, or even an animal. Margot sighed. If he were an animal, it would be considered kind to put him down. Now the poor man had to live this blank, meaningless life. And although he seemed quite content, it was very upsetting for everyone else. Margot had given orders to the nurse to keep him out of the way as much as possible. It was increasingly difficult to believe that Roland had once been a lively and amusing man with a successful banking career. That frail, stooped old man had once put on amateur dramatics and hunted to hounds on the wildest of horses. Gradually he had faded from her and was now unreachable. It was quite tragic.

Margot sighed again. Well, it was dreadful to grow old like

this, but it came to everyone. And at least she had only lost one child to the war. She still had two fine boys.

At the thought of her sons, Margot frowned. What on earth was going on? Augustus had arrived on Friday for the weekend, full of talk about an American girl he wanted to marry. She had never seen the boy in such a state – smiling and jovial and excited. Margot had been most worried. She was indeed anxious for both her sons to get married, she made no secret of that. But to an American! And to a cousin of Henrietta, which Margot did not take as a recommendation. Margot had always rather disapproved of her unconventional sister-in-law and felt that Henrietta's soirées and 'at-homes' attracted the most unsuitable – even louche – types.

Margot poured herself another cup of coffee. Now where was Masha? It was time the child got up.

Masha had arrived on Sunday afternoon to introduce her new husband to the family. Ambrose Etherington seemed a most suitable husband for her young Russian niece. It was marvellous that Masha had chosen to marry an Englishman, and a naval officer, too. He was clearly a high-flier and would probably be an admiral one day – perhaps even the First Sea Lord. Yes, Masha had done well.

Ambrose had motored back to London with Augustus on Sunday night, leaving Masha to stay down in Sussex for a few days. This pleased Margot, for it would be fun to have some young female company for a change.

As the old lady's thoughts wandered, Masha stepped out of the French windows carrying a book. 'Good morning, Aunt Margot.' She leaned down and kissed Margot on the cheek. 'Oh, how wonderful it is to see an English country summer again! There were times over the past few years when I never thought I would.'

Margot picked up the little brass bell on the trolley next to her chair and rang it.

Within seconds a maid in a black uniform, white cap and apron entered the room.

'Ah, Jane. Please get Mrs Etherington some fresh coffee, and I'll have a little more myself.'

The maid nodded and disappeared into the house again.

'That's not the same maid that you had before, is it? I thought she was called "Jane".'

Margot waved her hand dismissively. 'We always call our maids "Jane". It's easier to remember their names that way. Mind you, we're lucky to have anyone, whatever we call them. Ever since the war, it's been very hard to get any staff at all, let alone good staff. For some reason women just don't want to go into service in the way they used to. Some people blame the war when women worked at other things and now they prefer those jobs. It really makes life very difficult.

'We've been luckier than some. Laura Blenning has been without a cook for six months. At least things haven't become that bad at Avery Hall.' She shook her head. 'I'm too old for all this change. I find it hard to keep my feet in this new world. Maids have married officers; butchers and bakers have taken commissions and made gallant officers. People talk differently, too. It's not only the slang but all manner of unspeakable matters are now mentioned with bravado in public. Not to mention these new corsets women seem to think are dashing.'

She turned to Masha and smiled. 'I remember the last time you were here, playing clock golf with your cousins out there on the lawn. That must have been just before war broke out, six years ago.

'I was so sorry about your mother. Such a terrible business.'

Masha nodded and said nothing.

'But it's good to know that Nicolai is safe now. I heard that he was imprisoned.'

'He escaped to Finland and then made his way to Germany. He's in Heidelberg now, staying with Aunt Natasha, my mother's sister, who is married to a German.'

Jane the maid appeared again, carrying a silver tray with a silver coffee set on it. She placed it on the table next to Masha, who offered Margot some more coffee before pouring some for herself.

Margot waited until she was settled, then she took a deep breath. 'I want you to tell me about this American woman who has stirred up Gussie so much that he spent almost the entire weekend talking about her. I know she's a cousin of Henrietta's, but apart from that, who is she and what is she like?'

Her niece's face lit up at the thought of her new friend. 'Blanche is a charming person. She is very beautiful with hair the colour of bronze, and she's full of life. I liked her the minute I met her. Everyone else seems to, as well.'

Margot was silent but her narrowed eyes revealed her suspicions even before she spoke. 'Do you think she's a gold-digger? Gold-diggers can be perfectly charming, too.'

Masha smiled mischievously. 'I don't know if she is. I don't know if she has any money. Most Americans have it seems – or the ones I have met here. But does it matter? Gussie has lots, anyway. And besides, if Gussie is in love with her, then that's all that matters.'

Margot pursed her lips at Masha's embarrassing candour. Russians really could be uncontrolled sometimes. She had noticed that about their cousins before when they had come to stay. They had a tendency to say exactly what they meant, without regard to proper manners at all. 'He seems to have fallen in love very suddenly. It's all a bit rushed. It worries me.'

But Masha had not finished. 'But, Aunt Margot, I thought you wanted Gussie and Rudie to find nice wives and settle down.'

'Of course I do!' Margot sounded almost impatient.

'Then you should be pleased,' said Masha triumphantly.

'Oh, I'm not sure about them marrying foreigners.'

'Auntie Margot, how could you! I'm a foreigner!'

Margot smiled and patted Masha's hand. 'Oh, you don't count, my dear. You're half English, and you're family.'

Masha was not going to let this go. 'But what about Aunt Henrietta? She's American, too, a foreigner, as you say.'

'Indeed,' agreed Margot, 'but she doesn't like America and was determined to settle in England anyway. This young woman has only spent six weeks in Europe. Who's to say if she'll want to make Gussie move to America?'

She shook her head in disapproval. 'There are too many Americans marrying our men already. There aren't very many eligible English men left as it is, after this wretched war. Laura Blenning has four daughters to marry off, and goodness knows where she's going to find husbands for them.'

Margot had still not finished. 'And Gussie's feelings for this Blanche woman are not all that matters, as you suggest. We know nothing about her family or family circumstances. It's all very well Henrietta vouching for them, but even now Henrietta does not often . . .' She corrected herself, 'Henrietta rarely does what's right and proper. And since they are Henrietta's own family, she *would* vouch for them, wouldn't she?'

Masha sipped her coffee and let her eyes wander over the green English scene before her. Margot had not changed at all. The war had changed the world, but not Margot Champion.

'I've asked Rudie to meet her and report back. At least I can rely on one son's judgement even if the other has temporarily lost his. Then we'll find out what's what.'

Masha looked over at Margot, her dark eyes wide with delighted wonder. 'You've sent Rudie to inspect Blanche Hamilton?'

Margot nodded triumphantly. 'He's meeting her today. He and Gussie are having lunch with her at the Savoy.'

Masha fell silent. Sitting back in her chair, she tipped the dainty coffee cup to her mouth to hide the smile on her red lips.

It was tea-time when Margot was wheeled out in her bathchair on to the terrace. This time the table next to her was laden with cucumber sandwiches, Battenburg cake and brandy snaps filled with thick cream from the farm. Earl Grey tea was poured from silver teapots into porcelain cups and served with a slice of lemon.

Masha was walking around the garden admiring the flower borders when the maid appeared.

'There's a telegram for you, ma'am,' she said, handing Margot an envelope. 'It's just arrived.'

From a distance, Masha watched her aged and crippled aunt fumble as she opened the envelope with knobbly arthritic fingers. She saw Margot stare down at the telegram in her hands, without a word. Masha stepped towards her. 'Is something wrong? What's happened?'

Margot had slumped forward in her chair, her face expressionless. Staring in front of her, she handed Masha the telegram.

'It's from Rudie.'

The Russian held it with two hands and read the words

herself. Then she let out a deep husky laugh, and twirled around on her toes. She threw up her head to read the words aloud:

'IF GUSSIE DOESN'T MARRY HER I WILL STOP RUDIE STOP'

She laughed again. 'Well, both your sons have good taste!'

Margot looked disgruntled but she took a deep breath and sighed. 'I suppose I'd better meet this young lady. I'll invite her down for the weekend as soon as possible. Then I'll be able to make up my own mind about what's going on.'

CHAPTER 5

⮑⮒

Savannah, Georgia

October 1920

The soft autumn light blazed through the tall window in Blanche's home in Duffy Street, Savannah. The bed remained rumpled and unmade; her discarded clothes and undergarments lay in heaps on the floor and spread over the rocking-chair in the corner of the room.

Blanche was nearly ready. Her hair was piled on top of her head in soft tresses. Now for the dress. She took in a deep breath as her black mammy, Simmy, hooked her into her wedding dress, a glorious garment made of white satin and decorated in delicate embroidery and pearls.

Simmy was usually cheerfully chatty as she went about her business looking after Blanche and had been particularly happy to see Blanche back at home after her months away in Europe. Today, however, she was subdued and quiet.

'Whatever's the matter, Simmy?' Blanche wanted Simmy to share the excitement of the day but she could tell that the maid was unsettled.

'I'm just sorry that you're going away, Miss Blanche, and

you ain't taking me with you.'

Blanche turned to her. 'But you could. You could come with me if you want, Simmy, of course you could. Oh, I'd love you to come with me. Why didn't you just say?'

Simmy shook her head. 'I can't come with you, Miss Blanche. I never been out of Savannah, and I can't be going to no foreign country now. Besides, there's only white folk in England, that's what I heard.'

Blanche said nothing. She would genuinely prefer to take Simmy with her. It would be like having a bit of home with her, but it was true that she had not seen any black people anywhere on her trip to Europe. She would miss Simmy, there was no doubt about that. She had known her most of her life. But it was time – and necessary – to leave everything behind.

Simmy took a deep breath and let out a cheerful coo-ing sound. 'Well, I like that young man you've chosen for yourself, even if I do have trouble understanding him when he talks. And his brother, too. You marrying into a good family, that's for sure.'

Blanche smiled. 'Yes, I think so, too. Gussie is a good and dependable man.' What she did not say to her maid was that she had plans to mould Gussie the way she wanted him. Gussie had a kind and good heart but was a little rigid and conservative. He was well educated and extremely well versed in the classics but he showed little interest in modern culture. She felt confident that she could get him to enjoy modern art and literature, just as she did.

Simmy was thinking of something else. 'I'm sure glad for you, Miss Blanche,' she continued, 'after . . .'

A sharp look from Blanche made the words fade in her throat. Simmy felt a hot flush of embarrassment on her face. 'Why,' she exclaimed with exaggerated enthusiasm, 'this is a pretty dress. You're going to be the prettiest bride Savannah has seen in years! Wait there, now. Your mama wanted me to call her when you were ready.'

As Simmy left the room, Blanche walked briskly over to the rocking-chair and pulled out an envelope. She stood staring at it for a few moments. A look of frustration on her face. 'Do I send them?' she whispered aloud. 'Or do I keep them?' Indecision kept her standing there for a few moments. Then she heard her mother's footsteps coming down the corridor and she quickly pushed the envelope back into the folds at the back of the rocking-chair.

Blanche had been down to Avery Hall for several weekends with her mother to be inspected by Margot. She had been to church with the family and responded to Margot's grilling questions with charming fortitude. She knew she was on trial and she was determined to win her case. At last Blanche had been accepted as a potential daughter-in-law. It was, however, several weeks before Margot was prepared to say anything, because during that time she was waiting for information about the Hamilton family of Savannah, Georgia, which might have put a stop to the whole affair. But the news from Savannah – through her husband's contacts in New York – was, from Blanche's point of view, positive. Margot had to concede that although the Hamiltons were not wealthy by Champion standards (Blanche was certainly not one of the new American heiresses) her family was certainly comfortable enough to make it unlikely that Blanche was a gold-digger. From what Margot had observed of the girl, Blanche did not appear to have particularly expensive tastes and was unlikely to spend Gussie's considerable fortune foolishly.

And finally, Blanche did appear to be besotted with everything English and European. She did not seem to stop exclaiming at the beauty of the Sussex countryside and comparing it favourably with the hot, steamy Savannah, or extolling the culture and treasures of London – the theatre, the galleries and the music.

Margot did not have much time for cultural affairs herself (or had not before her arthritis made her almost immobile). She always went to the Summer Exhibition at the Royal Academy, of course, and to the opera, but these were really just part of the season and places to meet with one's friends.

No, she did not share the girl's passion for such things, though she did not mind it. She was not so sure if Gussie would be taking his new wife to the theatre very much, but never mind. The most remarkable fact about Blanche was that she did not seem to have the slightest concern about uprooting herself and moving to England, which was a great relief to Margot.

Once she had realised that there was no danger of Gussie being made to move to America, Margot had relaxed a bit, though she did question the mother, Mrs Hamilton, who had been invited down to the Sussex house again to discuss arrangements now that it had been agreed that the wedding should indeed go ahead.

The wedding would take place in Savannah, which would mean that Margot and her husband would miss it. It had been agreed that Rudie would travel out with Gussie to represent the family, and he could do some business in New York while he was there. The Champion brothers would get an opportunity to meet Blanche's family, especially the New York branch, who could be useful for the business at some point – one never knew. Blanche herself was to return home in September, six weeks before the wedding date, with her mother to prepare for the occasion. Margot never said anything but she did think that Rose Hamilton seemed remarkably unmoved by the prospect of her only daughter leaving home to live three thousand miles away. Most mothers in her situation would at the very least comment on it. Rose Hamilton seemed almost relieved, while at the same time being clearly attached to Blanche. It did not quite make sense but Margot was satisfied with the news from New York about the family, so she chose not to dwell on it.

The marriage ceremony took place in St John's Church in the middle of Savannah, and the reception afterwards was in the large drawing-room at the family house in Duffy Street. Blanche's Savannah friends and family – brothers, cousins, uncles and aunts – were all there, as were the uncles and aunts and cousins who had moved up north and had now travelled down to meet the Englishman who was to take their young Blanche away with him.

Rudie Champion watched Blanche from across the room, admiring her copper hair and dark brown eyes. She was a most attractive woman, he thought. Sensuality seemed to radiate from her body as she moved gracefully about the room. Gussie had certainly done well for himself, and the family were decent people too. The uncles – all lawyers or doctors – were clearly very fond of their niece, as were her two much older brothers.

Rose Hamilton, Gussie's new mother-in-law, appeared like a happy woman, too. She was more than handsome and probably a good indication of how Blanche would look when she was older – tall and dignified with pretty delicate features and porcelain skin.

'You will miss your daughter,' he said to her.

Rose nodded with a serious look. 'More than you can know.'

'Well, we'll look after her,' Rudie said cheerfully, sensing that Rose might burst into tears. He quickly changed the subject. 'I've met all the family except one of the uncles. Is there another of your brothers yet to arrive?'

Rose instructed the maid to carry more trays of lime juice for the thirsty guests. She looked around the room. 'Yes,' she said, 'my brother Hayward should be here but I haven't seen him at all. I don't think I even saw him in the church.' She reached over to touch the sleeve of a tall man standing near her. 'Jasper, have you seen Hayward? He did say he was coming.'

Jasper shrugged, and smiled ruefully at Rudie. 'I'm afraid our brother Hayward can be very unreliable,' he said. Jasper was in his early fifties with the distinguished look of the successful lawyer that he was. His suit was impeccably cut to hide the growing middle-age spread of his torso, the result of too many meals eaten at his gentlemen's club. To Rose, he murmured out of Rudie's hearing, 'It might be a relief if he doesn't appear. I still don't see why you had to invite him, after all that business. I had successfully got him out from under my feet and then you insisted on inviting him back. It's bound to cause more trouble.'

Rose lifted her chin defiantly. 'I know what you think, but Blanche is his niece and this is her wedding. Blanche has always adored Hayward and I know she'll be most hurt if he doesn't turn up. He has sent her a beautiful pearl necklace in a red velvet box. It's inscribed with her initials on the clasp. He knows how much she loves jewellery.'

Jasper grunted. 'Humph. Bought with my money, no doubt.'

Ignoring her brother's remark, Rose turned back to Rudie. 'Blanche loves jewellery, you know. Cousin Henrietta started it by giving her that magnificent English Wedgwood set for her sixteenth birthday.'

Jasper looked up, interested. 'Cousin Henrietta? Of course, Rudolph, you know our cousin in London.'

Rose gave him a critical look. 'Henrietta is Rudie's – and Gussie's – aunt by marriage, Jasper. I told you that.'

Jasper nodded. 'Yes, you did, but I had forgotten. Now there's a wayward woman.' He turned to his sister. 'I don't believe she's been back home since she left, has she? After all that business?'

Rose gave him a quick look of disapproval. 'She came home about fifteen years ago, when Aunt Sara died.'

Rudie tried to pretend that he had not heard anything, but Jasper's words lingered in his mind. He looked hopefully at Rose.

Rose was not about to tell him. She looked around the room and smiled cheerfully at him. 'Well, I'm sure Hayward will be here soon. I'll make certain you meet him when he arrives.' She moved away to attend to her guests, leaving Rudie with Jasper.

'You pleased about this match? Is your brother a suitable husband for Blanche?'

Rudie laughed. 'Gussie is a lucky man and I think he's well aware of that fact.'

The maid offered him a glass of lemonade. Rudie declined. 'I cannot believe this Prohibition business is real. I need a proper drink. Since I've been in America, I've been having dreams about large tumblers of Scotch whisky.'

'Yes, it's absurd,' agreed Jasper. He leaned towards the younger man. 'Later on, we'll go to the library and I'll be able to offer you something you'll enjoy. This business is absurd because it can't be banned. Anyone who wants a drink can make it himself or knows someone who can get some. But publicly we have to obey the law – I am a lawyer, after all

– I'm afraid it would be considered indelicate to be too open about it.'

Rudie nodded gratefully. 'Thank you, sir. I'll look forward to that later on.'

Jasper raised his eyebrows as he looked at him. 'Tell me,' he said, 'what does England think about America now that we've saved you from Germany? I've heard that there is some hostility towards us over there.'

Rudie hesitated and thought carefully before he spoke. 'If you want the truth, sir, there is some resentment. I think that what people in Britain mind most is that we and the French have been impoverished by the war and the Americans are richer than ever. Yet you're not prepared to cancel the war debts. Americans don't hesitate to remind us about how much we owe them.'

Jasper nodded. 'It is a lot of money – a billion dollars, I believe.' He squared his shoulders. 'Well, it was our help that saved the Allies from losing the war. Without us you would have been defeated.'

'Indeed,' Rudie agreed. 'I suppose it's the way America has to make the point that Britain is finished anyway. Never again will she regain the position of power and prominence in the world that she had before.'

Jasper leaned towards Rudie with a patronising smile. 'All the more reason to stay on America's good side,' he chuckled. 'And all the more reason to be delighted by personal alliances such as this marriage between my delightful niece and your brother. What better way to build international relations! Come now, let's celebrate, as we should.'

As Jasper turned to escort Rudie across the room, his sister Rose hurried to his side. 'You'll be pleased to hear,' she said tartly, 'that Hayward is not coming after all. He's just sent a telegram to say that he has been delayed.'

Jasper raised his eyebrows and grunted.

After the wedding reception, Blanche and Augustus took the train out to Savannah Beach, to the Hamiltons' family house where they were to spend a few days.

Rudie had joined the northern members of the party and taken the boat up to New York where he would visit some American book publishers before returning by liner to Southampton.

Now, for the first time, Blanche and Augustus were properly alone. The beach house was going to be the place Blanche missed most when she left Savannah to live as Mrs Augustus Champion in England. Although she enjoyed the society of her friends in Savannah, it was this house that held her heart. It had been built by her grandfather in the 1880s when the railway out to Savannah Beach was first laid. Then, as now, it was the family retreat from the steamy heat of the streets for weekends and holidays. It was here that Blanche had spent many hours as a child running free with her older brothers, catching oysters and blue crabs, rowing silently through the reedy marshes to watch birds, and to swim in the warm waters of the creek. The garden had old live oaks festooned with heavy drapes of Spanish moss, and Blanche loved to lie under these in the hammock, reading any book she could get her hands on.

Blanche was disappointed that Gussie was not as enchanted with Savannah Beach as she had hoped. He complained constantly of the humidity and heat – when Blanche thought it was hardly humid at all. Besides, there was a lovely cooling breeze off the sea. And when she tried to demonstrate how to catch the vicious blue crabs off the beach – with a chicken-neck tied to a piece of twine – his expression was more of disgust than admiration.

'You wade in up to your knees like this,' she said, hitching up her skirts to her thighs. 'Dangle the chicken-neck in the water like this . . . and when you feel a tug, yes, like this! you yank the whole thing out and fling it on to the beach behind you.'

She demonstrated her skills to her new husband with great pride. 'I've been doing this since I was five,' she said proudly, holding up the twine with a large angry blue crab holding on to the sodden raw chicken with a grip that could only be broken by banging the crustacean against the side of the tin bucket Blanche had brought along with her.

Gussie smiled disdainfully. 'Perhaps you're a bit old to be doing this,' he said, thinking of what his mother would say if she saw her daughter-in-law now.

Blanche looked at him and laughed. 'Why, you silly goose! Don't be absurd! You can never be too old to do something you enjoy.'

But the beach house did not amuse Gussie for long. He was happy to meet local members of society, Hamilton family friends who also had houses on Savannah Beach, but Blanche could sense that he was not engaged with the place. The visit out to Fort Pulaski was relatively successful as Gussie showed some interest in battles and wars but it was obvious that everything else – the exotic wildlife, the flowers, the extraordinary light on the water at different times of the day – left him cold. All the things that enchanted her, that made her heart leap upwards, seemed to leave him untouched. It saddened her but she put it down to his age.

One day, she suggested an expedition to a special place. She was secretive about what it was. 'I'll tell you when we get there,' she teased. 'It'll make it all the more intriguing.'

They travelled back to Savannah on the train and then set out of town in the Hamiltons' pony-trap.

Blanche sat next to her new husband waving to friends she

saw as they set off down Bay Street, through Yamacrow, the Negro section, and then turned a sharp right in the narrow uneven dirt road, lined with gnarled oaks from which hung soft tendrils of Spanish moss. Branches of the great trees, set nearly at right-angles to the trunks, formed a sort of canopy across the road, while streaks of sun fought their way through the leaves to strike at the ground like dazzling swords.

The road led to a shaded clearing not far from where an old house loomed up. The yellow river could be glimpsed in the background. Edging the tree-vaulted clearing were dirty red brick huts with tumbling chimneys and worn black roofs. These were the slave dwellings of another era. About twenty of the original sixty dwellings were still inhabited by Negro families. Small children played out in the red earth and their mothers peered out of their houses as the visitors passed.

They had come to a property in the centre of a five-hundred-acre tract along the southern branch of the dreamy Savannah river, west of the city. The house was a colonial mansion, built in 1830, though the plantation itself had been settled almost a century earlier. Sacked by Sherman's troops as he marched into Savannah during the Civil War, the house had not been occupied for decades, and was in a sad state of disrepair.

The pony-trap stopped and as the blacks stared at the latest visitors to the house, Blanche took Gussie by the hand and stepped out on to the red earth. They stood hand in hand in front of what was the colonial façade.

'My great-grandfather built this,' she said. 'My father remembered living in it as a boy, before the war between the states.'

Now Gussie was impressed. 'Your family owned this?'

Although the house was in a sad state, the general shape of the building remained: its ample front with columns, the staircase curling to the threshold.

'It's enormous,' murmured Gussie, eyeing it with admiration.

Blanche felt proud as she led him inside. They stepped carefully over the rotting floorboards, to find a vivid sight within. There were huge cobwebs, broken glass and crumbled stone. The four great pillars supporting the roof were cracked and weathered. The once green shutters of the tall windows were all but gone.

From the basement, accessible through caved-in ground-level doors, the ruins of the structure were clearest. Here the rotting of the flooring showed grim rafters, bare and gaunt. Soiled white walls rose above, merging with torn ceilings. Rooms remained only as grotesque suggestions. Hundreds of scrawled initials, names, addresses and inscriptions of all sorts, with dates, were mute proof of how long this once magnificent place had been considered a mere curiosity.

Blanche's expression was dreamy as she led Gussie through the building.

'In my great-grandfather's time, the gardens were a mass of blooms, extending down from the back of the house to the river. Visitors would arrive by boat and see this glorious vision first.'

They looked at the old garden. Now there were only tall reeds and twisted natural vines and a few stray blossoms.

Gussie shook his head. 'What a waste. What a loss!'

Blanche hugged his arm. 'But it's so romantic like this, don't you think? Whenever I come here, I imagine being back in the atmosphere of this place before the war – the warm sun, the cotton fields, fine ladies in hoop skirts and bonnets, and the gallant Southern gentlemen who courted them. Can't you see it all here? And if it were still lived in, and added to and modern, it wouldn't have any of that atmosphere. It doesn't bother me to see it as a ruin.'

Gussie shook his head. 'I'm afraid my imagination is not as fertile as yours, Blanche.' He took a few steps backwards to look up again. 'It's terrible what a war can do. It ruins families, it ruins family fortunes. Look at the English now. Look at Masha and what's happened in Russia. Your family was obviously badly affected by the Civil War – more so than the Great War – and it must have been a tragedy to lose this place, to have it ransacked by invaders. This house symbolised so much.' He squeezed Blanche's hand. 'Doesn't it make you angry that your family lost so much in a pointless war?'

Blanche laughed. 'Well, I don't think it was a pointless war – unlike many people in the South. It was about slavery and its evils. It makes me sad that my people lost so much during that time but my family did not lose their lives – and the slaves won their freedom. I think it was a good thing, though I know I'm in the minority when it comes to such thoughts down here, but I do believe it with a passion.'

Gussie laughed at the earnest look on his wife's face. 'Why, you're delightfully idealistic.'

Blanche shook her head. 'I'm not particularly idealistic. I just believe that there are some things in life more important than money.'

'Such as?' Gussie challenged her with a provocative grin.

'Such as art, truth and beauty. Such as freedom – in the broadest sense!'

Gussie pulled her to him and hugged her. 'And you say you're not idealistic! You are full of the dreams of youth. You shall no doubt learn soon enough that wealth is important to live in the way you want to, to enjoy a standard of living which enables you to appreciate art, truth and beauty,' he teased.

Blanche laughed. 'Well, you can teach me all that, and I'll teach you about higher things. We've obviously both got a lot to learn.'

They wandered around the grounds and stopped to look out over the river. 'My mother has given me several pieces of furniture to bring back with us, a set of dining-room chairs and a rocking-chair. They originally came from this house, so I'll always have a bit of Savannah with me.'

'Good,' said Augustus.

'You don't like it, do you?' Blanche challenged him. 'You don't like Savannah.'

Gussie smiled. 'I don't dislike it,' he said. 'It's a bit provincial for me, too small a society. I prefer places to be bigger and more anonymous. And I don't know how any work gets done in this heat and humidity,' he added, wiping the sweat from his brow. 'I would find it impossible. But I can see why you love the place so much and I'm touched that your affection for me is strong enough to allow you to leave it behind. You can, of course, come back to visit your family whenever you want.'

They climbed back into the trap and set off down the dirt track. Blanche smiled as she looked across the Savannah river. She was looking forward to the future, there was no doubt about that. She felt a sudden rush of warmth towards Augustus. He was kind and he clearly liked her. He would not try to take Savannah away from her – he would let her keep it in her heart. She smiled to herself as she felt a strange sense of omnipotence, a feeling that she could make anything happen, if she wanted it to. She would make Gussie love all the things she loved. It would be easy.

Two weeks later, Mrs Rose Hamilton stood on the dockside waving farewell to her daughter and new son-in-law. They were on a steamboat that would take them up to New York where they would board the liner to England. Blanche's trunks were packed with all her belongings, and the chosen pieces of family furniture had been packed up carefully and placed in the hold.

Looking at Blanche's pretty, excited face standing next to the stiff form of Augustus, Rose felt a twinge of anxiety. She hoped so much that the marriage would last and that Blanche would be happy. Nothing had ever been said between them but mother and daughter knew that conventional Augustus Champion was an unlikely companion for Blanche Hamilton. If there had been any choice, this union would probably not have taken place. Rose had to be glad it had, even if it meant losing her wonderful wayward daughter. Now England was to have her and Savannah would be an emptier place without her. But what happened had happened, and nothing could change that. Blanche had to move away to escape the secret that she and her mother shared. Only by going would the secret be safe and contained. That way, no one would ever have reason even to think about the matter again.

CHAPTER 6

London, 1921

In a small maternity home on London's Welbeck Street, at six o'clock one bright spring morning, Mrs Augustus Champion gave birth to a healthy 8lb girl.

For a first baby – and for such a relatively large one – it was a remarkably quick and easy birth, the nurses told Blanche as she settled into the pleasant room she was stay in for the next ten days.

Blanche lay back against the soft goose-feather pillows, holding her baby in her arms. She stared in wonder at the tiny creased face and ran her forefinger over the moulded lips, and examined one by one the miniature fingers with their jewel-like nails. Her pregnancy had been an easy one and although the birth itself had been unbearably painful, it had been mercifully short. Blanche had been taken in to the nursing home a week before she was officially due, and the baby had been born within three hours of her labour beginning, so it had all been fairly unexpected.

It was now mid-afternoon and Augustus was still in his office at the bank. He had telephoned the nursing home to say that he would be along to see his wife and child at around five o'clock.

Blanche kissed the baby's soft cheek. 'If you were a boy,

my darling,' she whispered, 'I think your father would be here earlier. I'm so sorry.'

Blanche's sorrow, however, did not show on her face as Mr William Fforde, the obstetrician, arrived to offer his good wishes to his patient.

He was a large man with a huge belly which was well covered by a carefully cut Savile Row suit. He had florid cheeks and wide silver sideburns. 'Congratulations, Mrs Champion,' he said. 'You have produced a perfect specimen.' He stood by her bedside and smiled down at her.

'Thank you, Mr Fforde,' replied Blanche. 'Even during the worst moments, I knew I was in safe hands.'

William Fforde smiled. 'Has Mr Champion visited yet?'

'He's on his way from the bank,' replied Blanche. 'It was all so quick, all such a surprise. The baby wasn't due until next week.'

Mr Fforde nodded. 'Babies come when they're ready,' he said. He looked at her hard. 'But I must say, for a first baby, your labour was remarkably short. You're a lucky woman.'

Blanche looked up at him and smiled. 'I am indeed a lucky woman. Look at my beautiful baby! My husband will be very pleased, I'm sure of that.'

'All men love to have daughters – just so long as you give them a son, too, at some point,' the doctor added with a twinkle in his eye.

Later that night, Mr William Fforde, obstetrician to London's fashionable society, retired to his study after dinner, as he did most evenings. There in the yellow light of the desk-lamp, he wrote the day's entry in the diary he had kept for over thirty years. They were neat black notebooks recording both personal and professional thoughts, notes for the autobiography he intended to write on his retirement. Certainly they were not for publication – there were too many details about his famous patients for that! No, he kept a diary because it was a habit, almost a compulsive one, which he had to keep up every day. He rarely failed to make an entry but if he occasionally did, he would feel quite agitated until he had caught up the next day. And some time, when he was gone, they would no doubt provide good material for a historian, who might enjoy them as an accurate account of obstetrics during this period of history when conditions for confinement and giving birth had changed so drastically.

Mr Fforde was tired, so he did not wish to write much. He simply noted that he had delivered a baby girl weighing 8lb 2oz to Mrs Augustus Champion and that labour had been consistent with his earlier observations about the lady, who was, he commented, with a sudden lapse of professionalism, a strikingly attractive woman, both in form and character. She had been a charming patient. No doubt he would be delivering another baby for her soon, as he was aware that her husband had been convinced that the child would be a boy.

Mr Fforde shook his head. The disappointment would be great. He had seen this so many times before, people wanting a baby of a certain sex and convincing themselves that it would be what they wanted. Then they went into shock when the baby was the opposite sex to what they expected.

He had little patience with such attitudes. He had seen too many pregnancies go wrong and thought that getting the baby out safely was the only concern anyone should have. That was his concern as a doctor, and he wished that his patients and their husbands realised it too.

He put down his pen and yawned. Well, none of it was his concern now. He had done his job for this baby and he would do it for the next. He hoped this baby had a good life.

As he closed up his notebook and slipped it in the drawer of his desk, he recalled the look on Mrs Champion's finely boned face. At least she had seemed very pleased with her baby, as any mother should. He smiled. That look of pride on the faces of his newly delivered patients was one that always gave the obstetrician immense pleasure. It was something that men, to their loss, could never know.

But Mr Fforde's immense pleasure was particularly personal. He had become popular among the British aristocracy immediately after the war when a whole generation seemed caught up with the frantic desire for an heir. He could guarantee an heir for £1,000. Many wives and mothers, desperate to replace the heirs they had lost to the fighting, were turning, at their late age, to Mr Fforde for his miraculous treatment. It was never discussed openly, only discreetly in low whispers among women at their luncheon parties, but he could do wonders with artificial insemination, it was said. He had particularly good sources of fertile sperm (bright young medical students, it was rumoured), and everyone was happy. The women had the babies to present to their husbands who were happy to believe the children were theirs, and Mr Fforde's practice flourished. No one ever commented on the fact that many of Mr Fforde's patients gave birth to children who looked remarkably similar to each other, or that they looked remarkably like the good doctor himself.

Augustus arrived to visit his wife promptly at five o'clock. The baby was to be kept in the nursery between feeds but Blanche had asked for her to be brought a few minutes before her husband was expected, so she was holding their tiny child when he appeared.

Augustus had arrived in a state of confusion. William Fforde had been right. Augustus had been so convinced that the child would be a boy, that he was about to become the father of a son, that he was utterly unprepared for the actual outcome. He managed a smile as he kissed Blanche on the forehead but his eyes betrayed the disappointment inside. He was disappointed with Blanche, he realised. He felt that she had let him down.

Blanche looked up at her husband with her large brown eyes. 'Isn't she beautiful? Just the most darling thing.'

There was a moment of silence, an awkwardness, during which Blanche waited for her husband to take the baby in his arms.

Augustus stood as if paralysed. Unprepared, he did not know how to act spontaneously. 'I'm happy that you're both well,' he said stiffly. 'I understand that you'll be staying here for about ten days.'

There was silence. An awkward shifting of weight from one foot to another. Then he tried. 'What name did we decide on for a girl?'

It was a disingenuous question, for he knew that all their discussions about names had been for a boy. They all swirled in his head now – Adrian, Rupert, Lennox. The list of girls' names had seemed irrelevant and unnecessary, of course.

'Evelyn.'

Blanche said it quietly but firmly, stroking the light brown down on the baby's head. The baby moved her fingers in strange slow clawing movements. 'Evelyn Gwendolen Champion. Don't you remember?'

The stay in the maternity home was a frustrating one for Blanche. The place was run under very strict rules, with the babies staying in the nursery away from their mothers until feeding time every four hours, when they would be brought to their mothers in bed.

Blanche hated it. At times she could hear her own baby crying – Evelyn's cry was a lower pitch than that of the others – and she would ache to get up and bring her back to bed with her to nurse her for as long as she wanted. But such behaviour was forbidden. Mothers had to stay in bed and get as much rest as possible, to regain their strength. The babies could only be fed every four hours, or they would get spoiled.

To Blanche it made no sense. It was a rigid, cruel system which seemed to be designed to make both mother and baby miserable. It seemed so unnatural. She thought of the Negro mothers back home who gave birth, and then had their babies with them at all times, even when they were working out in the cotton fields in the hot sun. It was commonplace to see coloured women feeding their babies out in the open, and certainly whenever the baby cried to be fed. It did seem the natural and right way to respond.

But the other mothers in the maternity home did not feel the same way. They accepted that was the way things were without complaint, and allowed themselves to be bossed around by the nurses as if they had no instincts of their own.

Blanche fought it as much as she could but finally gave in after being ticked off by the matron for picking up Evelyn in the nursery to cuddle her when she was crying.

'You'll spoil baby if you do that, Mrs Champion. If you pick her up every time she cries, you'll end up being her slave. She's got to learn from the start how to behave.'

'Why, she's only three days old!' Blanche looked at the matron with an incredulous expression on her face. 'She's too young to understand about behaving well or badly. You can't say she's being naughty, or good. You just can't apply such words to a new-born infant.'

Matron smiled patronisingly and removed the baby from Blanche's arms. 'We do things differently here in England, Mrs Champion. Now you get back into bed, it's time for your afternoon rest.'

Blanche returned to her room seething with a sense of injustice. She lay on her bed and tried to read a book but the words jumped about in front of her eyes. It was impossible to concentrate.

What a nonsense all this was. Rules, rules, rules. It was like being at school again. Rules always made her want to challenge them, or break them, like fences she found in her path. Just because it was the fashion to feed babies on this rigid four-hour schedule, it did not make it right. Poor little Evelyn, alone in her cot, having just arrived in the world after being warm and enclosed inside her mother for all these months. And poor Blanche, whose craving to cuddle the baby, to hold her tight and never let her go, was driving her almost to distraction.

She told this to Masha, who came to visit her that afternoon. 'It's quite unbearable,' she said. 'I'm going to have my next one at home, away from all these regimes.' She let out a defiant laugh.

Masha was sitting next to Blanche's bed. Dressed in a dove-grey silk suit and hat with a long black feather, she looked very elegant. Her eyes sparkled as she laughed at Blanche's protestations. 'Having the baby at home would be daring!'

Masha watched Blanche nursing the baby. The feeding had come easily to her and she had plenty of milk. Masha cleared her throat and leant forward slightly. 'Well, your little Evelyn is going to have a cousin.' Her voice was quiet.

Blanche looked up. 'A cousin? Oh, Masha, that's marvellous news. When?'

'I've just come from Mr Fforde's consulting rooms in Harley Street,' said Masha. 'He thinks the baby is due at the end of June.'

'Wonderful! Your baby and Evelyn will be so close in age, they're bound to be good friends.'

Masha smiled ruefully. 'Yes, provided Ambrose is not posted anywhere for too long.'

Blanche looked at Masha's wide Slavic face with its

high cheek-bones and strong features. 'You're happy with Ambrose, aren't you?'

Masha nodded. 'Yes, I'm very happy. I feel that my marriage has made up for so many of the disasters of recent years. I'll never forget those events or the people I have lost. They have condemned me to living with apprehension all the time, worrying about losing every cherished relationship. I have only recently realised how much confidence I have lost. I can hardly believe that I'll ever feel secure again. But Ambrose has helped me a lot. He is solid and dependable and I believe that with him I can slowly build up my confidence again. He has given me a reason to look forward to the future. Always kind and thoughtful, he is such a good man.'

She broke off. 'And you, Blanche? Are you happy with Gussie? I see you so rarely nowadays that I have little sense of how life is for you.'

Blanche raised her eyebrows. 'I envy you when you talk about your marriage like that. You and Ambrose are obviously well suited to each other, you complement each other. It's luck, I suppose . . .'

She paused and stared out of the window. 'Augustus and I are very different. Before I married him I thought he would change, I thought I could change him, that he would change for me. But I was mistaken, and I have to live with that. It's not a big mistake but it is a mistake all the same.'

Masha's eyes widened in dismay. 'I'm sorry to hear you say these words, Blanche. I'm so sorry. I never realised. Gussie is a good man even if he is a little conventional.' She let out a sudden laugh. 'He's delightfully conventional in his artistic convictions. I'll never forget him describe Claude Debussy as the man who writes all the wrong notes!'

Blanche nodded, forcing a smile to her lips.

Masha turned serious again. 'Do you think your marriage was a mistake?'

Blanche shook her head. 'No, I don't think that. No, I meant that my mistake was in thinking that people can change. I believed that I could make us have more interests in common, that I could influence Gussie in the way I wanted. But people don't change.'

'Of course people can change!' Masha's voice was heavy with emotion. 'Perhaps now that Gussie is a father, you will see a big change in him. He can be a bit – how do you say it? – stuffy, but perhaps fatherhood will make him relax and give him a sense of fun.'

Blanche laughed. 'We'll see, Masha, we'll see. Now, tell me your plans for the next few months, because I hope to see plenty of you. My mother is coming over from Savannah to see her new grandchild. She's planning to stay for a month, so I do hope you'll come and visit while she's here. She's very fond of you.'

'Of course, I should love to,' replied Masha. 'I remember her well.'

'She arrives in two weeks. She's leaving in two days' time.'

But Rose Hamilton never saw her new grandchild. On the evening of the day she sent the telegram to her daughter with details of her arrival, she went down with influenza. On the day she was due to leave Savannah for Europe, she died of the pneumonia that had developed as a complication of the flu.

Blanche received the news of her mother's sudden death on the day she returned home to the house in Devonshire Place. Evelyn was in the nursery with Nanny, and Blanche shut herself in her room for several hours. Her grief was private and contained.

Augustus was kind and considerate. He knew how fond

Blanche was of her mother and how much of a shock this news must be to her.

He knocked on her door and went in. She was sitting in a low chair staring out of the window. She seemed composed now.

'Will you go back home?' he asked gently.

Blanche shook her head. 'Even if I could with the baby so small, it takes too long to get there. I wouldn't be in time for the funeral.'

Augustus nodded. 'You may want to go back in a few months time, to sort out your mother's effects, to finalise things. You have my permission if you do.'

Blanche turned to look at him. Now he could see that her eyes were bloodshot and puffy. She shook her head. 'I have no desire to go back,' she said. 'With Mama gone now, I probably never will.'

Augustus looked surprised. 'Oh, but you are so fond of your family – your brothers, your uncles.'

Blanche shook her head helplessly. She looked at him standing so awkwardly by the door, twisting the gold signet ring on his little finger. She smiled.

'Thank you, Gussie,' she said quietly. 'Thank you, all the same.'

Augustus took a step towards his wife. Seeing her in distress like this touched something inside him. He did love Blanche, of course, he was proud of her beauty and vitality, and she was a fine hostess. It unsettled him to see her brought down as if the life had been beaten out of her.

He moved towards her and awkwardly placed his arms around her shoulders. Blanche turned to him and a surge of sorrow swept through her, forcing her to sob loudly and uncontrollably into his chest. For that moment they were as close as they could ever be.

CHAPTER 7

1922–1925

Augustus made his desire for a son obvious soon after Blanche's recovery from the birth of her daughter and her mother's death. He came to Blanche's bedroom night after night and would pull up her night-gown and place his whole weight on her, pushing up against her and into her without a word.

And without a word, Blanche would lie there waiting for him to finish, turning her head away to avoid his breath which carried the strong fumes of his night-cap.

She did not complain. This was her duty as a wife. She knew that, and was prepared to put up with it. But it seemed so soulless, this clumsy groping and pushing and the almost inhuman grunts and groans that went with it. She longed for him to kiss and caress her, to hold her tightly in his arms. And after he had finished, Augustus would lie still for a few seconds and then withdraw from her, from the bed and then from the room, returning to his own bedroom without a word.

It seemed to her that Augustus got no pleasure out of it either, as if it were a duty for him, too.

Blanche was left lying in the dark, praying that she would soon be pregnant so that he would leave her alone.

In fact, it took a long time for Blanche to conceive again. It surprised her that it did not happen at once, as it had before. But now she found herself disappointed each time the monthly shedding of blood happened. It made her sad, and at times she felt that her body was shedding tears of sorrow.

At last she did conceive. Her periods stopped and a visit to Mr Fforde's consulting rooms confirmed that another baby was on the way. 'You won't need any extra help from me, my dear,' the doctor said with a chuckle.

She lost the baby a few weeks later, waking up one morning to find her bed drenched with blood. The doctor prescribed plenty of bed-rest. They were unable to tell whether it was a boy or a girl. After that, Augustus's nightly visits began again.

In the meantime, Masha had given birth to a little boy whom she named Misha, and then, a year later, she had twin girls, Kyra and Irina. Blanche was disturbed and envious of Masha's fecundity but managed to be gracious about it because she cared for her. Although she did not see her often, they kept in touch by letter and her attachment to Masha grew quietly each year.

Little Evelyn was growing up. She spent her days with Nanny in the nursery, and was brought down to have tea with her mother each evening. At weekends she also saw her father, but Augustus was not particularly interested in her, though he was happy to play cards with her occasionally. Never having had sisters, he seemed awkward with his little girl, as though he did not have an understanding of a female child. Evelyn was a small, anxious-looking girl with large frightened eyes and a wary look.

Augustus's mother's health was steadily deteriorating. She was barely capable of walking and she now travelled around the village in a vast wicker bathchair on wheels pulled by an old donkey. Her energy had been sapped from her body and she spent large tranches of the day taking naps. But although her body was packing up on her, her mind was as quick as ever, and her criticism of Blanche was as sharp. 'What's wrong with that wife of yours?' she demanded of Augustus one Sunday as he drove her up the hill to church. 'Why can't she produce a son for you?'

Augustus shrugged. His mother always made him feel like a little boy.

'Perhaps she should try a bit of praying,' snapped Margot Champion. 'She hasn't been to church in years, and she doesn't even seem to be ashamed of the fact.'

Augustus did not say anything. He double-declutched and put his foot down on the accelerator, making the engine roar as they came round the bend to the churchyard.

Evelyn's third birthday had passed before Blanche was pregnant again. She had turned down Mr Fforde's quiet offers of assistance, and finally conceived. This time she held the pregnancy.

In spite of her experience the last time, and earlier determination to have a home birth, she allowed herself to be admitted to the Welbeck Maternity Home once again for her confinement. There, under the expert care of Mr Fforde, she gave birth to the much-longed-for son and heir.

Augustus's response could not have been more different from the previous time. He took the afternoon off from the bank and arrived at his wife's room with an enormous bouquet of pink roses for her.

'Well done, my dear,' he said. 'I am immensely proud of you both.' He leaned over and kissed her cheek.

Blanche smiled wearily. She was exhausted from the labour and she resisted the temptation to suggest to Gussie that he seemed proud of himself, as well.

But she, too, had a sublime sense of completeness. She held this new child to her breast and watched his miniature fists tense up and relax, his head dark against her creamy skin. She held him tight. This one she would not lose. This one she would keep for ever.

Blanche lay in the maternity home for twelve days. Her strength came back rapidly. Her spirits were high and each night she dreamed vivid dreams of Savannah, of the live oaks heavy with Spanish moss, red azaleas and pink bougainvillaea, the graceful, grey-brick houses around the city's squares, the sultry heat, the waterfront and the handsome sailing ships in the harbour. She dreamed of her old family house on Savannah Beach, of Fort Pulaski and the marshes of Tybee Island where she had caught crabs and watched the gawky white ibises perched in the trees.

Each time she awoke, usually when the nurse brought in the baby for a feed, she would feel a strange combination of sadness and happiness. She knew she could never go back to her old home but she was glad that she had retained Savannah inside her like this, so that it could be recalled as vividly as if she were actually there. It was a beloved part of her, as much as this child pulling at her breast.

Now Augustus had his heir and he did not seem worried about having a spare, his nocturnal visits to Blanche's bed ended with Adrian's birth.

Soon afterwards, Augustus's mother died. She had a massive stroke and passed away in her sleep.

The family gathered for the old lady's funeral at the village church and she was buried in the family vault in the garden of rest in the churchyard at the bottom of the Downs.

Now the Sussex house belonged to Augustus, who was keen to spend every weekend down there after a week of work in London. He enjoyed country pursuits and was happy to spend his hours hunting and shooting, or on his own in his wood-panelled study listening to Gilbert and Sullivan operas and reading Kipling.

Blanche, on the other hand, was not at first so keen on weekends in the country. She loved the London life and craved intellectual stimulation constantly. Her husband did not give it to her, so she relied on her circle of London friends who were interested in what Blanche thought of as the life of the soul.

In London, in the tall Georgian house in Devonshire Place, she regularly went out to the theatre or opera with Henrietta or her friends. She went to literary parties in Bloomsbury and art exhibitions at the fashionable Grafton Galleries. She read every new book that was published and discussed it eagerly with like-minded friends. At parties, she would dance and sing – she was a sparkling addition to any social gathering, her rich husky laughter a delight to all.

Everyone seemed to dance all day long. The *thé dansant*, started during the war, was still popular. Popular, too, was the waltz 'Destiny', which had been played endlessly before the war and had been heard by thousands of young men before they went to their deaths. Blanche's days were an endless round of visits, parties and social events dictated by the season. Occasionally a reluctant Augustus would accompany her to these gatherings but she was quite happy to go without him as an independent woman.

This was the time of the chintz dress, the chemise frock, cloche hats and silk stockings. Blanche had her portrait painted by Philip de Laszlo, the society portrait painter, and her days settled into a pattern, spending part of the week in Devonshire Place, and the rest of the time at the house in Sussex, which she grew to love. A full staff was maintained in both households, and increasingly, Blanche

invited her London friends down for weekend house parties.

On Friday afternoons groups of clever young men and
women would arrive from London in their motor cars or on
the train, or on motorcycles. These young people would fill
the house with noisy debates about the latest Noël Coward
play, Rebecca West's new novel, or T.S. Eliot's latest
poem. They discussed politics, and described their travels
in France, Italy, Egypt or even China. They were very
modern. There was no segregation of the sexes and men did
not linger over the port after dinner. Augustus himself tended
to withdraw from the company, preferring to take his port
into the quietness of his study where he could spend the rest
of the evening away from the tiring and tiresome talk. For the
talk was intense and heart-felt. There was a lot of discussion
about conditions in Germany. Some people said they felt
sorry for the poor old Kaiser, who was now chopping wood
somewhere out in the sticks. Gloomy types warned about
drifting into another war, while the optimists said that no
one would be fool enough to start another war ever again.

When they were not arguing and debating, they played
Scrabble in French and put on clever plays for each other at
night. Friendship was what they valued more than anything
in the world.

One weekend, Gussie's brother Rudie was among the
guests, arriving on his motorcycle. He often came and
Blanche had become very attached to him. He had a
sharp sense of humour and, as a book publisher, shared
her interest in cultural matters. The bond between Blanche
and her brother-in-law had always been strong and although
nothing had ever been said, Blanche always felt that after
Henrietta, Rudie was her main ally in the family when old
Margot Champion had been alive.

Saturday morning was fine and dry. Blanche was up early while her house guests slept after a late night of fiery discussions about the new Labour Government.

It was a habit of hers to go out into the garden first thing to inspect the herbaceous borders. She was peering at a delicate pink diascia and watching the fat bumble-bees busying themselves around the blossoms, when Rudie appeared beside her.

'Good morning,' he said, with a mocking flourish of the hand.

Blanche smiled and held out a welcoming arm. 'Your mother may not have liked me very much but she certainly liked her garden. She clearly had a passion for it, even if her taste was different from mine. This is a labour of love.' She waved her arm to take in the garden – two acres with numerous different areas with different styles and moods, from the formal garden with its star-shaped flower-beds on the south of the house, to the shrubbery garden to the east and the water garden beyond.

Rudie laughed. 'I think my mother's only interest was her garden.'

'What I find extraordinary is that there's no part of it where one can relax and read. I don't think Margot ever actually enjoyed the garden itself. I think she just enjoyed planning it and ordering around the gardeners.'

Rudie threw back his head and laughed as Blanche continued, 'I have great plans and I'm afraid your mother will be turning in her grave by the time I've finished with it.'

Rudie chuckled. 'I'll look forward to seeing what you do to it, then.'

Blanche laughed. 'You won't object?'

'Not at all.'

A silence came between them, until Rudie spoke. 'Is it easier for you now that my mother's gone?'

Blanche nodded. 'Of course,' she said. 'It's difficult to get on with someone who has an irrational dislike of one. She didn't like me simply because I came from America. I always knew that nothing I did would win her over. I knew that she would never like me. And that was hard, especially when I had lost my own mother.'

They walked towards the orchard and the field beyond. It was still early. The sky was a confident blue and the sun weak and hazy.

'Let's go up to the top of the Downs,' suggested Rudie. 'I feel like getting some proper exercise and I haven't been up there for a long time.'

Blanche did not hesitate. Her guests were well catered for and the children were with Nanny.

The chalky side of the Downs was steep and it took them a good half-hour to reach the top, by which time they were puffing hard. They flopped down on a patch of grass where the sun had already dried the dew. They were breathing heavily after the scramble, mouths open, hearts pounding.

'It feels so good,' gasped Blanche. 'It reminds me that I have a body and I'm not just a thinking thing.'

For a few minutes they lay on their backs in the grass watching the puffy white clouds race across the blue sky. The leaves of the trees rustled in the light breeze and a hawk circled overhead, watching out for the movement of small animals below.

Rudie sat up, hugging his knees. 'I love to look at the leaves on the trees in the wind. It always makes me amazed to think that they will never all be in the same position in the air more than once. They will never repeat that pattern. It's wonderful, just like this view!' He made a sweeping gesture with his arm. 'Imagine what the Romans thought when they came here, building the road from London to Chichester. It feels like being on top of the world. They must have felt so powerful.'

'They were,' laughed Blanche. 'It just confirmed it.'

After a while they got up and walked a few moments in silence. As she walked, Blanche pulled up long pieces of grass which she chewed thoughtfully.

'What are your dreams, Rudie?' she asked. 'What do you want from life?'

Rudie kicked a large lump of chalk with his shoe. 'What do I want from life? What most people want, I suppose. To love a good person, to do interesting things, to have well-rewarded and rewarding employment.' He turned to look at Blanche. 'And what about you? What do you want?'

'I don't know,' Blanche replied. 'I have so much already. I have a good husband, my children, enough money not to have to worry about it. I have an interesting life, and yet . . .'

As she hesitated, Rudie looked interested. 'And yet?'

Blanche shrugged her narrow shoulders. 'I don't know. I have so much already yet I want something more. I yearn for something else, though I can't tell you what because I don't know what it is.'

They had stopped on the ridge. 'Look, there's East Head and Chichester Harbour.' He pointed out in the distance where the sky and the sea seemed to merge. The curve of the land was like a shimmering mirage before her eyes.

Rudie continued to stare into the distance as he spoke. 'I'm not surprised to hear you say that. My brother is not the most exciting of men,' he said quietly.

'No,' Blanche agreed in a low voice.

'In fact, I think he's very dull.'

'Yes.' Blanche's voice was barely audible.

Now he turned to look at her. 'Are you disappointed with him?'

Blanche was quiet and thoughtful. 'I thought he would change, and I was wrong.' Then she added quickly, 'But he's a good man, and he means well.'

Rudie chuckled and grabbed Blanche's hand. 'Oh, you should have married the younger brother, then you wouldn't be wanting more now.'

Blanche pulled her hand away and laughed. 'Perhaps you're right, Rudie, but I made my choice and I must stick with it. Besides, I'm not sure that one person can make another completely satisfied. That seems too simplistic.' She tossed back her head. 'Come on, now, let's walk some more.'

Again they walked on through the woods and across the fields, disturbing the pheasants and partridges as they went. The birds rose into the air with a whirring of wings.

'Why did you marry Gussie?' Rudie was gaining confidence. His question was blunt and bold. 'What were you running away from in America?'

Blanche stopped abruptly and spun round, looking at him sharply, her eyes bright and startled. Then she relaxed and let out a soft laugh. 'Don't be so silly, Rudie,' she said. 'I married Gussie because I loved him.'

Rudie nodded and smiled. 'Of course,' he said, 'I know that.'

He took her hand again and pulled her to him gently. 'I'm going to do something I've been longing to do for years. Please don't slap me.'

Before Blanche could protest, Rudie was kissing her on the lips. She closed her eyes and allowed her body to relax against his.

The kiss lasted for less than ten seconds. Then Blanche pulled away quickly and started to walk ahead, her lips tingling.

They did not talk again. They walked back down the steep

side of the Down in silence. Blanche was feeling excited by
what had happened, and afraid of what it might mean. But
she also had a glowing inside. Never in all his embraces had
Gussie kissed her with such gentleness and passion. This
simple kiss had set something alight in her.

They arrived back at the house as some of the house guests
were just starting a game of croquet on the lawn. Others were
sitting on the terrace drinking coffee.

Blanche turned to Rudie and whispered fiercely, 'I have no
regrets but that must never happen again. I love you dearly and
I want you as a brother-in-law, not a lover, or even a husband.
Please, Rudie, say that you agree.'

Rudie laughed. 'Oh, you're safe from my attentions,
Blanche. Our friendship is quite safe. I'm actually getting
married myself later this year.'

Blanche looked up with interest. 'To whom? How wonderful! Is it someone we know? And what a shame your mother
isn't alive to see you settle down. She was always complaining
about your bachelor status.'

Rudie grinned. 'It's only because she isn't alive that I feel I
can get married. My fiancée is French and Mother loathed the
French even more than she loathed Americans. I had to wait
until Mother died before I could commit myself to Natalie. It
just would not have been fair to subject her to my mother's
hostility.'

'What a pragmatist you are!' Blanche laughed. 'Well, all
I can say about that cowardly behaviour is that you're lucky
your mother didn't live for another fifteen years, which her
doctor said was perfectly possible. That would have made it
difficult for you – and for Natalie.'

Rudie took her arm and guided her towards the house. 'Yes,
well fortunately we don't have that problem now.'

Blanche gave Rudie a playful push. 'A word of advice. If

you're about to get married, you shouldn't be going around kissing other people.'

'I thought we all believed in Free Love,' replied Rudie.

Blanche shook her head in mock disbelief. 'Free Love is a nice enough concept for debate, but I've noticed that in actual fact more men seem to believe in it than women.'

She started to run across the lawn. 'Come on, enough of this. I'll race you back. I can't wait to tell Gussie your news. I know he'll be delighted.'

The two ran fast across the garden, greeting the other guests as they came towards the house.

CHAPTER 8

~~

Sussex, 1926–1931

Blanche's garden was beginning to take shape. She had got rid of the dour shrubbery of laurels and skimmias and planted a wild-flower meadow. She gave curves to the lawn and built pergolas for roses and clematis to grow over, creating gateways into other areas of the garden, so that it became a place of mystery and discovery. The herbaceous borders were given fluid shapes and the wide formal garden, with its low box hedges, was reduced in size to give way to an avenue of rhododendrons and azaleas.

The lawns were redesigned, with half of them given over to long grass dotted with red poppies with paths of mown grass slicing through them. Overall, the effect was to give the eye a softer and more varied view, with soft curving lines that enticed one to follow them, to find out what was beyond.

Blanche found herself getting more and more involved in the garden. Whether in London or Sussex, her waking thoughts focused on the next horticultural project and how to tackle it. It seemed that all her passion and energy were being channelled into this one scheme.

Augustus did not like the changes and he was disturbed by Blanche's plans. 'I do wish you would leave some of it as it is,' he grumbled one morning at breakfast. 'By the time you've finished, the place will be unrecognisable as my mother's garden.'

Blanche laughed. 'Why, that's the whole point, Gussie!' She sipped her coffee and smiled so sweetly at him that Augustus had no idea if she was being ironic or not. He grunted and went back to his newspaper.

Blanche knew that Augustus did not really care about the garden, so long as it was well-tended and neat. And since he took no interest in gardening himself she knew that he would not interfere, even if he complained occasionally. He just could not understand why anyone should wish to alter anything that was perfectly acceptable already. And a bit of him also felt that Blanche was showing an unhealthy disrespect for his dead mother, but he would never say that to her face.

'There's a practical reason for making these changes, too, Gussie,' said Blanche. 'It's getting harder and harder to find gardeners nowadays – it's almost as difficult as finding a good cook. Apart from wanting to create my own garden, to my own design, I also want to create one that does not rely too much on the work of a huge team of men. Your mother's garden required a ridiculous number of staff just to maintain it. At one point, I know she had fourteen. I want something different that can be managed with very little labour. I'm spending many hours on it now but eventually I hope to be able to spend more time just wandering around and enjoying it.'

Blanche pored over books and literature from the nurseries. She went to the Chelsea Flower Show and visited gardens whenever she could, for ideas of her own. Her enthusiasm and passion surprised her but at some level she recognised that her obsession was a way of keeping certain internal passions under control.

Her children were a delight to her but she did not see a great deal of them. Evelyn and Adrian spent most of the day with

Nanny, and were brought down daily to say hello and to have a goodnight kiss before bed.

In the country she romped with the children on the lawn or walked around the woods with Evelyn on her fat Shetland pony and Adrian in the pram. She gave them everything they could want – dogs, cats, ponies and toys and puzzles to keep them busy throughout the day.

Evelyn was an inhibited child, who aroused protective feelings in her mother, especially since Gussie showed little interest in her and did not even attempt to disguise his preference for the boy. He was much more at ease with Adrian than with Evelyn. To Blanche, Adrian was like a golden child. He was beautiful to look at with honey-coloured skin and long dark eyelashes over his bright, dark eyes. His personality was lively and matched his quick brain. He was forever asking questions and dancing about, fired by the sheer excitement of living. Very advanced for his age in everything, he had learned to walk before he was ten months old and began talking fluently by the age of two. Adrian enjoyed the company of both children and adults and his permanently sunny disposition placed poor Evelyn in the dark shadows. Everyone paid a lot of attention to Adrian and little to her.

Blanche felt that no matter how hard she tried it would be impossible to make up for this unfair situation. She no longer said anything to Augustus because he indignantly denied that he treated the children differently. She was glad that Nanny was such a kind and sensitive woman who seemed to go out of her way to make Evelyn happy, but the sad look on Evelyn's face as she watched Augustus play and talk with Adrian made Blanche wince.

Blanche's marriage to Augustus had settled down as a functional arrangement. Augustus worked hard at the bank in the week and brought in the money. Blanche carried out her duties as a wife extremely well, running both houses and staff with skill and competence.

Augustus let her live the social life she wanted and was happy to appear at her social gatherings even if he did not want to get involved very much. He was also happy for her to go out with her friends, leaving him behind to his own company, which he preferred.

They were civil to each other and lived together with ease. But there were no feelings of love in their marriage. Blanche would sit opposite him as they ate dinner, watching Augustus cut his food with great precision and bring it to his mouth to chew fastidiously before swallowing. He was a man of habit in every way.

Augustus's views on social matters were also different from those of Blanche. In the village a half-witted girl had been made pregnant by her own father. The vicar had come to visit Augustus to ask his advice about the matter. Together the men decided to send both father and daughter away so as to avoid a scandal.

Blanche was not impressed and was visibly upset by this judgement. 'What good will that do to any of them – father, girl or baby?'

But her views were ignored and the family packed off out of sight.

And now, aged forty, Gussie was never going to change. Sometimes Blanche had to remind herself sharply that she must not complain, but she did her best to avoid such reflection because it took her too close to other matters too painful to think about. When she felt this happening, she would tell herself how lucky and how happy she was. She could not complain about anything; she had everything she wanted and had ever wished for.

And yet, she felt there was something missing, something

that Gussie could never understand. She had such powerful feelings inside her; she yearned for intimacy and passion. Every good piece of literature, every book she read, every piece of music she listened to, every play she saw, stirred up these feelings so violently that she would be frightened by their strength, feeling like a boat at sea without a mooring to hold her safe and secure.

It was when she was in such a state that she met Ivo.

In recent years, ice-skating had become all the rage. Blanche, who had grown up in a place where the temperature rarely touched freezing, was fascinated by the sport. In the winter of 1931 the temperature dropped well below freezing and stayed there for several weeks. Sussex was particularly cold; everyone pulled on extra woollen underwear and all the fires in the house were kept blazing for most of the day and night.

Blanche did not enjoy being cold but she did love the countryside touched by snow and ice and delighted at the silhouettes of the trees, black against the sky, their boughs edged with crystals of white frost.

The ponds and lakes had frozen over and the ice was thick enough for skating. Every day, Blanche went to the pond in the wood to practise. She had never done it before this winter but she quickly improved until she could skate confidently across the ice, her gloved hands clasped behind her. She could spin gracefully, her back straight, her arms outstretched. Occasionally the ice cracked and groaned deeply, the sound reverberating and echoing on into the woods beyond.

This pond was a private spot, surrounded by high rhododendron bushes which hid it from the footpath that ran all around it. Blanche loved the place, enjoying the solitude it offered, and in the spring and summer often came to sit on the bank to sketch and paint the scene. In the winter, she would stand and listen to the silence of the frosted water.

One day, she made her way to the pond and began to skate, slowly at first, and then faster, enjoying the cold air on her cheeks and forehead. Then she tried out some new steps, which entailed complicated backward jumps. She suddenly lost her balance and skidded. Her arms flapped helplessly as her legs shot out in front of her. She landed with a graceless thump on her bottom.

'That must've hurt!'

A loud voice boomed across the icy pond. As Blanche grimaced at the shock to her backbone, she looked up to see who had seen her embarrassing fall.

Standing by the gap in the rhododendrons with a black labrador by his side was a large tall man in a tweed coat. He wore a hat over his wild, wiry grey hair. 'Are you all right, my dear?'

Blanche tried to push herself up off the ice with her hands. One skate slipped backwards and she was down again, her legs splayed awkwardly beneath her.

The man had come to the edge. 'Having trouble? Here, give me your hand.' He held out a large gloved hand.

Blanche was blushing with embarrassment. It was as if she had lost all control of her limbs. She crawled unceremoniously towards the edge of the pond and reached up to catch the man's hand.

She felt his grip tighten as she heaved herself up on to her skates. Then she allowed him to pull her in and she sat down on the mossy bank.

'Thank you,' she gasped. 'I'm mortified. You must think me the clumsiest creature you've ever seen.'

She looked up at him with her large brown eyes, noticing immediately how brightly blue his own eyes were.

The man laughed. 'I would never think such a thing when I can't skate myself, or rather, won't. I wouldn't dream of risking my neck skating on any natural pond – and I never saw the point of buzzing around on a sheet of ice getting colder and colder.'

Blanche laughed back. 'I know it can look ridiculous but it can also be so graceful – like ballet.'

The man snorted. '"Can" is the operative word,' he said. 'Most of the time, people's movements are far from graceful – not,' he added hastily, 'that I could say that of you.'

Blanche glanced sideways at him. 'Why, that's pure flattery, sir, for you know it's not true, after what you witnessed a few minutes ago.'

The man thrust his hand out. 'Ivo Barnard,' he said. 'I'm sorry. I should have introduced myself.'

Blanche held up her hand for it to be squeezed. 'Blanche Champion,' she said.

'Champion? Are you one of the Champions of Avery Hall?'

'Indeed I am, sir,' replied Blanche, emphasising her Southern drawl. 'My husband is Augustus Champion.'

The man drew back and scrutinised her hard. 'Then I believe we have met before, Mrs Champion, many years ago at the home of my friend Mrs Henrietta Champion.'

Blanche looked at him, unsure of what to say. Then she smiled. 'So you're not a stranger, after all. Henrietta is my cousin. Forgive me if I don't remember, but were we introduced then, Mr Barnard?'

'We were indeed,' Ivo said and laughed. 'I remember that you had just arrived in England, and you enchanted the entire company by dancing one of those modern dances with great skill and expertise.' He smiled slyly. 'And a little more style, if I may say, than you have developed, as yet, on the ice.'

Blanche looked delighted. 'How extraordinary! Why haven't we met since? I've been in this country for eleven years now, and I see Henrietta several times a year. Why haven't I seen you at her house?'

'I've been away travelling for a long time. I've been to India, and then China and Japan. I'm a painter, and I've been away for years looking for new ideas and inspiration.'

Blanche was intrigued. 'So what brings you to this part of the world? To Graffham?'

'I've recently bought a small cottage here in the woods – soon after I returned home from abroad. I knew I wanted to settle away from London – London has too many temptations for a man like myself. I've just got my studio finished and the cottage into shape, and I'm pleased I made the decision I did. I've been doing some good work down here, away from the soot. But then,' he added, sweeping back his arm to indicate the landscape around them, 'how can this not be inspiring?'

Blanche pushed herself to her feet and tottered on her skates towards her bag and boots. 'Where is your cottage? I thought I had got to know everyone around here.'

'It's deep in the wood, down a very overgrown lane. There's no reason for you to know about it,' he said, 'unless you were looking for it. It used to be the gamekeeper's home.'

Blanche had laced up her boots and slung her skates over her shoulder. 'Well, it's been a pleasure to meet you – and I trust that you won't be describing my most undignified efforts on ice to any of our mutual acquaintances.'

Ivo laughed. 'I wouldn't dream of it, Mrs Champion. Trust me. I'll escort you to the main path.'

'Well, you must come and visit us, Mr Barnard. Would you do that?'

Ivo shook his head. 'Thank you, but I won't. I'm afraid

I'm rather shunning company nowadays. I'm getting very unsociable in my old age. But perhaps you'd like to visit me in my little home among the trees one day. You'd be very welcome.'

'Yes, I'd like that indeed,' replied Blanche. 'Now, I must get back to organise lunch. My husband gets so cross when it's late and our new cook is still settling in.'

They shook hands and parted. As Blanche walked back through the snowy wood, the image of Ivo's intense blue eyes remained before her. She felt quite unsettled by the meeting – and surprised by her reaction to this stranger in the wood. Though, of course, he was not a stranger. As he had told her, they had once been introduced by Henrietta.

As Blanche walked on towards home, she found herself reliving the encounter over and over in her head. She could still feel the strength of his hand as he helped her up.

She asked Augustus at lunch, 'Do you know someone called Ivo Barnard? He lives in a cottage in the woods.'

Augustus was concentrating on his bread and butter pudding. 'Ivo? He's moved down here, has he?' He grunted. 'Never had much time for him,' he muttered. 'A Bohemian. Not my type at all.'

He took a mouthful of food and chewed it as he thought some more. 'He's very unreliable, I think. He's been divorced at least once. Divorced the first wife, I think, and the second one died. I'm not sure. Well, that's one thing I am proud of. There's never been a divorce in our family and there never will be. I think it's dreadful the way married couples think they can break those vows they made at the altar.'

The breakdown of other people's marriages was a favourite subject for discussion with Augustus, along with the state of the family finances, which had just about survived the Wall Street Crash two years before.

Blanche knew that there was no point in arguing but she could not stop herself. 'But if two people are dreadfully unhappy together, surely it's better that they part than spend the rest of their lives making each other miserable.'

Augustus shook his head dismissively. 'No, no, there's never a good reason for divorce. Never.'

Blanche poured herself some water and sipped it from her glass. Whatever Augustus thought, she knew that he was wrong and she was right.

She decided not to ask any more questions about Ivo because they would probably only set Augustus off again. But Ivo intrigued her. She would visit Henrietta and find out about him from her. Henrietta always knew everything about other people, and was only too happy to tell.

CHAPTER 9

1931

'Ivo Barnard is a wonderful man, and a most talented artist.'

Henrietta sat back in her chair and talked of her friend with pride. 'His first wife, Eliza, was a witch. I don't know why he married her. Though she was very attractive and a talented artist herself, I think she felt eclipsed by Ivo's early success. She was horribly competitive and always seemed to me to be angry, so very angry that she did not get the acclaim she thought she deserved. Perhaps she would have been more successful if she hadn't married Ivo. I don't think two people of artistic temperament can live happily together. One is bound to be more successful than the other – though that isn't necessarily the most talented one,' she added, 'but in this case he was.

'Whatever was true in this relationship, Eliza drove him away from the house and finally divorced Ivo for adultery. He was well rid of her, though, for she was truly unsympathetic. I tried to be on her side at times, when I thought Ivo was being unfair, but she made it very difficult for people to like her. To her mind, everything was everyone else's fault, and unfair.

'It may be that she had a difficult time but I believe that

we make our own lives. You have to make the most of what you have yourself, and not expect anyone else to do it for you. Eliza just whined constantly and blamed everyone else for any misfortune she had.

'Ivo then married Dora, a most charming young woman, about a year before you arrived in London, I should say. She was an artist, too, a potter, but very young and modest about her talents. I always thought she was a little too much in awe of Ivo. She was going to have a baby but something dreadful happened. The baby burst her womb and they couldn't save Dora or the child. It was a terrible, terrible time.

'Ivo collapsed. He's always been a melancholic kind of fellow, with a tendency to have dark moods, but this was a total collapse, and I was very afraid for him, too. I really didn't think he would survive that time.

'But he did. He picked himself up slowly and began to paint again a little. I think his painting took on an extra dimension after Dora's death. It even had more depth. Then, soon after that he took himself abroad, to the Far East, where he stayed for years.'

Henrietta sat back in her high-backed chair and drew on her long silver cigarette-holder. She held the smoke in her lungs and then blew it out slowly through pursed lips. 'I've seen him only once since he returned. I've missed him a lot. He's an interesting man. My husband always liked him, too, so I got to know him well, as a family friend.'

She watched the cigarette smoke hanging in the air and then looked over at Blanche's pretty, open face. 'I don't think Gussie has ever liked him very much,' she added.

'No,' agreed Blanche. 'Gussie told me that himself. He said Ivo wasn't his type.'

Henrietta raised her eyebrows and nodded knowingly. 'That makes sense,' she said dryly. 'Ivo is far too complex a character for old Gussie.' She reached over to the table next to her chair. 'Now,' she said, 'I have just read Mr Lawrence's new book, the one everyone is scandalised by. It's been lent to me by a friend but I'm sure you can borrow it, if you promise to read it quickly. I shall look forward to hearing what you think of it. I can't really see what the fuss is about, myself.'

The following week the weather changed dramatically. The snow melted and frost dripped from the trees. The ice disappeared and snowdrops and early wild crocuses appeared in the woods on the banks beside the stream. The sun shone in a cloudless blue sky and the birds, thinking that spring had come at last, opened their throats and sang joyfully from their perches.

Blanche was determined to see Ivo again. She had been out riding on the common with Evelyn and Adrian on their ponies that morning, and in the afternoon they were going to play with their friends who were coming over from Midhurst. Gussie was in his study reading and Blanche told him that she was going off for a walk.

She set off through the wood to the path that Ivo had mentioned – through a tiny overgrown gap in the rhododendrons. The leaf mould was soft and damp under her leather boots. Occasionally there was a quick rustling in the undergrowth as a rabbit or a pheasant fled from her disturbing presence. Then she found herself walking along a ridge, with the ground dropping steeply to the right, where it led down to a small brook. On the other side were soggy green fields in which small herds of sheep and cows grazed.

The path cut round a group of ancient beech trees and there, several yards down in a small clearing, was the cottage, standing alone, surrounded by a wild and overgrown garden. Blanche could not understand why she had never encountered it before. It was like the witch's cottage in the story of 'Hansel and Gretel'.

She walked up to the door and knocked.

Ivo opened it. 'Why, Mrs Champion,' he said, standing back and bowing chivalrously, 'do come into my humble home.'

'I do hope you don't mind my just turning up like this,' said Blanche. 'I'm anxious not to disturb your work.' She suddenly felt nervous, and wondered if her forwardness was inappropriate.

Ivo shook his shaggy head. 'Not at all,' he said. 'I've recently finished a big painting and I'm just thinking about what I'm going to do next.' He stepped back. 'Do please come in. Can I offer you some tea or coffee? Or something stronger?'

Blanche sat in the small sitting-room on a squishy sofa while Ivo filled the kettle and put it on to boil in the small kitchen.

The whole cottage was small. It comprised two rooms downstairs, with the kitchen and bathroom built into a lean-to at the back. The narrow staircase was hidden away behind a door in the wall, and wound its way up to two small bedrooms above. Of the rooms downstairs, one was the sitting-room, which had book shelves covering the walls. The shelves had bowed under the weight of the books, which also sat in piles all around. The other room had a small table and two chairs, and a black piano in the corner.

Blanche looked around. 'But where do you work? I was looking forward to seeing some of your paintings.'

They're in my studio, across the garden. It's a separate building I added myself. It was the first thing I did when I bought this place. I'll show it to you in a minute.'

'This tea is delicious,' said Blanche, peering at the liquid in her cup. 'It's wonderfully delicate . . . unusual.'

Ivo smiled. 'It's green tea, and very special. I brought it

back from Japan where tea is revered. Did you know that the tea plant is related to the camellia bush? It was cultivated in prehistoric China and was probably first used as a vegetable relish there, as it was by your ancestors in the American colonies.'

Blanche was sat forward, her hands clasping the china teacup resting on her knees. 'No, I didn't know any of that,' she said.

She felt edgy, more excited than nervous, but she did not know why.

'Are you glad to be back home after all your travelling? Do you miss the Far East?'

Ivo shook his head. 'I don't miss it, not particularly. I'm glad to be back but I felt it was the right thing to do at the time. My wife and child had just died and I didn't know what to do with myself. It was only by going off to foreign places that I was able to hide from myself during those first few years. Then I got well enough to work again and found studying under the great Japanese potters very helpful for my own work.'

'But you're a painter primarily, aren't you? That's what cousin Henrietta told me.'

'Well, all art forms are of interest to artists. You'll find that many potters paint or weave, and many painters throw pots or sculpt. My main interest is certainly in paints and painting, yes, but I love to throw pots, or carve a shape out of a beautiful piece of wood. I'm primarily a landscape painter but I enjoy doing portraits even though they are not my strength.'

After their tea was finished, Ivo led Blanche across the garden to a wooden structure, like a summer house, which looked out across the ridge towards the fields and the South Downs beyond. 'This is my lair,' he said, standing back to let her step inside. 'This is where I am happy.'

A lumpy sofa had been placed against the far wall and was covered with exotic Persian fabrics and Indian cushions. On the wall opposite hung framed Japanese prints. Against another wall were canvases leaning against each other. Silhouetted against the window was a large easel.

Blanche was suddenly aware of his eyes running over her, scrutinising her shape and form. Embarrassed, she became more and more self-aware. She looked down at her feet and turned her head away so that he would not see her blushing face.

Nothing needed to be said. Why else had she come, after all? Ivo took her hand and led her to the sofa. She went without resistance, knowing what was about to happen.

He kissed her neck as he gently took off her clothes and then beckoned her to lie down on the sofa so that he could gaze down at her long white body while he undressed.

It was then that Blanche knew the distinction between marital relations and the act of love. Ivo was much older than her and his body was showing the signs of age, the flesh soft, the skin loose, but that made no difference to her pleasure. The warmth and strength of his body, the soft grey hairs on his chest and arms, the gentle way in which he touched and handled her body, inflamed her. The dormant passion that had first been kindled by Rudie's kiss the summer before was now fully unleashed. Blanche gave way to her impulses, letting go of all control, abandoning herself to her instincts. Never had she experienced such physical joy.

Afterwards they lay entwined on the sofa, half-covered with the colourful cloth. Blanche's heart pounded as she stroked Ivo's hirsute chest.

'What is happening to me?' she murmured. 'I have committed adultery, and I don't care.'

Ivo stroked her hair and nuzzled the top of her head. 'You're growing up, my dear. It's only by throwing off the shackles of our upbringing and learning to go with our spontaneous feelings that we can truly live life to the full. Any other kind of life is not worth living.' He pulled himself up and sat on the edge of the sofa. 'Now the next thing I want to do to you, apart from fuck you, of course, is paint that beautiful body of yours.'

CHAPTER 10

1931–1932

The early 1930s were happy years for Blanche. With careful management, Gussie was slowly building up the family fortunes to a comfortable level, allowing Blanche to live much as she liked. She spent half her time in London and the other half in Sussex. In London she moved in cultured circles, going to poetry readings in Bloomsbury, plays and art exhibitions. Her friends increasingly came from arty groups, many of them introduced to her by Ivo, rather than from society contacts of Gussie's.

She went on her own to most events, normally meeting Ivo there.

Her affair with him was an open secret among their friends, and they were frequently invited to parties and openings together. Ivo made Blanche feel alive. 'You must live your life to the full,' he urged her. 'It's imperative to experience everything at its most intense. That is what life is for.'

And Ivo himself did everything intensely. When he was not working on a painting he spent a lot of time socialising, visiting people, drinking vast quantities of whisky and smoking French cigarettes. With his wild laugh and flashing blue eyes, he was an entertaining guest whose presence was always welcome.

When he was working on a painting, he was completely different. Then he would shut himself up in his cottage for weeks at a time, seeing no one, working through the night, sleeping in the day, not shaving and missing meals. And when the painting was finished, he would want to see Blanche, to sink into her soft body and hold her tight, as though finishing the painting gave him a need to be contained. 'We have to try everything before it's too late,' he said. '"But at my back I always hear, Time's wingéd chariot hurrying near." Andrew Marvell, "To His Coy Mistress",' he added with a grin.

Blanche would then come every day, and they would make love on the floor of the studio, in front of the fire if it was winter, or outside in the fresh open air if it was fine and warm.

Ivo made Blanche aware of her body in a way she would never have imagined before. Before Ivo, her only experience of sex had, at the very least, been unrewarding and dismal. Gussie no longer troubled her in bed but in the past, when he did, his idea of love-making amounted to silent awkward groping and fumbling in the dark. And always seemingly reluctantly done in a way that had left Blanche feeling sad and alone. Ivo, by contrast, had an almost electrifying presence; he made her feel sexually alive in response. He kissed her deeply, he marvelled at her naked body, running his hands over her curved belly and limbs as if noting the structure of her bones and muscles beneath her white skin.

He nibbled her ears, ran his tongue over her legs. He lifted her up and kissed her neck. He always kissed her and prepared her for more, building up her own excitement until she was pulling him to her, taking the initiative, guiding him to her, kissing and caressing as much as he did. What she loved most of all was simply being held tightly in his arms, lying quietly with her head on his broad chest.

When she experienced her first climax, Blanche did not know what had happened. She felt possessed, taken over for several seconds, her body beyond her control. 'That was the strangest, most wonderful feeling,' she murmured into Ivo's chest. 'It went right through me.'

Ivo smiled and ruffled her hair. 'Women have it better than men. The female orgasm seems more generalised throughout the body. For men, it's localised.'

Blanche looked up at him, pushing her fingers through the thick curly grey hairs on his chest. Beads of sweat fell down her brow, her body pulled towards him, aching. 'For all these years I have missed out. I have to make up for it now.' Her hand moved down his belly. 'You've turned me into a whore, Ivo.'

Ivo laughed. 'That's the Southern lady in you, my dear. You're not a whore to want sexual satisfaction. Women are entitled to enjoy sex as much as men.' He clutched her hand. 'The trouble is, I'm not sure if I'm up to it again so soon. I'm getting on, you know. I'm not a young man any more. I'm sorry.'

They lay in each other's arms as the sun went down and the studio grew dim. 'That emotional rush we experience in sex,' he said, 'that intensity of pleasure, is what I strive for in my work. When a painting is going well, when it's building up to how I want it, the excitement in my veins is the same, and the feeling is like a sated release at the end, when the painting is finished, when it's perfect and how I want it. It is exactly the same as that ultimate sexual pleasure. Seek it in life and you will be much rewarded. That's what I mean by living life to the full. It's reaching that state of exhilaration in as many areas as possible. You feel it reading a great poem or novel. You can feel it listening to a brilliant piece of music, or looking at a great work of art. Seek and you shall find it.'

He kissed her cheek and pushed some damp curls off her brow. 'You have such a dull husband. You can tell that he's not interested in an inner life – he doesn't have one. He doesn't read books or listen to anything except Gilbert and Sullivan. He's a philistine.' Ivo laughed quietly. 'I doubt if he even enjoys sexual intercourse. But what you do get from him – and this is not to be ignored – is the freedom to live as you want. Take the opportunity while you can. He takes his duties as a husband seriously, which is good for you. He wants a pretty wife who will run a good house and help him look successful to the world. So long as you don't do anything to embarrass or expose him, you'll be able to do what you want.'

'I think he has a woman in London,' said Blanche.

'That wouldn't surprise me,' replied Ivo. 'But you should be happy with that. He won't begrudge you your affairs if he is getting whatever pleasure he needs from someone else . . .'

'So long as it's not someone I know,' said Blanche. 'I would find that hard to put up with.'

Ivo rolled over on top of her again. 'I very much doubt that he's seeing anyone you know,' he said. 'In fact, you can almost be certain that it's not anyone you could ever know.'

He kissed her gently. 'But what about you? You're being a little hypocritical, aren't you, having an affair with someone Gussie knows?'

Blanche giggled and ran her hands over his back. 'Oh, that's different,' she said.

'Come on, now, I feel my strength coming back. Let's

converse biologically again – the best kind of conversation in the world.'

Blanche threw back her head and let Ivo nibble at her long white throat. 'We must be quick,' she said. 'The new gardener and his family are arriving this afternoon and I've promised Evelyn and Adrian that they can come with me to see them settled into their cottage.'

EVELYN

CHAPTER 11

1932–1934

Blanche had been cutting down on the number of staff at the Sussex house and her newly designed garden demanded nothing like the work of fourteen gardeners, as had been the case in her mother-in-law's time. She now employed two but she had been anxious that one was a head gardener who was familiar with the kind of design she had created. Rather than the rigid shapes and colours of the formal garden, with large beds of flowers grown especially for cutting and displaying in the house, Blanche's grounds were now an enticing controlled wilderness, with shapes, colours, foliage and texture combining to lead the eye over a never-ending scene.

Matt Knight had spent many years working as the under-gardener to Melissa, an acquaintance of Blanche who had a large house in Chichester. Blanche had long admired Melissa's garden and had been pleased when Melissa herself suggested that Matt move on to her. 'He's so talented and he's not going to be head gardener here for a long time since Tony Jones is only in his early fifties and won't be moving on, I don't think.'

Matt Knight was a tall man of thirty-five. He had curly black hair and muscular brown arms. A good-looking man, Blanche noted. His wife was pretty, too.

Peggy Knight was small and lithe with intelligent brown

eyes and a small red mouth. She was to be the junior housekeeper in the house, overseeing the maids and the cook.
If she fitted in, she would eventually take over from Mrs
May, the current housekeeper, who was getting on and very
arthritic, and unlikely to keep working for much longer.

The Knights had one child of about Evelyn's age, a boy
named Frank. He was as dark and handsome as his father
but had a quiet brooding manner and always seemed to be
watching everything around him very carefully.

The cottage the Knights moved into was at the bottom of
the drive. It was small, with two tiny bedrooms on the first
floor, a tiny front room and a kitchen in a lean-to at the
back. The garden ran down to the road. Unlike the big house,
which had recently had electricity installed throughout,
the cottage remained without such modern conveniences.
Much to Blanche's disapproval, Augustus had refused to
put electricity in the cottage when the big house was done.
'It's an extra expense we don't need,' he had said. 'The
gardener doesn't need electricity. They can use candles and
lanterns just as they always have. Besides, they wouldn't be
able to pay the electricity bill and then we would have to
help them out.'

Blanche was not impressed at the time. 'It seems unnecess-
arily mean,' she commented. 'Our own house? Lots of the
small cottages in the village are getting electricity now.'

Evelyn was only truly happy when she was down in
Sussex. She enjoyed school enough but she had no close
friends there, and the concrete and buildings of London
made her feel quite claustrophobic at times. In Sussex,
where she came with her family every weekend and holiday,
she felt free because she could be left alone to escape, to
wander around the huge grounds of the house and to explore
the fields and woods beyond.

She was now eleven and a quiet, closed child. The moment breakfast was over, she pulled on her boots and set off for the woods and meadows with a basket and sketchbook. On her walk she would collect wild flowers to paint and subsequently press for her big scrapbook. There were bluebells and red campion and wild-beaked parsley, as well as violets and wild arums all in flower. She loved pushing her legs through the dew-soaked grass, listening to the blackbird's powerful morning song and watching the swallows swoop and turn over the small lake at the bottom of the hill. Some of the horse-chestnut trees were a mass of white blossom, and on the beech trees flowers were coming out that were scarcely distinguishable from the pale green of the foliage.

In the woods themselves, which were all part of the grounds, she had a favourite spot under an old oak tree, where she often sat for hours, sketching the branches above her, or interesting leaves or fungi she had picked up on the way. She would stay listening to the rustling of small animals in the undergrowth or the crashing of the pigeons through the trees. The wood pigeons would call softly to each other through the leaves, and she could see the cows, relaxed after their early morning milking, grazing in the fields below.

Out of the corner of her eye she was aware of some movement on the log on which she sat. It was a large wood ant carrying a twig twice its length, negotiating with some tenacity every obstacle that came its way.

She took out her sketchbook and drew the ant as it struggled up the log, over the bumpy terrain of the bark. She did not mind ants on their own, like this one. What she hated were the big anthills in the woods, creations sometimes three feet high, made up of leaf mould and twigs, similar to the one this ant carried, and as still as the water on the lake, until you poked it with a stick or, worse, stepped into it. Then swarms of angry ants would rush out, ready to defend their home, crawling up your leg and spreading out all around, sending alarm signals to ants outside the nest. The struggling ant, thought Evelyn, seemed to be far more confident than she herself ever felt in life.

She did not hear the footsteps behind her until Frank was right next to her.

'What are you doing, then?'

Evelyn jumped with alarm. 'Oh, hello,' she said shyly. She had not met the new gardener's son but she had seen him in the distance, wandering in the woods on a few occasions.

'I'm drawing this ant,' replied Evelyn. 'I need to do it quickly before it disappears.'

'What do you want to do that for?'

Frank's dark eyes looked at her steadily.

'For my scrapbook. I like to draw animals and plants. Then when I'm in London, where I go to school, they remind me of all the things that are here in the countryside. There's nothing like this place in London. There are some parks but the air is very dirty so very few plants can grow happily there.'

Frank stared at her, taking in her words. 'I've never been to London. It's a big place, is it?'

Evelyn nodded.

'Bigger than Chichester?'

'Much bigger than Chichester,' said Evelyn. 'Bigger than you can imagine.'

Frank looked thoughtful. 'I want to go to London one day,' he said. 'That's where fortunes are to be made.'

Evelyn smiled. 'That's what Dick Whittington thought anyway.'

Frank looked around him. 'Have you seen the moorhen's nest down by the pond in the woods?'

Evelyn shook her head.

Frank turned and began to walk away. 'Follow me, I'll show you,' he said.

So Evelyn followed the gardener's son along the soft path, through the rhododendron tunnel and down the steep incline to the stream. They followed the stream for a hundred yards, passing the bugle and plantains that were all in flower. Finally, they reached the pond, shining quietly in its secret spot surrounded by rhododendrons. Frank led Evelyn over to the stump of an old alder tree just at the edge of the bank. The moorhen's nest was made of sticks and pieces of dead reed. It contained one egg.

'What a messy nest,' said Evelyn.

'Sometimes they don't even bother to make their own, they just use other birds' nests.'

As Frank spoke, a moorhen appeared by the edge of the water, running swiftly, with its bobbing head and jerking tail. Disturbed by the children, it showed its annoyance with a sudden *'Prruk!'* as it slipped into the water, gliding away with its head still bobbing.

The children sat on the bank of the pond just where the stream ran into it, their legs dangling over the edge. 'There's good fish in this stream,' said Frank. 'I caught three trout the other evening.'

'I'd like to fish,' said Evelyn, 'but I hate the idea of hooks in the fishes' mouths.'

Frank shrugged. 'Fish are different,' he said. 'All animals are.'

He was looking sideways, towards a small bush to his right. Then a quiet chuckling sound came from his throat.

'What are you doing?' Evelyn stared at him, puzzled.

Frank put his finger on his lips, telling her to be quiet, and continued making the soft noise.

Then Evelyn heard a rustling in the bush. Some of the green leaves moved and a grey squirrel poked its head out, its beady black eyes bright and alert.

As Frank continued to make the sound, he put his hand into his pocket and pulled something out to offer to the squirrel, which now hopped tentatively towards him, stopping every now and then before continuing towards the boy's open hand containing the oats.

Within three minutes the squirrel was perched on Frank's arm eating its oats as he stroked it gently. 'Here, touch it gently. They like to be stroked.'

Evelyn ran her forefinger over the squirrel's back. She could feel the bony body beneath the fluffy coat. 'Is this your squirrel? Is that why it's so friendly?'

Frank shook his head. 'Not this one, I haven't seen it before,' he said with a grin. 'Animals just seem to like me. I don't know why. My mam says it's a gift, a charm.'

'Perhaps you should be a vet, then,' said Evelyn, impressed.

Frank shook his head. 'I want to get rich in the big city,' he said emphatically, 'away from the animals and the countryside.'

Frank's way with animals was impressive. As Evelyn spent more time with him she could not help noticing how dogs always ran up to him in the village as he walked past, and then did whatever he ordered them to do. Birds came and sat on his shoulder and picked nuts and berries he held in his teeth for them. He would hoot to owls and make them believe that he was a mate, and he and Evelyn would laugh when the answering call came through the night sky a few seconds later. Cats came and rubbed up against his legs or jumped into his lap if he was sitting down. The horses in the fields would follow and walk along behind him, nuzzling his back as if he were the leader of the herd, and even the most nervous pony would allow him to jump up on its back and ride around the field with no tack. Then the small beasts, the squirrels, dormice and rabbits, always appeared from the undergrowth when he made his peculiar chuckling whistle.

However hard Evelyn tried to imitate him or learn how he acted, she could not get it right. There was clearly something about Frank that all animals recognised. It seemed that this humble boy had an aura about him that attracted them as much as it did Evelyn.

Over the months, Evelyn and Frank became close friends insofar as their respective lives allowed. She looked forward to her weekends in the country all the more knowing that she was going to meet Frank and spend the entire two days outside with him, apart from mealtimes and when she went out riding on her pony.

She was poignantly aware of their differences – his torn and ragged clothes, his dirty fingernails and tousled, unbrushed black hair. She felt quite prim in her cotton skirt, white socks and shoes next to him. But she also felt close to Frank in a way she did not with anyone else. Perhaps she was just like all those animals, recognising this odd specialness in him. Something pulled her towards him and made her feel calm.

She was not happy at home. Her father had very little to say to her at mealtimes, which was the only time they met. He tended to test her on her spelling or mental arithmetic, as though he knew no other way of communicating. And her mother was always kind but tended to have her thoughts on other things, such as the next planting in the garden or a play she had seen the night before. And her brother Adrian was three years younger, and too young to be a proper companion. He was also becoming aware that their father preferred him and he was smug about the fact at times. It was no wonder that Evelyn became so attached to Frank.

It was Frank who first alerted Evelyn to the possibility of her mother's infidelity, and the unhappiness of her parents' marriage. Evelyn knew Ivo well. He was often around at the house, either in Sussex or London. She liked him because he did not ignore her. He talked to her, and did not seem to care that she was not pretty. Certainly he never commented on it, unlike everyone else. He was always friendly and seemed genuinely interested in her. But he was also rather noisy and very clever, which intimidated her at times. She could tell that her mother liked him a lot because she was always so happy and lively in his presence. They always had a lot to talk about and shared many interests. In spite of all this, it had never occurred to her that her mother's relationship with Ivo was anything more than friendly until Frank suggested otherwise.

'Does your pa know about what goes on?' He asked this cryptically one morning as they sat in their den in the woods – a hollow they had dug out of the hillside opposite the badgers' setts.

Evelyn turned and stared at her friend. 'What do you mean? Know about what?' But even as she asked, she knew what he meant, or at least she felt she knew, even if she would not at that point have been able to put it into words.

Frank pushed his hair off his forehead. 'About your mother and that artist man? The one that lives in Fox Cottage.'

'You mean Ivo Barnard?'

As she asked it, to her surprise, Evelyn knew exactly what

he was talking about. It was as clear as light. Even though she had never acknowledged it to herself and no one had ever said anything about it, Frank's question made everything seem as clear as the blue sky above the canopy of trees above them. Of course her mother and Ivo loved each other. It was so obvious to her now that Evelyn felt stupid for never realising it before. It all fell into place – Ivo's frequent presence, the happy bantering and jokes, the intense conversations, none of which went on between her mother and father.

All of a sudden, Evelyn felt a deep sorrow for her father because her mother did not love him. No wonder he was so bad-tempered and mean all the time. Other things seemed to make sense – her father's coldness, her mother's sharpness. It was to be some time before she realised that matters were not as black and white as they appeared, that one thing did not necessarily lead to another.

Initially, Evelyn was angry with her mother for her unfaithfulness and found herself siding with her father. She tried to be friendlier to him herself. She would watch him at Sunday lunch, carving the joint by the dark mahogany sideboard. His face would be set with concentration as he endeavoured to cut the leg of lamb before him in flawless slices, just as his father used to. The juices ran down in rivulets, bursting forth as the sharp knife cut into the sealed flesh.

One Sunday, the lunch party was relatively small, as only ten guests were staying that weekend and four of these had taken themselves off sailing at Del Quay in Chichester Harbour that day.

Blanche sat at the end of the table, dressed in a pale blue silk suit she had worn at church that morning. She was laughing and looking very spirited, as she always was in the company of her friends.

Evelyn watched her mother with a hardened feeling in her chest. Mama was so cruel to treat poor Papa so unkindly. Papa must be dreadfully hurt to have his wife betray him for another man.

Evelyn said very little at lunch, allowing Blanche and her friends to discuss Virginia Woolf's new novel and the art exhibitions they had seen in London, as well as the situation in Germany, which was getting very worrying, they all agreed. Augustus told them that he was particularly concerned with the collapse of the German banking system, which he was sure would lead to major upheavals. Others talked about the hunger marches in Britain and the awful rates of unemployment everywhere.

Evelyn ate her food silently, wishing that she were in the nursery eating with Adrian. Since she had turned thirteen, she was expected to eat with the adults, and she hated it. They all talked so much and had so many opinions about everything, yet half the time the matters that worried them seemed very remote from their world. They were not hungry, they were not unemployed. None of these awful situations ever seemed to touch them, in fact. It seemed almost smug of them to be worrying about these things from their positions.

Her gaze drifted to the garden through the French windows. She looked out over the terrace and rockery and on over the sweeping lawn, with its swathes of long curving grass. Suddenly she saw something moving fast across the neatly cut lawn. It was a big black horse. A human figure chased after it.

Augustus had also seen it. 'What in the name of God is that?' He dropped the carving tools and wiped his hands. 'My god, it's Jupiter! Jupiter's out!'

The astonished guests watched as Gussie disappeared out

of the room and reappeared in the garden outside running fast after the excited black horse.

'Oh dear,' said Blanche, jumping up to finish carving the meat. 'That's Gussie's new hunter. He only arrived this week.'

Evelyn was on the edge of her seat. 'May I go and help him, Mama? Please?'

Blanche nodded. 'We'll keep your food warm. Off you go.'

Evelyn ran out of the house and down to the tennis court at the bottom of the garden where she could see the fiery black gelding trotting up and down, his nostrils flared, his tail held defiantly high in the air as he trotted around, occasionally breaking into a canter with a high-pitched squeal or kicking up his legs in a joyful buck.

Augustus was standing on the grass, one hand outstretched towards the horse. Every time he moved towards him, Jupiter eyed him, rolled the whites of his eyes and turned on his back legs with a wicked squeal before galloping off again, to then stop and stand in a provocative pose, ready to dash off if they tried to reach him.

'Bloody animal!' Augustus was angry. 'I'll whip him when I get him.'

Frank had reappeared with a rope and a handful of oats. 'Oh, he's just playing, sir. Remember he's only three, he's green, just a baby still and he likes some fun.'

Augustus was not appeased. 'He's either going to damage himself or ruin the garden. Look at how he's cut up the tennis court already.'

'I'll have him out in a minute, sir,' replied Frank.

Evelyn watched with admiration as Frank walked up to the sweating horse with his heaving black flanks, making his curious chirruping noises deep in his throat.

The animal snorted and stepped back, throwing up his head defiantly.

Frank walked towards him, one hand flat, offering the little pile of oats. The other hand held a rope behind his back. 'There's a good boy, then,' he cooed, walking right up to the horse. The oats were accepted; he gobbled them up and visibly relaxed. Frank positioned himself close to his head and gently slipped the rope over the horse's neck.

Realising suddenly that he was now caught, Jupiter pulled back and shook his head but Frank held the rope firmly.

Evelyn smiled. 'Well done, Frank,' she called. She looked over at her father, waiting for him to congratulate Frank on catching his valuable horse but Augustus was scowling.

'Right, now take him back to the stables right away. After my lunch I want an explanation as to how the animal got out of his stable in the first place.'

Frank stared at Augustus with a blank expression on his face. Evelyn was struck by how he did not respond quickly and deferentially to her father's orders in the way most servants did. Then she watched the boy lead Jupiter back to the stables without a word.

Augustus sniffed. 'Incompetents!' he muttered, as he turned to go back to the house and his lunch table. 'They could have ruined that animal.'

'But we don't even know how he got out,' Evelyn reminded him. 'And Frank was brave to catch him when Jupiter was so upset.'

'No, we don't know how he got out,' agreed Augustus. 'But when we do, someone will be punished.'

Evelyn caught her breath in her throat at these harsh words. Her father was so angry all the time. It seemed to her that he almost wanted situations to arise that resulted in someone being punished.

'Well, at least Jupiter didn't do too much damage to the garden,' she said, 'except the tennis court. Mama will be relieved about that.'

'It was lucky that it's been so dry recently. Otherwise he would have cut up the lawn,' said Augustus. 'But no doubt your mother will be pleased,' he repeated, with a sarcastic edge to his voice. 'No doubt indeed.'

He stopped in the hall where large portraits of his mother and grandmother were hung. In the middle was the portrait of Blanche by Philip de Laszlo, painted soon after her marriage. Augustus looked at the row of women – all strikingly handsome, in the bloom of young adulthood. He turned to Evelyn and placed an arm around her shoulders. She smiled at him eagerly, expecting a special fatherly remark from him at last.

'Aren't they lovely?' He looked down at his daughter. 'You do at least have your mother's eyes,' he said flatly.

He let go of her shoulders and walked back into the dining-room to finish lunch. 'Anyone need some more meat before I sit down?' he asked the assembled crowd.

Hurt and mortified, Evelyn followed him into the room and slipped into her seat. Then she struggled through the rest of her lunch in silence, the food sticking in her throat like lumps of chalk.

Her father's remark had struck deep. She was not a beauty and never would be one. She had no charm like her mother. She had nothing. Any trickle of confidence she might have had drained from her. In an internal struggle to keep some sense of herself, she decided that she did not care if her father was hurt by Blanche's infidelity. In fact, it would serve him right if he were.

CHAPTER 12

1936

It was a while before Blanche became accustomed to Ivo's moodiness. Over the years she had gradually come to recognise the pattern, a period of intense energy, when he would work night and day on a piece of work, making love to her whenever she visited, talking and laughing with an intensity that awed her. Then these periods were followed by increasingly subdued moods – long hours of sleeping, of silence and withdrawal. These could go on for weeks, when Ivo would shut himself up in his cottage and not come to London at all. He did not wash or shave and it seemed that he could barely get himself out of bed.

During these times, Blanche continued to visit him, organising one of her maids to clean up his cottage for him, holding his hand as he sat sadly in his armchair, staring out at the garden with blank eyes.

Often during his dark moods he talked about his wife Dora who had died pregnant with their child. He blamed himself, he told her, it was all his fault. She had been so small, surely she had been too delicate to carry another human in her womb.

Blanche would tell him not to be silly, that women were designed to bear children, and that what had happened to Dora was an accident of nature. It was certainly not his fault, he was certainly not responsible for her death. She would pray silently that the black cloud would lift before it enveloped him even more.

Then suddenly it would be gone. Blanche would return one weekend and walk through the woods to Ivo's cottage, wondering what state she would find him in, dreading the worst. Then Ivo would throw open the door with a warm greeting, freshly bathed and shaved with clean clothes and looking as if nothing had ever been different.

'Blanche! My darling!' he would exclaim, pulling her to him and kissing her on the lips. 'Conversation at last! I was getting tired of talking to the trees, and I don't think they thought much of me, either.'

With an overwhelming sense of relief, Blanche would sit down and relay all the news from London, all the events and happenings, since he had sunk into the gloom, and Ivo would be alert and interested.

'And now,' he said, pulling her gently towards him, 'I want to devour you, I want to sink inside you.' He slipped his rough painter's hands under her blouse and squeezed her. 'I'm back from the dead,' he said, stroking her white skin. 'You have kept me alive all this time, my darling Blanche.'

Ivo had another deep depression after he had received the news that an old friend had died in Spain fighting the Fascists. He became very morose and pessimistic again, talking about the terrible situation in Germany and the appalling state of the world. 'And while all these things are going on, all that people want to talk about is the King's mistress!'

'I think they do care about what's going on abroad,' Blanche said gently. 'Gossip about Mrs Simpson is just a distraction. After all,' she added with a light laugh, 'she is another American, someone to blame.'

For once Ivo did not respond to her banter. He remained

slumped in his chair. A dirty glass tumbler and half a bottle of whisky were on the table beside him, the letter from his friend's widow still in his hand.

'Too many people die,' he muttered with slurred words. 'Too many people die young.' He could hardly focus on Blanche as she gently prised the letter from his hand to read it herself. 'Only good people die,' he moaned. 'Only bad people survive.'

Blanche helped him to bed and sat downstairs watching the dusk fall on the garden. The sky was pink and the light falling on the plants had a soft pinkish hue.

Life was so difficult, she thought. Here was Ivo, so talented and clever, so successful and acclaimed, yet periodically so desperately unhappy that he did not want to live. Blanche loved him very much but she knew she could never live with him. He was far too much of a handful. She did not love Gussie but she could live with him; his dullness never changed.

Ivo sank into his gloom for a few weeks and then slowly surfaced again. It was then that he announced that he was going to Paris to study print-making under Picasso.

'It's the place to be,' he said, 'and I feel I need to perfect my print-making skills.'

So off he went, as he had gone off to the Far East after his wife had died, to bury himself in art and creation, warding off the fear of death that tormented him when he was at his lowest.

Blanche understood why Ivo had to go and she knew that she would miss him for the year he planned to be away. She continued to live a busy life in town and invite friends down to Sussex for large weekend parties. All sorts of people came. They played tennis and clock-golf and croquet. In the evenings they played bridge or canasta and sang songs at the piano, or they read quietly in the library, or listened to the wireless or gramophone in the drawing-room. They sat around in groups having heated discussions about the state of Germany and Chamberlain's policy of appeasement of Hitler. They argued about Spain and Franco and whether they should go out to risk their lives like so many of their friends.

One hot August weekend, Blanche invited down an artist called Olive Porter, someone she had originally met some time ago at an art exhibition in Bond Street, and then again at a poetry reading in Bloomsbury.

Olive was a tall woman with an oval face and large, protruding grey eyes. She had thick brown hair worn wound up in a purple turban. She wore loose kaftan robes around her statuesque body and leather sandals on her feet. She had strong views on most subjects and emphasised her points with wild gestures, hands dipping and weaving in the air as she spoke. Her voice was particularly distinctive, too; it was slow and deep and rather masculine.

Blanche was fascinated by Olive who was, at forty-six, ten years older. She was married to a viscount and had several children, now grown. After the war, she had been a talented and successful spiritualist and had been besieged by miserable widows and desperate wives whose husbands were missing. She was also said to have a gift for reading people's palms. She was a patron of the arts and gave generously to a number of impoverished painters and craftsmen, having set up a trust to help those who needed financial aid to build a studio or kiln. She was a great admirer of Ivo's work and owned several of his big paintings.

'Ivo is a truly great artist,' Olive told Blanche as they walked around the garden on Saturday after lunch. 'His work will live on after him, there's no doubt about that.'

She swept her arm round in an extravagant gesture. 'It's wonderful to come down to this part of Sussex where he paints. This scenery is so familiar to me after seeing the paintings. I have several of his landscapes. There's one I particularly like, of a pond surrounded by bushes. Is that near here? I've always wanted to see the spot that inspired such a work.'

'Why, it's very close by,' said Blanche. 'It's where I first met Ivo, years ago, when I was trying to learn to skate. I'll take you there if you like.'

Olive smiled. 'Can we go now?'

The two women walked down the drive of the house. Blanche smiled at the gardener's boy who was playing horseshoes in the small garden of his parents' cottage. 'Good afternoon, Frank,' she called.

Frank looked up and, with a moment's hesitation, waved an arm. 'Afternoon, ma'am,' he called.

They turned down the footpath into the wood. They stopped for a moment to watch a blackbird sitting on its nest at the top of a high hawthorn bush, before pushing their way through the thick rhododendron bushes to the pond. There, at last, it was before them. They paused again to look at the scene. One part of the pond was covered with yellow water-lilies and their broad shiny leaves, and behind them rose an imposing army of tall rushes, nearly six feet high with blue-green stems and knotted clusters of brown flowers.

At last they reached the pond; the water shimmered like glass. A mallard, disturbed by their arrival, sprang clear of the water and flapped low across the lake with straight, rapid, powerful swishing of its wings, and a loud '*Quack!*'

Olive let out a light gasp. 'Oh yes,' she said. 'I know it so well. His painting of the pond in the wood was the first one I bought. I have often walked around this pond in my head – the pine trees, the rhododendrons, the reeds, the lilies. What a place!' She stopped and sat down on the mossy bank, stretching out her long brown legs.

'Come and sit down!' she said, patting the mossy spot beside her.

Blanche settled next to her, and sat hugging her knees as the two of them watched the coots and moorhens creeping among the reeds on the far bank. A pair of mallards appeared, swimming regally in front of them, tipping upside down in the water every now and then in their search for fish below them.

Olive lay back to stare at the sky. She sighed deeply. 'Are you happy, Blanche?' she asked quietly.

Blanche was puzzled. 'Whatever do you mean?' She did not know Olive well enough to laugh such a question off.

'Are you happy?' Olive repeated her question. 'Are you fulfilled?'

Blanche looked slightly askance. 'Why, yes, indeed.' She was aware of an odd settling in the air, a tension building up between them.

Olive ran her finger along Blanche's bare arm. 'Your skin is so white, pure, pure white.'

Blanche did not flinch. Her arm tingled under the touch. 'Well, in the Deep South ladies are taught to cover up and stay out of the sun at all times. My grandmother used to carry a parasol even in the moonlight.'

Olive laughed as her finger travelled slowly up Blanche's shoulder. Her voice was soft and caressing. 'Beautiful.' Her voice was quiet. Then she sat up quite abruptly.

Blanche was watching a moorhen launch itself into the water and tried to ignore Olive's soft lips on the back of her neck. But instead of being repelled, she could feel herself trembling with an excitement building up inside her, tightening her skin.

Olive's hand reached up and stroked Blanche's cheek. 'You are so beautiful, you know, an exquisite example of feminine beauty.'

'Thank you.' Blanche's voice came out as a hoarse whisper. Inside a voice was telling her to see it through, to see what would happen, not to run away.

'Look at me, Blanche.'

It was clearly an order. Blanche turned to face Olive, and was caught by the look in the older woman's dark grey glowing eyes.

So when Olive's lips touched hers, she did not pull away. Instead, she responded.

'What does your husband do to you, Blanche?' Olive murmured. Her fingers were undoing the buttons on Blanche's blouse. 'Does he touch you here, Blanche?' She stroked Blanche's neck and ran her hand down to her breast.

Blanche was almost quivering with excitement. She breathed hard as she allowed Olive to kiss her lips, her neck, her breasts.

'Does he touch you here, Blanche?' Olive slipped her hand between Blanche's legs under her skirt. Her fingers were searching, probing.

Blanche lay back in silence and let Olive make love to her as she wanted. She lay passive, staring up at the blue sky above as the older woman's lips and hands moved over her body, removing clothing, caressing and squeezing and stroking.

'Just lie there, that's right,' crooned Olive. 'Don't do anything. I'll do it all. I'll look after you.'

When Olive took off her own clothes, Blanche caught a glimpse of her sun-tanned skin. Olive was brown all over, nut brown against Blanche's own porcelain skin. She gave in to the sensations, the pleasure. It was not for her to think about the morality of what was happening. She wanted to go with it, to experience this, making love to another woman. It was something she had often wondered about, knowing a few of Ivo's Sapphist friends. She had been unaware of this tendency in Olive until now, but that did not matter. Their arms were entwined. Olive's body was strong and lean and smooth. Blanche closed her eyes and concentrated on the smoothness of their contact, the creaminess of their skin. Women's bodies together. In a dreamlike state, it struck her as quite wonderful.

As Blanche felt the tension building up inside her, she smiled. She found herself thinking of Ivo away in Paris. How much he would be amused by this scene by the lake! And no doubt he would want to join in, too!

Afterwards, when they had dressed and brushed the moss and twigs out of each other's hair, they walked back to the house. On the way they saw Evelyn and Frank by the path. Evelyn was crouching over something. Frank stood near her, a smile on his face.

'Hello, darling,' Blanche called out. 'Are you enjoying the woods today?' She had a sudden flash of fear that the children might have witnessed the scene between her and Olive, but she did not need to worry. They had obviously been preoccupied with another matter.

Evelyn swung round, her eyes ablaze with excitement. In her hands she cradled a small grey squirrel. 'Look what Frank has given me! He says it's been rejected by its mother and it's too small to look after itself. I'll look after it and bring it up. Isn't it sweet?'

She held out the grey rodent for the two women to see. Olive, a town woman, drew back. 'I've always thought of them as rats with fur myself, just as pigeons are rats with wings. All nasty and diseased.'

Blanche laughed. 'Oh, Olive, these are clean animals here. Perfectly clean and healthy.'

'I can keep it, can't I, Mama?' Evelyn looked earnestly at her mother.

Frank stared at his boots, his hands clasped behind his back.

The animal's beady black eyes were bright and pretty. Blanche smiled. 'I have no objection but you'd better not bring it into the house because the dogs may go for it. And,' she added, 'keep it away from your father. He thinks squirrels are only good for shooting.'

Evelyn's eyes shone with happiness. 'Thank you so much. I'll keep it in the stables. See how it sits on my shoulder and nibbles my ear? It's the sweetest thing.'

'Well, I must get back to see how everyone else is getting on and supervise dinner. I'm sure there's time for a game of tennis before the afternoon is up.'

Olive lit a cigarette and drew the smoke deeply into her lungs. 'I'll leave the tennis to the others, I think. It's not the sort of exercise I like,' she said with a sly look at Blanche. She indicated towards Evelyn's disappearing figure. 'It's a shame she hasn't inherited your looks,' she said. 'She takes after her father.'

Blanche sighed. She did not wish to discuss Evelyn's looks with anyone. She did not want to because she did not want to admit that she was herself saddened by Evelyn's gawky face and weak chin, and frightened-rabbit expression. No, Evelyn was no beauty. One thing that disturbed Blanche was that she had no experience of plain looks in her family. All the women were good-looking, and the men, too. Adrian, the boy, had inherited the well-proportioned features, strong brown eyes and fair hair of his grandmother and he was going to grow up to look like one of her uncles.

At the thought, Blanche stopped herself going further. Adrian was going to succeed at anything he did in life. He had the intelligence and the charm that would take him far. Evelyn was different. There was a fragile sadness about her daughter that made Blanche want to pick her up and envelop her in a protective hug, to keep her safe from the cruelties of the world. The child was so shy that she was almost paralysed in social gatherings, and Gussie's insensitivity towards her had not helped to build up any confidence she might have. In fact, his attitude towards his daughter had probably contributed to, if not caused, many of Evelyn's problems.

Blanche had no idea why Gussie was so unpleasant to the child. Surely he did not still resent her for not being the boy he had expected? And he had Adrian, after all. You would think he would be happy with his boy and enjoy Evelyn as his daughter. But Adrian's outstanding charm and talents seemed to highlight Evelyn's shortcomings all the more. It was very unfair.

Perhaps if Evelyn were outgoing and charming and beautiful, Gussie would treat her differently. But she was none of these things and nothing the child did seemed to improve matters. Blanche used to think that Evelyn would grow into herself, grow in confidence as she got older, and gradually become at least handsome, like the ugly duckling. But this had not happened; in fact, as Evelyn grew older she seemed to shrink in every way – at least in the company of her parents. She had a feeling that Evelyn was a different person when she was with other people.

Blanche wished she could help Evelyn develop into the person she wanted to be, the person she was happy to be, but she did not know how. What she did realise, to her surprise, was that it was probably a good thing that her daughter was so friendly with the gardener's boy. If she weren't, she would have no friends of her own age at all, since she did not seem to be interested in them. But goodness, how Blanche wished that Gussie would be a little less hard on her.

That night at dinner, Blanche watched Olive flirting with her friend James Beale, a quiet publisher who had recently been through a divorce. Earlier, during cocktails, Olive had made a drama of reading his hand, telling him that he was about to fall in love. Blanche had to avert her eyes and try not to notice. Poor James was to be another conquest for Olive, just as she herself had been. Since their walk earlier, Olive had barely spoken to her, and her whole behaviour towards her had changed. It was as if, having seduced Blanche, Olive felt she could discard her, and walk over her like some fallen enemy. Blanche felt annoyed and ashamed that she had been taken in and led astray like that. To Olive she was now no more than a trophy.

Evelyn's squirrel very quickly became as tame as a dog. It ran along behind her when she went for walks and rode on her shoulder when she went out riding. It chattered to her in an odd rumbling squeak and nuzzled her cheek when it was happy.

The highlight of the summer holidays was to be a visit from Masha and her three children, Misha, Kyra and Irina. Masha's husband now commanded his own ship and had recently been stationed in South Africa where the entire family had stayed. Now he was being posted to Hong Kong and the children were being sent to boarding school in England. They were arriving in Sussex for an extended visit.

Blanche had not seen Masha for some years and she was pleased that time had been kind to her. The two women fell immediately back into the close friendship they had shared before, though Blanche was careful not to tell Masha about her affair with Ivo. She did not want Masha's family loyalties divided by such details.

At Masha's arrival, Gussie turned into a different man. He

emerged from his dour shell and became, for him, outgoing, fun and energetic. He quoted Shakespeare and John Milton, even the romantic poets, surprising everyone. Masha always had this effect on him, as though her presence reminded him of the fun he and his Russian cousins had had in the past. Perhaps in loving Masha and paying her so much attention, he was honouring all the forebears who linked them together. Whatever the reason, everyone, even the maids, commented on Mr Champion's sudden good humour.

Many events were planned for Masha's stay. They motored down to the beach at West Wittering, swam in the water and then caught crabs and shrimps as the sun set on the horizon, making the water glow pink, and the tide went out leaving shallow sandy pools around the breakwaters.

They went sailing at Del Quay and ate picnics on the sand-dunes around East Head. On another occasion they climbed the Downs and walked along Stane Street, the old Roman road running from London to Chichester. They also went to the races at Goodwood and Fontwell, and visited Brighton and the Royal Pavilion before walking on the stony beach and fooling around on the pier. Bodiam and Arundel Castles were visited combined with a walk in Petworth Park. A trip was made to the Roman villa at Bignor, with its two courtyards covering four acres, which was discovered by a farmer in 1811 when ploughing the field with his oxen. They all marvelled at the exquisite mosaics of the dolphin, the gladiators and the mournful Venus.

At the house they had tennis matches and golf tournaments, and fiercely contested games of badminton. In the evenings, chess and backgammon were played followed by rowdy sessions of charades, and discussions about the state of Europe. There were musical evenings when the children played duets on the piano and sang solo recitals for the pleasure of the adults.

Everyone seemed very happy. Even Evelyn smiled for much of the time. Her cousins were deeply impressed by her squirrel. Blanche had moments of extreme happiness, when she felt everything was good and complete. This was the perfect family life.

Adrian's birthday was coming up. It was his eleventh. To most of the world, Adrian was an easy-going, straightforward boy who enjoyed straightforward pleasures. Good at every-thing he did, it was generally agreed that he was destined to make his mark on life. Adrian was not, however, quite how he seemed to others. He had started out at his prep school as the cleverest boy in the class and for several years had been accustomed to coming top in every test and exam. He excelled at sports and was captain of both the rugby and cricket teams, and was generally admired as an all-rounder. Then another boy joined his class, who was equally bright and who began to compete with Adrian for the position at the top of the form.

The boy, Roland, was not an athlete and he was not handsome. He was, however, exceptionally clever, and it was not long before Adrian felt threatened. Used to sweeping up every prize and award, his position had never been challenged before. Now this little runt in thick glasses got slightly better marks than he did.

This made Adrian feel angry. During the summer term, he felt himself getting more and more anxious about the exams at the end of June. He was determined to beat Roland. He worked himself into a frenzy as they approached.

The day before the exams started, Adrian began to feel dizzy and sick, and he felt relieved to be able to take himself to the medical room to see the school nurse. The nurse was used to pre-exam nerves and she allowed Adrian to lie down in the sick bay for an hour before she packed him off to his last chemistry lesson before the exams. Having no sympathy from the nurse left Adrian having to admit that he was not coming down with influenza, as he had hoped. He put on his shoes and gloomily left the medical room.

Inside, he was in turmoil. He had been so convinced that he was too ill to sit the exam that the very thought of sitting down at the desk the next day and turning over the paper made him panic. He had to get out of it somehow. In the chemistry lab came the solution. Standing at the back of the lab, when he was sure no one was looking, he tipped a beaker of boiling water over his right hand. He let out a cry and dropped the glass beaker on the floor with a crash. The chemistry master was by his side in a second, and thrust Adrian's badly burnt hand under some cold running water.

Back in the medical room, the nurse bandaged up Adrian's blistered hand without a word. She was in no doubt about what had really happened but she kept quiet. She had seen it all before. It was always the really clever boys who could not cope with the fear of failure and developed mysterious illnesses that made it impossible for them to compete. But few people understood that.

Thus Adrian escaped the humiliation of not coming top in every subject that term. Everyone was sympathetic and said how unfortunate it was but it did not really matter since the exams were not important anyway, not like the Common Entrance to public school which he would do in a year's time.

Evelyn herself was not as keen on her brother as everyone else seemed to be. Just in the last year, Adrian had become quite cocky, as though all the praise and admiration had gone to his head. Before long he had developed an arrogance at home that was quite unpleasant. He was rude to Nanny and the servants, and contemptuous towards Evelyn herself, while remaining perfectly charming to people whose opinions he cared about. He made remarks about Evelyn's developing figure, taking delight in her acute embarrassment, and once, when her menstrual blood had seeped through the back of her white skirt, Adrian took great delight in pointing it out to her in a room full of people.

So whenever Evelyn overheard her parents' friends extolling Adrian's virtues, she would feel an angry hardness in her chest at the unfairness of it all. If only they knew, she would think. Then she would feel guilty and tell herself that Adrian would surely grow out of such mean behaviour and that she ought to be kind to her little brother.

For Adrian's birthday, a large family dinner was planned, with globe artichokes from the garden, cold partridge in aspic, roast suckling pig, poached salmon, pears in chocolate sauce and fresh strawberries picked that afternoon.

It was the hay-making season. The week before, the hayfields exuded a warm smell of marguerites and clover as the scythes cut through the grass, their soft swishing sound disturbing the corncrakes nesting on the ground. After cutting, as the hay was left to dry, the smell changed to a sweet mustiness. Now it was time to bring it all in for the winter, and for the last two days the farmhands had been gathering it in from the fields.

The children always loved helping out with the hay harvest, in the heat of the day, riding aloft on the seat of a spidery metal horse-rake above the hindquarters of a fat black Shire horse. On the ground the children were expected to help by lifting up the heavy sheaves of corn, already tied up swiftly and skilfully by the stronger men, and carry them one under each arm to the pick-up spot in the middle of the field. These sheaves were then bundled into larger clumps and built up into high haystacks in the middle of the far field until it was time to carry them to the big hay barns for the winter.

The children took it in turns to drive the horses, pulling hard on the reins to steer the massive animals in the right direction.

At lunchtime, as the gong from the house signalled lunch for the children, the men settled down under the trees with their handkerchiefs of food and stone jars full of elder-berry wine.

On the final day of hay-making, the children gathered around the terrace gulping down cool lemon barley-water as the adults sat in wicker chairs sipping tea from white porcelain cups.

The cousins were excited at the prospect of staying up with the grown-ups to eat the great feast in honour of Adrian, the birthday boy, and they jostled and teased each other noisily. That summer there seemed to be a plague of large rats in the farm buildings, and the cousins discussed with relish increasingly elaborate and daring ways in which they might trap and kill the rodents.

Blanche was heartened to see how Evelyn was smiling so much, her cheeks showing an attractive glow. She really seemed to emerging from her shell at last. Perhaps she simply needed to be with children she knew and liked, she thought. Then she was confident enough to come out of herself.

Even Gussie, she noticed, was responding to Evelyn's dif-ferent behaviour. On one occasion, he grabbed his daughter's hand and kissed her cheek, as if to prove to his cousin Masha that he was a good family man.

It was Evelyn who suggested the fatal game in the first place. Perhaps things would have worked out differently if she had not. Who can tell? But it was Evelyn, with her newly acquired confidence who took the lead and shouted out her idea.

'Hide and seek!' she shouted. 'We must play hide and seek! There's time before dinner,' she said urgently. 'We can play for half an hour and then come in and get ready for the evening.'

The grown-ups laughed and said that it was all right as long as Nanny agreed and provided the children gave themselves time to have baths and change into their special clothes for the evening's activities. It was agreed that because of the shortage of time, they should all stay within the confines of the garden. Since it had been her idea, it was suggested that Evelyn was It.

At first, Adrian objected. 'It's my birthday, I should be It,' he complained.

Augustus laughed. 'Well, let's be fair and toss a coin. You can't argue with a coin.'

Much to Adrian's annoyance, Evelyn won the toss. She covered her eyes and counted to one hundred as the other children scattered themselves out across the lawns, the shrubberies and behind the greenhouses in the kitchen garden.

They were having fun and no one played too seriously, so Evelyn was able to find the others without too much trouble. That was everyone except Adrian, who had decided to foil his sister by going outside the garden into the nearest hayfield. That way he would get his own back for losing the toss.

Then time had run out, and Nanny was urging them to come in to get washed and dressed for dinner. The children called Adrian's name, telling him to show himself, the game was over, they had to go in to get ready. They called and called, cupping their hands over their mouths to make the sound carry across the garden but their cries were answered only by the echoes of their own voices.

As dusk fell, annoyance at Adrian continuing to hide turned into worry. Then worry turned into fear. The adults joined in the hunt just as the maids were putting the finishing touches to the dinner-table. Dressed in their dinner jackets and long dresses, the grown-ups spread out over the grounds, all calling Adrian's name.

Night came. The feast had been long cooked but stayed on the sideboard and table. The children were fed in the kitchen and sent to their rooms. A search party was made up of men from the farm and estate. A group of them went out into the dark, torches blazing in the night as they looked in vain for the master's son. In the house, the adults paced the room, anxiously waiting for the news that did not come.

It was two days before they found the boy. It was the thatcher who discovered him, when he arrived to fix the straw thatch on a haystack to protect it from the autumn rains. Investigating the oddly shaped stack, he found Adrian's body right down inside, suffocated and crushed by the weight of the hay that had collapsed on top of him while he was hiding. His fingertips were scraped to the bone in his effort to pull himself out, his eyes, nose and lungs filled with hayseed. According to the old men in the village pub that night, Mrs Champion was advised by the police not to view the child before he was taken away, for half his face had been eaten by rats. It was left to her husband to identify his son.

The next morning, Evelyn's squirrel scuttled in jerky movements, foraging for food around the smooth green lawn just outside Augustus's study. Augustus had been up all night, poring over photograph albums with photographs of his son, or staring out of the window, his face collapsed with grief.

As he became conscious of the rodent moving about on the lawn outside his window, he felt a growling rage building up inside him.

Perhaps he did not know that it was his daughter's pet.
Perhaps he did. Whatever the case, he moved, without any
expression on his face, to the cupboard in the corner of the
room and reached for his shotgun. It was always loaded, so
all he had to do was aim and fire. Gussie was an excellent shot
and could not fail to hit a target so close.

Thus the bereaved household was woken that morning by
the loud blast of a shotgun. Thinking that Augustus had shot
himself in his grief, Blanche ran downstairs, prepared to find
another dead person. When she saw that he had merely killed
a squirrel, she burst into tears of relief. It was only the sight of
Evelyn's face at breakfast that made her realise that it was no
ordinary squirrel. But Blanche had no strength left inside her
to reach out to her daughter and comfort her. After all, she and
Gussie had just lost a child. How could the loss of an animal
be compared to the loss of a child at any time of one's life?

That evening, Blanche sat in her bedroom staring out of
the window at the misty Downs in the distance, the line of
the horizon delicate and sharp. Her body was numb, her eyes
glazed. Almost in a trance, she found herself picking up her
jewellery box. There, in the bottom, were the Wedgwood
brooch and earrings, and pretty brooches Gussie had bought
for her over the years. From a separate compartment at the
back, she pulled out a red velvet box and opened the lid. A
small pearl necklace lay curled up inside like a little snake.
It was untouched, unworn.

Blanche stared at it for a few seconds, and then shut the lid.
'They are not related,' she murmured to herself firmly. 'There
is no connection.'

She placed the red box back in the jewellery case and shut
the lid. Annoyed that it had even come to her mind after all
her efforts at control, she vowed never to look at it again.

The funeral of Adrian Champion became part of Graffham's

history. For generations the villagers would sit under the heavy oak beams in the Forester's Arms and talk about the sombre cortège of black carriages pulled by glossy black horses with black plumes on their heads, transporting the boy's coffin and the funeral party from the big house along the road through the village and up the hill past the village shop and bakery and on up to the church at the bottom of the Downs. There were at least fifteen carriages filled with women in black gowns, their hair covered with black veils or silk hats, sniffling children of various ages dressed in funeral garments, and the men in dark suits with black armbands on their upper arms. Henrietta had managed to come chauffeured from London in her black clothes, her bathchair in the back of the motor.

Behind the family, friends and estate workers, in honour of Augustus's position as Master of Hounds, came the huntsmen on their horses. They wore black armbands which showed up dramatically on their pink coats, and the whip controlled the pack of hounds with low whining calls from his horn which had the impressive effect of making the hounds calm and subdued as though they too knew it was a sad and tragic occasion.

Behind them came the staff from Avery Hall, their heads bowed, their faces blank with grief at the sadness of the young boy's death. Following in small clumps came the other villagers, most of whom had connections with the estate and farm going back generations. The Champion tragedy was shared by the entire village.

Evelyn would also remember the white expressionless faces of her parents, far gone and untouchable. Her father seemed frozen, unable to say or do anything. He moved like a machine, guided in and out of the church by Blanche, who also kept her feelings hidden beneath a controlled surface. She seemed composed, in control. But no one in the world could know how deep the pain went.

After the funeral and burial in the family vault in the graveyard at the foot of the Downs, when Adrian was set-tled alongside his grandparents and great-grandparents, the friends and family gathered at the house. Evelyn was grateful for the presence of Masha and her three children. Masha's husband Ambrose was too far away with his fleet to come back for the funeral but he had sent a telegram expressing his heart-felt condolences.

Masha looked weepy and subdued but she was the one who retained the strength to take charge and organise the staff, making sure that the family and friends were served appropriate refreshments, as were the domestic staff who, with mixed feelings, drank to the memory of the young master downstairs in the butler's pantry.

Sudden death, and especially the death of a child, splits a family in many ways. The shock that envelops each person is almost physical, like a blanket that makes it impossible for the person inside to be touched by anything. They walk around in a daze, detached from the world, hardly believing that anything will ever be normal again, that banal decisions will be made, such as what to wear or what to eat. It is hard to believe that anything in the world will ever matter again, that a funny joke will ever be appreciated, a piece of music stir the emotions or the simple song of the nightingale in the dark of the night be uplifting. Pain of the heart isolates everyone from each other.

All these pleasures were denied to the members of the Champion family for many months. For weeks they had nothing to say to each other, and they avoided each other's company, alone in their separate misery.

For a few weeks, Masha became Blanche's backbone.

Because she herself had suffered so much in the past she was well-equipped to know when to step in and when to stand back.

She accompanied Blanche on walks through the woods and they talked about Adrian as a boy and the things he had said and done.

'The world has lost a leader,' Masha said. 'But his short life was a good one.'

Blanche did not reply. She stared ahead of her, neither seeing the glorious display of pinkish-white blooms on the wild rosebushes nor hearing the blackbird's sweet song in her ears.

Masha sighed. 'And you know,' she said gently, 'you could have another child, you're still young enough. You could if you wanted to.'

Blanche stopped and turned towards Masha. Tears rushed to her eyes. 'There's no replacing a child, however old it is when you lose it. It's an impossible thing to do. I know that. Adrian is gone. He will never be replaced by another.' Her voice cracked.

Masha placed her hand on Blanche's arm. 'Perhaps I put it the wrong way,' she said. 'I didn't mean you could replace Adrian, put him out of your mind. No, Adrian will always live on in our hearts. I just thought that you and Gussie could easily have more children if you so wished.'

Blanche pulled a small lace handkerchief from the folds of her skirt and blew her nose. 'Yes, we could,' she sighed wearily, 'if we so wished.'

HENRIETTA

CHAPTER 13

⤫

1937

In early 1937, Blanche went to visit Henrietta in London. She had not seen her since Adrian's funeral. It had been a challenge for the old lady to attend the funeral, for her mobility was so limited by arthritis. Now she was worse, and housebound, confined to the two ground-floor rooms of her vast house in Regent's Park and looked after at all times by a nurse-companion. Her hearing was poor and it was only possible to communicate with her by shouting down a large horn held to her ear. But her eyesight was still good and she read as avidly as ever. In her hands that morning she had the new Rosamond Lehmann novel, *The Weather in the Street* – 'a marvellous tale of a failed marriage, an adulterous affair, and an abortion,' she said with a chuckle. 'That will get the tut-tut brigade going! You can borrow it.' Henrietta's fondness for Blanche had also not diminished. She always had time for her young cousin and fellow Southerner, and the sadness inflicted on her by old age was invariably lifted by Blanche's visits.

'I got a letter from my Uncle Jasper this morning,' said Blanche. 'He was writing to send his condolences about Adrian and he enclosed this clipping from the *Savannah Morning News*. I'm sure it'll be of interest to you.'

Blanche dipped into her handbag and pulled out a piece of

newspaper. Holding it in her fingers, she began to read. 'The famous Hermitage plantation near Savannah has been bought by Henry Ford to add to his own plantation in Richmond, Georgia.'

Henrietta clucked and nodded. 'The Hermitage! Well, I never! A relic of the old past has been snapped up by a man who made his fortune by investing in the future. Now, that does make me laugh.'

She paused. 'Well, I'm pleased the place will be restored to its former glory. I was born just after the war between the states so I never saw it before when it was my grandparents' home. I used to visit it as a child and my father would get angry at the state of it and the fact that we no longer lived in such style.' She shook her head. 'Oh my, people were so bitter about that war. I can't say that the house meant that much to me but I did feel sorry that so many people lost their lives at that time.'

'I took Gussie there just after we got married in Savannah,' Blanche said. 'He thought I should be angry to have been done out of my birthright.'

Henrietta peered at Blanche. 'We all know that worse things happen than losing a birthright,' she murmured. Then she paused. 'How are things now, my dear? You've had a terrible time. How are you all?'

Blanche shrugged and studied the hands in her lap, glad that for once tears were not welling up in her eyes at the reference to Adrian's death. 'We're getting on,' she said quietly. 'Everyone says that time heals. There's a scar but it is healing, thank you, Henrietta, though I think I shall have a pain in my heart for ever.'

Henrietta nodded sympathetically. 'Well, just let me know if you ever want me to do anything for you. That's what I'm here for, my dear.

'Now, what other news from home? Presumably Jasper sent the clipping along with some family news . . .'

'Yes, indeed.'

'Jasper is the doctor, yes?' Henrietta used to know exactly who everyone was in the family and what they did, in spite of not being home for nearly forty years. Now age had muddled the details in her head, so she had to check carefully to ensure that she knew who she was talking about.

'No, he's the lawyer. He sends news of his grandchildren – they're all slightly older than Evelyn. The eldest is at Harvard Medical School and the next one is about to go to Yale.'

'All clever, our family,' muttered Henrietta.

'He also says that Uncle Hayward has died. Apparently no one knows the circumstances of his death as no one had seen him for some years. According to Jasper, there are a lot of debts left behind that had to be honoured. He died a few months ago, somewhere in Nevada.'

'How sad.' Henrietta had turned her head to look out of the window as she recalled the young man. 'It seems that Hayward did not make much of his life. I remember him as a lively little boy, always funny and making people laugh. He used to do the most outrageous things which made his mother reach for her smelling salts on a regular basis. I have often wondered what went wrong with him.'

Blanche was staring out of the window, her thoughts elsewhere. Her face was pale and grim. Her voice was soft as she spoke. 'Yes, he was my favourite uncle. As a child I adored him. I even wanted to marry him. There was something so mischievous, so young and different about him that set him apart from other grown-up folk.' She fought back the tears that were threatening to flood her eyes, hoping that Henrietta could not see them.

Henrietta laughed. 'What made Hayward so special was

that he ignored all the rules. You have to be a special sort of person to be able to do that, but . . .' she lifted a warning finger in the air '. . . you have to be strong or the rest of the world will crush you for it if it can. Society doesn't like people who ignore its codes of behaviour. Believe me, I know! And I'm afraid that's what happened to Hayward, and he suffered. He never escaped their clutches, and was punished.'

Her voice was almost inaudible as she added with a faint smile on her smooth aged face, 'But I was lucky enough to escape.'

Blanche looked at her, hoping to hear more. 'What did you escape from, Henrietta? I've never heard you talk like this.'

Henrietta laughed. 'Perhaps you're just old enough to understand now. And perhaps I am old enough to want you to know what happened. Otherwise, I could die and you would never know. People take so much with them when they die. All that learning and hope and love. I want you to know and to understand. I have got something to show you.'

She picked up a large folder which lay on the table beside her. 'I got the maid to bring these down from the attic for you to see.' She handed the folder to Blanche and closed her eyes while her cousin pulled out a pile of newspaper cuttings and began to read.

New York Times May 13, 1892

McALLISTER – GARMANY – In the City of New York by the Rev. Arthur H. Judge on the 22 day of August 1887, Conrad Hall McAllister of this city and Henrietta Larcombe Garmany, daughter of the late George W. Garmany of Savannah, Ga.

*   *   *

New York Times – May 13, 1892, p.1

MARRIED FIVE YEARS AGO
Ward McAllister's Younger Son has a Wife

The father greatly surprised and displeased by the news – Miss Henrietta Garmany of Savannah the bride – a well-kept secret.

The marriage notice printed in *The Times* this morning stating that Conrad Hall McAllister and Miss Henrietta Garmany of Savannah were married in this city on August 22, 1887 will doubtless be read with surprise by a great many people.

Conrad Hall McAllister is the younger son of Ward McAllister and Mrs McAllister is the daughter of the late George W. Garmany, a prominent lawyer of Savannah, who died in the spring of 1888, having no suspicion that his daughter Henrietta was married. The secret has been kept absolutely.

Mrs Garmany has, since her husband's death, lived in Savannah in the family house with her son Howard, who is a lawyer, her daughter and her three younger sons, who have been absent from home part of the year studying at Princeton. The fact of the daughter's marriage was known to nobody in the family except the daughter herself.

Mr McAllister became engaged to Miss Garmany immediately after her graduation from Miss Cary's school in Baltimore, with the approval of the entire Garmany family. Miss Garmany was scarcely eighteen years old at the time.

Ward McAllister opposed his son's engagement on

the grounds that the young man ought not to enter into such a condition of life until he should have so established himself in a profession as to be able properly to support a wife. The young people became engaged in the autumn of 1886, and this fact was known in the families. It now transpires that the marriage followed in August of the next year.

The reason now given by the husband and wife for marrying was that they wanted to make sure of each other beyond an accidental separation, and the reason for keeping such strict secrecy was the opposition of Ward McAllister to the match.

During all the years since the engagement Mr McAllister was a frequent visitor at Mrs Garmany's house, where he held the footing of a prospective son-in-law. Mrs McAllister passed none of her time in the company of Mr McAllister except in the presence of her mother or some other chaperon. The news of the marriage has come as a complete surprise to the family of the bride and Mrs Garmany, it is said, is much distressed at the sensational features of her daughter's marriage.

Ward McAllister when seen last night declared that he had nothing whatsoever to say upon the subject of his son Conrad's marriage. He finally stated, however, that the first announcement of the fact had come to him on Sunday from Albert Gallup, his son's lawyer. Mr McAllister said that he had always opposed his son's marriage with anybody, not specially with this young lady, whom he had not the honor to know, but with anybody, because his son was not able to support a wife.

He said that he did not know where his son was at present. The last time he had seen him was last Saturday. He said he knew absolutely nothing of his son's wife and had never known her family in Savannah, although he lived there years ago, and had often visited in the city since then.

When asked if his son would still be a welcome visitor at his home, Mr McAllister said he could not answer that question.

Dr Richard Garmany, a brother of Mrs Conrad McAllister, now lives at 40 West 40th St. He said last night that the announcement of the marriage had come to him as a complete surprise within a very short time. He said that Mr and Mrs McAllister had determined to make the matter public but he could not say why they had come to this conclusion.

He said that the secret marriage was a matter of great regret in the family and that it was possible that his brother Howard, as present head of the house, might have something to say in the course of a week or so. He declined to make public any details of the affair, saying, however, that his actual knowledge was very limited. He said that he saw his sister last Wednesday, when she called at his home, but that she and her husband had not remained as guests in his house while they were in town together.

Where they had staid he did not know, nor could he say where they were at present beyond the fact that they were not in town. He said his sister was in high health and spirits and that he could form no idea why she had elected to disclose her marriage at that present time beyond the conjecture that she happened to take the fancy to do so.

New York Times – May 14, 1892, p.8

Story of the McAllister-Garmany Marriage Notice

*   *   *

Its publication demanded by Frank Garmany, a brother of the wife – a strange affair from beginning to end – off on a Tour.

The reason for the announcement of the marriage, so long concealed, of Conrad Hall McAllister and Miss Garmany of Savannah, was given yesterday by Frank C. Garmany, the brother of the bride. Mr Garmany is a general agent of the Equitable Life Assurance Company and was seen in his office at 120 Broadway.

He said that the facts in the case had been made public at his demand – made as soon as he heard of the marriage – because he was unwilling that his sister should remain in a position that was embarrassing to her, even if not compromising.

Mrs McAllister is the only daughter among a family of seven children and has always been allowed to have her own way. While still a schoolgirl at Mrs Cary's Academy in Baltimore, her companions used to tease her about being engaged to somebody or other from New York, and it is probable that Miss Garmany became engaged to Mr McAllister before she left school. At all events, their engagement was announced at her home directly since her leaving school.

His father absolutely refused to consent to his engagement but the young woman was so infatuated with him that she married him secretly and because he had no means of supporting her, remained at home in her mother's house, with her husband's consent, maintaining her character of single woman and going about as usual in Savannah Society, where she was much admired because of her beauty and vivacity.

She received much attention, and yet contrived to keep most of the young men at a convenient distance. Three of her admirers, however, proposed marriage to her, as time went on, and in these emergencies she wrote to each young man addressing him a letter, in which she told him she was already married and required of him that he should keep her secret.

So it came about that while no member of her family except herself knew about her marriage, the fact was known by a few persons outside, and although they did not betray her confidence, yet an indefinite idea got abroad, little by little, that she was married.

So matters went on until December of last year when Frank C. Garmany of this city wrote to his sister asking that she break the engagement because Mr McAllister did not appear to be worthy of her, inasmuch as he did not seem to be able to keep his engagements.

The sister wrote back confessing that she was already married to Mr McAllister, and giving the date of the ceremony. This was the first knowledge of the marriage.

The excitement of the affair caused Mrs McAllister to break down with nervous prostration and hence the matter has been delayed until now. Meanwhile, Mr McAllister has made unsuccessful efforts to persuade his father to assist him financially and to remain friends with him in his married state. But it is well known to certain persons in town that Conrad McAllister is not a favorite son either of his father or his mother, and his relations in the family are so unhappy that it is extremely improbable that Mr and Mrs McAllister will ever be received by Ward McAllister in his home.

Mr and Mrs McAllister were last seen in town the day before yesterday in a cab on 5th Avenue. Mr Frank C.

Garmany said that they went away from town in a train which left between four and six o'clock in the afternoon. He would not say where they had gone but said that he had seen them on Thursday and had suggested several directions for their journey, which is to be as extended as convenient, for they wish to get away from everybody who knows them until the talk shall have subsided. It is not probable that they will return to the city for a long time; they may go to Savannah later, or perhaps to Europe.

It has been intimated that Ward McAllister objected to the marriage because he considered the family of his son's wife inferior to his own. Mr McAllister's exact standing in New York Society is perfectly well known, and that of the Garmany family is equally well known in Savannah, where the late George W. Garmany was well known as a cotton dealer before the war. Mr Garmany was a rich man whose fortune shrank with other Southern fortunes after the rebellion and at the time of his death he was in comfortable circumstances, but not rich.

His only daughter has enough money in her own right suitably to care for herself and to assist her husband in getting upon his feet should he make an effort to do so. While masquerading as 'Miss Garmany' at home, Mrs McAllister had her own horses and carriage and enjoyed life very thoroughly among her friends.

Her brother Howard is a lawyer in Savannah and lives at home with his mother. He has been in this city the past few days, pending the publication of the marriage notice. The second brother is Dr Richard J. Garmany of 40 West 40th Street. Dr Garmany is a physician of reputation in town and a Fellow of the Royal College of Surgeons in

London. Mrs Garmany was a Miss Larcombe from the New England family of that name. The Garmanys were originally from South Carolina.

New York Times – May 16, 1892, p.2

—That McAllister Marriage—
—The Groom's Attorney says the Couple will not live together—

The report in the morning paper yesterday that Conrad McAllister and his wife had gone on their bridal tour and would return to the city in a few days was denied, Albert Gallup, attorney for young McAllister, said last evening.

'Conrad McAllister and his wife have not left the city together and he has not been seen in the city since early last week. I have it from the lips of Conrad McAllister that he has not seen his wife since the announcement of their marriage. He is not with her and has no intention of living with her. I do not know where his wife is but I do know that she and her husband are apart and will remain as such. I have it from Mr McAllister that they have never lived together.'

'Will there be a suit for divorce?' Mr Gallup was asked.

'I am not able to answer that question,' was the reply. 'All that I can say is that despite the fact that the marriage was bona fide Mr and Mrs Conrad McAllister will remain as far apart as if they had never been married. He perhaps can explain how this is to be and the explanation will have to come from him. I had a telegram from Mr McAllister yesterday. He is at

Yonkers and I have no idea when he intends returning to the city.'

New York Times – May 17, 1892, p.8

—Young McAllister's Marriage—

—What Lawyer Edward Lyman Short says about it—

The exclusive publication in *The Times* yesterday of the interview with Mr Albert Gallup, attorney for Conrad Hall McAllister, created no little gossip in social circles. The announcement that young McAllister would never live with the pretty young woman he secretly made his wife five years ago came from Mr Gallup as the mouthpiece of his client.

Edward Lyman Short, attorney for Mrs McAllister, seemed not only surprised but chagrined at the disclosure made by McAllister through his attorney. To the reporter of *The Times*, Mr Short said:

'I do not care to discuss the marital relations of Conrad McAllister and his wife. It does seem to me that the public has been sufficiently amused with this affair. Less than ten days ago, Mrs McAllister expressed to me her dread of the newspaper discussion which would follow the announcement. It was her hope that it would be short-lived. She is not in the city, and I don't care to say where she is, for she has been annoyed too much already.

'It was my understanding with Mr Gallup that there was to be an end to all this talk and let this annoying discussion of a purely personal matter die out.'

'Is it true that there will be a proceeding for divorce

and, if so, by which of the parties will it be insti-
tuted?'

'I know nothing about the private intentions of either
of them. There is no little lack of truth in much that has
been said about this matter, and this attempt to fathom
and analyse the feelings, motives and future intentions
of McAllister and his wife has not been in any means a
veracious success.'

Mr Gallup said yesterday that he had written a letter to young McAllister at Yonkers, but whether he
could be found in the village or some distance out in
the country with a friend he did not know. He said,
though, that McAllister had no intention of returning
to the city until all the gossip about this marriage had
subsided.

New York Times – May 10, 1895

—Mrs H. H. McAllister Asks for a Divorce

Savannah, Ga. May 9. Mrs H.H. McAllister today
filed a petition for divorce from her husband, Conrad
Hall McAllister of New York, son of the late Ward
McAllister.

Mrs Conrad Hall McAllister is related by birth and by
marriage to many of the most prominent families of the
south. She was Miss Blanche Garmany of Savannah and
is about 28 years old.

She had been the daughter-in-law of Ward McAllister
five years before the fact was announced.

Young Mr McAllister's name has been used in many
stories of late, especially when Mrs Lillie McCall sued
him for $100,000 for breach of promise of marriage. The

suit never came to trial. There have been rumours that Ward McAllister compromised it.

New York Times – February 13, 1898

Early March, Miss Henrietta Garmany, the divorced wife of Conrad Hall McAllister of New York, will be wedded once more, this time in Savannah. The prospective bridegroom is Anthony P. Champion of London, a member of the firm of Henry Champion, Sons & Co., bankers.

Miss Garmany met him in Egypt. She is now in Europe but is coming home soon. Her divorce from Conrad McAllister was granted a few years ago. It was the sequel of a secret marriage to him in New York.

When she had finished reading, Blanche shook her head and looked up at Henrietta. The old lady was staring at her intently, her eyes bright like a bird's, waiting for her response. 'What a sad story,' Blanche murmured.

'Now you know why I hate America.' Henrietta's voice was suddenly hard and firm.

'But how did it happen? How did it come about?'

Henrietta's mouth twisted ruefully. 'It was a bit of fun. I was a headstrong girl and I thought it was a lark. I never expected to be treated in the way I was, either by society or my family, and certainly not by Conrad. I thought I knew him but I was deluded. My brothers were bad enough, so censorious and unkind, but my cousins were, too, though not your dear mother, of course. But Jasper, your uncle Jasper, was particularly unpleasant about it all. He was very strait-laced generally and made out that I had brought shame upon the family name. How dare I? He was more concerned about his reputation than my feelings, as I recall.'

Blanche sighed. 'He was always like that, I believe, very moralistic and upstanding. I remember him being very critical of my uncle Hayward for his behaviour.'

Henrietta raised her eyebrows and smiled. 'But my, how lucky young women are today. They don't suffer anything like the number of restrictions we had. They can smoke and drink and enjoy all manner of sexual freedom. That was all denied us in my day.' She chuckled quietly. 'Jasper must be quite shocked by modern life.'

Blanche laughed and nodded. 'I'm sure he is but I don't know that life for young women in the American South is quite so liberal. They are years behind the times down there. They always have been, and they're proud of it, too!

'You haven't been back for so many years. Have you ever missed America?' she asked quietly, shifting the conversation.

Henrietta shook her head with a light grimace on her thin aged lips. 'I miss the sun over the Savannah river in the evenings and I miss the soft-shell crabs. Apart from those two things, I don't believe I miss anything. I've never wanted to go back home, and I never have, except once.' She looked at Blanche intently. 'What about you?'

Blanche turned away with a quickness that did not go unnoticed by Henrietta. 'I do miss it, of course. I miss my mother – but she's dead anyway. I miss my brothers but they keep in touch by writing. Yes, I miss Savannah Beach and the crabbing and all the things I did there as a child. I miss the weather, though not the humidity, of course!' She sighed. 'No, I think I'm happy enough here on this side of the ocean to stay a while longer.'

'Yes,' breathed Henrietta. 'Exiles have to be prepared to accept sacrifices.'

The nurse made a quiet entrance into the room. 'Oh, it's

time for my afternoon nap, Blanche. Do come and see me again. I always enjoy your company. It is tedious getting old, you know. One's energy goes on mundane things, like dressing, leaving no energy to do the interesting things of life. So tedious.'

'But you're not old,' protested Blanche. 'And you're as fit as a fiddle!'

Henrietta raised her eyebrows cynically. 'I feel as old as God,' she sighed. 'In my family, the women all die young. They all die in their late sixties. I'm on borrowed time.'

Then her expression became more serious. 'In fact, my medical news is not very good, which is one of the reasons why I asked you to come today. I have a tumour that looks bad. I have not told anyone else this – and I'd appreciate it if you did not mention it to anyone.'

The shock of Henrietta's news made Blanche's thoughts jump about at random. 'Perhaps the doctors are wrong. They're often wrong about these things, you know. A friend of mine was told she had six months to live, and lived for another four years.'

'There's no mistake,' Henrietta replied firmly. 'The doctors are correct in their diagnosis. No, I don't want any unnecessary fussing about it. It gives me the chance to put my affairs in order, and I wanted to explain what I've done about my will.

'I've left half my estate to Masha because she needs it to educate all those children and her husband, wonderful though he is, is not paid a fortune in the Navy. I've left a little to Gussie and Rudie as my dear nephews but they were left plenty by their own ma and pa. The rest I'm leaving to your Evelyn.'

'Oh, Henrietta, why that's very kind and unexpected.' Her voice sounded insincere. It seemed inappropriate to be talking like this, and she felt she was gabbling, her tongue not connected to her thoughts.

Henrietta shook her head again. 'No, it's not kind. I've watched that child from birth and I have always liked her. But I've always felt she needs protection. Money won't save her from all the evils of life but it will cushion her. The only stipulation will be that she can't have it until she's thirty. That's just to stave off the gold-diggers, though I know you can find gold-diggers at any age!' She chuckled.

'Now, goodbye, my dear, I'm so very sorry about Adrian but you are a strong person and I know you will survive. Gussie, I'm not so sure about.'

Blanche nodded. 'He's taken it very badly. I hardly feel that I can reach him any more.'

'Have another baby.'

Blanche shook her head. 'That's not the answer . . . but maybe . . .' Her voice tailed off.

'You're still young enough. How old are you now?'

'I'm thirty-eight.'

'There you are! You're a spring chicken. My mother went on producing children until she was forty-eight. Just tell Gussie to do his duty. Anthony and I were never to be blessed with children, which was always a great sadness to me. But it meant that we could travel the world, which we would not have done had we led a more conventional life. Our lives were certainly enriched by that. If you can have children, have them.'

Blanche got to her feet and kissed the old lady's cheek. Her skin, barely touched by the sun's rays was soft, white and smooth. 'You're tired. I must go now.'

She stepped out into the bright light of the afternoon feeling sad at the thought of losing Henrietta. She could not bear the idea of her dying, and talk of wills was unsettling.

Blanche turned into Regent's Park and walked across the green field to watch several girls playing rounders. A group of boys kicked a football around. Now she had filled the gap in Henrietta's past. At last she knew why her cousin had left Savannah and settled in Europe. Yet what had Henrietta actually done? Her so-called crime seemed so tame! Such had the mores of the times changed!

As she walked along the lakeside and watched the ducks and swans gliding on the water, she found herself wishing that she could unburden her own secret on to Henrietta. It would be a fair exchange. She knew that she could trust Henrietta but she still did not dare. The secret was inside her, under control. Once you let out a secret, once you confide in someone else, however much you trust them, the control of that secret is gone. Other people can do things with it, and you cannot stop them. Perhaps you just get too old to care in the end. Or the control slips.

A threesome of uniformed nannies pushing their charges in large black prams walked past. Blanche's thoughts switched to the idea of babies. Henrietta's words about having another spun in her head. Perhaps she should think about that seriously . . .

To Blanche's surprise, Gussie agreed that a holiday together might be what they both needed. They decided to go to Bavaria, to a small guest-house Gussie used to visit every year with his parents, who loved walking and the mountain air. He was always very fond of the hotel-keeper and his wife who, it turned out, still owned it. When the letter arrived confirming their reservation, the hotel-keeper had also written a note saying how much he was looking forward to seeing Herr Champion again after all these years.

Sadly their trip was not a success. Gussie had been keen to

see his beloved Bavaria again before a war in Europe, which seemed imminent, began. He and Blanche were shocked by the sight of the banners stretched across the streets in every town bearing the words: 'The Jew Is Our Enemy'. She was terrified by the sight of the thuggish Hitler Youth goose-stepping down the streets and the nasty bullying ways of Hitler's supporters.

Herr and Frau Konig hated the Nationalist party and were not afraid to say so. They welcomed Blanche and Gussie and told them with much sadness about the goings-on since Hitler had become Chancellor.

Herr Konig was a fat, florid-cheeked man with bright blue eyes and a white moustache. 'I'll give you an example, Herr Champion, of how things are – and how dangerous these people are . . .' He lowered his voice and looked around the dining-room. 'You'll remember I used to have a big flagpole outside on the hill in front of the guest-house. It flew the flag, the Bavarian flag.'

Gussie nodded. 'I used to help you hoist it every morning when I was staying.' He looked puzzled. 'But it's not there now, is it?'

Herr Konig shook his head. 'That is my story. A few years ago, a Nazi official came and told me I had to fly the Nazi flag as well. He made it clear that I had no choice. He even handed me a Nazi flag to put up. It was the same size as my flag, so I got a bigger Bavarian flag and flew that on top of the smaller flag with the swastika below.

'Well, a few months later, another official came to tell me that the swastika had to be no smaller than the Bavarian flag. So I pulled out my old flag and flew that. A few months after that they came and said that the Bavarian flag had to be smaller than the swastika. That was it. I was fed up with this nonsense. So you know what I did? I took the flagpole down altogether.

So now there can be no more arguments, no more bullying.'
He slapped his fat belly triumphantly and laughed. 'Now that
official can go and make trouble for somebody else.'

The couple laughed at the hotel-keeper's proud act of
defiance. But then he leaned forward. 'But it's all very bad
here, my friends, very bad indeed.'

The Champions walked every day and enjoyed the fresh
air. They enjoyed the food and the concerts given in the
hotel every evening. It was a relaxing time but in other
ways the holiday was not a success. It had been an unspoken
agreement between them that this trip offered an opportunity
to re-establish sexual relations with the aim of producing
another baby. Blanche had decided that if she had another
child, it would never be a replacement for Adrian. It would
be loved and wanted for itself.

Gussie never uttered a word about it, but the fact that he
was willing to enter his wife's bed after twelve years was
evidence enough that he was hoping that there would be some
result from it.

In spite of his efforts and Blanche's patience, Gussie was
unable to find the passion in his heart to make love to his
wife. He tried hard enough, every night in the dark, but their
conjugal efforts ended each time with Gussie heaving a deep
sigh of despair and rolling off Blanche.

'It's no good,' he said one night. 'It's no good.' For the first
time ever he held her in his arms and stroked her hair.

Blanche lay beside him wondering whether she should try
to coax him to excitement and use the tricks she had learned
over the years with Ivo but she was afraid that Gussie might
accuse her of infidelity, even though she was pretty sure he
knew about Ivo anyway. She herself had suspected for some
years that Gussie visited prostitutes in London. Presumably
he was not impotent with them and, she thought with some

irony, they probably aroused him with all sorts of tricks, too. So absurd that a wife could not do such things with her own husband!

Anyway for her it settled the matter. They would not have another child, which was just as well, really. For if it were another girl, and not a boy, just how would Gussie take it?

While her parents were in Bavaria, Evelyn was left in Sussex in the company of her nanny.

She spent much of her free time with Frank, who had recently expressed a desire to learn tennis. Every morning, she instructed Frank in the game, showing him how to hold the wooden racket as though he were shaking hands, how to keep his eye on the ball at all times, where to position his feet, and how to wait until the exact moment to hit the ball in the centre of the racket. She laughed a lot and got a thrill out of having to touch his strong body as she pushed him into the correct positions.

But Frank did not laugh. He concentrated hard and listened to her every word about running for the ball, putting his weight on the correct foot as he made his strokes, and always positioning himself so that he could run forward rather than back.

Within a day or two, they were able to play a tolerable game of tennis together. Although Evelyn won the first few, Frank improved at an astonishing rate, the determination etched on his face as he began to win.

They played every day, morning and evening. The staff were worried.

'Wouldn't you like to invite Sophie St Clair over for tea?' Nanny said one day. 'I really don't think your parents would be pleased that you're spending so much time with the gardener's boy.'

'His name's Frank,' sniffed Evelyn. 'And I don't even like Sophie St Clair. She's a dreadful snob.'

The morning her parents were due home, Evelyn helped Mrs Knight do the flowers for the house.

Although Blanche preferred to see flowers growing in their natural state, her husband expected to see arrangements everywhere in the house, as had his mother in the past.

The special beds for the cut flowers were high above the house, beyond the vegetable garden and the greenhouse, well out of view. There the irises, gypsophila, stocks, sweet williams, cornflowers, bellflowers and cock's comb were grown in straight rows, ready for cutting when the household demanded it.

The flower arrangement was one of Mrs Knight's chores, which she did every other morning in the flower-room beyond the kitchen. Her husband would bring in the blooms which he usually presented to Blanche for her approval during his morning session with her, when he would discuss what needed to be done in the garden that day. That morning, he had brought in a magnificent bunch of floral offerings, which now lay on the sideboard ready for trimming and arranging.

With nimble fingers, Mrs Knight cut the stems and pulled off the unnecessary leaves. She gave Evelyn the scissors and explained the principles of flower arranging. 'The last lady I worked for taught me how to arrange flowers properly,' she explained. 'It's an art in itself, she used to tell me. You have to think about what it all looks like together. It has to be balanced, she used to say. You have to think about proportion, so everything looks right in relation to everything else. You need contrast, with the colours and textures, and you need what she called "harmony". That, she always explained, was what you have achieved when the display makes you feel pleased. If it looks good and it gives you pleasure, then you've got it right.'

Evelyn loved to work alongside Mrs Knight. She cut and trimmed the plants methodically, enjoying Mrs Knight's quiet presence beside her. She threw away the dead and dying blooms from the vases brought in from the various rooms and poured the rancid green water down the stone sink in the corner. Mrs Knight was a quiet woman with a gentle demeanour. She had a pretty, round face with a white scar down one side, the result of a kick from a cow as a child on the farm where her father had been the hand. She was happily married to her husband, and was generally content with her lot in life. Her only sadness was that she had only ever had one child. 'It was God's decision, not ours, that we should only have Frank,' she told Evelyn.

'Frank's becoming very good at tennis, Mrs Knight,' commented Evelyn, pulling leaves off the stalks.

'Is he indeed?' Mrs Knight was bemused by Frank's interest in the game. 'I don't know where he thinks he's going to play tennis when you're not around.'

'Oh, it's always good to be able to play any game,' said Evelyn, missing the irony in the woman's voice. 'I'm just so impressed by how good he is and how quickly he's progressed.'

Mrs Knight smiled. It was a mixture of pride and bemusement. 'Frank seems to be blessed with so many talents,' she said. 'I don't know where he gets them all from because they don't come from me or his father.'

'But that's good,' said Evelyn.

'Perhaps,' replied Mrs Knight, 'but it makes me worry about him at times.'

'What do you mean?'

'Well, I worry that he gets ideas above his station. He's so good with the animals, he should be thinking seriously of getting a position on the farm.'

Evelyn shoved the flowers into the vase and tried to make some arrangement out of them, adjusting one stem here, moving another there. Was the balance right? Was it all in proportion? 'But he does well at school, doesn't he?' she said. 'Why shouldn't he think of doing something different from his father and get out of service?'

Mrs Knight turned on the tap to let a rush of water into another large cream-coloured vase. 'I just worry about him sometimes,' she said. 'I don't think people should hanker after more than what the good Lord has given them.' She shook her head in a sorrowful manner. 'But Frank doesn't seem to understand that. He wants to move to the city and make lots of money.'

'What's wrong with that? Wouldn't that make you proud of him if he bettered himself?'

As she said it, Evelyn blushed. 'I'm sorry,' she added hastily, 'I really didn't mean it that way.'

Mrs Knight shrugged. 'Some call it bettering themselves but when you lose your roots you can lose everything if you're not careful. Frank's a country boy. The city indeed!'

'Frank wouldn't do that, he wouldn't lose his roots,' protested Evelyn. 'He loves the country.'

'Mmm,' murmured Mrs Knight, clearly not convinced.

Evelyn was bothered by these remarks. 'But if everyone accepted their station in life, nothing would ever change.'

'No, that's right. And so it shouldn't,' returned Mrs Knight emphatically. 'You, for instance, will no doubt do what your mother and grandmother did before you: marry a suitable boy and start your own family. If you had any idea of being one of these blue stockings, or something like that, your parents wouldn't like it one bit.

'Frank's ideas worry me to death sometimes. He likes too many things, too many objects. He tells me he's going to have a Rolls-Royce like Mr Champion's one day. Well, I don't know why he thinks that or how he thinks he's going to get enough money for any motor car, let alone one like that. I don't want to think about it. He's a bright lad but sometimes I think he's got something missing in that head of his. Now, help me carry these out to the hall chest and I'll do the rest. Thank you, Evelyn, you've been a grand help.'

EVELYN

CHAPTER 14

1937–1938

The holiday in Bavaria had not helped Augustus's mood. The Nationalist tension in the country combined with his conjugal failure, plunged him into a prolonged depression and triggered another bout of deep mourning for his son Adrian. The gloom descended on him like a thick fog but it manifested itself mainly as bad temper. He went to his office at the bank each day, was snappy with his clerks and secretary, and came home in the evening, ate dinner in silence and retired to the drawing-room to read *The Times* before going off to bed.

His sense of virility was restored fairly rapidly by returning to the foxy young woman in Soho who knew how to arouse him with the clever tricks and secret routines he could ask only her to carry out. She did it well and his sexual appetite was sated. His impotence with Blanche would not have bothered him if it had not meant that there would be no male heir to his house and estate. Adrian was gone, and Blanche could not arouse him. It was her fault and it made him burn with a rage without words from the moment he awoke to the moment he dropped off to sleep. Even when he was concentrating on his work, it simmered in the background. He was angry with her, with Evelyn, the whole world. He would fall asleep and have fierce nightmares in which Adrian's face, eaten by rats, would leer at him in the dark.

On Fridays, after lunch at his club, he motored down to Sussex, where he went out with his shotgun and dogs, or his fishing-rod, and disappeared except for meals. He sank into a reclusive, moody existence, cut off from much of the world outside.

Evelyn was even more terrified of her father than ever. She knew that he blamed her for Adrian's death, if only because it was her idea to play the hide and seek that prompted her brother to hide in the haystack. At meals, she barely spoke to him and he never addressed her.

Evelyn's relationship with her mother, however, became closer that summer. Her mother's grief was something Evelyn could try to comfort, which she did, and Blanche responded in turn. Blanche knew that Evelyn blamed herself for Adrian's death and she knew that Augustus blamed her too. Over and over again she tried to reassure her that it was not her fault, that it had been an unfortunate accident. Apart from that, Evelyn's grief at the loss of her brother was not even mentioned, as though her grief as a sibling did not count. But she felt lonely, suddenly an only child, the only representative of her generation, without any ally at all. She had never been particularly close to Adrian and he had been rather mean towards her in the months before his death, but he was her brother all the same.

For the period after the trip to Bavaria, Blanche was also rather withdrawn. She stopped entertaining in London and invited nobody down to the country. She read endlessly, the works of Freud, Edith Wharton, Tolstoy, Jane Austen, Trollope, as if to discover the reason why her son had died. She took up needlepoint and created exquisite designs based on the shapes and colours of the plants in the garden she loved so much. Generally, she became more reflective.

By the time the gloom of bereavement had finally lifted, Blanche Champion had changed. To other people she was the same but she was aware that the secret, private side to her character had grown, and she had a tendency now to be more thoughtful and quiet, to withdraw from the world and live in her head as she had never done before.

To Blanche's relief Ivo finally returned home from Paris after studying print-making with Picasso for a year. They met in the wood one day. Blanche had not seen him since his return, though she knew he was back because he had had sent her a postcard from Paris telling her he was on his way home.

For months after Adrian's death, Ivo had written long letters urging her to be strong and positive about the future. 'It's proof of how well I am that I can be advising you in this way,' he wrote. 'But even I believe there is a future. You must hang on to that thought.'

Now he was standing before her, a broad smile on his rugged face. His hair was wild and almost completely white now. 'Blanche, my dear!' Ivo held out his arms and hugged her. 'How are you? I was planning to visit you today. How opportune to meet in the woods we love.'

He kissed the top of her head and pushed her back so that he could look at her face. 'You are such a beautiful woman, Blanche. I think it's time for you to sit for me again.'

'But you painted me before,' Blanche laughed, 'when I was in the bloom of youth. Now I'm old and middle-aged.'

Ivo laughed. 'You're more beautiful now that life has made its mark on you. Your face is more alive, more interesting. No, I like the idea of painting you ten years on. In fact, I think I should paint you every ten years.'

Blanche rolled her eyes. 'God forbid!' she exclaimed.

'Will you sit for me again? Come and sit in my studio while we make conversation – and perhaps a little love!' He smiled warmly and squeezed her waist provocatively.

'Ivo!' Blanche twisted away from him, but the laughter in her eyes told him that she would.

Evelyn still played tennis with Frank, who had become very accomplished. They played long sets in the summer sun, evenly matched. Evelyn loved the heat of the sun on her arms and legs, running for the ball across the grass as it hit the ground and the sharp twang as it hit the gut strings on the racket in a good return.

She also liked to watch Frank as he served, his tall frame poised against the sky, concentration on his strong face, his dark eyes fixed on the ball.

She was proud of his progress, for she had taught him. He was a natural athlete and a responsive pupil but she knew she had been a patient teacher.

Afterwards they would sit in the shade and drink lemonade made by Cook.

'You're doing well,' said Evelyn.

Frank knocked his racket against his knee. 'Perhaps I'll play in championships one day.'

Evelyn laughed. 'You goose! Why do you have to be so competitive? Isn't it good enough that you can play for pleasure, with me?' She looked at him, suddenly shy.

As she spoke, she noticed that Frank's attention was elsewhere. Turning in the direction of his gaze, she saw her father, returning from a walk with the dogs, coming towards them. Her stomach lurched. As he recognised his daughter's companion, Augustus frowned with anger. 'What do you think you're up to? Get off my court!' he yelled. His face was red with rage.

'But, Papa,' protested Evelyn. 'We've been having a very good game. Frank has become very accomplished at tennis. I taught him. We're very well matched now . . .'

Augustus was not interested. He marched up to Frank, who stood staring at his father's employer with a nonchalant look on his face.

Augustus snatched the wooden racket out of Frank's hand. 'How dare you be so presumptuous as to play with my daughter!'

Evelyn pulled on his arm. 'Oh, Papa, please, don't!'

Frank stood for a second, facing Augustus before turning and walking away without a word or expression on his face.

Evelyn's throat tightened painfully as she watched the boy's broad back disappearing down the garden.

'What do you think you're doing, playing with the servants?' Augustus's fury was beyond control.

Evelyn knew that there was no point in trying to explain. She picked up her racket and ran back to the house, salty tears streaming from her eyes.

That night in her room, with the anger still burning inside her, she picked up her racket and with a little silver penknife her Uncle Rudie had given her for her birthday, she began to etch an 'E' on the varnished wood, chipping away the bits with care. It was easier than she thought it would be and after half an hour she had etched more. She stared at her handiwork with trembling pride. It was a work of such defiance – private but public as well. And the message had surprised her: 'E loves F'.

They had to stop playing tennis together. It was not just Augustus's disapproval but that of Frank's parents, too. On hearing what had happened, Mr and Mrs Knight banned Frank from playing tennis as well.

At first Evelyn thought that she and Frank should try

playing in defiance anyway but then she realised that there were too many servants around who would know and possibly tell. And who knew what would happen then?

Instead of playing tennis, Evelyn and Frank began to go for long walks together around Ambersham Common or across the Downs. Frank quizzed Evelyn about London on these outings. He wanted to know what it was like – the sounds, the sights, the smells, the views.

'It's impossible to describe, really,' replied Evelyn. 'It's noisy and crowded and very dirty. There are people rushing about, and concrete and soot everywhere. Cars, buses and hooting, and filthy air from the chimneys. Sussex is so much more lovely. It's the place I prefer to be in.'

Frank was not to be put off. He looked dreamily into the distance as he shook his head slowly in disbelief. 'London sounds so wonderful, so alive, so much where things happen, so much where a man can do something interesting.'

Evelyn looked at him with a teasing smile on her lips. 'It's very different from Midhurst, you know. Unimaginable.'

Frank scowled. 'I know!' he snapped. 'I know what it looks like. I've seen photographs.' He strode on ahead as if offended by her teasing tone.

'Then why do you ask?' Evelyn was bewildered, and anxious not to annoy him. She had hurt his feelings, and was sorry. 'I didn't mean to seem superior,' she said softly.

Frank spun around on his heels, his dark eyes glowing. 'Your life is so different from mine. You have no idea what life is like for most people. You spend your time going up and down to London as if it's the easiest thing in the world. You never have to worry about holes in the soles of your shoes or how to fix them with layers of cardboard which may make them last just a little bit longer. You've probably never even seen a darned sock or a patched shirt, except worn by one of your father's servants. Anything you want, you have, because you have money. Or because your father has money.'

Evelyn stared at him, taken aback by his outburst. 'But that's not my fault. I can't help the way I was born.'

Frank was shaking his head. 'That's not what I was saying. That's not my point.'

'Well, what is your point, then?' Evelyn's voice rose in pitch with anxiety.

'The point,' Frank said, spinning round and catching her hand,' is what money can do. It's money that buys you the freedom from poverty, it buys you the freedom to make choices.'

'Well, yes.' Evelyn was uncertain about what was going to happen next. Frank's strong hand grasped hers in a firm grip. She squeezed his back, her heart pounding in her chest.

'One day I'm going to be rich,' Frank whispered, coming closer. He looked down at her face. She could smell his breath. It was sweet and musty, like grass.

'I'm sure you will,' she murmured, her eyes watching his red mouth as it came down on hers.

His lips were moist and soft. Frank had kissed many of the maids, and gone further with several, so he knew what to do. But he was careful not to go too far with the master's daughter. A kiss or two was enough for her, and the scent of her body was different. It was so good – clean and pampered. So rich.

He ran his hand gently under her skirt and along her leg and he squeezed her breasts gently. 'You smell so good,' he breathed.

Evelyn was ready to give herself up to him if he went any further, so she was relieved when he finally pulled away and suggested they get back home. She was shocked to feel that she would have been incapable of telling him to stop. That just went to show what an honourable person he was, she thought, touching her numbed lips in wonder. His passion had changed her appearance!

They walked home through the woods, avoiding the roads so as not to be seen together. They kissed each other on parting and set off for their respective homes – Frank to the gardener's cottage where his mother had a pot of mutton stew and boiled potatoes on the black stove ready for him, followed by stewed fruits picked from the garden and the hedgerows. Evelyn was off to have a bath before changing and emerging for an uncomfortable half-hour of drinks followed by a stiff formal dinner with her parents. The food, served by a servant, would be mushroom soup, followed by chicken Kiev and baby beans, then crème caramel followed by cheese. All of it served by servants, who hovered in the background as their employers ate.

As usual, the conversation was about family and the situation in Europe. Germany had annexed Austria and two members of the government had resigned in protest at the Prime Minister's policy of appeasement.

Augustus barely addressed Evelyn throughout the evening, until the end as the cheese and grapes were placed on plates before them.

'I've decided it's time you were sent to finishing school, Evelyn,' he said. 'We had originally planned for you to spend some time in Germany but the situation there is too unstable, so I've arranged for you to go to Madame Lemarchand's Academy in Switzerland, where you will learn French and German but be taught by native French and German speakers, not Swiss. After that, you will go to Florence to perfect your Italian and, because your mother thinks it important, to learn about art and music.'

Evelyn looked at her father and then across at her mother. Blanche's face gave away no emotion.

'It's all been arranged?' Evelyn asked. 'Without any discussion with me?'

Augustus nodded. 'Yes.' He pushed down on the Stilton and cut a thick, crumbly slice which he placed carefully on his plate. He picked up the grape scissors and snipped off a bunch of plump purple grapes which he placed next to his cheese.

'But you haven't asked me if I want to go,' protested Evelyn.

Augustus buttered a cheese biscuit and scooped some Stilton on to it. 'Of course not,' he said, 'you have no choice in the matter. You know perfectly well that a properly brought-up girl goes to finishing school to learn the essentials.'

Evelyn looked defiantly at her father. 'They don't all go to finishing school, Papa,' she said. She lifted her chin. 'Some,' she said provocatively, 'go to university.'

Augustus threw down his knife so that it clattered on the plate. His mouth was set in a straight line, his face flushed with annoyance. 'No daughter of mine is going to university. You're catching that train from Victoria Station next week and you'll be away for a year. This can hardly be a surprise to you. You've always known that this is what is expected of you. In our family, that is what happens.'

Evelyn stared at her plate. 'You mean with the females.' But she knew there was no point in protesting. 'I just thought you might have discussed it with me first. I don't seem to have any choice.'

Augustus looked steadily at her. 'No,' he said, indicating to the servant to take away his cheese plate, 'you don't. And,' he added, looking at her with undisguised hostility, 'it will get you away from that boy. It seems that only sending you away will keep you apart. You'll see in no time how ridiculous you are to be friendly with him. You'll soon see what sort of man you'll want to marry, someone who is educated and cultured, someone with means. It will all be clear to you when you return. You'll despise that boy when you get back, I can assure you. You'll be embarrassed that you ever had anything to do with him.'

'Gussie!' Blanche frowned at the savagery of her husband's attack on Evelyn. But Augustus ignored her. He dropped his napkin on the table in front of him. 'Come, Blanche, we'll have our coffee in the drawing-room. Evelyn, some day you'll be grateful to me for arranging this for you. I shall await with pleasure the day when you thank me.'

Upstairs, Evelyn was undressed by her maid whom she then dismissed.

Her mind was filled with thoughts coming from all directions. They swirled in the dark hole in her head, twisting and tangling around each other. She had to go to Europe. It was true that she knew all along this was planned for her but it was the way it was done that hurt her so much. There was no discussion, no courting of her opinion. No choice. What was it that Frank had said? Money gave me choice. Well, she certainly had no choice in this, or any choice in the way her life had already been mapped out for her, not only by her parents but also by generations of rich people before her.

Money brought choice for men, perhaps, but not much for women. And money did not buy the one thing Evelyn craved more than anything – love, her father's love.

She touched her lips again, where Frank had kissed them that afternoon. Throughout dinner, she had tried to stop the food touching her lips because she wanted the juices from his mouth to stay there for ever. She wished that she had not had a bath earlier that evening so that his earthy scent would still linger on her skin. But the maid had already drawn it for her and she could not think of an excuse for avoiding it.

She had to leave Frank, and she knew she had no choice. She knew that nothing in this world of hers, of her father's, would or could allow them to be together as equals. Frank was the son of a servant, and nothing could change that.

It would be good to get away from her family, at least, to see Europe and to break this pattern. In London, she had no friends, and in Sussex the only person she wanted to be with was Frank. Something had to be done. And it would be different and interesting to live in another country. At least she would be away from her father, and perhaps she would make new friends. The spirit of her mother rose up inside her to encourage the timid Evelyn, urging her to look forward to this new adventure, the beginning of something new and different, something that might bring her happiness.

CHAPTER 15

1939

Blanche began to sit for her new portrait in April, when Ivo's studio was warmed enough by the big black wood-burning stove in the corner for her to be able to sit poised in a thin gossamer dress without shivering. Her hair was pulled back to emphasise the elegant bone structure of her head.

Ivo stood in front of her, his easel between them, mixing his oils and squinting at her in the afternoon light. The portrait he had painted of Blanche ten years before hung on the wall by the window. It showed her young and fresh, wide-eyed, graceful and serene.

She still had reservations about allowing Ivo to paint her again. 'I think I'd rather be preserved in my twenties. Who wants to look at someone worn out by life?'

Ivo laughed without taking his eyes off the canvas in front of him. 'Worn out by life! My dear, you surely exaggerate. I know you've had your share of tragedies but I think it too strong to suggest that you've been worn out by life. Think of some of those servants and labourers of yours – why, they look about fifty when they're only in their twenties. If you want to see someone worn out by life, you have to look at a person who does manual work and doesn't have others waiting on them hand and foot, night and day.'

'Of course, you're right,' Blanche replied contritely. 'I didn't mean to be facetious.'

'You don't need to worry. As I've said before, you are more lovely now than ever. You have lived more and learned more over the years, and it shows on your face. Experience is beauty.'

Ivo walked over to his model and manipulated her face carefully, so that he had it in the exact position. 'I am doing a life-study of Mrs Blanche Champion,' he said with a chuckle. 'Didn't I tell you? I plan to paint you every ten years until one of us dies.'

Blanche smiled, trying not to move out of her position. 'We'll see about that,' she said dryly.

'Oh, I'm going to do it,' replied Ivo with some emphasis. 'Such a series of paintings will reveal a lot about us both.'

Blanche's sittings would last for a few hours at a time. While Ivo mixed his paints and applied the layers on to the canvas, they talked. They talked about ideas and thoughts, and whether there would be a war in Europe. They talked about their friends, about Henrietta, whose health, after a heartening period of remission, was suddenly deteriorating again. They talked about Evelyn and how she was getting on in Switzerland and how much she was looking forward to going to Florence in the spring. Blanche said she planned to visit her at some point. They talked about Gussie and his moods, his bad temper and selfishness, and about their London friends, and analysed the latest books and plays they had read and seen. They never tired of conversations they could have. The session was over when Blanche was beginning to wilt and Ivo's energy was petering out. Then Ivo would produce some cheese, pâté, a loaf of fresh bread and a bottle of delicious wine from the ice-box. They would eat together in the studio and then make love on the thick sheepskin rug spread out on the wooden floor, and lie entwined and naked, drowsy from the wine.

The portrait gradually took shape. Ivo was an extraordinary painter who deserved his reputation. Not only was the picture a true likeness but, like the first one, it went far beyond the face, to the character inside. It captured the intelligence and mystery in Blanche's eyes, the fresh bloom on her pale skin, the delicate arch of her neck and the exact curve of her lips. The comparison between this and the earlier picture was interesting. Now the skin was looser around her jaw, that was true, and there were faint lines between her brows and around her mouth, but Blanche had to agree that it looked as if she had more substance, more character than her younger self. She certainly looked calmer, more confident. And she agreed with Ivo that if given the choice at a party, she would rather meet and talk to the older woman in the new picture than the younger woman in the old.

'But you wouldn't mind being introduced to the younger one today, either,' she teased. 'I remember what you can do to a young girl's heart.'

Ivo stroked her arm thoughtfully. 'Oh, I'm not up to so much of that any more,' he said. 'I live more with my brain than my loins now. But a pretty and intelligent woman . . .' He laughed. 'Well, I can always be persuaded.'

He turned and smiled. 'Actually, my dear, I seem to be pretty much faithful to you nowadays. Have been for some years, really.'

Blanche looked at him in disbelief. 'I'm not sure I believe that.'

'It's true,' insisted Ivo. 'I haven't slept with another woman for at least three years.'

Blanche was silent as she pulled on her stockings and clothes. She felt a tight feeling of power inside her, a pride that Ivo regarded her as his prime woman, even though they had always agreed that free love did not allow for sexual jealousy.

Her feelings were changed a few weeks later when she went for her final sitting before heading off to Italy to visit Evelyn. She arrived at Ivo's cottage to find it empty. Ivo had left a note saying that he'd walked down to the farm to get eggs and milk and that he would be back soon. He added that Blanche should make herself comfortable while she waited.

Blanche went to the studio and as she waited she began to look through Ivo's work, the unframed water-colours of the woods, the familiar glades with browns and golds and purples, the copses and the commons with the South Downs in the distance. These were the imperfect paintings, the ones Ivo did not exhibit or sell, ones he never showed to anyone except Blanche, and the perfect ones, the ones he liked too much to part with.

At the back there was a box full of prints made while Ivo was in Paris. Here he was experimenting more with the human form. There were nude studies of men and women, some of them very good, she thought. He had spent his time in Paris well. Blanche knelt on the floor, picking her way through them, admiring Ivo's skill, his gifts, his genius. She felt so proud of his talents. She was proud of him as her friend, as her lover.

Curious to see Ivo's other work stored at the back of the studio, she pushed behind a curtain that contained some large canvases of oils. She pulled one out and stared at it for a few seconds before she realised what it was. A full-sized painting of a reclining nude woman stood before her. The woman had a black cigarette holder in one hand, while the other had dropped carelessly over her thigh which was covered with a diaphanous blue scarf, in a gesture that was both modest and provocative. She stared out at the world with a heavy seductive gaze.

Blanche knew that look. It was the look of a woman who had just got out of bed with a man who made her happy. She was staring at the artist with that gaze. She was in Ivo's studio, surrounded by objects familiar to Blanche. She knew that look and she knew that woman. It was Olive Porter. Olive and Ivo! How could he?

She peered at the back of the canvas. The date was May 1937, just after he came back from Paris. Ivo had made Olive gaze like that at him. Blanche could only too easily imagine what he had done to her to make her look like this seductress. Her rage built up inside her. How dare he! How dare he take Olive to bed and then tell her, Blanche, that he had slept with no other woman for three years. And Olive, of all people, she who made love to anything that moved!

She picked up her bag and was walking towards the door when Ivo arrived.

As he opened his arms to embrace her, she pushed past him in a fury, and disappeared down the path, leaving the astonished Ivo to work out what had happened in his absence.

In Florence, Evelyn felt that she had never been happier. She had loathed the months at Mme Lemarchand's Academy in Switzerland, where she had been drilled in the manners of a society hostess, taught to make small talk, how to eat 'difficult' foods, such as a peach or an artichoke, and the correct table settings for different kinds of dinner parties. She was also taught flower arranging, not the fluid sensitive arrangements Mrs Knight had taught her but rigid displays which seemed to her to have no cohesion whatsoever. She certainly never felt a sense of pleasure at the work she was supposed to do – no feeling of 'harmony', as Mrs Knight would have put it. And on the one occasion she did try something with some fluidity to it, Madame told her off because there was no 'order to it'.

Evelyn made no friends during this period, for she felt she had nothing in common with these other daughters of wealthy fathers whose ambition was to marry a rich man and live the life of a society hostess that they were training for. Evelyn always felt like the odd one out. The only pleasure she got from being there was becoming fluent in French and German, and seeing the Swiss countryside. The sight of it made her skin tingle. The students were only supposed to learn the techniques of water-colour, but Evelyn loved to set out her easel outside and paint the mountains and valleys or close-up details of the edelweiss and saxifrage and tiny Alpine irises. She discovered that she had a talent both for painting and for language, neither of which her fellow students seemed to care about. Most of them spent their time comparing their address books to see which friends they had in common, whose country estates they had spent weekends in and what they intended to do when they came out. Most of them were pretty and pampered and spent much time in front of mirrors discussing each other's physical strengths and weaknesses. They thought Evelyn, with her lank hair and mousy face was a lost cause, particularly since she did not seem to care one bit about her appearance, or finding a rich husband. They could not think why she had bothered to come at all, or why she spent her days reading French literature. She was a mystery to them.

In Florence, however, Evelyn found freedom. Realising the importance of gradual independence, Blanche had arranged for Evelyn to stay in a *pensione* recommended to her by a good friend, and to attend the Italian Institute every day for her studies.

Thus Evelyn found herself with a room of her own over-looking the Piazza del Duomo, with the life of Florence below her window. In the mornings she would sit on her balcony in the weak sunshine, and drink cappuccino and eat fresh bread and butter, taking in the white, rose and green-black marbles of the great cathedral and the bronze doors of the Baptistery. The cries and shouts of the Florentines setting about their business filled her with joy. She wished she could live like this for ever. After her meal, Evelyn would practise her Italian on her landlady, Signora Rangoni, before setting off for a morning of Italian lessons at the Institute. In the afternoons, she was free to go to the great art gallery in the Uffizi to look at the pictures, or to go to the Pitti Palace, or wander around the churches, sketching and painting the architecture and the local scenes. She wandered over the Ponte Vecchio to look at the goldsmiths' and jewellers' shops, or the Ponte alle Grazie, the city's strongest and oldest bridge, with chapels and oratories perched on its piers. Over the weeks she became familiar with all the names of the great Italian artists, starting with the works by the greatest trio of Tuscan painters at the beginning of the fourteenth century – Cimabue, Duccio and Giotto.

Every evening, she walked across town, through the narrow streets, and headed for the Piazza della Santo Spirito in the heart of the Oltarno. There she would sit in the busy piazza and admire the unfinished façade of Brunelleschi's stately church of Santo Spirito. She would sip a coffee and watch the children sailing home-made boats in the slowly dripping fountains and the old ladies sitting on the stone benches where they gossiped, knitted and crocheted. When she was hungry, she would cross the piazza for a meal at a bustling trattoria owned by Signora Rangoni's brother-in-law, Vittorio.

Vittorio Rangoni took the safety of this young English woman very seriously. He had a table in the corner set aside for her and he warned off any Italian men who threatened to show too much interest in a vulnerable-looking woman sitting alone with her books and food.

Evelyn would read her books while eating a plate of pasta followed by salad washed down with a glass of chianti. She read Plutarch, Dante, Vasari, Ruskin, steeping herself in Italian culture. Sometimes, if the trattoria was not too busy, Vittoria would come and talk to her about Italy. He explained how the Romans and Neapolitans detest the Tuscans. 'They think our accents are uncouth,' he said laughing. 'But the English,' he said, waving his arms around dramatically, 'have always liked us. And they call Firenze the "City of the Lily". So we like the English, too.'

He talked, too, about Mussolini and told Evelyn that he did not like *Il Duce*.

'They say his brain is addled by over-indulgence in women,' he said with a roguish laugh.

As Evelyn blushed at the sexual reference, Signor Rangoni bent down and whispered in her ear, 'We must be careful, too. There are plenty of spies around who report unfavourable remarks about *Il Duce*. Everyone must be careful when they speak.'

At other times, he would tell her about his passion for opera – Verdi and Puccini, especially – and sometimes he would amuse her and his other customers by singing arias from *La Traviata*, and explain how at times of the *festa*, after lots of chianti had been drunk, the men and women would sit outside in the piazza and sing choruses from *Aida*.

Then after supper, because the light was going and Evelyn's *pensione* was on the other side of the river, Vittorio always insisted that Evelyn was escorted home by his fifteen-year-old son Marco. At first Evelyn thought this tall, handsome boy was mute, for he uttered not a word on their journey back to the *pensione*. When Evelyn asked him a question he only answered with a grunt and a shake or nod of the head. But after she heard him having a heated conversation with his father one evening at the trattoria, she realised that he was just acutely shy. Shy like her. She could sympathise with that.

In Florence, Evelyn felt so grown-up, so free. As she became fluent in Italian, it seemed that the foreign language had liberated her. Everywhere she went she talked to the Florentines, surprised by her own lack of shyness. It was as if the language gave her some protective armour that for once made her fearless of the world. So she could feel for this handsome Florentine boy, Marco. She recognised in him the person she was at home.

In the early mornings, as Evelyn set off for the Institute and the city was bathed in golden sunshine, she felt her chest fill with happiness. It was a strange sensation, but it intoxicated her. Never had she felt so glad to be alive. Here, in this city of such beauty, with so many beautiful honey-coloured buildings and works of art, and with such a history, she felt there was a reason for living. The experience seemed to flood through her body, filling up a void and giving her something solid that was her own. She was growing up

It had been planned for a long time that Blanche should come out to Florence to visit Evelyn. Blanche also loved Florence, which she had visited when she first came to Europe with her mother, and she had been back a few times since. But a telegram announcing Blanche's imminent arrival by train came much earlier than Evelyn had expected.

Evelyn was looking forward to her mother's visit. After months of not being close to anyone, she realised that she yearned for conversation and contact with someone she knew well. She enjoyed all her discussions with the Rangonis and the Florentines in the markets but she was aware of needing another outlet, so she had kept a diary, which had provided her with a channel for her thoughts. She wrote once to Frank, while she was in Switzerland but she did not feel that she had much to tell him about her life there – it seemed so far removed from Sussex and his experiences. Frank never wrote back and Evelyn was surprised to realise that she was rather relieved. She sent him postcards periodically, to show that she had him in mind, and she wrote about him in her diary. Most of what she wrote acknowledged the feelings she felt for him and the hopelessness of the situation. Her father would never allow what he saw as such an unsuitable match, and nothing would ever make him change his mind.

After a while, she stopped writing about Frank and focused on her life in Florence and how much she was enjoying it. Now she could not wait for her mother to arrive so that she could share it all with her.

Evelyn was waiting on the platform as Blanche stepped off the train. Blanche was impressed to see her daughter looking almost radiant and waving enthusiastically at her. They hugged each other warmly. Blanche called for a porter who hurried over and collected her many suitcases and bags.

Blanche was to stay at a smart hotel near Evelyn's *pensione*. 'I'm at an age when I like my creature comforts,' she said with a laugh when Evelyn suggested that she stay at the *pensione* with her. 'Besides,' she added, 'you don't want your mother right on top of you. You have your own life to lead, and I don't want my visit to interfere with that.'

Evelyn was touched by her mother's concern for her social life, and protested that Blanche's presence was hardly going to disrupt the rather regular programme she had set for herself, particularly since her classes at the Institute were now over.

Evelyn felt great pride in Florence as she took her mother

around it, showing her not only the famous sights, which Blanche had seen before, of course, but also the smaller, secret treasures she had discovered in her months there, such as the Brancacci Chapel in the Church of Santa Maria del Carmine and the Porta Pisano, the fourteenth-century bridge that stood behind one of the few surviving sections of the old city wall. She took her around the Uffizi, telling her about the history of Italian art, and pointing out her favourite paintings in the great galleries.

Blanche was impressed by Evelyn's grasp of Italian, which seemed to give her a new confidence. It was Evelyn who led the way everywhere, buying tickets, asking for directions, ordering food in restaurants. She could hardly believe that this was the shy daughter she had put on the train at Victoria Station only six months before. All this time in Europe was evidently beneficial.

However, Blanche was concerned that Evelyn seemed not to have made any friends during this time. Certainly she had not made friends at the finishing school, and Evelyn seemed to have nobody she cared for in Florence, apart from the landlady and the owner of the scruffy trattoria on the wrong side of the river. Yet there were many English and American people in Florence. 'Surely you have made friends with other people learning Italian at the Institute,' she said.

Evelyn shook her head and looked at her mother with some anguish. 'I'm sorry, Mama, there's nobody there I care for very much.' She pushed her tortellini around her plate. 'I thought I had come here to learn Italian, not meet English and American people.'

Blanche smiled reassuringly. 'Of course, darling, you were not sent here to meet English people. It would just have been nice if you had met a few you could continue to be friends with back home.

'Well, tomorrow we have both been invited to dine with the Armstrongs up in Fiesole. They are having a dinner in my honour, which is very kind of them.'

Blanche had given Evelyn their address for her to contact them while she was there, but Evelyn had never bothered. She was not interested in meeting English people while she was in Italy. She felt a sinking feeling in her chest. 'Oh, do I have to go, Mama? I really don't feel I'm up to a dinner party.'

'Nonsense!' Blanche was suddenly impatient. 'I know you don't like social gatherings in the way some people do but it is important to know how to handle them. Only by experiencing them will you learn that. And you never know, you may even end up enjoying them . . .'

The Armstrongs' villa was on the winding road up to Fiesole, the pretty town on the hill above Florence that occupies the site of a Roman settlement. The villa itself was set back from the road behind tall brick walls covered with bougainvillaea. Beyond the tall metal gates, there was a terraced garden filled with bright flowers, and dramatic views of Florence in the valley below.

For Evelyn, the dinner was a nightmare, hurtling her straight back into her shell. She could not bear sitting at the table with two stuffy diplomats on either side of her and having to make conversation. She did not feel knowledgeable enough to engage in the serious talk about the political situation in Europe, and she sat mostly silent, feeling like a bored and boring child waiting to be allowed to leave the table.

The food was awful, too. It seemed that although the Armstrongs' cook was Italian, she had been taught to cook English food because Teddy Armstrong did not like foreign dishes. So, after months of eating the most delectable flavours she ever could have imagined, Evelyn sat at the lavishly set dinner-table and ate flavourless mushroom soup, indifferent chicken à la king, overcooked boiled potatoes and cabbage, followed by treacle pudding.

Evelyn watched her mother across the table, in full swing. Blanche loved any social occasion, and could command a room of people without dominating it. Her conversation was clever and broad, light and serious. She could impress anyone.

After the men had drunk their port and smoked their cigars, they joined the ladies for coffee in the drawing-room. Just as they appeared, the bell on the gate rang out into the night.

Jenny Armstrong turned to Blanche with a smile. 'We have a visitor,' she said. 'He's just arrived in town and I told him he was welcome to come for dinner but he insisted on coming after the meal.'

Blanche looked up and her mouth dropped open in surprise as Ivo Barnard walked into the room. He shook hands with the other guests, kissed Evelyn on the head, and grasped Blanche's two hands and pulled her into a corner.

For a moment she glared at him but this was not the place to be angry. 'I'm cross with you still,' she said quietly.

Ivo cocked his head. 'I know you're cross with me. You ran away and then rushed off to London, and now you're here. And I still don't really know why.'

They walked out to the terrace beyond which the lights of the city competed with the starry sky. 'You have to tell me why you're cross with me.'

Blanche sipped her coffee. 'Olive,' she said. 'I know I've no right to be jealous or possessive but I was hurt when you said you had not been with any other woman for three years, and there was proof that you certainly had been with Olive.'

Ivo looked at her quizzically. 'What are you talking about?'

'Her portrait,' replied Blanche. 'Nude and seductive.'

Ivo looked at her as the explanation finally became clear.

He threw back his head and laughed. 'You think I slept with Olive Porter?'

'It's obvious. You've only got to look at the expression on her face in that picture and,' she added, glancing at him sideways, 'I know you.'

Ivo came close to her and leaned on the balcony. 'You don't know me enough, my dear. I have never found Olive attractive and I have never been to bed with her.'

'You haven't?' Blanche had been so convinced that she was right. She had never imagined the situation could be otherwise. She felt a sudden film of shame creep over her.

Ivo laughed. 'No, I haven't. Olive commissioned me to paint her. I did not want to because I suspected she had some ulterior motive. I quoted an enormous price, hoping that would put her off, but it did not. She paid me in advance, in cash. She told me it was for her husband, for the bedroom, so she wanted it to be a full-size nude in order to excite him every time he looked at it. I think she was also trying to convince her husband that she only had thoughts for him. That's why she insisted on looking as she did.'

Blanche narrowed her eyes. 'I'm beginning to believe you, but why didn't you tell me at the time? And how is it that I never saw Olive down in Sussex?'

'She came in the week, usually, when you were generally in London, and she told me that no one was to know about it. It was a secret. And I keep my secrets,' he added with a broad smile. 'She has bought a lot of my paintings. She likes to think of herself as my patron, I think. It was only right that I keep it a secret if that's what she wanted, even from you.'

'And why is it still in your studio?'

Ivo shrugged. 'She's never collected it. We had a row soon after the painting was finished. You know she likes all that spiritualist nonsense. Every time she sat for me she talked about seances and how she could make contact with dead people. She's really believes this rubbish. Anyway, she told me one day that she had made contact with my wife Dora, and she said Dora wanted to speak to me. At first I laughed it off but she became so persistent in her suggestions to have a seance so that I could make contact with my dead wife that I'm afraid I lost my temper completely, and asked her to leave. She took offence and stormed off.'

Blanche watched Ivo carefully as he spoke, then said: 'It wasn't just that, was it? I think there is something more. That doesn't really explain why it's still in your studio.'

Ivo turned to her and, taking her hands in his, he smiled. 'You are perceptive, as ever. What I have told you is true, she did keep pestering me about seances but I never responded. Then on the final day I think she must have got desperate. She tried to seduce me. She simply walked across the studio and dropped her gown to the floor, waiting for me to do something. I said no.'

'You did?'

Ivo nodded. 'I did indeed. It will interest you to know that she told me that you had seduced her one weekend when she came to stay. I was in Paris at the time. She said she felt she had a right to seduce me, too, to make us all one: the Holy Trinity, I suppose,' Ivo snorted.

Blanche looked horrified. 'I never seduced her! That's a lie!'

Ivo chuckled. 'Don't worry, my darling, I never believed her. The world is divided into those who seduce and those who are seduced. You would never seduce anyone, while Olive is a praying mantis.

'Anyway, I think she took offence because I didn't give in to her, and she left her portrait there, presumably as a constant reminder of what I had missed. She'd paid me for it, so I didn't really care, though the canvas does take quite a bit of precious space.

'Perhaps she's changed her mind about presenting it to her husband, who knows? It doesn't bother me. I've been paid and it's there when she wants it, though I suspect she's changed her mind about continuing as my patron in the future, which is a shame. All artists need patrons.'

Ivo placed his hand on the small of Blanche's back. 'You shouldn't have been snooping in my studio.'

'I wasn't snooping!'

'Whatever,' he replied. 'My point is that you saw something you did not know about and you jumped to absurd conclusions, and then never gave me a chance to explain. That's why I've had to come all the way to Florence – to explain.'

Blanche smiled into the darkness. 'You came all the way to Florence to explain this to me?'

'Well, I had to find out what was going on, didn't I? I couldn't finish your portrait because I need you to sit one more time, and you rushed off. I came out to bring you back. It took me four extremely pleasant days to get here.'

Blanche turned around, leaning against the balcony. The city of Florence glowed in the basin behind her and the light from the house glowed in her eyes.

'I'm flattered,' she murmured.

Ivo smiled back. 'It's my pleasure. But I want to finish the painting when we get back.'

Blanche turned to him and looked up with her dark eyes. 'You shall,' she said softly, 'you shall.'

Evelyn sat on the sofa wishing that she could leave. She could feel exhaustion sweeping over her and the dullness of the evening had made her even more tired. She had watched her mother mingle and mix with the other guests and had, as ever, been aware of how much Blanche sparkled in public. It made Evelyn feel even gloomier. She could never imagine holding the attention of a roomful of people in the way her mother could. She had always hoped that that kind of social ease would come to her as she grew up. But far from getting better, she seemed to be growing increasingly awkward and gauche in company.

She was aware of having made a bad impression on all the guests here. They did not think a young woman of her age should be spending her days studying and reading, and nothing more. 'There's plenty of time for study and looking at paintings,' said one retired diplomat, 'but young people have to have fun, too. You should be getting out a bit, making some friends.'

'That's what my mother thinks,' murmured Evelyn gloomily.

'And she's right,' the old man said. 'Now, your mother certainly knows how to have fun – always has.' He reached over and patted Evelyn on the forearm. 'And I'll tell you, my dear, we should all be having fun while we can. When the war starts – and there's no two ways about that – it won't be fun for anyone. I may be an old fart but I'm not a fool, whatever my wife thinks,' he added with a sad chuckle.

Evelyn smiled gently at him. 'You're right. I'll try to remember.'

She looked through the doors to the balcony at Ivo and Blanche flirting with each other outside, old lovers, but also good friends. There was something both touching and threatening about the sight. Evelyn longed to have someone pay attention to her in such a way but she feared that however hard she tried, she would always fail to match her mother's engaging personality, and that no one would even notice her, let alone love her.

At last the opportunity to escape came when Ivo finally offered to drive the Champion women home to their rooms in the city. Driving down the hill into Florence in Ivo's blue coupé, their tongues loosened by the fine wines, their laughter scattered out into the night.

'If you arrived this morning,' demanded Blanche, 'why didn't you arrive in time to eat dinner at the Armstrongs'?'

'Because I wanted to eat some decent Italian food,' replied Ivo, causing Evelyn to giggle in the back of the car. He continued, 'The Armstrongs have taught their cook to produce the most disgusting meals I have ever tasted. It's ridiculous to be eating English food when you're in the land of good cuisine. It's even more ridiculous to bc eating bad English food. I'll wager that their cook can produce perfectly good Italian meals in her own home.'

Blanche laughed. 'Yes, Jenny boasts about how she taught Bruna to cook English meals. I can't imagine that Jenny's much of a cook herself – any more than I am. I don't even know how to boil an egg!'

'How things will change for you if a war starts,' said Ivo.

'Oh, the war. Everyone talks about the war.'

Ivo grimaced. 'Well, it's not going to go away just because we ignore it.'

'Actually, I find that a lot of things do go away if you don't think about them. Eventually they just aren't there any more,' said Blanche.

'Not this time, my darling. Not Hitler, however much you try not to think about him.'

He pulled the car up outside Blanche's hotel. 'Here you are,' Ivo said with a laugh. 'We'll finish this argument tomorrow. Now I'll take Evelyn on to her *pensione*, and then I'm going to see an old painter friend of mine.'

Ivo escorted Blanche to the hotel door and Evelyn moved to

the front passenger seat. 'Marvellous woman, your mother,' said Ivo as he got back in. 'Such a free spirit, and such force of character!'

Evelyn clasped her hands together and nodded. 'Yes,' she said faintly.

Ivo was quiet as he manoeuvred his car through the narrow Florentine streets and parked outside the dark *pensione*.

'Are you going to be able to get in?'

'I have a key,' replied Evelyn.

Ivo opened the car door for her and walked her to the door, holding the back of her elbow. 'Is something the matter?' he asked gently. 'You seem a bit quiet.'

Evelyn spun round, tears glistening in her eyes. 'I'm always quiet, didn't you know? I never talk very much because I have so little to say. I feel so inadequate next to my mother. Everyone tells me how marvellous she is in so many ways. I want to be like her so much, but I don't know how . . .' Her voice tailed off as she dropped her head and fidgeted with the door-key in her hand.

Ivo smiled and pulled her to him in a great bear hug. 'You don't want to be like your mother, my dear, and that's certainly not what I meant. You must concentrate on being yourself, not anybody else. You'll only be happy in life if you follow what's right for you – within reason, of course!' He gave her an avuncular kiss on the cheek. 'Know thyself,' he whispered.

As Evelyn snuggled into her bed that night, her thoughts were on Ivo and what a splendid friend he was to her mother. Her mother was entitled to have someone like Ivo, someone who was more than a friend, and more than a lover. She fell asleep wondering if she would ever have someone like Ivo in her life and what, with all this talk of war, the future held for any of them.

CHAPTER 16

Sussex, 1939

Evelyn returned to England at the end of May to find the subject of war on everyone's lips, though few people believed it would actually happen. She was unsure about what to do with herself in the future and the uncertainty about the state of Europe made it even more difficult for her to make up her mind. A Ministry of Supply had been set up and there was now compulsory conscription for men aged twenty and twenty-one.

She returned to the house in Sussex, choosing to spend the summer there rather than London. It all seemed very much the same but also different as she looked at it through the eyes of someone a year older and a year more experienced.

Mrs Knight filled her in with all the news downstairs. Frank, she said, had got himself working at the wood mill in Midhurst, and was putting up with it even though he did not like it that much. 'Probably not good enough for him,' she said with a mixture of affection and exasperation. 'He knows he's never going to earn enough to buy a Rolls-Royce with those wages.'

The surprise news was that Evelyn's horse Megan, a nine-year-old Welsh cob, was about to foal. It had been decided by Harry, the head groom, that while Evelyn was away in Europe, it would make sense to have Megan put into foal.

'If you have a spare horse, you put it into foal and then you have two spare horses,' he said with a chuckle. Harry looked as though he had spent all his life on a horse. His short legs were so bandy it was a wonder that he could walk at all.

The mare ran with the stallion rather late in the season, and now she was due to foal any day.

Evelyn was thrilled, and awaited the birth with childlike excitement. She had always adored her ponies, and the many hours she had spent riding quietly over the Downs and Ambersham common or through the woods, had given her a profound knowledge and love of that area of Sussex.

It was only a few days after her return that the stable boy ran to the back door to inform Evelyn that Megan's foal was coming. Evelyn had given instructions to be told when the mare went into labour as she very much wanted to witness the birth.

It was nine o'clock and dinner at the house was finished. Evelyn ran up to her room, pulled on her slacks and a shirt, and ran down to the stables.

Megan was lying on the ground. Her haunches were heaving, dark sweat flecked her coppery flanks. Her tail curved around at an awkward angle. Every now and then she pushed her head forward and let out quick snorts through her nostrils. Her lower jaw was dropped.

Harry crouched by her head talking quietly to her in encouraging tones. 'There you are, Miss Champion,' he said. 'I'm afraid she's having a bit of trouble here.'

Evelyn frowned at the horse lying in the yellow straw. 'What's the matter? Will she be all right?'

As she spoke, Megan grunted, blowing air noisily through her nostrils. Her sides shuddered again.

Harry stroked her ears and looked up at the stable boy. 'Run and get Frank. I think he'll be a help in here now.'

As the boy ran off towards the Knights' cottage, Evelyn watched Harry soothe the mare and thought how little she had seen of Frank since she had returned from the Continent. His job at the wood mill meant that he cycled to Midhurst every day. On the rare occasions they passed each other, their communication had been awkward and self-conscious. It was as if Frank felt that Evelyn was now a different person, having travelled to lands that he would never set foot in and learned the polished ways of a world he was not part of. He had drawn back, respectfully, or perhaps resentfully.

For her part, Evelyn also felt shy and awkward. She now spoke three foreign languages and had tasted and savoured other worlds. She had left as a child and come back as a woman. How could there be anything other than a widening gap between them? That, she reflected, was precisely what her father had hoped for.

She glanced into the yard as she heard the sound of running steps. Frank and the stable boy were at the door.

'Frank!' called Harry. 'Come and talk to the mare while I get this foal out. It doesn't seem to want to come out by itself.'

Frank nodded to Evelyn. 'Evening,' he said. Evelyn was struck by how much it was like the way his father greeted her; on the surface with respect but with an undertone of resentment.

'Hello, Frank,' she said.

Frank went straight to the mare and held her head-collar firmly, talking in a low voice into her ear. Harry moved around the mare's rear and pushed his arm under her tail and deep into her body.

Megan jumped and snorted again, throwing up her head. Her ears were flat against her head, her nostrils flared. She was obviously in pain but unable to shout out like a human. Evelyn was aware of her own face twisted in sympathy for this creature. Then gradually, the effect of Frank's presence could be seen on the horse. As he stroked her ears and neck and talked gently to her, her breathing slowed down and she seemed to be calmer, less panicked. Every now and then she pushed her head and neck forward and snorted but otherwise she seemed happy to be close to Frank.

Harry had begun to pull. 'Got it, here,' he said. 'It's stuck but at least it's the right way round. I've got the front hoofs.'

The mare shuddered and heaved herself up, front legs first. She kept turning her head to look at her sweaty flanks, and stamping her back legs in pain.

Frank was holding the leather head-collar, gripping one side while continuing to talk soothingly to the mare and stroking her neck.

Harry was pulling hard. 'Here it comes,' he said.

Megan seemed to have braced herself for this stage. Harry stepped back, pulling the foal from its mother's body, a huge translucent bag through which its dark coat and front legs could be seen. Finally, it slipped out and fell to the ground like a heavy sack. Harry held on to it, trying to break the fall and Frank let go of Megan's head so that she could turn around and see her foal.

Instinct made the mare turn with a soft snicker and immediately begin to lick the foal, cleaning off the semi-transparent caul to reveal the damp dark coat underneath.

She continued to wash her offspring tenderly as Harry pulled out the dark bloody afterbirth.

'It should stand up in a minute,' said Harry. He moved over to the foal and lifted its tail. 'Good, a filly,' he said with a grin on his wrinkled face. 'I prefer fillies. Hello, poppet,' he crooned.

They all watched the mare and her foal, touched by the mare's tenderness. Megan began to nudge her baby, urging it to get up on its feet. The foal responded, pushing its haunches into the air and trying to push up from its front knees. But every time it tried, it wobbled for a few seconds in mid-air and then dropped down again.

It tried several times before Harry said, 'It's having trouble. It should be up by now.'

'Its legs don't seem to be strong enough.' Evelyn was suddenly worried about the animal.

'It's wearing itself out like that,' said Frank as the foal collapsed again into the straw.

That there was something seriously wrong with the foal was evident after half an hour. It just did not have the strength to stand on its own legs. Harry held it up, clasping it around the belly, but the moment he let go, it sank slowly on to the ground again.

'Perhaps it needs a rest,' suggested Evelyn, her joy at the sight of the birth now turned to worry. The mare continued to nuzzle and nudge her baby in an encouraging way.

The minutes, then hours ticked by. Harry and the stable boy had to leave to feed the other horses before it became too dark outside. 'I'll stay with her tonight,' Harry said. 'They need to be watched.'

'I'll stay with them,' volunteered Evelyn.

Harry shook his head. 'You don't need to do that. That's my job. I can't let you spend your night in a stable!'

'But I want to,' insisted Evelyn. 'I feel I can't leave her like this. I want to make sure they're okay.'

'All right, Miss Champion, just so long as it's all right with Mrs Champion.'

Evelyn ran up to the house and told her mother what was

happening. She knew that Blanche would not object. It was the sort of spontaneous action her mother liked.

She was right. Within ten minutes she was back in the stable with blankets, a Thermos of hot milky tea and a tin of ginger biscuits to sustain her through the night.

Frank had left by the time she got back. 'Gone to have his tea,' explained the stable boy. 'He said he might look in again later.'

Evelyn settled into the corner of the stable, watching the foal, which was now lying on its side breathing slowly. As she watched it, she willed it to get up on its feet. 'Please get up,' she whispered. 'Please be normal. You have to live!'

Harry came in again with a bowl of hot bran mash and some hay for the mare. 'You all right, then, Miss Champion? It's going to be a long night. Would you like a cup of tea?'

By midnight, Evelyn was feeling very tired. Nothing more had happened. The foal lay on its side. Its mother nuzzled it with a soft snicker every now and then to encourage it to move. Evelyn's eyelids kept drooping as she fought off sleep. She felt it her duty to be there doing the watch. She felt increasingly gloomy about the likely outcome; deep down, she knew that the foal would not survive. It gave her an overwhelming feeling of hopelessness.

Not long after the stable door opened again and Frank appeared with a blanket and another Thermos flask.

'I've come to keep you company, if that's all right,' he said. 'I'd like to keep an eye on these two.' He nodded at the mare and foal.

'But what about your work?' she asked. 'You have to get up early in the morning.'

'I'll be all right,' Frank replied. 'It's these two we have to worry about.'

'It will be all right, won't it?' Evelyn hardly dared ask. She dreaded the answer.

'The longer it takes for the foal to get up, the worse it is,' replied Frank, stroking the mare and crouching down to caress the foal. 'The danger is that if it doesn't start moving around soon, it'll get pneumonia.'

Evelyn's heart seemed to move in her chest. 'Then what can we do? Isn't there something else we can do?'

Frank shrugged. 'Not much. We can just watch and help it get up when it tries again and get it to feed.'

The two sat in the dark stable, with a gas light casting a soft light around the stable walls. Weird shadows danced around the wooden roof.

'How do you find working for a living?' Evelyn felt keenly that she wanted to get over this awkward feeling in front of Frank.

Frank shrugged. 'It's not up to much,' he grunted. 'It's not going to get me anywhere.'

He paused and then added, 'But I'll probably join up pretty soon. If there's going to be a war, I'd like to be in there from the start.'

Evelyn nodded. 'A war will change everything. It's frightening to think of it, but quite exciting, too, to have the future so uncertain.'

Until recently, Evelyn had felt that her life had been mapped out for her, with no chance of deviating off the path. Her own desires and dreams had no place in that life. But she knew that even though a war would be a terrible thing, it could offer her opportunities she would otherwise never have, opportunities beyond her father's influence. These were thoughts in her mind she dared not tell anyone about. But they offered her a future where she had thought there was none. Evidently, Frank thought the same.

The foal lived just nine hours. After a while, it gave up trying to stand. It lay in the golden straw, its fluffy brown tail occasionally twitching as it grew visibly weaker by the minute. The mare stood over it, watching it, breathing over it, as if she sensed something was wrong. At about five in the morning, as the birds were waking up and the cows had begun to low, uncomfortable and eager to be milked, the foal's breathing became laboured as the infection crept into its immature lungs. It had no resistance against the disease and after an hour's battle, it gave out a great sigh, its body shuddered and then was still.

Evelyn knelt down to hold the foal's head in her lap, stroking it. Tears fell down her face. 'Don't die,' she whispered, 'please don't die, you have to live!'

But she knew it was useless. The foal's eyes were glazed. Dead. The life had drifted out of it. Almost dizzy from lack of sleep, she could not hold back her tears of loss, yet another loss in her life.

'It's gone,' Frank said. 'Nothing can be done. It can't be saved now.'

Frank's quiet words forced Evelyn to accept that the evening that had started with such excitement and anticipation had ended in a morning of tragedy and sadness.

Harry the groom appeared not long after the foal had died. 'It's what I feared,' he said. 'When they don't get up straight away to feed, you know it's unlikely they will later. It must have had something wrong with it that made it impossible to get up. It just didn't have the strength. It wasn't supposed to live.'

Megan was sniffing the foal and pushing it with her nose. 'She's going to be very upset for a while,' commented Harry. 'She's ready to nurse her baby and it won't be there for her.'

Harry spoke in such a matter-of-fact way. Evelyn did not

dare speak in case she burst into tears. Her throat was constricted as she held back her grief.

Frank picked up his blanket and ran his fingers through his black curls. 'I'd better get off now. There's nothing I can do. I'll come and see the mare tonight, when I'm back from the mill.'

As he left, Harry began to pick up the foal by the hoofs, and dragged it towards the stable door. 'It's probably best for you to go home now, Miss Champion,' he said. 'I'll see to this. I'm sorry it ended like this, I'm sorry we've lost this one.'

Evelyn gathered up her blanket. 'What will you do with the body? Do you bury it?'

'Oh no, you can't bury something like this – the animals would just dig it up, the foxes and the dogs. No, it goes to the Kennels, to the hounds, all the dead animals do. They'll come and collect it this morning. The quicker it goes the better. Then the mare can recover.'

Evelyn turned on her heels and ran to the house. Out of sight and sound of the stables she let the sobs of sorrow rumble up her chest and tumble out of her throat.

Masha had arrived home from South Africa only a few weeks before England declared war on Germany. The family was all together in Sussex when they heard the news, that Sunday lunchtime. They were enjoying pre-lunch drinks in the drawing-room. For a few minutes after the announcement on the radio there was silence; nobody said a word. Augustus pulled himself to his feet. 'Well, now it's started and now we can get it over and done with.'

Blanche was quiet and Masha sighed and rubbed her chin. 'Well, I shall definitely be taking my children to America. Thank goodness we have family there, and Henrietta's legacy. Blanche, are you sure you won't come with us?'

Before she died, Henrietta, anticipating the difficulties on the future horizon, had arranged a fund to be set up to pay the passage across to America for any member of the family who wanted to go. Masha and her four children had been ready to go for some time, just waiting for the word.

Blanche smiled and shook her head. 'I'm sure, Masha. I chose to make this country my home, so here I shall stay and share its fate.' She smiled at her cousin. 'It will be strange thinking of you living with my brother and his family up in New York, but I'm sure the war will be over in a few months. I'll bet it's over by Christmas – not long enough to warrant a major upheaval.'

CHAPTER 17

Sussex, 1940

The New Year came in bitterly cold, bringing with it scattered showers and hard frosts. The ponds and rivers froze, bringing out the skaters in their crowds, wrapped up like cocoons in woolly hats and coloured scarves, enjoying a sudden and exhilarating sense of freedom in the otherwise drab and suffocating atmosphere of wartime. For a few hours the cold crisp air on their faces would blow away the everyday anxieties of war, of gas masks, identity cards, ration books, and the safety of loved ones far from home. Gliding and skidding across the echoing ice, it was possible for many of them to be intensely happy to be alive, almost free from care. But they knew that this next year was different. After the phoncy war, the real war was about to begin.

By May, the fear of invasion had intensified. More women and children were evacuated to the countryside. Signposts were taken down so that no one knew where they were coming from or going to. Poles and wires were planted in fields to stop gliders. The black-out dominated everything. Church bells were now to be silent except in the case of an invasion. Everyone was on the look-out for spies and for German parachutists landing in the night.

Soon after war was declared, Blanche had joined the

Women's Voluntary Service and was to spearhead the local salvage drive, encouraging everyone in the surrounding villages to ransack their houses and barns for scraps of paper, metal and rubber which could then be used for the war effort.

Blanche drove around the Sussex roads in a battered old van picking up dustbins filled with different forms of waste for the war effort. She learned to quote the government statistics without hesitating: one newspaper would make three twenty-five-pounder shell cups; sixty large cigarette cartons made one outer shell container; one envelope made one cartridge wad; and twelve letters made one box for rifle cartridges. 'It's extraordinary to see how much can be reused,' she commented. 'It just goes to show how much we normally waste during peacetime.'

Evelyn was keen to join the Land Army to work on the land with other young women, but Augustus was having none of it. 'I'm not having you being used as a groundsheet for some officer,' he grunted. 'You're still too young to be called up. Why don't you stay at home until you are mobilised?'

Evelyn was annoyed by her father's attitude and she suspected that he simply wanted her to stay at home to look after him now that her mother was working so hard in the WVS.

Augustus was now retired from the bank on the grounds of ill-health, as his heart was not strong, so they closed up the London house and remained in Sussex for the duration of the war. Evelyn was impatient to work. 'I want to do my bit,' she said, 'and I'd rather do something I enjoy doing that is also important war work than be directed to some job that I don't like. I would hate to have to make parachutes or shells.'

Augustus was unsympathetic. 'It's probably wise not to expect to enjoy work at any time,' he said caustically, 'especially during a war.'

In April, Germany invaded Denmark and Norway. The Germans seemed to be coming closer and closer. Now it appeared that air-raids on London were certain.

In anticipation of the Blitz, a second wave of women and children was evacuated from London to the countryside. Through the WVS, Blanche had been busy helping to organise the arrival of the evacuees in Pulborough and to find homes for them all. This time, she and Evelyn decided to take in some evacuees themselves.

It was Evelyn who had first made the suggestion when the evacuation programme was announced. She was anxious to do more for the war effort than simply giving blood at the local hospital. Taking in some little Londoners seemed like a simple gesture, since there was plenty of room in the house. And as they had the kitchen garden, and were almost self-sufficient, feeding the extra mouths would not create a problem. Blanche agreed.

They first saw their evacuees standing scruffy and frightened, clutching their gas masks with grubby hands, as they stood in the church hall at Pulborough where they had been shepherded after arriving off the train from London.

The atmosphere in the hall was like that of the cattle market held each week outside the station, with the local people standing around and choosing the children they thought suitable for them. Farmers were choosing hefty lads who looked as if they'd be assets on the farm; county ladies chose strong-looking girls who could be helpful around the house. Evelyn was immediately struck by the sight of the timid threesome, huddled together in the corner, wide-eyed, like frightened kittens.

'Let's take those ones,' she whispered to Blanche. 'It doesn't look as if anyone else wants them.'

The group comprised two skinny girls called Ellen and

Susan, aged ten and eight and their little brother Bobby, aged seven. When their names were called, they stepped forward, clutching each other in fear. They had pasty white faces and dirty hands. Their clothes were worn and ragged.

Evelyn knew what they were thinking. She knelt down next to them and smiled. 'Don't worry, you're not going to be split up. There's plenty of room for you all at home.'

The elder girl looked up at her with sharp brown eyes. Her cheeks were streaked with grime. 'Well, our mam said we had to stay together,' she said, 'we're not allowed to be separated.'

Evelyn nodded. She was glad to be able to carry out their mother's wishes. Too many siblings were being split up by evacuation officers who chose to be much more officious than Blanche could ever be. They bossed the children around as if they were sheep, regardless of the youngsters' feelings.

The presence of the children in the house was a pleasure. Evelyn delighted in their wonder at the countryside and the animals on the farm. They'd never been outside London before, having always lived in the slums of Hackney, and for the first few weeks they were fascinated by the strangeness of the place.

There were problems, too. The children tended to sleep in the same bed together, as they did at home, and they often wet the bed. They threw stones at the chickens and ran around the house playing noisy games until Augustus emerged from his study, his face red with rage, to bellow at them to be quiet. He would never have agreed to taking on these children if Blanche had not told him that if they did not offer, they were likely to have evacuees placed with them, without being given any say in the sort of children they got. Even then, he thought they should be looked after by Nanny rather than his wife and daughter, having heard from their neighbours that their evacuees were infested with lice and did not know how to use a toothbrush.

Evelyn and Blanche were having none of it. For once, they were able to ignore Augustus's views on the matter. These three, while a little wild and wilful, were rather attractive, Blanche thought. Evelyn was delighted with them, and it gave Blanche great pleasure to see the three children curled up around her daughter's feet as she read stories to them. They were intelligent children and they were enthralled by *Peter Pan*, *Alice in Wonderland* and the Greek myths.

Evelyn read to them, played with them, and taught them table manners. Within weeks, with their skin clean, their hair washed and cut, and dressed in good clothes, they looked like different children. Their faces had filled out and the pallor of their skin had given way to a fresh healthy bloom. They grew in confidence each day, and while they remained inseparable, they exhibited a spontaneous gaiety which delighted Evelyn. She recognised it as something she had never had herself. When the farm manager turned up to complain that the children had fitted their gas masks on to the sheep in the field, she could only laugh, she thought it so funny.

She took them for walks in the woods, and taught them to ride her old pony. They went with her in the pony-trap to shop in Midhurst, and she showed them the stream on the common where they could fish for small trout.

Looking after the children gave Evelyn a sense of purpose that had been missing since her return from Italy. She had decided that what she wanted to do with her life was teach. She knew she was good with children and thought that her knowledge of languages would make it possible to get a position of some kind in one of the many schools that had been evacuated from the cities.

Augustus, however, would not hear of it.

'No daughter of mine needs to work,' he insisted every time Evelyn brought up the subject. 'You just need to find a good husband and men don't like to have wives who work,' he said, as though ignorant of the call-up of all the healthy young men in the country. 'And you're better off here, looking after your mother and me,' he added.

The domestic arrangements at the house had changed quite considerably since the outbreak of war. All the young staff had either been called up or had left to volunteer for war work, leaving the running of the enormous household to old Mrs May, the housekeeper, Mrs Knight and a few other elderly retainers.

With the loss of her cook, Blanche herself had had to learn to cook very quickly. She began buying *Good Housekeeping* magazine which was full of advice for women like her, and in no time she learned how to make custard and pastry, and how to make the best use of the food rations available to them. It surprised and pleased her that people were happy to eat the meals she produced. 'I've always felt that I could never survive on my own, without servants,' she said. 'Now I think I could manage all right.'

Blanche learned to cook all sorts of offal – sweetbreads dipped in flour and fried, pigeon pie and rabbit stew. She made puddings with supposedly highly nourishing 'beastings' from the dairy, the first yield of a cow that has calved. She had done all the fruit and vegetable bottling herself and now rows of bottles were lined up neatly on the larder shelf. She and Evelyn made jam from strawberries and gooseberries and raspberry and quince jelly from the fruit of the old quince trees. Life took on a rhythm of survival – the relentless pace to keep going with practical tasks, leaving herself little time to think about what the future held for any of them. It was better that way, to concentrate on the present, with no time for the future, and certainly not for the past.

It was Blanche who cooked Saturday lunch a couple of months later when the children's parents came to visit. They came by train to Pulborough, having bought 'Visit to Evacuee' cheap-day return tickets.

Evelyn went to pick up Mr and Mrs Brown from the station. The children, who had discovered some challenging trees in the woods to climb, had not been interested in coming to meet their parents. At first this had puzzled Evelyn but then she decided that they were worried about their parents' visit and wanted to avoid thinking about it for as long as possible.

She spotted the couple as they got off the train. Mr Brown was a small man with close-set eyes, ruddy cheeks and a beaky nose. He wore a badly fitted suit, and a hat over thick brown curls. He was well over forty and therefore had not been called up. His wife was small and slight and she wore a thin coat and clutched a shawl around her shoulders. She blinked nervously as Evelyn advanced towards them with a smile of greeting.

'Mr and Mrs Brown? I'm Miss Champion.'

Mr Brown stared at her and then looked around. 'Well, where are my kids?' he demanded in an accusing tone of voice.

'Oh, they're back at the house,' said Evelyn. 'I think they thought the journey would be too long,' she said apologetically, 'and they were rather engrossed in a game of hide and seek.'

Mr Brown frowned. His wife looked up at him anxiously. Evelyn noticed how scuffed his brown boots were.

'Well, that's a fine greeting for their own parents,' he said in a thick Irish brogue.

It was like this for the rest of the day. Evelyn took the Browns home for lunch with their children and her mother.

Not wishing to meet the couple, Augustus had arranged to have lunch in his study.

Blanche and Evelyn ate in the kitchen with the Brown family. The parents sat silent and rigid at one end, watching their children eating their way through the fresh chicken and potato salad that Blanche had produced. Evelyn noticed Mr Brown raise his eyebrows every time one of the children said 'please' and 'thank you', and he almost got to his feet when Ellen, the eldest, politely asked if she could get down from the table.

'Oh, right little madam, you are,' he sniffed.

Blanche and Evelyn glanced at each other in bewilderment. They could not understand why the parents were not grateful and impressed to see their children well dressed and well fed, with their hair trimmed properly, and showing off the manners that they had learned in their short time there.

Blanche tried unsuccessfully to engage the Browns in conversation, asking them about how Londoners were coping. 'I've hardly been up to London since war was declared,' she said, 'and I do miss it. We closed up the London house the following week.'

Mr and Mrs Brown made no response.

After lunch it was clear that they wanted to leave as soon as possible, and Evelyn drove them back to the station. She continued to try to make contact. 'Do visit us whenever you want. You are most welcome. You have lovely children,' she said brightly. 'I do hope they continue to enjoy staying with us. We certainly like having them.'

Mr Brown sniffed. He had been looking thoughtful since lunchtime, and had hardly said a word after mumbling goodbye to Blanche at the front door. 'I think we want them back,' he said quietly. 'We want them back home, not out here in this place!' He looked round him with a contemptuous expression on his face.

Evelyn did not know what to say. She put her foot down on the accelerator and passed a donkey cart ambling along the road in front. 'I think you'll catch your train all right,' she said brightly. We're in plenty of time.'

The children returned to London the following week. The Browns complained to the evacuation officer that their children were being spoiled and they wanted them back at home, so the three were to be put on the train back to London.

The children had only been staying for a few months but Evelyn felt a terrible sense of loss when they left. She kissed them all on the cheek and hugged them. They were confused and silent, unable to understand why they were being ferried back and forth, just when they had got settled in to this big rich world they could never have dreamed of. 'I'll never forget you,' whispered Evelyn as she crouched down to their level. 'And you can come back whenever you want.'

The two younger children smiled and stared at her but Ellen, the ten-year-old, stepped forward and threw her arms tightly around her neck. 'I'll come back,' she said. Then she whispered, 'I don't want to go home, I love it here.'

Evelyn squeezed her hand. 'But your parents want you home,' she said, 'so that's where you belong.'

She waved to the children as the train pulled out of the station and watched as it disappeared from view. Once it had gone, she felt a heaviness pulling her down, and a powerful and distressing feeling of emptiness.

She turned on her heels and walked slowly back to the car. She had not realised quite how bereft she would feel when her little charges had gone. The lump in her throat and the tears pricking her eyes came as a shock.

As she drove home she knew that she had to do something for herself instead of waiting passively for something to change.

The next morning she bicycled to Midhurst to give blood at the Cottage Hospital. She had done this once a month since war had been declared. She had become quite friendly with one of the nurses there, a young local woman called Mavis. Mavis read women's magazines obsessively so was full of the latest tips for managing with wartime shortages. She told Evelyn about making her silk stockings last longer by washing them in methylated spirits and storing them in an air-tight jar. She showed her how to make mascara from burnt cork, taught her how to make underwear out of old bits of parachute silk, and revealed the secret of making effective scouring powder by crushing fresh egg-shells.

These and more she would relay to Evelyn as she lay on the bed with the needle in her arm, squeezing the wooden baton to encourage the flow of blood out of her veins. 'You know there's a job here at the hospital,' she said one day. 'You might like to apply for it. The girl who was doing it has volunteered for the WAAFs, and walked out on us. We desperately need someone to do the filing and keep the records. It's considered essential war work, so you'll be settled for as long as you want, if you like it.'

Evelyn looked at her hesitantly. 'But I can't type. I've had no training of any sort.'

'Oh, I don't think that matters,' said Mavis. 'They just need someone who's efficient and organised, and reliable.' She lowered her voice. 'Quite honestly, Alison was not at all reliable – she always had some complaint or other which kept her from coming in, and I think they're glad to be rid of her. Now, you strike me as someone who would be very steady and reliable, just what we need.'

Evelyn smiled. 'Well, I'm flattered that you've even thought of me . . .'

Mavis was instantly embarrassed at Evelyn's hesitation. 'Oh, I hope I haven't insulted you. I expect it's a bit beneath you, really, I just thought . . .'

'No, no, it's not beneath me at all,' Evelyn replied quickly. 'Not at all. I'd love to be considered for anything that would be helpful. Just tell me how to apply.'

Mavis grinned. 'Once I've finished with you here, and you've had your cup of tea, I'll take you to meet Matron. Oh, I do hope it all works out!'

Evelyn started her job at the Midhurst Cottage Hospital the following week.

Her mother was pleased for her, her father was silent.

'Gussie has no choice in the matter,' Blanche said later as they washed up the dinner dishes. 'He knows that if you aren't in work you're likely to get called up anyway. And even if things do get bad, I expect your job will be considered essential in any circumstances, so you are not likely to be sent away.'

Evelyn quite liked the idea of being sent away from home, of not having any choice, but she knew that she was lucky to have got as far as Midhurst.

In August, the Battle of Britain began, with a full-scale air-attack on south-east England. In an air battle over Dover harbour, fifteen German planes were shot down. The inhabitants of the Home Counties saw battles raging over their heads every day, with twisting vapour trails creating complicated patterns in the sky. Bombers swooped over the Downs, making a deafening noise as they roared up into the air and off into the distance. Sometimes faint bursts of machine-gun fire reached their ears, and sometimes a shower of empty shell cases came clattering down to earth to be scooped up by a rush of local children. Then the air-raids on London began, night after night, with incessant bombing, which then spread to all major towns, ports and docks. The civilian casualties were heavy.

Blanche heard about what was going on in London from her friends who occasionally came to stay for the weekend, arriving on the train jammed with servicemen, and clutching their ration books as a contribution. Over the course of the weekend, they would describe the bombed-out buildings, the homeless families, the smoking ruins, the damaged water pipes spurting water across the roads, and the horrors of the air-raid shelters.

Ivo was particularly observant about life for ordinary people, having been appointed a war artist, along with Henry Moore, John Piper and various others. His task was to create a visual record of life on the home front. He travelled around the countryside and to all the big cities to paint and sketch faithfully what he saw. Some of his stories about the air-raid shelters kept his friends laughing well into the night. 'The other week in Bristol, there was a woman who was so anxious about the raids, she could talk about nothing else. Then every time the sirens went off she would pee on the floor and burst into tears.' Sitting round the dinner-table, Blanche and her friends laughed at this human tragedy. 'But people do the most extraordinary things when faced with death. The desire to procreate in the face of death is almost an impulse. All these public air-raid shelters are supposed to segregate men and women, but it's impossible to keep everyone apart. Why, the other day, while I was sketching a young family settling down for the night, a man came rushing into the women's section, saying that his mother had just been killed in front of him and he needed to find his sister. When he tracked down his sister, this man, completely demented with grief, climbed into bed with her and fucked her! The rest of us stood around, half embarrassed and half sympathetic. We didn't know what to do.'

Blanche laughed. 'I don't think anyone would know.'

'I don't think you should use such language in front of Evelyn,' Augustus muttered with a frown.

'Don't be such a stuffed shirt, Gussie!' Ivo retorted. 'Evelyn's quite old enough to hear adult language, aren't you, my dear?' He smiled warmly at Evelyn, his blue eyes twinkling in the candlelight. 'With a war on, don't you think that the last thing we should be worrying about is a few honest Anglo-Saxon words, my dear chap?'

Augustus looked disgruntled and laid his knife on his plate. 'I think I shall retire,' he said, withdrawing from the company and disappearing to his study.

As Augustus left the room, Ivo grinned. 'Let's have some music. Evelyn, will you honour us first?'

Blanche felt awkward about the incident but she knew that with Gussie out of the way they would have a much more enjoyable evening. With a twinge of disloyalty, she had a sudden longing to be with Ivo for ever. Then, fortunately, the feeling was gone.

Unknown to Blache, Augustus was spending his time in the study reading serious books. She would have been surprised. Now retired from the bank, and not fit enough to do much for the war effort, Augustus had all the hours of the day to occupy himself. He still enjoyed his outdoor pursuits of shooting and walking but the extra time for solitude was strange to him. At first he found it disturbing, as unwelcome thoughts and memories shouted at him from inside his head. His disappointments in life, the losses, the failures, the awful fact of another world war, seemed to weigh down on him with relentless cruelty. He longed to walk through the woods with his gun in the crook of his arm and his son by his side. He imagined grandchildren bearing the family name far into the future, and generations of Champions making a mark on British life long after he was dead and buried.

He spent many hours in his study, sitting in an armchair and staring out of the window at the sweep of the lawn and the outline of the misty Downs looming in the distance like a sleeping dinosaur. He could judge the seasons by the colours of the field on the top of the highest Down in the distance. At first it was newly ploughed and brown. In the spring it turned a bright green as the young corn shoots sprouted from the ground. Then a darker green, turning gradually to a deepening yellow as the corn ripened in the summer sun. Then the activity in the field, as the corn was cut and gathered, brought sad reminders of that fateful harvest when Adrian had died. Then, finally, when the crop was in, the burning of the stubble left the field looking like a blackened battle-ground until the rich earth was ploughed and brown again, ready for the oncoming winter.

It was during this time that Augustus rediscovered the great literature of his childhood. He had been sent away to boarding school at the age of seven, and there he remained until he went up to Oxford. He had never been particularly happy at school but he was well behaved and, unlike Rudie, a conformist. He was a prefect and head of house, and his school life was uneventful and predictable. Then at Oxford he had read history, and again he worked hard, kept out of trouble, and achieved the second-class degree his tutors expected him to get, before moving on to his position in the family bank.

Now, in his late fifties, he found himself remembering the classical education of his youth. He still had the books on the shelves in his study. One day he took down a copy of John

Milton's *Paradise Lost*, and he began to read, astonished by how familiar the words were to him after so many years. The story of Satan's rebellion against God and the tale of Adam and Eve in the Garden of Eden moved him to tears, as it never had as a boy. Milton's epic made sense to him; it spoke to him.

Fired by the knowledge that he could find strength inside himself, he began to read the books in his library. He re-read the old volumes on the shelves, the classical Greek literature, the Romantic poets, Shakespeare. He suddenly saw everything afresh. What he had been taught at school he could now understand himself. Wordsworth's work showed the love of commonplace things, and an ease with the use of ordinary speech. In the works of the ancient Greeks, he appreciated their economy of words, direct expression, subtlety of thought and attention to form. He read the works of Sir Philip Sidney, and saw now for himself why his tutors had presented this sixteenth-century poet as a model of correctness, clarity and measure, and why Sir Walter Raleigh had referred to Sidney as the Scipio, Cicero and Petrarch of their time.

Augustus's reading fortified him. He realised at this late age the value of living below the surface of everyday life, of the sustenance that came from knowledge of history and literature. He had always taken it for granted. It was only now that he fully recognised why a good education for a man had value in itself. And he was glad to have had it. It was ironical that the very education that had given him such inner knowledge had also made it impossible for him to express any of these feelings at all. He could appreciate great writers expressing feelings but nothing in the world could induce him to express emotion himself.

Augustus's reading was generally in secret. He did not discuss it with his wife, for it seemed a world apart from her.

Blanche's literary interests were focused entirely on modern writers. She always read the latest books from Elizabeth
Bowen, Rosamond Lehmann or Daphne du Maurier, and
could discuss the poetry of Auden and Isherwood late into
the night. However, her knowledge of the classics was limited. He realised that he had a deeper knowledge of all of
Shakespeare's work than she did, merely because he had had
to read most of the plays, poetry and sonnets at school. It was
a strange situation. Augustus was aware that people thought
him a Philistine, whereas in fact he knew that the works he
enjoyed and wanted to read and re-read were the true classics,
written by men who recognised universal truths regardless of
the age in which they lived. He did not wish to waste his time
reading books that did not contain thoughts that touched him.
His reading became his secret joy, and he did not care what
people thought of him.

   One day, Augustus had been reading Kipling's poems
which he found particularly moving, as Kipling, too, seemed
to express an empathy with common experience. It was 'If'
that really triggered something in him as he read it:

  If you can keep your head when all about you
  Are losing theirs and blaming it on you;
  If you can trust yourself when all men doubt you,
  But make allowance for their doubting too . . .
  . . . If you can dream – and not make dreams your master;
  If you can think – and not make thoughts your aim,
  If you can meet with Triumph and Disaster
  And treat those two impostors just the same . . .
  . . . If you can fill the unforgiving minute
  With sixty seconds' worth of distance run,
  Yours is the Earth and everything that's in it,
  And – which is more – you'll be a Man, my son!

As the words filled his head, he realised that he was crying. His father had read this poem to him when it was first published in 1910, a stirring message from father to son. Now Augustus suddenly thought of his own son and had a sudden urge to visit Adrian's bedroom.

Since the day Adrian had died four years before in 1936, his bedroom had remained as it had been when he was alive. Before the war, when they still had staff, the room was cleaned and dusted once a month by one of the less superstitious maids, as several of them were too frightened to go into the room which, they whispered to each other, was haunted. During the first year after Adrian had died, the year of anniversaries, Blanche would go into his room once a week and sit alone on the single bed in the corner and think about her son and how different life might be if he were still alive. She would stare out of the window at the brooding misty outline of the Downs, and feel so desperately sad that she knew there were no words even to describe how she felt. It was not a feeling she could share with anyone, not one that she wanted to share with anyone. Then she would rise wearily to her feet and walk out of the room, closing the door firmly behind her, shutting the sadness in so that it could not escape to taunt her. Then, sometime in the middle of the second year, Blanche's visits tailed off, and soon the room was never visited at all.

Augustus had not been into Adrian's room since the day he died, though it had been Augustus who had originally ordered that it be left untouched until further notice.

Now he walked up the front stairs and through the darkened corridor past the master bedrooms. Turning right, he passed into the west wing. He felt in a trance, as if pulled towards Adrian's room by some force beyond his control.

Standing outside, he took a deep breath, unsure of how

he was going to react when he entered. Then he turned the brass knob.

The door creaked as it swung open. The room seemed deathly still. He switched on the light and walked in. It smelt musty and the dust caught in his nostrils as he looked around at the small bed in the corner, and the mahogany desk by the large bay window. Augustus walked over to the desk and opened the top drawer. Inside were penknives and bits of string. The other drawers were filled with shrivelled conkers, toy guns, a small chess set and several packs of cards. In the bottom drawer, there was also a bottle of blue ink, a Parker fountain pen and pads of paper with strange coded writing, now faded with age. Augustus smiled. Adrian always had been keen on spying and secret codes. Now his eyes flooded with tears again and Kipling's words repeated themselves in his head – 'If you can dream and not make dreams your master.'

He sat down heavily in the chair and put his head in his hands. Dreams, dreams. Some lines of poetry, some Wordsworth came to mind, and he began quietly to quote:

'There was a time when meadow, grove, and stream,
The earth, and every common sight,
To me did seem
Apparelled in celestial light,
The glory and the freshness of a dream.
It is not now as it hath been of yore;—
Turn wheresoe'er I may,
By night or day,
The things which I have seen I now can see no more.'

Augustus sat at his son's desk murmuring the words of the poem and he had a sudden and vivid recollection of a moment in his own childhood. He had been about seven, and had become overwhelmingly determined to have a secret place away from his younger brother where he could have private thoughts and be alone. He decided to build himself a little shed in the woods. He chose a spot hidden under some thick holly and spent several hours drawing different designs for it. He knew exactly what he needed, all the wood and nails, and perhaps a carpet for a floor. Full of inspiration, he bicycled into Midhurst to buy the first supplies. There, at the builder's yard, he saw the perfect padlock and chain. Those would keep everyone out of his private place! He bicycled back home with the padlock in his basket. He felt he was embarking on a great project.

Then somehow, the shed never got any further. Augustus kept the padlock and chain for years and eventually used it to lock one of the paddock gates. He always felt rather ashamed of this project that he had started but never finished – a sin in his household.

But now he thought back to the boy he was then and it seemed extraordinary that he, Augustus Champion, had been that little fellow, so full of fresh dreams and enthusiasm, fuelled by an unshakeable belief in himself. What had happened to that boy? Well, Wordsworth understood. Growing up seems to be a form of corruption, or contamination. We start off so free, and then we are slowly enclosed and trapped by our circumstances. Was there no escape for him? He was trapped, he knew that, unable to respond to anything without reference to his background and schooling. And that was why he had such a difficult time understanding Evelyn and her dreams. When dealing with her he could only think about what his mother would have expected of her granddaughter, and the answer to that was the conventional education of an upper-middle-class girl, designed solely to find her a suitable husband. Augustus knew that he was simply incapable of thinking beyond what he knew was right and safe. For a moment, he despised himself for it.

With a sigh, he closed the drawers to the desk and left the room. Tomorrow he would give orders for it to be cleared out and turned into a proper guest-room. It was absurd to keep it as a shrine.

During the Battle of Britain, the Midhurst Hospital was suddenly full of British soldiers recuperating from injuries. They came to Midhurst on the final leg of their journey back to the Front, staying for several weeks or months at a time, depending on the severity of their injuries.

The camaraderie in the hospital was a joy to Evelyn. She loved working with all these dedicated nurses and doctors, and caring for the brave soldiers who came into her life for a brief time and then disappeared. Many of them became attached to the staff at the hospital and kept in touch if they could. The walls of the office were covered with postcards bearing cheerful messages.

Evelyn bicycled to Midhurst and back every day, enjoying the freedom that full-time work could bring, with its responsibilities and routines. She enjoyed her pay packet, too, and would often happily join her off-duty workmates for a drink in the pub after work. For the first time since being in Florence, she felt she knew what it was like to be an independent adult, though when she returned each evening to the house where her father's word came first, that exhilarating feeling would fade away, leaving Evelyn feeling frightened and sad.

One day she was surprised to receive a letter from Frank, from an unspecified location. His handwriting was well-formed and confident. 'I hope you don't mind me writing to you,' he wrote. 'But apart from my parents you are the only person who might be interested in receiving anything from me.'

Evelyn was puzzled by these words but concluded that Frank wanted to write to her to prove to himself that he was still alive and had a future. It must be so frightening for all those young men out there. She wrote back and told him that she was delighted to hear from him and that he should continue to write. She then described the disaster with the evacuees and her new job at the Midhurst Hospital.

The hospital began to take in patients from the armed forces who had been transferred from the Army hospital in Basingstoke, men who had nearly recovered from their injuries but needed a few more weeks of convalescence before going back to the Front. Michael was one of these men.

It was Mavis who first mentioned Michael to Evelyn one morning when Evelyn arrived for work.

'We got a few more soldiers in last night after you'd left,' she said with a smile. 'One of them's a real charmer.' She looked knowingly at Evelyn. 'Your sort, really.'

Evelyn blushed. 'Whatever do you mean?' she asked, uncontrollably embarrassed by her friend's remark.

Mavis giggled. 'Oh, I don't know,' she said, 'he's just a bit posh, really, that's all. I've got to get these bedpans sorted out, I'll see you later.'

Later in the day Evelyn met Michael, the new patient. He was tall, with dark brown hair, a thick moustache and pale blue eyes. She noticed him first walking past her window as he took a stroll around the overgrown gardens of the hospital. The place had once been a private house, owned by someone who loved plants, and who had created a paradise of a garden within three acres. But because of the war there was little time for gardening and it had become unkempt and over-grown. But it was like a lush jungle. There were walks through woods and arbours, bluebell woods, a water garden and gentle slopes of rock displaying alpines flowering at all times of the year. It was a perfect, quiet place for the patients to take their fresh air.

Evelyn noticed this new patient walking slowly, his head held high, smoking a cigarette which he held lightly in his long elegant fingers. As she stared at him he turned his head and caught her eye through the window. Evelyn blushed and quickly went back to her work.

She was aware of him coming into the house again and walking past her doorway. From the sound of his steps she could tell that he had wandered into the day-room, where the patients were free to read the newspapers and magazines, to play cards and games, or play on the old piano in the corner.

Soon the sound of the piano reached Evelyn's office, bright and cheerful music she recognised. She got up from her desk and walked down the hall to the day-room. The new patient sat upright at the piano, absorbed in the keyboard and the music he was creating.

She stood by the door listening until he had stopped. He must have sensed her presence because as he finished he turned to look at her and smiled before turning back for the final notes, which he finished with a kind of bow to the piano.

'That was beautiful,' said Evelyn. 'I love Chopin.'

The man jumped to his feet. 'How do you do?' He walked over with his arm outstretched to shake her hand. 'Michael Peart,' he said.

Evelyn quickly shook his hand. She was not used to shaking patients' hands, so she was caught off-guard. 'Oh, how do you do? I'm Evelyn Champion.'

'And you're a pianist?' The steely blue eyes were fixed on her as if he were giving her his full attention. His good looks were striking. It flashed through her mind that he looked a bit like Clark Gable.

'Not really,' she laughed. 'I do play myself but without much skill. Before the war, I preferred to go to concerts and listen to the true musicians playing great works. You are very good.'

Michael bowed his head modestly. 'Thank you,' he said.

There was a silence between them which Michael quickly filled in. 'You work here, do you?'

Evelyn nodded. 'Yes, I help in the office, doing the filing and administration. I came to give blood and was offered a job,' she laughed. 'Now I really ought to get back to my work or it will pile up and get completely out of control.'

Michael went back to the piano and as Evelyn returned to her desk, she could hear the sound of more Chopin drifting up the hall. She felt oddly excited by the brief exchange, and she kept hearing Mavis's words in her ears – 'Your sort, really'. What was it that had made her say that? What did she mean?

After that she saw Michael several times a day. He would drop in to say hello whenever he went out for a stroll in the garden, and he often came by the office to ask for a stamp for a letter he wanted posted. He always offered her a cigarette, even though she refused, and she found herself looking forward to seeing him each day, and hoping the footsteps on the marble floor in the hallway were his. Before long, she could distinguish Michael's footsteps from other people's.

Late one afternoon, he came into her office and sat in a chair while Evelyn finished talking on the telephone. 'Would you like to come out for a drink in the pub after work this evening?' he asked as she got off the phone.

Evelyn was flustered. 'Oh,' she stammered. 'Are you allowed? I don't think you're meant to leave the hospital grounds.'

Michael laughed. 'So what are they going to do if they find out? Give me a detention? I'll just say I've been reading in the garden. The grounds are so big, they can hardly search the whole area, even if they want to. We can slip out of the gate behind the wood and go for a quick drink at that pub down the road.'

Evelyn was suddenly excited by the thought. Her eyes shone as they looked straight back at him, into those blue eyes. 'All right,' she said, 'I'll meet you by the gate at six o'clock.'

In the pub they sat in a corner and talked. Michael told her that he had been just about to go up to Oxford University when the war had broken out. 'Once this damn war is over and I've finished my degree, I want to go into the Foreign Office.'

Evelyn told him about herself, about how frustrating but also liberating the war had proved for her. 'I'm anxious to use my languages in some way,' she said.' It seems like such a waste, otherwise.'

It turned out that Michael was also a good linguist and spoke not only French, German and Italian, but Spanish, too. And in the darkened corner of the pub they began to converse in these foreign languages, becoming so wrapped up in communicating in the different tongues and enjoying another drink or two, that they did not notice the uneasy atmosphere in the bar as the other customers glanced at them and then at each other. They did not notice the landlady whispering to her husband and then disappearing to the back room where the telephone was. They were enjoying each other's company too much to notice the two constables arrive at the pub and come into the bar to talk to the landlady, and they certainly did not notice the landlady leaning over the bar and pointing a finger at them as she whispered to the policemen.

Suddenly, their conversation was interrupted by the presence of two uniformed men standing over them. 'Excuse me, Madam, Sir,' one of them said, after clearing his throat.

'Would you mind stepping down to the police station with us, please? We have some questions we'd like to ask you both.'

Evelyn looked up at them in puzzlement. 'Whatever's the matter? We haven't done anything wrong.' She was aware of the other customers staring at them as they were escorted out of the bar.

'Just come with us, Miss,' replied the policeman. 'We can sort it out at the station.'

Michael squeezed her arm and leaned towards her. 'I think I can guess what's happened,' he said. 'Don't worry, it'll be all right. Just do as they say for the time being.'

They spent half an hour in Midhurst police station being questioned by two excited local bobbies as suspected foreign spies. Once Michael and Evelyn had established their identity and credentials, the disappointed policemen allowed them to leave, with a sharp warning not to converse in foreign languages in a public place in the future.

Once outside, the couple ran down the steps of the police station and collapsed on the grass, helpless with laughter. Evelyn felt deliciously close to Michael at that moment.

That evening, at supper, Augustus was complaining about the sausages Blanche had served up.

'They're full of bread. You might as well have toasted them,' he grumbled.

Blanche shrugged. 'With the meat shortage, I suppose anything goes,' she said.

Evelyn laughed, her spirits were high. 'Well, perhaps you'd like some marmalade with your sausages, Papa, instead of mustard!'

They all laughed, giving Evelyn the confidence to recount her earlier adventure with Michael.

Blanche was struck by how alive her daughter looked as she spoke about this new friend of hers. 'Perhaps you'd like to invite this young man to lunch on Sunday,' she said.

Michael came to lunch the following weekend. Evelyn sat at the table watching him as he talked to her father about his family and future career. It did not take long to establish that Augustus knew Michael's uncle, who was an investment banker in the city and a member of his London club.

Michael's credentials brought instant approval. After the war, he told them, he intended to take up his place at Oxford to read Greats, before going into the foreign service to become a diplomat like his father and grandfather before him. Augustus surprised Blanche by initiating an animated discussion about Ancient Greece with Michael. She was astounded by the depth of his knowledge, which he had kept quiet about before.

After lunch, they settled down in the drawing-room where Michael played Schubert at the grand piano while Evelyn sang. Evelyn had a sweet voice – not particularly strong but pure and true all the same. As she sang, she felt her heart lifting and a strange sense that the music was like a golden cord linking her with Michael at the piano.

Then they went for a walk, the two of them, through the woods towards Petworth. The sky was grey and there was a fresh wind making darker clouds race across it. But the rain held off. On Lavington Common they came across several clumps of mushrooms. Michael ignored most of them but one caught his interest and he bent down. Taking a silver penknife from his pocket, he sliced the fungus half an inch from the ground. '*Boletus edulus*,' he said, 'penny bun or cep. Fry this up with your butter ration, and you'll have the most delicious taste in your mouth for a week.'

They wandered on through the woods, picking the fungi as they found them. Evelyn took off her cardigan and used it as a bag to collect their edible treasures. Then, under a small group of birch trees, spread across several yards, was a carpet of golden chanterelles. 'You're going to have a feast tonight,' said Michael.

Michael came out to the house several more times during that month. The last time he came he kissed Evelyn under the oak tree by the stream in the wood. She had been waiting and hoping and, when it happened, it seemed as though she had found true happiness at last. Here she was in love, she had to believe, with a man her parents clearly approved of. Her father frequently told her what a good sort Michael was. It seemed that for the first time in her life, Evelyn was doing something right.

Michael's kiss lingered on her lips for the rest of the day, and when she bathed before dinner, she did not wash her face for fear of wiping away his scent. Her head was spinning with excitement; it hardly seemed possible that Michael could reciprocate her feelings. Yet he had kissed her and run his hands over her breasts and hips, and told her that she had pretty eyes.

The following week, Michael was told by his doctors that he was fit to return to the Front. He took Evelyn out to the pub and told her that he would write to her every day. He held her hand and stroked the back of it as he told her what a joy it was to have found her.

Evelyn believed every word he said. She wept tears when they said goodbye but she comforted herself with the thought that he would be talking to her regularly through his letters.

Michael's first letter arrived within a week. It was short and factual, though he did add in a PS the words: 'I miss you'.

He never wrote again.

Every day Evelyn waited for the post to arrive, and there would be nothing. She became convinced that he had been killed in action until she confided in Mavis, and told her friend about her feelings for Michael.

'I wouldn't waste your time pining after him,' Mavis replied bluntly, as she folded starched pillowcases into a pile.

Evelyn stared at her. 'But I thought you liked him. You did when he first arrived here.'

Mavis pursed her lips. 'I did but then I changed my mind,' she said. 'He was shameless, the way he carried on. I didn't want to say anything because you seemed so happy, but all the time he was going off to see you at your home, back here he was carrying on with another nurse. Shameless, he was, but I think the war does that to a lot of men. They lose all sense of themselves and what's right, because they might not be around tomorrow. Mind you, it's not just men, either.'

Evelyn bicycled home very slowly that evening. On the way she stopped and got off her bike in the middle of Ambersham Common. In a daze, she sat on a hump of purple heather hugging her knees and thinking about what Mavis had told her. She knew it was true. She knew that she could not try to convince herself otherwise. Michael was a fraud. He had used her as a source of amusement, as a means to have some decent meals and good wines at her parents' house, and to have a limited sexual encounter with her. And all the time he was probably going all the way with some of the other women – nurses and other staff in the very place where she worked every day. Evelyn bit her lip as she chastised herself. It was her own fault for being so foolish. How could she have seriously thought that a man like that could be attracted to *her*, someone so timid and dowdy? What ridiculous folly!

CHAPTER 18

1945

Frank came back home at the end of 1945. The village had lost several boys in the war – the two Tucker brothers, killed on the same day in different parts of the world, the Boxsall boy, and Jim Murray. Tom Robinson was reported missing and since no word had been heard for some time, the most pessimistic villagers believed that they should expect the worst.

Others came home injured or shattered, certainly different, to homes that were different, where the women they had left behind had shown themselves to be capable and independent, able to survive without men in the house. That was difficult for some.

Others came home bathed in glory for their courage in battle, more confident of their own abilities, looking forward to what the new world ahead of them had to offer, and sure that they were to be rewarded for their efforts in the fight against Hitler.

Frank was certainly one of the latter. He had won more decorations for bravery than anyone else in the village. The Army had recognised his talents, and he had very quickly been made an officer. He had thrived in a world where he was able to succeed on the basis of his own skills and he was determined that he should continue like that.

'Frank has big plans for the future,' said Mrs Knight a few days before he came back. She was ironing the white damask napkins and folding them carefully away in the drawer. 'He says the Army will pay for his education now, so the sky's the limit.' She sniffed. 'That's what the government promised us last time – jobs and homes for heroes. What did we get? Millions out of work and dreadful poverty. I'll believe it when I see it . . .'

Watching Mrs Knight's servant's hands, reddened by scrubbing and cleaning and scouring, Evelyn listened with interest, surprised that she felt rather nervous about Frank's return. He had been writing to her throughout the war, and over the years the letters had become more fluent and confident. They were generally very straightforward and factual (insofar as the Army censor allowed him to convey any facts) and sometimes Evelyn had a peculiar sense that he was writing to her in order to practise his writing skills and trying out his ideas, as some people write a diary.

Certainly his handwriting had changed – had become more mature and he talked quite philosophically in a way that she could not imagine him using to his parents. Who else could he talk to about the meaning of life and death without being laughed at? But whatever cynical twinges she had, she was touched that he wrote to her so consistently and regularly. Perhaps he did care about her but after the humiliating business with Michael, Evelyn did not dare even consider such a thing.

Evelyn had been feeling very low over the past few months. Perhaps the end of the war had brought with it a future of uncertainty for her. While the country was at war, her duties were clear, and her own plans could be put on hold, with no danger of coming into conflict with her father. But now everyone was being demobbed and the new beginning stood before them, Evelyn wanted to think about what she was to do herself. She longed to go to teacher training college and go on to teach languages in a school, but whenever she broached the idea to her parents, her father would roar his disapproval. 'I'm not having my daughter going out to work,' he said. 'No women in the family have ever been out to work and never will. There's just no need.'

'But I've been working all through the war,' Evelyn protested. 'I've been working long hours and bringing home a pay packet.'

'And now the war's over, your work is over,' said Augustus emphatically. 'You're not needed any more. Women have got to go back to their homes and make way for the men again. The men need jobs, not the women. You just have to find yourself a husband and then you'll be glad to have been born into your position.'

Evelyn turned away miserably and took herself up to her room. There she sat on the edge of her bed and contemplated the future. She was not allowed to gain qualifications for a job, and she did not want to get married. She did not know any men she liked enough to marry and she certainly did not think anyone was interested in marrying her. What did she have to offer? She was not pretty or lively and she could not believe that anyone would ever find her interesting enough to propose to. Her experience with Michael had shaken her already fragile confidence in herself, and her father's constant dismissal of her dreams and desires had worn her down. She realised, as she sat watching the rooks circling their rookery in the wood, that she was actually afraid of men. Her father had shouted at her too many times in her life, he had thwarted her ambitions, and forced her into this narrow life path regardless of her own feelings. She realised now that she had no faith in herself at all. She had nothing to offer anyone; the thought made her very sad. The only man she was not afraid of was Frank. He treated her like an equal. Her father would never agree to her marrying him, yet Frank was the only man she could ever feel comfortable with.

Evelyn saw Frank a few days after he returned home. She was taking the dogs for a walk in the woods and as she went past the gardener's cottage at the end of the drive, Frank emerged from the house, grinning at her in greeting. 'Hey there! You going for a walk? I'll come along, too, if you don't mind.'

Evelyn found herself blushing and she put her face down and pretended to fuss the dogs which were eager to jump up at Frank, the man with the way with animals. Frank spoke to them and they squealed with pleasure, rushing on ahead of the two as they turned into the road and down into the woods.

'So, here you are,' Evelyn finally said. They walked along, comfortable in each other's company.

'Yes, back to civvy street.'

In his time away, Frank had changed physically. He had broadened out and become heavier, which befitted his six-foot frame. He also appeared more confident, which was not surprising, thought Evelyn. Everyone has had to grow up very fast and no one more so than the men out fighting.

He talked about the war very little. His thoughts were focused on the future now, and when he talked about it, Evelyn could almost see the excitement exuding from him.

'Now I want to become a barrister,' he said, 'and I'm determined to become a KC before I'm forty. I had a mate in the Army, a commissioned officer, whose family are all KCs – his father, his uncles and his grandfather before them. He's told me what an interesting life it can be – and how much money you can make. The law interests me like nobody's business and I know I can do well in it.'

Evelyn was surprised and impressed by the passion with which Frank spoke about his ambitions. It seemed so extraordinary – and wonderful – to hear the gardener's son having such dreams as though they were a real possibility. Perhaps that was a good thing to come out of the war – an equalising of the social order, so that everyone could get the chance to have an education and the better jobs that it could lead to. How ironical it was that she, who had every material comfort and was regarded as privileged, should be denied such opportunities by her own father.

'And what do your parents think of your plans?' she asked. 'They must be pleased for you.'

Frank shrugged. 'I don't know. My mother thinks I'm aiming too high. She says I'll have a fall. My father won't talk about it. I don't think he likes the idea of his son doing something different from him. He thinks I should be happy with my lot and not rock the boat. And perhaps he thinks I'm putting him down because I don't want to stay stuck in the country, and I don't want to be a gardener or a farm hand, or any of the other things my family have always been. It's as if I'm saying it's not good enough for me.'

'Well, you are,' replied Evelyn, 'in a way.'

Frank turned to look at her. 'Yes,' he said, with a smile, 'I suppose I am.'

They walked on through the wood, over Graffham Common and on past the pond and Barnett's Mill. There they stopped for a while and sat by the mill pond watching the great crested grebes glide over the silvery water. 'Odd to be a bird,' said Frank. 'Just to live instinctively, without thought. The whole war can pass you by without it meaning anything to you.'

'Plenty of humans can do that, too,' murmured Evelyn, 'never questioning what they do.'

They sat silently for some while, listening to the wind rustle the trees, and watching the occasional fish rise on the surface of the water.

'Did you miss all this tranquillity while you were away?' Evelyn asked.

Frank picked up a stone and flicked it into the water. It dropped to the bottom of the pond sending a series of circles drifting out across the surface. 'I didn't miss it at all,' he said. 'I kept my thoughts on the future and what I was going to do when the fighting was over. It was the best way to concentrate the mind.'

He rolled over on to his front, chewing a long piece of rye grass. 'I saw such terrible things over the past few years, things that make other things seem so unimportant. When you see someone with his legs blasted off and bleeding to death, or friends with their intestines protruding from their bellies and begging to be shot to be put out of their misery then the ordinary things we think about mean nothing. How can it matter how a man speaks or what sort of home he came from when confronted with that? And when you're all fighting together, we are all the same, with the same goals and fears. Now the war's over and I intend to carry that in my head. The war has given me the chance to get an education and to get on in life. Before the war, I could never have had such an opportunity. And I know that I am equal to all men – even the posh ones whose bacon I saved on more than one occasion. It's a good feeling and I look forward to the future in a way I've never felt before, because now I can see how to achieve what I want.'

Evelyn listened to him with admiration. His dark eyes were glistening with passion as he spoke.

'I think it's wonderful,' she whispered. 'And I'm sure that you'll get what you want.'

There was another silence between them as Frank stared out across the field. He started to say something, and then stopped himself.

'What were you going to say?' Evelyn knew that it was something to do with her.

Frank shook his head. 'I don't know if I can. I thought I could but I just don't know.'

'Oh, go on, tell me, please,' Evelyn pleaded.

Frank sat up and tentatively took her hand. 'I would never have dared ask you this before but now I'm not afraid. Please answer as honestly as you can, I won't mind.'

'Well, what? How can I answer unless you ask me?' Her hand was burning in his.

Frank took a deep breath, his eyes fixed on hers. 'I would like you to be part of my future, Evelyn. It seems like madness but I'm asking you to be my wife.'

Evelyn's heart jumped as she felt gripped by a combination of excitement and fear.

'I know your father will say no,' continued Frank, 'so I don't know how you can say yes.'

Evelyn leaned into his side and rested her head on his shoulder. 'I will say yes,' she said. 'It's reckless, but so what? I'll talk to my mother and see how she reacts. Perhaps she'll be happy to persuade Papa that it's all right.'

Frank looked at her with his dark eyes searching hers. 'Are you sure? Don't you want to think about it overnight?'

Evelyn laughed. 'No, I don't need to think about it. Like you, I know what I want. It's just that I don't yet know how to get it. But I do have one question before I broach the subject at home . . .'

'Yes?'

'I really want to work, to teach. I need to go to teacher training college first and then find a job. My father is utterly opposed to women working. I just want to find out what you think. I don't want to find myself married to a man who holds my father's views about women and work.'

Frank smiled. 'It's only women of your class who are not expected to work by their men. Working-class women, like my mother, always have, ever since they were children. I would expect you to work, especially while I'm building my career. I have to do my law exams and then be accepted to do my pupillage in chambers and work for nothing for a year before I can get tenancy then take on cases of my own. So things will be tough for a while and we certainly won't want to have children for a long time.'

'Well, I have a bit of my own money,' offered Evelyn. 'That would help towards keeping the wolf from the door for a bit.'

'And we have to live in London. That's where I want to study and that's where the work is.'

'I'm happy with that,' Evelyn said and smiled. 'I like London. I can train and then get a job there.'

They kissed on the edge of the pond, bathed in the dying light of the day.

Afterwards, they walked slowly back to the house, silenced by the gravity of their agreement. Evelyn felt an almost physical lifting of her chest, a deep happiness that perhaps she had found an escape from the world she had been trapped in for so long. She had to talk to her mother and get her support first, but she felt confident that Blanche would be on her side.

Evelyn was right about her mother. When Evelyn told her about Frank's proposal, she was silent for a second or two before smiling and opening her arms to embrace her only child. 'My dear, how can I be anything except happy for you? Frank's an ambitious boy and clearly did well in the war.' Like many people, Blanche liked the equalising effect of war honours. 'If you're happy with him, then I'm happy for you.'

'But what about Papa? He's not going to respond in the same way . . .'

Blanche sighed. 'No, he's not,' she said flatly.

Evelyn threw herself on the sofa, placed her hands behind her head and stared up at the ceiling. 'But, Mama, I love him so much. I didn't realise until recently how much we are meant to be together. We've spent most of our childhoods together, and although we come from such different backgrounds, we understand each other so well and have the same attitudes towards things.'

Blanche looked at her daughter's animated face as she spoke and was touched by the passion in her voice. 'Well, you know what I have always thought, darling, that you should follow your heart first, don't let rules and conventions restrict your life, or you might miss out on something you'll regret later.'

Evelyn jumped to her feet and hugged her mother. 'Thank you, Mama, thank you.' She paused and looked anxiously at Blanche. 'So what about Papa? How am I going to tell him what I want to do? Should Frank come and speak to him first?'

Blanche shook her head emphatically. 'No, no, I don't think that's a good idea. If anyone can persuade him it will be me,' she said. 'Let me have a word with him and sound him out. There may well be a way of getting him to see how much it means to you.'

Evelyn hugged her mother again. 'Oh thank you, Mama. I knew you'd be on my side.'

Blanche looked down at her with surprise. 'Of course I'm on your side,' she said, 'you're my child.'

'Well, I don't always feel that Papa is on my side,' replied Evelyn, 'and I'm his child, too.'

Blanche nodded. 'I'll try to bring it up this evening. I shall have to prepare myself carefully, as I don't want to get it wrong.'

However well Blanche might have prepared herself, she would never have persuaded Augustus. As she started to speak, as she mentioned Frank's name, she could see the scowl appearing on her husband's brow as he waited for her to finish. Even then, he could not wait because once he had heard enough to grasp what was being suggested, he threw down his newspaper and let out a great roar that made Blanche jump with surprise.

'How dare you even entertain such an arrangement? How dare you support the girl in such a ludicrous plan? Marry Frank Knight? Marry the gardener's son? Who do you think we are? What do you think everyone will think of us if our only daughter marries such an imbecile? Is it because you're American that you can't see how outrageous an idea that is?'

Blanche shook her head and, although stung by Augustus's jibe about being American, tried to keep calm as she spoke. 'Don't be absurd, Gussie. Frank is not an imbecile. He's a bright boy who is about to study law. He's done very well in the war and has come home showered with honours. And I'm not worrying about what other people think, I'm concerned about what Evelyn wants and what will make her happy. She hasn't had the easiest of lives and she's very unsure of herself. Her devotion to Frank does seem to be one consistent certainty.'

Augustus snorted. 'Devotion to Frank! How dare you! The boy's nothing but a gold-digger. He's not wanting to marry Evelyn for any strengths of her own – good god. The girl has no looks to speak of, and acts like a scared rabbit most of the time. He can only be after her money. He knows a good thing when he sees it . . .'

Blanche listened to her husband ranting at her without bothering to contradict him. She knew that it was pointless to argue, she was not going to win him over. And there was also a slight nagging feeling inside her that Frank did have another motive for marrying Evelyn. It was not a financial one, Augustus was wrong about that. Frank was not a gold-digger but she did fear that Frank wanted to marry Evelyn to get back at Augustus, to score in that way. She would never say such a thing to Evelyn and she just prayed that even if she were right about this hunch, Frank still loved Evelyn for what she was. That, surely, had to be true. Augustus was wrong about that.

They finished their cocktails in silence. Blanche decided to work out some other plan but she hardly knew where to start. She sat in the soft light of the floor-lamp, pushing back the frustration she could almost feel as a lump in her chest, and then shivered as she felt a sudden flash of guilt. She felt guilty for not paying enough attention to Evelyn, guilty for not having defended her daughter enough, and guilty for not having stood up to Augustus in his worst and most rigid moments.

For a few moments, she felt almost limp with inadequacy. What sort of a mother was she to let matters develop to this stage? Could she not help her daughter more? What sort of a mother was she? The question bounced around her head like a ball, dragging up unwelcome memories with all their own questions that had gone unanswered for so many years.

Blanche looked up at her husband to check that he had not noticed the brief look of anguish on her face. Then she recovered her composure and rose to her feet.

'We can eat in five minutes,' she said, walking to the door.

'I think it would be a good idea if we don't discuss this matter at dinner.'

Augustus looked up. 'I agree,' he said, 'and as far as I'm concerned, the matter is closed.'

Nothing was said at dinner or afterwards. Evelyn looked in vain for some clue as to whether her mother had raised the subject with her father.

It was only as she was going to bed that Blanche had a chance to say something. 'Don't raise your hopes, darling,' she said. 'He's being very difficult, and I just don't know if I can make him budge.'

The next day Evelyn was slipping out to meet Frank. She had brushed her hair and put on some lipstick. Perhaps it was the lipstick or perhaps it was the look of eagerness in her face that alerted Augustus as she dashed past him in the hall. Whatever it was, he called her back into his study.

Evelyn meekly came into the room and stood in front of him, her hands behind her back, her head bowed.

'I hope you're not running off to meet that Knight boy.'

The patronising way in which he referred to Frank annoyed Evelyn. She lifted her head, raising herself to her full height, and thrust out her chin. 'What if I am? I can meet whoever I like,' she said, quite taken aback by her sudden boldness.

Augustus nodded. 'You can meet whoever you like, that's true, I can't stop you doing that. I can't control you. But what I do control and can control is your money. If that boy is interested in you, it's because he's interested in your money. My money. Well, if you don't have any money he can lay his hands on, you can be sure he'll go away.'

Evelyn scowled at him in fury. 'How dare you say such a thing! Frank loves me for what I am. We've known each other almost all our lives, so we do know each other.'

Augustus snorted. 'This is quite preposterous!' His face

had turned red and his mouth had turned into a downward curve. For a moment, Evelyn hesitated. Her father looked as though he was going to have a heart attack he was so angry.

But she persisted, trying to placate him by talking in a softer tone. 'I love him, Papa. And I think we could have a good life together.'

Augustus started to point his finger at her. He was shaking, his rage fuelled all the more by his daughter's continuing defiance of him. 'All I will say is that if you marry Frank Knight, I shall make sure you're cut off without any of my money. Then we'll see how much he wants to hang around. I know his sort. I've seen his sort before.' He hesitated and held his hands out to Evelyn. 'My dear,' he said, 'I beg you to listen to me. I know you think I'm old-fashioned but I assure you that I'm concerned about your welfare. I do care about you, even though I find it hard to let you know that.' He stumbled over his words and looked away, embarrassed by this tiny expression of feeling.

Her father's softening was not going to deter Evelyn. She took a deep breath and braced herself. 'I'm sorry, Papa, but I'm going to see Frank now. If you want to punish me for loving someone, then that's up to you. I'll deal with the consequences when I meet them.' With that she turned and went out of the door. The fresh evening air felt like a cool balm on her hot cheeks.

Evelyn spent the early evening with Frank. She told him about her father's reaction and his warning about her legacy. 'It doesn't bother me,' she said. 'Even if Papa does cut me off, I have a small inheritance from my grandmother, and more from Aunt Henrietta when I'm thirty. We'll make do while we get through our studies. And once I've got a job, I'll be bringing in something while you finish getting qualified. We can live modestly, and we'll get by.' She laughed and hugged

Frank's arm. 'You know, Papa just cannot believe that you're not after my money – or his money as he sees it.'

Frank smirked. 'No, I'm not after his money. I'm going to be making plenty of my own one day. Plenty. Then we'll see if he accuses me of being a gold-digger.' He laughed to himself. 'Then we'll see who's right.'

Evelyn smiled, relieved that Frank had confirmed what she thought she knew – that he was not after her money. They hugged each other tight.

'Right,' said Evelyn, an unfamiliar feeling of confidence rising through her, 'I'm going back and I'm going to tell my father what we plan to do. I'm sick of always giving in to him. I'm going to tell him I'm marrying you and nothing can stop me.'

When Evelyn returned to the house, she found the place in turmoil. She learned that ten minutes after she had left, Augustus had had a stroke. Blanche had found him lying on the floor of his study, half-paralysed, opening and shutting his mouth like a fish, unable to speak. The ambulance had been called and they were waiting for it to arrive at any moment.

Evelyn was distraught. The sight of her father being carried out on a stretcher made her panic. She walked along beside him holding his hand. 'Oh, Papa, I'm so sorry,' she wailed, 'I'm so sorry. You'll be all right.' Tears trickled down her cheeks. 'You'll be all right. Everything will be all right,' she kept saying. The terrified look in his eyes would haunt her for ever, and she wept as she recalled his last words to her – that he did care about her. It was the first time that he had ever come close to saying that he loved her.

That night was the longest that Evelyn had ever experienced. She slept fitfully, for ten, fifteen minutes at a time, waking with a sudden jerk. Her thoughts churned in her head. Sometimes she found herself praying for her father to recover, to get back to normal, as it had been before. But then she would find herself imagining more battles with him about Frank and what she did with her life. Sometimes, she would be imagining that her father did not recover, and that she never again had an argument with him. How liberating that thought was! As the excitement of such a possibility caught her, she would chastise herself for thinking such things and force herself to pray for his recovery. But underneath it all, she felt a terrible shock at having been the probable cause of her father's stroke. 'If I had not defied him, he would still be here, and not in hospital,' she told herself over and over again.

The next day Evelyn and her mother visited Augustus in hospital. He was barely conscious and did not recognise either of them. They sat on either side of his bed for half an hour and then left.

'It's all my fault,' confessed Evelyn in the car home, 'it's my fault this has happened.'

Blanche shook her head. 'No, darling,' she said quietly, 'you did not make this happen. It was going to happen at some point. You are not to blame yourself.'

Frank was curiously unsympathetic. In fact, he barely said anything comforting to Evelyn when she told him the news. This annoyed her.

'Aren't you going to at least express some sympathy?'

Frank looked at her with genuine surprise. 'What for? Your father hated me and made his feelings clear. I can't now say how sorry I am.'

Evelyn frowned. 'Well, you could say that you were sorry because I'm upset.'

Frank shrugged. 'That's just an absurd convention. It means nothing. Besides, he hasn't exactly been a loving father to you,' he said flatly.

'But that's mainly because he did not know how to be loving.' Evelyn defended her father, confused by all the feelings she had.

'Doesn't that amount to the same thing?' Frank sounded harsh. 'The end result was identical, regardless of the reason.'

Three days later, Augustus had another stroke in the night and died. The hospital telephoned Blanche at six o'clock the next morning. When she put down the telephone receiver, her face was white.

Evelyn had been listening from the top of the stairs and could tell from her mother's voice that it was the end. She walked slowly downstairs, wrapping her dressing gown tightly around her.

'He's gone.' Blanche blurted out the words, her sentence ending as a choking sob. 'He died at half-past five, half an hour ago.' She turned to embrace her daughter and the two women clutched each other in their sorrow.

Frank's response to Augustus's death again hurt Evelyn when she told him.

'Well, now we're free to marry when we want,' he said.

Evelyn frowned at him. 'How can you say such a thing? Papa's only just died and you're talking about getting married.'

'I'm just telling the truth,' he said. 'There are no obstacles now. Your mother's not going to stop us.'

'I know it's the truth,' replied Evelyn, 'but it's a bit tasteless to talk about marriage at this point, even before the funeral.'

Frank grimaced. 'Sorry,' he said with a sarcastic edge to his voice, 'you have to remember that I haven't been brought up with a sense of taste, like you.'

'Frank!' Evelyn was shocked at the bitterness in his voice.

Frank pulled her to him and kissed her. 'Look, the old man's dead. We're free. It's what you wanted, isn't it?'

Ducking her head to the side, Evelyn pulled away from him. She was shocked by his callousness. 'He was my father,' she said quickly. 'I didn't want him dead. He was my father after all, and you should show some respect for him now he's gone. I know he was difficult but I was still his daughter. One can go on loving someone even when they make you unhappy, and I do think he cared for me, in his way. I do think that now.'

Frank sniffed. 'I don't have much time for sentimentality, that's all,' he said.

Evelyn was quiet. She felt as though she had been hit on the head, so dazed was she by the bereavement. How difficult it is to admit that you do not feel something you are supposed to feel, and Evelyn could not admit even to herself that she did not like her father. He had been unkind to her for most of her life, first for being a girl and not even a pretty one, second for being responsible for her brother's death, as Augustus had seen it, and third for not marrying a man who could act as a substitute son for him. Augustus had never given her a chance. However hard she tried, Evelyn always felt she could never win his love. His death had released her from his control but convention prevented Evelyn from ever admitting that she was glad. Convention also prevented her from admitting that she did not like her father. She loved him, and longed for him to love her, but she did not like him. One is not allowed to admit to such feelings. And yet he had told her that he did care for her, so late in the day. Too late. The saddest fact of all was that now her father was dead, the chance for them to be reconciled and happy with each other was gone. Their relationship could never change. It was now set in stone, like the engravings on the stones in the overgrown churchyard.

*   *   *

The day of Augustus's funeral was overcast and grey. A fine drizzle blanketed the Sussex landscape as the small group of mourners followed the coffin out of the church and into the graveyard.

As the coffin was placed in the family vault alongside his son and his parents, Blanche, looking exceptionally elegant in her black dress and veil, glanced across at her daughter. Evelyn's red eyes and blotchy face revealed her sorrow.

Blanche was sensitive enough to know that Evelyn still blamed herself for her father's death, but she hoped that time would ease the pain of that guilt and that now she would benefit from being free of his control.

Among the mourners were several of Augustus's colleagues from the bank, some of the local gentry he used to hunt and shoot with, and family members. Ivo had also come. Blanche had not seen him for some weeks and was touched to see him slip into the church. She knew that he was there more for her than for Augustus. Ivo had never had any time for Augustus, and his tolerance of him had decreased rapidly over the years.

Ivo himself was looking his age. His craggy handsome face seemed grey and gaunt. We're all getting old, thought Blanche, as she smiled at Rudie who was walking across the grass to speak to her. He had arrived only just in time for the service, and had come alone without Natalie, whom Augustus, following his mother's views, had never liked.

Rudie grasped Blanche's hand and kissed her on the cheek through the veil. 'My commiserations,' he said. 'I'm sorry.'

Blanche smiled wanly and squeezed his hand back. 'Thank you,' she whispered. Then she glanced sideways at him. 'When I die, I don't want to go into that thing . . .' She indicated the grey vault. 'I want to be cremated and have my ashes scattered on the Downs above here.'

Rudie nodded. 'Where we used to walk?'

'Where we used to walk,' Blanche agreed, 'and where I walk every week. It's the most beautiful place. When I walk up there, along the ridge looking down across the countryside, I feel as if I'm on top of the world.'

'I feel the same,' murmured Rudie. 'And I've missed it all these years.'

The vault was being closed. Four hefty men lifted the granite lid and it settled on its base with a grating sound which made Blanche shiver. Her new life was beginning.

Drinks and lunch were served at the house, and after the guests had gone, Rudie stayed behind. He planned to drive back to London that evening. He and Blanche had tea together in the library, overlooking the lawn, now wet with the drizzle, and the gardens beyond.

'Your garden is a masterpiece,' Rudie said with admiration. 'I remember when you started to plan it all those years ago.'

Blanche laughed. 'Yes, Augustus didn't approve at all. He said your mother would be turning in her grave.'

Rudie sighed. 'Oh, Augustus. He didn't approve of anything, did he? He was really just afraid to take risks. He was afraid to step off the beaten track that had been marked out by our ancestors. So showing disapproval to any new ideas was an easy way of keeping them at bay.'

Blanche smiled. She was exhausted after the events of the past week, the shock of Augustus's death and the sudden flurry of organisation that was necessary, informing everyone, organising the funeral, and sorting out his belongings and papers.

'Thank you for staying on, Rudie,' she said. 'It's good to see you after so long. Perhaps we'll see a bit more of you and Natalie now. I'd love to get to know Natalie properly at last. But you live so far away.'

Rudie had moved to Cornwall, where he had been running a small printing press with his wife. Augustus had more or less cut Rudie off because he considered that Rudie's lifestyle was bohemian, something that Augustus abhorred.

Rudie coughed and looked suddenly awkward. 'I'm sure we can manage to meet more than we have in the past,' he said quietly.

They were silent for a while. Then Blanche spoke. 'It's going to be so strange without Gussie. The entire household was run around his daily timetable. You could set your watch by his movements.'

'Gussie was always set in his ways, even as a boy. He was my mother's favourite because he did everything by the rules, and never rebelled. I've often thought – and forgive me if this is an inappropriate time to say it – that I should have married you.'

Blanche raised an eyebrow at him.

'I'm serious, Blanche, though it's all too late for anything to be different. But I have always carried a bit of guilt inside me because I think I should have married you. I shouldn't have let you marry Gussie. You were far too good for him, and I think you would have been much happier with me.'

Blanche chuckled. 'Oh, Rudie, you're very kind. I'm touched that you feel that way. But don't feel guilty. It's very possible that you're right, that I would have had a more enjoyable life as your wife – certainly it would have been more fun. But I was very happy to be Gussie's wife. He gave me what I needed at the time, he gave me the wealth and freedom to live life more or less as I have wanted. He could be difficult at times, but at least I always knew where I was with him. No, don't feel guilty, Rudie, it was my choice and I have no regrets.'

Rudie nodded. 'Good, I'm glad to hear you say that. Then perhaps it's me.'

Watching Rudie's face, Blanche thought he appeared troubled. There was a worried look in his eyes. She did not want to pry so she kept the conversation general.

'Do you regret that you and Natalie didn't have any children?'

Rudie shrugged. 'None chose to come along. It was a sadness for both of us but it made no difference at the time to my feelings for Natalie. She's the woman I married, and I loved her then.' He hesitated.

Blanche placed her hand on his arm. 'You loved her "then"?' Is everything all right between you and Natalie now?' Blanche's voice was low and gentle.

Rudie looked hard at her, revealing a deep anguish. He placed his hand over hers and let out a heavy sigh. 'The fact is, Natalie has left me,' he said flatly. 'She's gone off with someone else.'

Blanche touched his arm. 'I'm so sorry. Do you want to tell me about what happened? Don't if you don't want to.'

With his hands clasped together, Rudie dropped his head and shoulders slowly as if in shame. 'It was going on before my very eyes, and I failed to see it for months. But then I suppose it was a bit unusual. As you know, Natalie is a Catholic, at least brought up as such, though when we married she was pretty much lapsed.

'Our marriage was very happy at first but when no children came along, Natalie became increasingly bitter. She blamed me entirely and, without going into detail, I completely lost my confidence as a man. She made me feel emasculated so, in effect, I became so, thus proving her point.'

Blanche listened, fascinated but appalled.

'We did not have marital relations for years, though in every other respect we got on very well, running the press and the business, working with the authors and designing the books. We slept in separate rooms and so avoided possible conflict.

'Then last year Natalie began to go to church again, the Catholic church, where she went to Mass every Sunday, and in the week, too. She told me that in her old age she was feeling a spiritual need that was being met by her old religion. I believed her and, although I'm not a great fan of the Catholic church, I respected her desire for spiritual fulfilment – we all need it in some form or another at some point in our lives.

'Well, to cut a long story short, it turned out that she was not going to church to commune with God so much as to meet someone she had started an affair with.'

Blanche let out a sympathetic gasp. 'Oh, Rudie, how could she?'

Rudie sniffed. 'It took a long time for me to realise what was going on. I was so stupid about it. The person she was meeting was a woman. When I realised this, I didn't think it through. I wasn't bothered, though I did vaguely wonder why she was meeting a woman in secret. It never occurred to me that it could be a sexual relationship until later. This woman was someone I knew myself. She had left her husband and family already. Now she and Natalie have set up home together in a cottage on the coast. They say they don't care about what people say, which is fine. This other woman claims to be able to read the future, and she says they were destined to be together.

'So here I am, an abandoned, emasculated creature, so pathetic that my wife prefers a woman to me.'

Blanche felt outraged on his behalf. 'So who is this person? What does she do?'

Rudie grimaced. 'She's an arty type. She used to live in London until she moved down to Cornwall.'

'Do I know her?'

'You might have come across her. In fact, you probably have.' Rudie sighed. 'She's called Olive, Olive Porter.'

Even before Rudie said the name, Blanche knew who it was. 'Oh, I'm sorry,' she said. 'That woman has been nothing but trouble to me in the past.'

'Well, that's my story. I don't want you to feel sorry for me. I haven't told anyone else. I'm running the business on my own and I'll let the gossip take care of itself. I shall probably sell up and move back to London. I feel like cutting myself off from Natalie completely, The idea of bumping into her in St Ives is too much to bear.' He grinned ruefully. 'So you see, it's a rather good thing that we don't have children. Matters would be more complicated and painful than they already are.' He squeezed Blanche's hand.

'You know there is still a little bit of me, deep inside, that regrets not having grabbed you when you first arrived in London all those years ago. Just think how different my life would have been if I had. And how different yours, too!' He was getting morose.

Blanche shook her head and pulled her hand away with a smile. 'It's a dream, Rudie, just a dream,' she said gently.

'Well, it's a dream I'll carry with me for ever,' replied Rudie. 'Ah, here's that lovely niece of mine,' he said as Evelyn came into the room.

Relieved to change the subject, Blanche held out her hand towards her daughter. 'Have you heard Evelyn's news, Rudie? Has she told you that she is engaged to be married?'

Evelyn looked at her mother with surprise and then a wave of adoration rushed through her. This was the first time in the chaos of that week that Blanche had referred to her marriage. She had been waiting anxiously for her mother to bring up the subject. Now she had and she had shown her approval. Evelyn smiled broadly at her uncle. So out of the sad events of the week, something good had emerged for her. She was now able to marry the man she loved, and make her other dreams come true. She could not remember ever having felt so happy.

CHAPTER 19

1947–1959

Evelyn and Frank were married in the Chelsea Town Hall, a quiet civil wedding with two strangers from off the street as witnesses. This had been Frank's idea, and Evelyn had gone along with it, even though she was aware that both her mother and Frank's were hurt to have been left out in this way. Then they moved into a small mews house in Chelsea, given to them by Blanche as a wedding present.

At first, life seemed blissful to Evelyn. She started her course at teacher training college while Frank began to work for his law degree. They enjoyed living in London, which was slowly picking itself up after the devastating years of war. In the evenings, they went to plays in the West End or to the cinema to see the latest films from America – *My Darling Clementine*, *The Big Sleep* and *Notorious*. At weekends, they took the boat to Greenwich or wandered along the Embankment, or visited the National Gallery. Their house was compact and cosy, furnished with furniture from the Champions' old London house, which Blanche sold soon after Augustus died. She had bought herself a flat in South Kensington, so she was close enough to Evelyn and Frank when she was in town, and wonderfully close to her favourite spot in London – the Victoria and Albert Museum. She still

kept up with modern fiction, and read the new novels of
Graham Greene and George Orwell with admiration and
enthusiasm.

The newly-weds lived on the small amount of money
Evelyn received from her grandmother's legacy. Much more
money was coming to her from Henrietta but, according to the
terms of the trust, not until she was thirty, in 1951.

Frank had been noticeably annoyed by this news. He had no
understanding of trust funds at first and didn't understand why
Evelyn could not have the money set aside for her when she
wanted it. It took a lot of explaining before he finally accepted
that they were not going to have much for a while.

'I'm not going to be earning anything for a long time,' he
said. 'It's a long training but worth it in the end.' Frank had
no doubts about his future success as a barrister.

Evelyn was not worried. 'Once I've done my exams I'll be
able to get a job teaching, and we can live on my earnings.'

Frank grunted. 'They're not going to be much,' he muttered. Having been casual about them initially, he was now
clearly disgruntled by Evelyn's lack of available funds.

For the first couple of years life was good. Frank excelled
in his studies and came top in all the law exams. His plans for
the future grew bolder each month. Evelyn meanwhile had
passed her teacher training exams and found herself a job in
a small private girls' school in Kensington where she taught
French and Italian to sixteen-year-olds before they went off
to finishing schools in Europe. Although the girls were not
studious, they were a cheerful lot, and Evelyn discovered that
she could inspire them to produce good results for her. Above
all, she loved the fact that she was working. Every day as she
closed the blue front door and set out, she would feel grateful
for having been able to escape the stuffiness of her life in
Sussex. She had always known that work offered her an

escape from the dreary life of a wealthy young woman, and now she had been proved right.

Yes, life was good and they were happy. Until Evelyn discovered that she was pregnant.

At first she went to see the doctor because she had been feeling ill for some weeks. She felt run-down and tired and achy, as if she had influenza. When the doctor examined her and told her that she was going to have a baby, she refused to believe it.

'But we've been taking precautions,' she said in bewilderment. 'We've been so careful, I really don't think it can be possible.'

The doctor chuckled. 'It's always possible, Mrs Knight, no precautions are one-hundred-per-cent safe.

'I'll let you into a little secret. I always assume that any female patient aged between sixteen and fifty-five is pregnant until proved otherwise.'

Evelyn laughed. 'So it's definite, is it?'

'From my examination, I would estimate that you are about sixteen weeks' pregnant.'

'Sixteen! That's four months.' Evelyn was calculating dates in her head. 'That means the baby will be born in May.'

'Yes,' said the doctor. 'A summer baby. That's very good timing.'

But it was not good timing at all, as Frank pointed out that evening when Evelyn told him her news.

'What are we going to live on?' he demanded. 'You'll have to give up work. I thought you liked work.'

Evelyn stared at her husband, perplexed by his reaction. Instead of being delighted and excited, as she was, he was acting as if he did not want her to have a baby at all.

'Well, I do like work, Frank, but I also wanted to have

children, at some point.' Her hands passed protectively over her belly. 'This one has just come along a little sooner than expected.'

Frank glowered out of the window, his mind clearly trying to work out how to deal with the situation. He looked rough and brooding; handsome and unpredictable.

'Aren't you going to say that you're a little bit pleased?' she ventured.

Frank's reaction astonished her. He turned towards her, his face flushed. 'No,' he said simply, 'it's just not the right time. This could mess everything up.'

'Mess what up?'

'My plans, that's what. My plans for everything. If you have a baby, you'll have to stop working and what are we going to live on? We weren't supposed to start a family until I was earning properly.'

Evelyn moved towards him. 'Not all plans work out the way you want them to,' she said. She tried to place her hand on his arm, but he pulled away.

His eyes were blazing as he glowered at her. His upper lip quivered. 'My plans have to work out,' he said. 'Now you've spoiled them.'

'*I* have spoiled them? *Me?*' Evelyn looked aghast. 'It takes two to make a baby,' she said, 'in case you didn't know, a country boy like you.'

Frank did not respond. He frowned and looked away. 'It's just come at the wrong time,' he said.

Evelyn sank on to the sofa, her early happiness drained out of her. She cleared her throat and looked sadly up at her husband. 'Well, the baby's coming whether you like it or not, we'll just have to plan around it. I had plans, too, you know. I was hoping to work for several years before starting a family. You know how much I've always wanted to work. But now those plans will have to change. Looking on the bright side, at least I've got a qualification. I can go back to teaching whenever I want to,' she said, looking hopefully at her husband.

Frank was not to be cheered. He was cold and withdrawn for the rest of the evening and she hardly saw him for the rest of the week as he was working late in the library every night.

The arrival of their son Jamie marked the end of their relationship, though no one saw it like that at the time. The baby was born in the same maternity home where Evelyn had been born twenty-nine years before. It was a difficult birth, with a high forceps delivery, which left Evelyn feeling that her insides had been pulled out. The baby cried all the time, and Evelyn found herself crying with him, both for herself and the baby, in whom Frank showed very little interest. It was doubly upsetting since his behaviour reminded her of her father's distant behaviour towards her.

Their financial state had forced Frank to take on a job working as a solicitor's clerk and studying for his exams during the evenings. Evelyn had a lonely time at home on her own with the baby, seeing her husband very little. And when she did see him Frank was beginning to seem indifferent to her, even unpleasant. And he still ignored the baby. Even in her unhappy state, Evelyn was surprised by how little control Frank had over his feelings. They seemed to be just below the surface with him, ready to erupt at any moment. Sometimes she found herself wondering if this was because he was, in spite of his sophisticated veneer, still essentially rough and unsophisticated, or whether he was simply spoiled and used to getting his own way. Whatever the case, his behaviour worried and alarmed her.

One day his anger and frustration spilled over into violence, and he hit her. Jamie was about three months old. Frank came back from work one day looking very tired and angry. He had had a row with one of the solicitors and threatened to hand in his notice. He took his temper out on Evelyn, snapping at her so much that she stopped trying to talk. The baby started to cry in his bedroom and Frank swore angrily at him.

'Shut up, you,' he bellowed. 'Or I'll give you something to cry about.'

'Frank!' Evelyn was shocked. She pushed herself between Frank and the baby's bedroom. 'How can you talk like that?'

Frank hesitated for a second. Then he stared at her and a strange growl rumbled up his throat and came out as a terrifying roar as he lunged at her. 'Get out of my way, you stupid bitch!' His arm swung across in front of her, catching her jaw and sending her reeling against the wall.

She stood, dazed, staring at him and cradling her smarting jaw in the palm of her hand. 'Don't you ever do that again,' she hissed. 'Don't you ever do it again!'

Frank sniffed. 'I'll do what I like in my own home,' he said. Then he picked up his books and walked towards the front door. 'I'm going to the library,' he said. 'Don't wait up.'

Frank still had his eye on a career at the Bar, and he had, over the years, transformed himself as far as he could. He had perfected the accent, he wore the right clothes. However, he had not anticipated how easy it was to be revealed as an outsider. If asked about his education, he was trapped. If he told the truth, he was despised. If he lied and said he went to some public school, he would invariably find that they knew someone there, if they had not gone there themselves, and his ignorance of the place would be obvious.

Frank became nervous and prickly. In spite of his evident genius at the law, it was generally agreed among the other lawyers that he was not quite one of them and would not fit in. Frank's applications for pupillage were always passed over in favour of a candidate whose background was similar to that of other barristers in the chambers.

Frank's frustration at all this was profound. These prejudices prevented him from progressing through the door of his chosen path – his route to riches and fame. As the rejections continued, his bitterness grew. These confident men scrutinised and judged him with a callous ease that reminded him every time of Augustus, his wife's father.

He knew it was not Evelyn's fault, but Frank's rage was too strong to control. He associated her with these men who refused to let him become one of them. They belonged to a club he could never join but it was many years before he could accept that fact.

In the meantime, Evelyn had been anxious to have another baby. Once Jamie had been born, she had been keen to have another child quite soon, to avoid a long gap between them. She had always regretted the four-year gap between her and her brother Adrian; they had almost been like only children, never playing together or being close friends.

But this was not to be. For many months nothing happened. Then the doctor confirmed another pregnancy, which Evelyn lost the next day. A dragging pain in her back preceded the rush of blood that marked the end of the little life inside her.

Evelyn's sadness was profound but she felt unable to talk to anyone about it, not to her mother, and certainly not to her husband, who had just received another letter of rejection.

When the nanny brought in two-year-old Jamie for his evening play with her, Evelyn could barely respond to the child's demands. She sat listless and quiet, steeped in her own misery, while Frank took his rage elsewhere.

After another two miscarriages, Evelyn was finally able to hold the pregnancy. Her doctor told her that he thought she would have this baby on the day that Frank was finally accepted for pupillage in a small chambers. It was a far cry from the big chambers he had originally set his sights on, but at least it was a start. He was in, or almost in.

His tutor at college had been concerned about Frank's lack of success in being accepted as a pupil. John Bourne was an intelligent man who admired Frank's intellectual abilities but knowing only too well the prejudices at the Bar, he was concerned for the young man's future. In fact, while Frank was having so much trouble finding pupillage, he had done his best to persuade Frank to give up his ambitions to go to the Bar, and to settle for being a solicitor instead.

'You can do very well as a solicitor,' he said, 'and you could get a job and start earning now. If you continue trying for the Bar, it will be some time before you start earning anything.'

But Frank was not going to be put off. Despite John Bourne's warning that being accepted into a chambers after he was properly qualified was another major hurdle ahead of him, Frank was determined to stay on the path he had chosen. Fired by his success in the law exams and an unwavering belief that if you really want something, you can get it, he was not to be put off.

'I'm set on becoming a KC,' he said. 'I set out to do that and that's what I intend to do.'

John Bourne sighed. It was obvious the young fellow had to learn about life directly; he was not going to take any advice from him.

'Just let me know if you want me to write any letters of recommendation for you,' he said.

John Bourne felt sorry for Frank. Here he was, a youth of brilliant natural intelligence but none of his top marks in all his exams meant as much as the fact that he came from the wrong side of the tracks. He had disguised whatever accent he must have grown up with now with a neutral tone of indeterminate origin but the fact that his background was different from that of most law students, and especially those headed for the Bar, was a major problem for him. John Bourne could tell this from his lack of ease at social gatherings, and the prickly manner of talking to his peers. And although his clothes were the same as everyone else's, there was something about them – their newness, perhaps – which told those sensitive to such matters that they were not worn with the ease of someone who had grown up with them. Frank had no worn brown corduroys, no scuffed brown wing-tips, no fading green tweed jacket with leather patches on the elbows. Frank's clothes were spotless, clean and spruce and because of that he stood out like a beacon amongst his peers.

John Bourne was keen to warn Frank not to aim too high. He knew what it was like and he wanted him to avoid the disappointment he himself had experienced as an ambitious young man in his early twenties. As it was, he had gone on to have a satisfying and lucrative career before turning to teaching in his later years. But he too had come from the wrong background and had been convinced that he of all people would overcome that. It took experience to make him accept the truth, and he now wanted to spare this brilliant young man the same disappointment. But it is the nature of ambitious young people that they refuse to listen to others. They are different; life is not the same for them.

So although John Bourne was happy to take Frank out to the pub to buy him a drink to celebrate his getting pupillage, he knew that the next stage – being accepted in chambers – was far harder. He told all this to Frank many times but he knew he could not thwart any ambitions. As far as Frank was concerned, his career was launched.

But John Bourne's warnings came true. After a good year

in which Frank did his pupillage and Evelyn gave birth to a little girl, Josephine, life turned bad.

Having fully qualified for the Bar, Frank was interviewed at twenty chambers and not one took him on. His growing bitterness revealed itself more and more, and the evident resentment simmering below the surface at the interviews added to his problems as a candidate.

As the rejection ate into him, Frank became increasingly angry. He rarely had a good word for Evelyn or the children. Evenings were spent in uncomfortable silence. It was now clear that he and Evelyn had nothing in common.

Soon Frank started to stay out late and come back in the early hours of the morning dishevelled and smelling of drink. He finally gave up trying for chambers and took a lowly position in local government, almost as if to spite himself. Then, as if to make up for the dullness of his working day, he began to gamble, betting with larger and larger sums of money. Sometimes he won, often he lost but he was not worried. Evelyn's private income was large, so he spent it with abandon. It was almost as though he were getting his own back on his dead father-in-law and his kind by squandering the family fortune so carefully built up over generations. In many ways Frank was obsessed with money. It represented the power he craved and since he was being prevented from making large sums for himself he became reckless with it. Not only did he continue his night-time gambling in the West End casinos but he also began to put large amounts into risky enterprises.

Evelyn watched her husband's behaviour with a growing sense of helplessness. Finally, soon after Josie's fifth birthday, she suffered a major collapse.

Looking back, the signs had been there for some years – the deep gloom after Josie had been born, the periods throughout the years when Evelyn would sit in the dark staring out of the window, not responding to requests from the children, the naps she took most afternoons, even when there was no evidence of having exerted herself in any way. She had no friends, and her listlessness grew as her marriage crumbled. She was isolated from the real world, trapped in the hostile world of her mind.

Then she began to weep. The smallest frustration or difficulty would bring it on – a recalcitrant child, an impatient shopkeeper, or a dismissive Frank. Evelyn would feel a tide of hopelessness sweep over her, pounding her down so that she wanted to throw herself on the ground and let the world trample on her even more. She had no interest in existing; she had no belief in herself at any level, as a woman, as a mother, least of all as a person.

She hired au pairs to look after the children, sturdy competent girls from France or Germany, who quickly assessed the situation and responded accordingly, taking the children under their young wings and propping up their mother as best they could. There was no point in discussing Mrs Knight's condition with Mr Knight, as they rarely saw him, but occasionally they were able to get in a word to her mother.

Blanche became increasingly anxious about her daughter, as she recognised the signs. But when she tried to talk to Evelyn, she was confronted with a defensive wall. Evelyn would never admit that anything was wrong and so she never saw any reason to visit the doctor, as her mother urged.

So Blanche watched with concern, keeping in touch with the current au pair in case anything serious happened.

Finally it did, two weeks after Frank had told Evelyn, in a less than sober state, that he did not find her attractive and in fact never had.

Madeleine, the au pair, returned home one day having

fetched the children from school, to find the house reeking of gas. She pushed the children into the garden with strict orders to stay there, and went to investigate.

They said it was an obvious cry for help because Evelyn knew what time Madeleine would be returning. She knew that she would be rescued. And she was. But her action took matters out of her control, and she was sent to a psychiatric hospital to recover, while Jamie was sent off to boarding school and Josie went to live with Blanche down in Sussex. Both children were told that their mother was tired and needed a good rest for several months.

It is hard for a child whose mother tries to commit suicide. Josie was just old enough at the time to understand what had happened but she was too young to understand why. She could not know what had driven her mother to such a desperate action. All she knew, or felt, for many years, was that her mother did not love her and Jamie enough to make her life worth living. They themselves were not important enough to her to keep her alive.

Josie was lucky to spend the next six years of her life with her grandmother, Blanche, who managed to fill much of the void in Josie's young heart. Jamie was not so fortunate. Packed off to boarding school, he just had to get through on his own and develop his own armour against the world.

Blanche made an agreement with Frank that it was better if he did not have too much contact with his children, at least for a while, until their lives had settled. Frank visited Josie and Jamie one holiday and then the contact stopped. He was not interested in his children, he was not interested in his wife's family. He remained intent on pursuing his career at all costs. When the question of divorce was raised a few years later, he was happy to go along with it. Frank was not a family man.

BLANCHE

CHAPTER 20

1960–1966

Evelyn was in and out of mental institutions for about six years. She would stay for several months and then re-emerge, frail, fragile and a little stunned, to stay at her mother's house in Sussex, where efforts were made to keep life running as smoothly as possible.

These periods of recuperation never lasted long. After the first few days, when Evelyn was visibly making an effort to concentrate on the world around her, and to talk to her young daughter and appear as though nothing were wrong, the depression would creep up on her again, gently pulling her at first, reaching out with its tendrils to embrace her entire body and gently squeeze, like a boa constrictor, until it was impossible for Evelyn to think about anything except herself and the nightmare she was trapped in.

Others would observe her terrified glances, the tense twisted mouth, the hands clutching the back of a chair for support. And they would know that it would not be long before her bags were packed again and she would be led gently into the motor car to be taken back to the hospital, the only place where everyone felt she was safe, and where Evelyn felt she was safe from herself.

Blanche talked to the doctors on a regular basis. They shook their heads and shrugged. They suggested treatments which sounded barbaric to Blanche but they did, at times, seem to help Evelyn a little. So after having electrodes placed on her temples and an electric current shot through her, Evelyn would come home again, looking fragile but with a fierce burning look in her eyes that showed that there was still some spirit inside. Then, after a few days or weeks, the burning light would flicker and die and Evelyn would wander about looking listless and heavy-hearted, her shoulders bowed as though she carried a sack of earth upon them.

Josie had become used to seeing this woman, whom she called Mother, coming and going in her grandmother's house. She could not remember her mother being any different from this, so she expected very little from her.

The true mother in her life was her grandmother, who looked after her and doted upon her as much as she could wish. Josie went to Graffham village school and had friends in the area. When she was eleven, she was to go to Midhurst Grammar School. She had dogs and a pony and all the games and toys she could wish for. Her grandmother took her riding on the Downs and played tennis on their tennis court. She built a swimming-pool behind the house, so that the place was like a glamorous holiday camp to which Josie brought her friends.

Josie was aware that the arrangement was unusual. She never saw her father, but then many of her friends in the village did not have fathers either, if they had died in the war. Josie felt nicely different because she knew hers was alive. She still remembered him from a time long ago when they all lived together. She could recall his black curly hair and fierce dark eyes, and the way he could whistle and have all the dogs in the area throw themselves at his feet. She remembered him carrying her on his shoulders and whistling at a blackbird, which came hopping over to talk to them. She remembered his face, sort of. When she tried to see it in her mind's eye, she wanted it to be a kind smiling face but it was impossible for her to pull up such an image. The face she saw was always scowling, and frightening. His voice was deep and loud, but this too she remembered as harsh and angry when he spoke to her, not like the soft, kind tone he used when he spoke to animals.

No one ever mentioned her father to Josie, so she never asked about him, though she often wanted to. She sensed that he had been unkind to her mother, the poor creature who came periodically to the house, and she sensed that he had not been a suitable husband. Occasionally she picked up snippets of conversation between adults in the drawing-room about the 'situation' and slowly, over the years, she put together her own portrait of her father.

She made herself not mind. She told her school-friends that her father lived abroad, working hard to support the family while her mother was not well. She made herself believe that. She had a father, of course she did, it was just that she never saw him. But one day they would meet and be kindred spirits, she knew they would. One day, they would be together and he would see what a wonderful daughter he had had for all this time, and he would be glad.

Perhaps the years had made her wiser but Blanche was acutely aware of the need to mother Josie in a way she had not mothered her own children, particularly Evelyn. Evelyn's confusion, her failure to get a grip on the world, she feared, came from not having been given enough of her parents' time as a child. Blanche could not be sure – perhaps all this fashionable talk about Freud and Bowlby was no more than a fad, but she felt that Evelyn had been given a raw deal and that at least she was in a position to ensure that this was not repeated with Josie. Jamie was another matter. He had been packed off to boarding school some years ago and was now as remote as a visitor's child – polite, withdrawn, lacking in spontaneity. Angry.

When Evelyn was small, Blanche had been too busy living her own life to play with her children more than convention allowed. She had not passed on to Evelyn the idea that it was crucial to develop an inner life in order to survive the world. Or perhaps she had. Evelyn had been so happy during her time away in Italy just before the war. It was Gussie's conformity that made it impossible for her to bloom and flourish. And it was she, Blanche, who had failed to stop her spirit being crushed.

'There may not be much I can do about Evelyn now,' Blanche said to Ivo one morning as they sat at a small table outside his cottage sipping coffee, 'but I may yet be able to do something about her daughter.'

Ivo rubbed his grizzly beard. 'You mean prevent yourself making the same mistake? You're lucky. Not many people get that chance. Usually it's passed down to the next generation and it's out of your hands.'

Blanche looked at her friend and was conscious again of how age was catching up, had caught up with him. The muscles on his strong frame were wasted and the skin on his neck hung down in loose folds. He did not look well and the persistent hacking cough seemed to drain him of so much energy.

She smiled at him. 'Dear Ivo, you seem to care so much.'

He looked up at her sharply. 'Of course I care!' He frowned. 'How can I not care about you and your family?'

'But not as much as you care about your independence,' Blanche said gently.

Ivo glanced sideways at her, acknowledging his rejection of her dream for the future, for the two of them together. He turned away with a soft sigh. 'I'm too old to be someone's husband again,' he said. 'I'm too old to fit into another world. You know you're a social animal and essentially, although I may appear like the life and soul of the party, I'm an old misanthrope. I need my silence, my gloomy moments, my frustration and my rages. Like Baudelaire, I have felt the wind of the wing of madness, and I think I quite like it, even though it torments and frightens me, too. I need all this, and I need to have it alone. I cannot inflict it on others. In fact,' he said, smiling ruefully, 'I don't want to be anywhere near anyone else in those moments. Not because I'm embarrassed or concerned. It's because they are part of me. I need them and I don't want to share them with anyone else. I don't even want people to experience them, to witness them – least of all you, my dear.'

Blanche raised her eyebrows. 'I witness quite a few of them.'

Ivo chuckled. 'If only you knew the depth of them. If only you knew about the aching solitude, the sudden seizures of anxiety that grip me.'

Blanche looked at her friend as he spoke. He was right, she did not know what he felt like. Ivo's madness – for it was a form of madness – was incomprehensible to her. All she could do was react gently when it took him over, whether in its high or low form.

After coffee, as Blanche washed up the cups in the sink, Ivo came up behind her and caressed her back and buttocks, nuzzling the side of her neck hungrily.

Afterwards they lay on the rumpled bed, their legs entwined.

'We have been loving each other for over thirty years,' said Blanche.

Ivo sighed. 'I'm not what I was.'

'Neither of us is,' she replied.

'No, but our histories remain the same,' he said, rolling over to face her.

Blanche stared up at the ceiling. 'Events may be the same,' she said, 'but how you perceive them can change.'

Ivo pushed himself up on his elbow to observe her. 'And what about your past, Blanche?' He was suddenly serious. 'You are so open and so honest, and yet . . . there's something you always hold back. There's something about you, something inside, that you've never let me get a glimpse of.'

Blanche turned to him and held his intelligent eyes with hers. Did it matter any more? Secrets and their consequences could lose their power with time. What she hid deep inside her seemed almost trivial now, though the feelings that went with it could never be described as that. The fear, the betrayal, the sorrow. Contained inside her for all these years. How could she possibly let it all out now? Just the prospect of bringing them to the surface made her nervous, unsure about how she would cope.

And yet, here was Ivo, her best friend, and a man of infinite honesty, who was not interested in gossip or scandal, and who would certainly not go running off to tell the first mutual acquaintance he came across the secret of Blanche's youth. And yet, it was frightening. Once you tell someone a secret, it's gone from you, it's not yours any more. You tell one person, who may or may not tell another. You are no longer the one who makes the decision about whether to tell or not. Blanche had hung on to that decision for all these years and she was frightened to let it go. Yet she loved Ivo and trusted him as she trusted no one else. Sharing a secret is an intimate gesture, if done right.

Even admitting that there was a secret was a big step. Blanche leaned over to Ivo and kissed him, rubbing the grey hairs on his chest with her hand. 'I shall tell you, Ivo, one day,' she whispered. 'I'll tell you all about it.'

Ivo was motionless for a moment, as though stunned by this quiet admission. He gripped her arm and rubbed his leg down hers. 'Just tell me before I die,' he said jovially. 'There's no need to rush it.'

In the spring of 1965, Masha came to stay with her two grandsons, her daughter's children. Her husband Ambrose had been killed during the war and she had remarried, a rich American lawyer, and stayed on, raising and educating her four children as Americans. Now an American citizen herself, her visits to Europe had become rarer as the years passed. She came this time to give her grandsons an adventure, and to introduce them to Europe and their family there.

Masha was still as beautiful as ever – slender and lithe, with her large black eyes and delicate white skin. Though her black hair had turned white, it was thick and abundant and she wore it up in a becoming style that framed her broad Slavic cheek-bones.

The boys, the children of Masha's daughter Irina, were about Josie's age – William a couple of years older, Jack a year younger. They were open and friendly and very happy to play with their British cousin, even though she was a girl.

Seeing that they all got on so well, Masha suggested that they go off on a short motoring trip to Wales and the West Country. Josie jumped at the chance. She was enjoying the company of these boys who were so unlike her sullen, spiteful brother who despised her simply because she was a girl. These boys treated her as though they did not even recognise her gender, but she was particularly athletic and agile and very good at throwing and catching balls.

The trip was a great success. Blanche and Masha had the novelty of being able to talk at length to each other day after day, like the old days, and the children played happily together and never argued. The party saw Stonehenge at dawn, Tintern Abbey at dusk, and climbed every ruined castle on the Welsh Marches which they came across. Josie loved every minute in the company of her American cousins. She wished they were her brothers, rather than Jamie. And at night she would pray that she would wake up and be the sister of these boys. For the first time in her life, she felt she had a taste of what it must be like to have siblings and an ordinary family life, with good-humoured teasing and willing playmates at the ready.

On their last night, in a small hotel in the Brecon Beacons, the two women were in the sitting-room. The children were in bed and Blanche and Masha were sitting by the open fire. It was a cold night with an unexpected frost, and the fire was needed to warm the chilly room.

Blanche looked at her friend and smiled. 'It's been so good to see you again, Masha. I've enjoyed your visit enormously. I only wish you lived here, rather than America. We see each other so rarely, and although I know we are good at corresponding, it's not the same.'

Masha bowed her elegant head and nodded. 'Yes, I know what you mean, but you are almost the only thing I miss about Europe.'

Blanche looked sceptical. 'You can't really mean that,' she said, 'especially after you've just been showing the children some of Europe's greatest treasures. There are no Stonehenges in America.'

'That's true, you're right about Europe in that respect.'

'Well, that's a lot, don't you think?'

Masha sighed, and ran her fingertip along the arm-rest of her chair. 'For me, America represents the future, the future of the world, the future for my children and grandchildren. Too many ghastly things have happened on this side of the

Atlantic. I feel safe in America. I feel protected. You must remember that I lost my mother and my family homes in terrible circumstances. I myself nearly lost my life. My Aunt Natasha, who married a German, committed suicide when the Russians marched into Berlin in forty-five. Europe is simply too full of bad memories for me.'

Blanche sniffed. 'It's funny, isn't it, that you say America is your future. You see my family all the time, you know my family better than I do. America is my past. Europe was and remains my future.'

The women stared into the flames of the fire, and were quiet for some time. It was Masha who broke the silence. 'I do miss you, Blanche. I miss the companionship we had when we were young. It's lovely to see the boys and Josie getting on immediately as though they recognise something in common in each other, whether it's a family bond, or whatever.'

'We've been through a lot in life,' said Blanche, 'both of us.'

Masha turned to her. 'I want to tell you something that I've never talked about before. I want to tell you because you are the only person I can think of who would understand quite what it meant to me. It was so long ago, and even now the anticipation of telling you is making tears come to my eyes, but I don't want to keep it inside me any more. I need to tell you.'

Blanche looked intently at the other woman.

'I was engaged to be married just before the Revolution in Russia. My fiancé, Alexei, was an officer and was caught and imprisoned. But he was freed when Denikin's army arrived. We were so happy at his release that we decided to celebrate with a big picnic. We took hampers and blankets and a samovar into the woods near my parents' house. We had several friends with us and a lot of vodka was drunk by them all. They began singing and dancing the *lezghinka*, and then firing their guns into the air. Alexei pulled out his revolver and pointed it at his head. He called my name. "Masha," he called. "Do you love me?" And a moment later he called, "Russian roulette? Shall I play? After my luck today, I can only win."

'I had already started answering his first question when he called out the second one. I was tipsy myself and could not think quickly enough to stop, to change my words. I shouted out "Yes," meaning yes, I loved him. He must have taken it to mean yes, play the game.'

Masha lowered her eyes and shook her head slowly. 'That stupid game. There was one bullet in the barrel. The bullet blasted Alexei's brains out. They were falling out of his skull. Alexei fell in the mud and I didn't know what to do. We all stood there staring at him. Then I knelt down and tried to stuff his brains back inside. It was terrible. Useless and terrible.'

Masha's words came out as a whisper in the otherwise silent room. 'Alexei's family blamed me,' she continued, her voice growing fainter. 'They blamed me because they said I told him to pull the trigger.' She looked up at Blanche with such a pained expression on her face that Blanche almost rose from her chair to comfort her. 'But I was saying yes, that I loved him.'

She swallowed hard and let out a sigh. 'I have never told anyone that story since I met Ambrose and escaped with the British fleet. I have kept it inside me for over forty years. But it hasn't gone away. Sometimes I still dream that scene over and over again, either asleep or awake. And I still can't bring myself to change what I shouted. I couldn't shout No, I don't love you, and stop Alexei pulling the trigger because it wouldn't be true. I loved him dearly. And I can still feel the texture of his soft brains on my fingers . . .'

The fire was dying down. Blanche waited a few minutes

before rising to her feet to stoke it up again and throw on another log.

Now Masha was smiling through her teary eyes. She lifted her head and sat up, as though she had thrown off a hat. 'There, I feel better now. How strange. I've dreaded telling anyone for all these years, and now I've done it, and nothing's happened.'

'Well, you must know that you're not responsible for Alexei's death.'

Masha shrugged. 'It feels as though I was. That's the problem. But telling you now has made me think that perhaps I can change the way I feel about it. That's what I had hoped. I had hoped that the many years that have passed would make it possible to admit it. Age can be a marvellous thing.'

Blanche found herself shivering in the confessional atmosphere of the room. If she were to tell anyone what lay curled up deep inside her, like a viper, it would be Masha, not Ivo. Masha was a woman, she was her family. Masha knew Blanche's own family in America better than she herself did. The moment she allowed it to be a possibility, the urge, the desire, gathered strength inside her. Suddenly she felt it could be a form of liberation. She could let that viper unfurl itself and see what happened.

'That's a very sad story.' Blanche gave her cousin a sympathetic smile. 'But you are clearly not to blame for what happened.'

Masha shrugged her narrow shoulders. 'I know.'

There was a silence for a while, apart from the wood crackling in the flames. Finally, Blanche spoke. 'I used to be good at forgetting things that I did not like. I used to believe that if you try hard enough, you can make yourself forget unpleasant events. I perfected a technique for refusing to think about things I wanted to forget. Even as a girl, I could

forget that my father had scolded me simply by pushing away
the memory, almost as if I can put a spell on it to make it
vanish. I have done this all my life. Throughout my marriage
I ignored things about Gussie I didn't like and only believed
what I did like. I dealt with Adrian's death in the same way.
I refused to think about it in the belief that it would be erased
from my memory.

'For a long time, this worked but lately I've come to realise
that these things don't go away just because you want them to.
They return in dreams and in unexplained feelings and thoughts
that come to me in the night. It's naïve of me, no doubt, but
it worked for sixty years of my life. Perhaps now I'm better
able to accept some of the more terrible things that happened.
And some of them need to come out, they need to be told. I
can hold them in no longer. You know I'm not religious and
never have been particularly so, but perhaps I'm experiencing
a kind of need to confess. Perhaps it's actually a fundamental
part of being human – to clear the conscience.'

Masha was looking at her intently. 'What is it you want to
confess, Blanche?'

Blanche sighed. 'I know now that one never forgets anything. It's always there in your mind somewhere, waiting to
emerge again. The only relief is that time and age seem to
change the importance of secrecy.'

'Tell me, Blanche.' Masha's voice was gentle, coaxing.
'Tell me what bothers you at night.'

And so it was that, on that chilly April evening as the fire
crackled in the grate, and foxes sniffed around the chicken-run
and owls glided over the moonlit Welsh mountains, Blanche
found herself telling Masha what had happened to her nearly
half a century ago.

JOSIE

CHAPTER 21

1966–1990

In the mid-1960s, a pharmaceutical revolution enabled Evelyn to emerge from the mental institution that had been her home for so many years and begin to live a relatively ordinary life. The new antidepressants freed her from the regular courses of ECT and the confines of the psychiatric wards. Now her doctors had discovered that one particular pill worked well for her. So long as she took her medication at the prescribed times, she would remain balanced and steady, able to live a normal life, they said.

It was a terrifying but exciting prospect for Evelyn. She felt that so many years of her life had been wiped out by her illness that she found every moment now so precious. She was anxious to make up for the lost time, to be independent, to get a job, to enjoy what the world now had to offer her.

She bought herself a small house in London, in Dartmouth Park, Kentish Town. Jamie was about to start in the sixth form at school and twelve-year-old Josie was set to move in with her mother and go to Camden School for Girls.

Evelyn found herself a job teaching French at a sixth-form college in North London. Her daughter returned to live with her and gradually she found herself becoming part of the world again.

Blanche was pleased and relieved. She had thought that Evelyn was destined to spend the rest of her life in and out of that dreary and depressing hospital.

So Josie studied for her 'O' levels and, being a sociable child, made many friends at school. It all seemed strange, though. Having spent so many years living in the oddest family circumstances, she could hardly believe that she now lived an almost normal life. A few of the girls at school had parents who were divorced, so she was not even so odd on that score. She felt embarrassed that she never saw her father, that he never showed any desire to see her or Jamie, but she could live with that. Initially she pretended to her friends that he had died but then she discovered that another girl with divorced parents never saw her father either, so she owned up. She had a mother, she told herself, and an adoring grandmother. She shouldn't pretend there was more. What she had was enough.

So Evelyn's strength and confidence grew by the week. Although in her youth she had never been described as good-looking, in middle age she seemed to have grown into her looks. Perhaps it was the spirit of excitement, of having become part of an interesting world again, of being independent for almost the first time, but she felt reborn, and it showed in her eyes and the bloom on her skin.

It was not long before she struck up a friendship with another tutor at the college, a divorced man called Tony. They began to spend all their free time together, going to exhibitions and plays and films.

Josie liked Tony. He was a tall gangly man with thick grey hair, warm brown eyes and a deep laugh. He always talked to her when he saw her, and showed a genuine interest in her friends and schoolwork.

Josie was happy for her mother, and only slightly anxious

when Tony asked Evelyn to marry him. Initially Evelyn hesitated, unsure of what her children would say. When she asked Josie her views, her generous-hearted daughter was positive. 'You must do what makes you happy, Mother. We're too old for you to worry about us.'

'I worry about how Jamie will react,' said Evelyn. 'He hasn't exactly been friendly towards Tony, at any point.'

Josie hugged her. 'You must do what you want, Mother. That's what Grandma would advise, isn't it?'

Evelyn nodded ruefully. 'She advised that in the past,' she said. 'I took her advice – and I wanted to – and it turned out to be a disaster.

'However, I understand now that my decision to marry your father had more to do with getting away from my own father and everything he stood for, than actually doing what *I* wanted to do.'

She smiled at Josie. 'It's a wonderful thing to gain insight with age,' she said.

Josie hugged her. 'Oh, get married, Mother. Don't worry about Jamie. He won't agree with anything anyone wants to do.'

Tony and Evelyn announced their engagement the following week.

Josie was pleased for her mother, and perhaps a bit selfishly she was glad that this would relieve her of some of the responsibility for keeping an eye on her and making sure she was safe and happy.

As expected, Jamie was not so gracious. Now at Oxford, he had adopted a pompous and arrogant manner. 'What does Mother want to get married for?' he demanded of Josie. 'This man Tony hardly earns anything. I just don't see the point of it.'

'People don't just get married for money, you know,'

Josie replied, trying not to show her irritation. 'And Tony makes Mother happy. He's a good companion to her. Surely you want her to be happy and cared for?'

Jamie shrugged, making it clear to his sister that he thought she was being wet. Any mention of feelings was dismissed by Jamie as sentimental tosh.

Fortunately, her son's lack of enthusiasm did not prevent Evelyn going ahead with her plans. They were to be married in a register office, and then have a blessing in the church. It was all arranged.

Then, a week before the wedding date, Evelyn and Tony were driving back from Sussex after visiting Blanche. They were involved in a car accident and, both unconscious, were taken to hospital. Evelyn recovered with a broken leg and a scar down her cheek. Tony lay in a coma for a week and when he emerged he could not recognise Evelyn as someone he knew. He certainly did not remember that he was due to marry her.

It took a month before he had regained his memory but for those agonising weeks it seemed to Evelyn, and to her mother and daughter, that the bright lights on the horizon had been put out for ever. Evelyn was in agony, convinced that her brief chance of happiness had been extinguished. She chastised herself for even hoping for such a chance. Pessimism was by now so ingrained in her way of thinking that she felt she could expect only cruel blows from fate. She had no right to happiness of any sort.

Fortunately, Evelyn was wrong. Tony did regain his memory completely. He emerged from hospital, a little frail, perhaps, but impressed by the devotion of Evelyn and her family. He and Evelyn were married in the autumn and had a honeymoon in Italy, two weeks in Tuscany, where Evelyn felt she reclaimed some of her lost life. They had eight years of a contented marriage – more, Josie would remind her mother, than many people manage.

Tony was a mild-mannered man whom insensitive people might incorrectly dismiss as weak. He avoided arguments and was not aggressive in any way. He was, however, a man of great internal strength. Brought up by a strong and loving mother, he always had a belief in himself. He suffered no self-doubt but this confidence came with no arrogance. He knew what he enjoyed and pursued his interests with a passion. The divorce from his first wife had been traumatic, but also a relief after years of being told he was not a real man because he did not overpower her in bed.

In Evelyn, Tony saw a fragile person with a fierce intelligence that needed to be coaxed out. He wanted to look after her, to build her up and encourage her to be herself, and this he did during their happy eight years of marriage. He was astonished by the breadth of Evelyn's reading in European literature. She knew her Balzac, and Flaubert and Genet. She could talk with great authority about the works of Dostoevsky and Pushkin, Hermann Hesse, Franz Kafka and Alberto Moravia – her greatest love since his early work was censored by the Fascists. In return, Tony introduced her to the modern American writers he was discovering at that time – Philip Roth, John Updike, Kurt Vonnegut and Gore Vidal. He encouraged her to read the new women writers – Margaret Drabble, Doris Lessing, Iris Murdoch, and the work of the new wave of feminists – Germaine Greer, Sheila Rowbotham and Juliet Mitchell, which he was very interested in.

Evelyn read these feminist books with interest but always finished them with a sigh. 'I was born too early for all this,' she would say. 'If I had read these when I was a girl my life might have been very different, but I doubt it.' She cuddled up to Tony on the sofa and he rubbed her head affectionately. 'It's Josie's generation that will benefit,' he said. 'You'll just have to make do with me for now – a man who cooks you supper and washes up as well. Not very masculine pursuits, I know, but who cares?'

Evelyn smiled. 'I'm afraid Jamie cares a lot. I can see him wincing every time you put on an apron to cook supper. It goes against everything he's been taught all his life.'

'Well, luckily he doesn't live with us, so he doesn't have to see it every day. I like cooking and you don't. It has nothing to do with being male or female. I'm glad to see that Josie doesn't seem to have any problem with it.'

Even if Jamie rejected him as a member of the family, Josie did not. She grew to love him greatly. Tony was an excellent step-father to her, almost making up for the fact that she hardly had a father at all. He had never had children so it was a joy for him to find himself with a daughter. He enjoyed taking her to the cinema and the theatre. He helped her with her homework and always came to her school to watch her if she was acting in a play or playing her flute in the school orchestra. He listened patiently to her complaints about her fickle girlfriends and gave her advice about troublesome boyfriends. When Josie finally went off to university, she felt she was leaving behind a true set of contented parents, an odd feeling after her mother's years of illness and unhappiness.

Then Tony died suddenly of a heart attack, in the mid 1970s while Josie was starting her final year at university. She would never forget the telephone call from her mother that freezing November morning. While Evelyn was waiting for the ambulance to arrive, she telephoned Josie in her student house, and told her how Tony had got up to make her an early cup of tea, as he always did, and she had heard a loud thump. Running downstairs, she found Tony lying on the floor, his head bleeding profusely where he had hit it as he fell. 'I know he's dead,' she said flatly. 'There is no pulse. I know they won't be able to do anything to save him. I must go now, the ambulance is here.'

Josie put down the telephone and wept. She knew too that there was no hope, that Tony was dead. She cried for the loss of a father she loved, a man who had shown her how kind a man can be. But she also wept for her mother and the future. How was Evelyn going to cope now that she was on her own again?

In fact, Josie's fears turned out to be unfounded. The eight years of marriage to a good man had given Evelyn an inner strength that withstood Tony's death. She was still prone to bouts of depression and could spend days in quiet gloom, but otherwise she remained relatively stable. Her medication was effective and she never had to return to the hospital again.

Josie remained close to her grandmother until Blanche finally died in 1983, aged eighty-four. Until then, she had continued to visit her at weekends and when she could no longer drive her car Josie would take her on trips to all the places Blanche had taken her as a child – the Roman Palace at Bignor, bird-watching at Pagham Harbour, the theatre at Chichester, and the wildfowl at Arundel.

Josie was heart-broken for many weeks, and for several days after her grandmother had died she dialled her number every evening just to hear it ringing in the house she had loved so much.

Josie carried memories of Blanche with her for the rest of her life. She remembered her as a relatively young grandmother teaching her at eight years old to ice-skate on the frozen pond in the woods. It was a freezing January day and Josie had had a red woollen scarf wrapped around her neck and thick red gloves. Blanche glided over the ice, her hands clasped behind her back, looking as elegant as a young ballerina. Viennese waltzes belted out from an old gramophone placed on the mossy bank.

Josie remembered her on Easter Sunday every year, hiding large chocolate eggs and carefully wrapped presents around the garden for her and Jamie to find. Even when she was well into her sixties, she was climbing the big oak tree at the end of the garden to hide the largest Easter eggs out of view. She remembered climbing into her grandmother's four-poster bed with its embroidered linen curtains to snuggle up as Blanche read wonderful stories to her from the Arabian Nights, or fairy-tales by Hans Christian Andersen.

She remembered her grandmother telling her about flowers in the garden and how to propagate any kind of plant. She showed her the wild spotted orchids on the Downs and taught her how to recognise trees from their outlines against the sky. She taught her the songs of birds, taking her out to Ambersham Common one night to hear the territorial churring of the nightjar. She taught her to identify the song of the nightingale and the mistle thrush, and what their eggs looked like.

Her most moving memory was of Blanche's friendship with Ivo Barnard, the old painter. By then he was an old man, older than Blanche and well into his eighties. But he was still full of life, very funny and lively. He would come over to the house for a drink, and Blanche would laugh like a young woman.

Once Josie was playing by herself in the garden and she saw Blanche and Ivo walking across the grass together. Whitc-haired and stooped with age, they both leaned on their walking-sticks, peering at the flowers in the borders or looking up to admire the clouds in the sky.

Josie watched them from afar and was astonished to see Ivo place an arm around Blanche's shoulders and nuzzle her neck. Blanche then turned towards him, and Josie was even more astonished to see her lift up her lips to his. Old people kissing!

Josie stepped back to hide behind a tree, terrified that she might be seen and thought to be spying. She felt both appalled and excited by the sight before her. It changed her view of her grandmother for ever, and this was why, when Jamie was so dismissive of Blanche's love-life twenty years later, Josie knew he was wrong.

Ivo died a couple of years later, and Blanche was very sad. Josie vividly remembered seeing tears in her grandmother's eyes for several days after the news that Ivo had been found dead in his studio, paintbrush in hand.

'Perhaps the worst thing about getting old,' she told Josie as they ate supper one evening, 'is losing one's friends.'

But in spite of her sadness, Blanche did not allow herself to be dragged down by Ivo's death; after all, she still had Josie to bring up. She bounced back, determined that life should be as good for her granddaughter as possible.

She took her to London to see the sights: to Westminster Abbey, the Victoria and Albert Museum, St Paul's Cathedral. She took her to the National Gallery, and talked to her about paintings and why some pictures were good and some were bad. She took her to piano recitals at the South Bank and the Wigmore Hall, always making sure they got the best seats from which they could see the pianist's hands on the keyboard. And then they would have lunch at Simpsons in the Strand or tea at Derry & Tom's roof garden. She took her to Paris for a week where they saw the Mona Lisa and Notre Dame and spoke French. And she took her to Florence where they stayed with her old friends the Armstrongs in a villa in Fiesole, overlooking the city. The Armstrongs liked to tell Josie about how they remembered meeting her mother just before the war, during which all the bridges across the Arno were blown up except, thank goodness, the Ponte Vecchio.

As Blanche became older, Josie's memories changed. She remembered her grandmother gradually slowing down. First Blanche stopped being able to climb the Downs any more, then she needed naps in the afternoons. When her eyesight deteriorated, she had to stop driving, as she was no longer safe on the road.

Well into her teens, Josie did not see Blanche so often, so when they did meet she was always more aware of the changes each time.

Old age is cruel to everyone. Elegant Blanche now dropped food down her front and was too blind to notice the stains. Her slender hands were liver-spotted, stiff and knobbly with arthritis. Although her eyesight was getting worse, her hearing remained sharp, so she spent hours listening to the radio. 'I'm well up on the events of the world but I have no friends alive to discuss them with any more,' she complained to Josie.

She always looked forward to the visits from her grand-daughter but she often talked about death. 'I've had enough,' she said. 'There's hardly anything left for me to do. I'm too old to walk far or read. I can't live on my own for much longer.

'I often take myself for walks in my head, along the streets of Savannah and around my parents' house. It's a pleasant enough way to spend the time but I have had enough, and

I think it may be a sign. I feel as if my life is coming full-circle.'

Until the day she died, Blanche remained an engaging character. Although her body began to fail her by degrees, her mind remained bright and alert until her heart gave out during an afternoon nap one summer day. Her daily help found her in the garden chair, her hands were clasped together in her lap, her eyes closed as if in sleep.

Josie retained vivid memories of her grandmother's house, too. She could always see and hear the tall grandfather clock ticking in the hall. She could remember the tartan picnic rugs and the tortoiseshell hairbrushes on the dressing-tables; the chamber pots, no longer needed, hidden in the bedside cupboards; the crisp laundered linen sheets that were icy cold to slip into in the middle of summer; the bath salts in a jar on a rosewood table; the heavy green silk curtains, and the large hall chests that contained the family's tennis rackets and golf clubs. Such memories always fuelled her imagination as she thought about her mother and grandparents living in the house in the old days.

Evelyn's cancer was diagnosed in early 1990. Josie knew that, unlike many people, her mother would not even try to fight the disease. 'I've battled with too many other demons in my life,' Evelyn said wearily. 'I have no more strength left inside me.'

While Jamie scoffed at this defeatist attitude, Josie was more understanding of her mother's position. 'I would probably feel the same way, if I'd had such a life, too.'

Who knows whether Evelyn's decision to give in to the cancer, not to put on the armour of battle and fight to the very last, meant that she died more quickly? She died three months after the diagnosis, in a hospice in Hampstead. She had not fought the disease, so she did not feel it had defeated her. It was, thought Josie, the right way to go, for her.

Josie sat in her grandmother's rocking-chair and thought about her family's past. Here she was with no history to speak of. She was thirty-five and had little to show for it. By the time her grandmother was this age, she had moved across the Atlantic, married a foreigner, had two children and created an exquisite garden in the grounds of her country house. Even Josie's mother, Evelyn, had done more than Josie – she had become fluent in two foreign languages, married and had two children, and had been divorced. To Josie at that moment, even getting divorced seemed like an achievement in someone's life. At least it was a marker of some kind. It was not so long ago, she thought, when the life expectancy of the average woman was about forty, when simply giving birth could be a matter of life or death.

Josie felt almost a sense of shame at her lack of achievement. For whatever reason, she had just let herself drift through life without any real thought. She had never been driven by ambition or goals. Unlike her friends, many of whom seemed to map out their lives when they were students, working out what they expected to do by the time they were twenty-five, thirty and thirty-five. Both male and female friends seemed to have personal and professional goals that they could reel off without thinking – earning £30,000 by the time they were thirty, getting married and having a baby before they were thirty-two, owning a flat, then a house, travelling the world, working in a foreign country. They all seemed so focused. It seemed to Josie that everyone else looked at the world and saw endless opportunities for themselves. She had never seen her life as one path with interesting hurdles to clear. Her life just was.

It was more like being on an island in the middle of a pond and being unable to swim. She did not have a clue about what direction she should or could be moving in. She did not think she had the means to move anywhere now, even if she did know where to go.

Josie had gone dutifully through school and university, a diligent but not outstanding student. She always had enough friends of both sexes, always more of a follower than a leader. She would go with gangs of girls to try on clothes at Biba in Kensington and spend the rest of Saturday afternoons hanging out in Kensington Market, the ultimate cool place.

Generally, however, she was a self-contained character without a strong need for close friends, happy with her own company, happy to spend the evening watching television or reading a book. Like her mother and grandmother, she was a great reader. Like Blanche, she enjoyed reading contemporary fiction, her favourite writers including Margaret Atwood, Angela Carter, Clare Boylan and Fay Weldon. If she had a novel in her hands, she was never bored.

Over the past few years with Andy, she had had plenty of time to herself in the evenings, while he was out 'networking'. She had a few boyfriends at university but met Andy at a party to celebrate the end of her finals. They had remained a couple for twelve years. Looking back now, Josie could see the same passivity in her relationship with Andy. She had always let him take the lead, deciding on what film they saw at the cinema, where they spent their holidays, whose parties they would go to, whose dinner parties they would not go to. She had endured hours sitting quietly in smoky pubs while Andy and his mates argued about football and put up with freezing-cold journeys on the back of his smart Harley Davidson on trips up to Scotland or Wales.

There were times when Josie knew that Andy was sleeping with other women, and she put up with it, knowing that he would return to her in the end. At the time, she was almost proud of her tolerance. Now, it shamed her. How could she have put up with it for so long? How could she have tolerated such treatment?

Andy was a bright and talented young man whose career was soaring. An aggressive award-winning journalist, he had recently been put in charge of the weekend section of a national newspaper. It was clear to all who knew him that, if he played his cards right, he was headed for a senior position in the future.

As his success grew, Andy's treatment of Josie had grown worse. Perhaps he compared her unfavourably with the young female journalists on his paper, ambitious women who were only too willing to succumb to Andy's charms if it meant that their own careers would not suffer as a result. Andy's life became increasingly interesting; Josie's seemed more inward-looking. Their interests grew further apart. Andy lived in the exciting world of the media, meeting new people, making news, causing controversy, while Josie worked quietly at her publishing job and did not care for any of the media parties that Andy loved so much.

Well, now it was all over. Finished. Andy was not for her. It had taken a long time for her to accept it, even longer for her to do something about it. Now she knew for sure that Andy was not for her. She knew that she did not want a man like him, a cocky, overbearing person who was used to getting his own way. No, now she recognised that a man more like her step-father, Tony, would be better suited to her, a kind gentle man who was not afraid to show his maternal side.

Josie had grown up with the feminist movement of the

seventies, and she had also learned from her mother's experience. She would never call herself a feminist but she had absorbed enough of the feminist message to know that she should not rely on a man for her happiness. Indeed, now she saw that it was precisely because she had just stayed with Andy that she had been unhappy, without exactly knowing why.

Although she did not even know if she wanted children, she did feel uncomfortable about the fact that her mother died before she, Josie, had given birth. Only a few weeks before she been moved into the hospice, Evelyn had expressed a sadness about that. 'I'm sorry I'm not going to live to see you become a mother,' she said one evening when Josie had come to visit. It was a warm summer evening and Evelyn had been helped out into the garden by the nurse who now looked after her in the day, placed in a chair and wrapped up in a maroon mohair blanket Evelyn had bought in Ireland on a happy trip with Tony.

Josie had blushed and looked away. 'Oh, Mother, you have four grandchildren from Jamie already.' She tried to laugh it off.

But her mother shook her head. 'That's not what I meant. It's not more grandchildren I want. It's seeing you move up a generation. A daughter as a parent is different from a son. Not better, but different.' She sighed and shut her eyes, resting her head against the back of the garden chair. The setting sun cast a pink light on her face, making her pallid skin look almost healthy.

Looking at her mother's face, thin and wizened by the disease, Josie knew that if she ever did have children, they would not be with Andy. She resolved there and then to do something about her feebleness. Her mother had a reason for being weak. Josie did not. She would make a decision about Andy.

It turned out to be surprisingly easy. A few days before Josie took Evelyn to the hospice in Hampstead, she left a note for Andy to see when he came home, telling him that he could move his possessions out of her flat. She would stay at her mother's house for a couple of days and when she returned she expected him to have moved out.

Andy did not argue. He took his books and LPs, his CDs and his portable television, and the clothes he had kept at Josie's. He knew it was over and that it had been for a long time. Like many men, he just had not had the nerve to end the relationship himself. He was glad that it was Josie who had done the deed. Then he could be blameless.

The rocking-chair's movement was smooth and regular. As Josie thought about the end of her relationship with Andy, she felt a twinge of satisfied pride. She was not entirely passive, after all. It had taken courage to end it and it was not as difficult as she had thought. The world did not cave in. Her friends still spoke to her. She resolved there and then to remember her grandmother's spirit and to try to be bolder in life, to take chances, even risks. She knew that if she did not, her life would be over in no time and it would amount to nothing. It would not mean anything to anyone.

CHAPTER 22

London, 1990

The house had been on the market for only a few weeks when Josie received a serious offer for it. It was from a youngish couple – probably in their early thirties and certainly younger than herself, she registered bleakly. They had a young child and another on the way. Dominic Turner was something in advertising and his wife had been a graphic designer before having her first child. Since then, she told Josie rather proudly, as she stroked her protruding belly, she had chosen to stay at home and look after their child rather than have some stranger do it for her.

Josie did not take to these people. They were too confident, too directed, too sure of who they were and where they were going. They made her feel old and inadequate, even incompetent for not having sorted out her life at this stage. She did not take to them but was pleased that they came back two more times to look at the house, showing genuine interest. She kept reminding herself that it did not matter that she did not like them, just as long as they bought the house and took it off her hands.

The estate agent rang one morning to say that the Turners had offered the asking price and, subject to the survey, were anxious to move as soon as they could. This was possible, since they were cash buyers and Josie was not in a chain either.

She telephoned Jamie to tell him the news. Her brother grunted down the phone. 'If they're offering the asking price, perhaps we weren't asking enough for it.'

Josie hesitated. 'So do you want me to refuse this offer and put the house back on the market at a higher price?' She tried not to sound irritated.

'No,' replied Jamie. 'Liz and I need the money. Accept the offer – but make sure these people don't try to bargain you down in any way. People can be sharks.'

'Yes,' responded Josie, recalling Jamie's gleeful boasts of having beaten down the price of his own house when he was buying it. The vendor was an elderly lady for whom the property had become too much, and she finally got fed up with Jamie's constant complaints about the condition of the house and knocked ten thousand off the price for a quick sale. Josie still felt an angry tug whenever she thought about the way he had treated that poor old dear.

Moments after speaking to Jamie, Josie's telephone rang again. It was her American cousin, Will. 'I'm in town for a brief visit,' he said. 'Any chance of seeing you tonight for a meal?'

Josie let out a shriek of pleasure. She loved Will's impromptu visits which happened once a year or so, when he had a meeting in Europe. Ever since he and his brother had come to England with their grandmother, Masha, when Josie was living with Blanche, Will in particular had maintained contact across the ocean. He had travelled to Europe quite a bit as a teenager. He spent a term at London University and now his work frequently brought him across the Atlantic. He and Josie had a close friendship. He often telephoned and wrote funny letters, enclosing amusing clippings out of the *New York Times* or cartoons from the *New Yorker* for her to chuckle at. He was a clever man and now a lawyer specialising in international law.

Josie had not in fact seen Will for a couple of years, since just before his wedding when he had come to London with his fiancée, Kelly. In spite of her best efforts to like her, Josie had not taken to Kelly. She was very attractive with long black hair, dark blue eyes, white skin and deep red lips, but she was also a fiercely jealous woman. She was clearly jealous of every one of Will's friends and acquaintances from his time before her appearance on the scene. She stayed by Will's side, showing little interest in anyone else, and looked threatened whenever his attention strayed from her. When Josie asked Will about his old girlfriend Mimi, with whom he had stayed friends for many years after splitting up, Will had mumbled that he had not really seen many people since Kelly had arrived on the scene. It was evident that it was all his old friends, male and female, that Kelly had a problem with. And she certainly could not cope with Will's closeness to his British cousin.

The first night the three of them had sat up talking late into the night. Andy had been around for supper but had left to go to a club. Josie did not expect to see him again until the next evening.

At about eleven, Kelly yawned and held Will's hand. 'I'm tired, honey,' she said, 'you ready to come to bed?' She got to her feet and stood over Will, waiting for him to follow.

Josie watched with interest. Will looked up at his future wife with a peeved expression on his face. Josie waited and then felt the sweet twinge of victory as Will, having hesitated, shook his head and sat back on the sofa. 'No, I want to keep talking to Josie,' he said. 'We haven't seen each other for a while and have a lot of family news to catch up on.'

Kelly frowned and her lips twisted into a crooked line. She hovered for a moment by the sofa. Then she shrugged and sat down again. 'I guess I'm not so tired,' she said.

She stayed up hanging on to Will's arm while he and Josie continued to fill each other in on news of the family and other mutual acquaintances.

Josie had been saddened by that incident, thinking that if Will was not careful, he would not be allowed to see anyone not approved by Kelly. So when she heard nine months after the wedding that Will had walked out on Kelly, she was surprised to find herself relieved and secretly pleased.

That evening Josie and Will met in Chinatown where they feasted on hot and sour soup, deep-fried squid, roast duck and Singapore fried noodles, and filled each other in on their news. Josie told Will about the final split with Andy, and how she had suddenly become aware of the contempt with which he had treated her for so long. She told him about his habit of putting her down in front of other people, and how he criticised her line of argument, or laughed cruelly if she asked a question he considered stupid or naïve. He had long ago ceased to compliment her on her appearance but instead frequently made derogatory remarks about a dress not fitting her properly or her hairstyle being old-fashioned. The final straw, however, was when he walked out of the sitting-room and switched off the light even though she was still in there reading on the sofa.

Josie laughed when she told Will this last detail. It was painful but so very absurd! She did not, however, go into Andy's cruelty in bed, for it was both too intimate and too humiliating for her to confess to her cousin. She did not want him to know that she put up with Andy waking her up in the middle of the night to have sex, even when he had been out late and had come home stinking of beer and cigarettes, and he knew that she had to get up early in the morning to go to work. She kept quiet about how he frequently bullied her into performing oral sex on him but rarely repaid the favour. It had become worse and worse. He used to drop his clothes on the floor and expect her to run around after him, doing his laundry and cooking his meals. Josie was fond of Andy's mother but she often cursed her for failing to bring up her son properly. Then one day something had snapped in Josie. When her mother's cancer was diagnosed, she knew she had to put an end to the relationship. 'I knew I couldn't look after my mother while I had Andy on my hands as well. It was the perfect excuse. I told him it was over and that I meant it.'

Will smiled grimly, appalled to hear what his cousin had had to put up with for so long. 'And perhaps you realised that you had to look after yourself as well,' he said.

'Yes, and now I thank God I did so before we went too far down the line. The older I get the harder it seems for me to act. Most of the time I just let myself drift because I don't want to be responsible for my actions. At least my mother's illness pulled me up. Otherwise I might have gone and married Andy in spite of the way he behaved towards me. I think at one point I felt that if we got married then things would improve, but of course that's stupid. In fact, it's only with hindsight that I've come to realise quite how badly Andy treated me. I was *such* a fool to put up with it.'

'We can all be fools when we are afraid of being alone,' said Will. 'My marriage to Kelly was not dissimilar but I made the mistake of getting hitched legally.'

Will then told Josie about his disastrous marriage and quick divorce. 'I think I was fortunate to realise very early on in the marriage that it wasn't going to work,' he said, 'so at least there were no children involved. I could get out fast.'

He shook his head. 'I still can't believe how I got hitched up with someone like Kelly. She was so jealous. She hated all my friends and if I was just a few minutes late home from the office, she would berate me, and whenever I went away on business, she would call me or make me promise to call her at every opportunity. I felt completely trapped. I can see now that she is a deeply disturbed person but I was blind to it all until it was too late.'

Josie laughed. 'Well, I can't say I'm sorry. I think she would have done her best to drive a wedge between us, too.'

'My grandmother was horrified by the whole business. I wouldn't be surprised if it helped to send her to her grave – she died about six months after I walked out on Kelly. She was upset that I wouldn't even consider a reconciliation. She said that there had never been a divorce in the family and it would bring so much shame on her. I guess she was worried about the gossip among her Long Island friends. I was sorry to upset her, because I was very fond of her, but I knew that any attempt to go back would be a mistake. And I told her that.'

'I liked Masha,' said Josie. 'She always brought me wonderful chocolates when she came to visit Grandma when I was living there. And she was always so beautifully dressed and elegant, even though she was old. My grandmother used to tell me stories about Masha's escape from Russia after the Revolution – it always seemed so exciting and romantic. And there was a terrible story about her fiancé playing Russian roulette and blowing his brains out.'

Will was fascinated to hear the story. 'It's odd that I've never heard that story before,' he said when Josie had finished, 'but then my grandmother never talked about her past – you probably know more about it than I do, or even my mother. I always got the impression that Grand-mother cut herself off from her past. America was her home, even though she was well in her forties when she went there. She adopted a new identity. She denied her European connections; she could speak three European languages but never used them and even chose to speak English with an American accent.'

'Yes, my grandmother used to complain that Masha came over less and less. She was very fond of Masha.'

'That reminds me,' Will said, looking thoughtful. 'Shortly before she died, my grandmother told me something about Blanche and why she originally left America and never came back.'

'Really? As far as I know she never told anyone.'

'I remember now. Your grandmother was already dead – I think she died the week before I got married – because Masha said something about keeping secrets for dead people. When I asked her what she meant, she told me that Blanche had had to leave America as a young woman because of a scandal. She had had a love affair with a man and a child had been the result. She was forced to give up the child and leave for Europe.'

Josie listened with astonishment and growing excitement. 'There was always supposed to be some scandal but we never knew what it was. Our great-uncle Rudie once told me that he was determined to find out before he died but if he did he never told me. And he died about ten years ago. I've always imagined that she had some lost love, an affair with someone she was not allowed to marry. I've never heard anything about a child . . . That makes it even more intriguing.' She laughed. 'It seems I know more about your grandmother's life than you do, and you know more about mine than I do. That's family gossip for you.'

She laughed at the irony, but something was niggling at her, some memory of her grandmother in her dotage, as she became frail and weak.

'What you've just said reminds me of something,' she went on. 'It reminds me of a conversation I had with Grandma about boys. It was not long before she died. I had been complaining about my brother, as usual, and telling her how selfish and unhelpful he was. She was a bit dreamy that day and she started murmuring about sons. I remember being confused because she stared out of the window and said, "I have lost two boys." When I asked her what she meant, she looked at me for a second and then changed the subject. I remember it because at the time it gave me a jolt. She was usually so lucid and clear and did not say things she did not mean, but in the last few months of her life she was slipping a bit. Her memory was going. She became forgetful, and would repeat things she'd told me before or not remember what she had been told. I started worrying that her mind was going, and I think she was afraid of going senile. She made jokes about it but I could tell that she worried about it more than she let on.

'Then she made this odd remark, which she never repeated again. It was so strange. It was well known that she had lost a son, my uncle Adrian, who suffocated in a haystack while playing hide and seek as a child, but as far as I knew she had only had two children – Adrian and my mother. I asked my mother about it and she just dismissed it as senility and said that Grandma was probably referring to her two boys, meaning the men in her life – her husband and her son. She said that a lot of women do talk like that.'

'A lot of women do talk like that about men, whatever their relationship is with them,' agreed Will.

'Not Grandmother,' Josie said. 'She just wasn't that type

of woman. I remember thinking that at the time. But what you've just told me about the scandal suddenly makes sense of her remark.'

Josie pictured her grandmother, a beautiful young woman, like the person in those portraits of her painted by Ivo Barnard. In the very first one, she looks over her bare shoulder straight at the viewer, shrewd and provocative at the same time, giving out a strong sexual message while retaining a veneer of reserve. What did that face say? What secrets lay behind those large intelligent eyes then?

Josie smiled at Will. 'It's very romantic, isn't it? She had an affair, probably with someone completely unsuitable, and she found herself pregnant. Then the poor thing had to give up the child and was hauled off to Europe to get away from the unsuitable man and to find a husband thousands of miles away.'

'It must have been scandalous at the time. Sleeping with someone before marriage in those days would have been unheard of in her circles.'

Josie nodded, remembering Blanche with proud affection. 'Grandma was always a rebel. She defied convention, so it was in character.'

'I wonder what happened to the child,' said Will. 'If that is really true, there's some aunt or uncle of yours wandering around this planet.'

'I don't suppose we'll ever know. Certainly I have never heard any reference to anything in my grandmother's papers, and my mother never suggested that anything like that had happened. She always maintained that her mother came to Europe to see the sights, and for no other reason. She thought that Grandma never denied the scandal rumour because she liked to have this mystery attached to her past.'

As they finished off their Chinese food, Josie suddenly

felt upset. 'It seems to me that my grandmother did so much in her life, enjoyed it fully and had wonderful experiences. Yet here I am, aged thirty-five, and I haven't done a tenth of what she did. Apart from my gap year, I've barely travelled, I've been in an unsuitable relationship for too long and remain indecisive about what I should do about it. I'm better educated than she was but what good has that done me? I've got a fairly interesting but low-key job in a poorly paid industry. I don't have the drive that some of my friends have, to apply for bigger and better jobs and increase my salary and stress levels. I just plod along through life, and very little happens. Blanche used to tell me that you have to make things happen in life, and I've always been afraid of that. I prefer to let other people make the decisions and I go along with them.'

Will listened to Josie's forlorn speech and grinned. 'It doesn't always have to be like that.'

Josie sipped her jasmine tea. The flowery aroma spread up her nostrils. 'Clearing out the house has made me think a lot about my life suddenly. I've never really thought about it very much but I've been so aware of what my grandmother and my mother went through, I've been trying to imagine how it would look to someone like me, a descendant, going through my belongings and trying to make sense of my life. And it doesn't amount to much at all. In fact, it's pathetic.' She shrugged her shoulders. 'Besides, at the rate I'm going, there won't be any descendants to go through my belongings, so I shouldn't even be worrying about it.'

'It certainly sounds as though you need a break,' Will said gently. 'You know, clearing out a house when someone has died is bound to be difficult. And your mother only died four months ago.'

Josie looked at him and smiled. 'Yes, it's not so long

ago, I suppose. I'm probably only sounding so gloomy because I've finally had a serious offer for the house. It makes me feel very relieved that I'll be getting the place off my hands at last, but also rather sad that it really is going, along with all its memories and associations. I felt that way when Grandma died and the house in Sussex was sold. I found it very hard to accept that it was no longer in my family and it meant that I could never walk up the drive or play on the tennis court or climb the trees in the park. It wasn't even so long ago – maybe seven years – but I felt I owned it because I had spent so much time there as a child. I have no reason to go to Sussex any more but I did drive down there once a few months after the house was sold, and I felt like a stranger shut out in the cold. I stood in the road by the driveway, and it made me feel choked up to hear the sound of little children running around in the garden. It was almost unbearable. Then a woman came out of the cottage at the end of the drive and greeted me. I didn't tell her what my connection was with the house but she told me that she had been evacuated there briefly as a child during the war, and had recently fulfilled a lifetime's wish to return. She was now the housekeeper and her husband the gardener. It made me feel very excluded.

'I shan't feel quite the same way about the London house, because I was older when we moved there, but I shall feel bereft all the same. It will feel like chopping off a finger or some other part of me.'

Will picked up a final mushroom with his chopsticks and popped it into his mouth. He swallowed and smiled at his cousin. 'I know so little about your family life, Josie,' he said. 'You were always with your grandmother when I saw you. I hardly knew your mother. I know she wasn't very well – at least, not well enough to look after you, but no one ever said exactly what the problem was. Was she mad? Whatever that means. I used to have fantasies that she was like the first Mrs Rochester shut away in the attic, yet whenever I did see her she seemed rather ordinary and mild.'

Josie sighed and fiddled with the uneaten noodles in her bowl. 'I had an unconventional upbringing by all accounts, though at the time it did not seem very strange. It's only looking back now that I see how very odd it was. And of course I only know the details from my grandmother and a little from my mother.'

While Josie described her parents' marriage and her childhood, Will listened with great interest. 'That's all very tough,' he said. 'It must have been sad to feel that you couldn't bring friends home. Did you go to your friends' houses instead?'

Josie shrugged. 'Hardly. I think I always felt guilty about leaving my mother alone, and even when she had married Tony and I was at university, I worried about her all the time. It's probably no coincidence that I bought a flat close to her in Kentish Town when I got my first job and started earning a living.' She sighed. 'In some ways I feel that it's only now, when my mother has died, that I've been liberated and allowed to break free.' She grimaced and shrugged. 'Pathetic, isn't it? It wasn't my mother's fault but that's the way I felt about her. I needed to protect her. Now she's dead and my role has disappeared. It makes me feel adrift and rather lonely. But in lots of ways I've always been a loner. I've had to be. Even with the few boyfriends I've had, I've never let them get very close, for fear of it all going wrong. That way I couldn't be too badly hurt when it didn't work out with them.'

They were feeling stuffed from their meal. They paid the bill and walked out into the night and wandered around Soho and Covent Garden before saying goodbye again. 'Perhaps I'll make a trip to America next year,' she said. 'Once all this is over, I should have some money from the estate, and I'll blow some of it on a holiday.'

Will nodded. 'Perhaps we could do a trip somewhere different – up to New England, or down south even. Let me know what you're planning, and I'll make sure I'm around.'

They said goodbye at Piccadilly Circus tube. Josie watched her cousin go down the station steps and felt a dragging sense of loneliness. She had to do something to her life to make it change course. She could not let it just seep away until she died. Something had to happen.

When she got home to her flat, the red light on the answer machine was blinking. She played back the message. It was a complete surprise. *'Josephine, it's your father, a voice from the past. Will you please telephone me either tonight or tomorrow.'* He added a long-distance telephone number for her to call.

Josie hesitated for a few moments, then bracing herself, she picked up the telephone and began to dial an oddly familiar number. Then she stopped and replaced the receiver. She needed to prepare herself properly; she should not just jump to attention and ring up her father as though nothing had ever happened. No, she had to be cool about this.

She poured herself a glass of cold water from the tap and sat down in the rocking-chair which now graced the sitting-room of her flat. She rocked gently backwards and forwards. It was so comfortable, it was lulling her to sleep. Her father had called her. What on earth could he want? She thought about the conversation with Will about her grandmother, and she remembered suddenly the tiny package she had discovered in the back of this very chair several weeks before. She had a strong feeling that it was connected to her grandmother and some of the matters she and Will had been discussing that evening. Could it offer a clue? In her effort to sort out the house, Josie had completely forgotten about the little packet. Where was it now? Then she remembered having placed it in her grandmother's jewellery box. There it was!

Josie picked up the small envelope, yellow with age, and gently opened it. There inside were the tiny mittens made of white lawn cotton. Around the top were pale blue silk ribbon ties, and across each mitten, in minuscule and exquisite embroidery, was the word 'Cooper'.

Josie stared at these tiny items, turning over the envelope in her hands as she wondered about this find. It looked as though the envelope had been pushed down into the chair, in the crack where the back and the seat met, a long time ago. How many years ago, she wondered? And why were they there?

The envelope had a name written on the front: her heart was racing as she picked up the telephone, all thoughts of her father gone, and called Will at his hotel.

CHAPTER 23

⁓⁓

Savannah, Georgia 1990

Josie and Will arrived in Savannah in the evening, after a flight from New York via Atlanta. The air was pleasant but it had a steamy tropical feel which was unfamiliar to Josie.

After booking into their hotel, they strolled about the wide shaded streets and around the fine squares where large old oaks, magnolias and pines grew. The charm of the houses was inescapable, with their small entrance stoops and recessed doorways with fanlights. The city had been much restored in recent years and parts of it seemed too sanitised and precious to Josie's eyes. But when she let her imagination drift, she could see her grandmother as a young girl in white clothes, walking with her mama down Oglethorpe Avenue, or driving around the leafy squares in her horse and carriage and waving to her friends.

They walked along the waterfront which gave them a sweeping view of the river that had been the reason for the founding of the city by James Oglethorpe in 1733 and had given Savannah its name. He chose well when he decided on the high land above the bluff on a graceful crescent of the river, just fifteen miles from the sea. The city was carefully planned, showing traditions of Georgian England in its compact brick houses, grilled gateways and half-concealed gardens. Encircled by pine woods in those days, and set amid dark moss-curtained live oaks, the city was rarely touched by ice or snow.

'It's strange to be here,' said Josie, 'and to think that I'm walking on streets that my grandmother and great-grandmother walked on years ago. To think that they looked at this same view of the river, or walked across these same squares, with their own thoughts and worries and concerns. And the smell is so wonderful!' She drew in a deep breath, savouring the tang of the salt winds off the water blended with the scent of gardenias, magnolias and luxuriant tropical palmettos, oleanders and azaleas.

Will nodded. 'I always find it hard to imagine what it was like to live in earlier times. Perhaps it's because I'm a lawyer with no imagination, but I'm incapable of putting myself in the shoes of people who thought the world was flat or who could not read. It's a sad failing on my part.'

Josie laughed. 'It is indeed a failing. You should work on it. I always find it a wonderful thought that no matter how sophisticated or educated people are, they still have the same basic needs and feelings. This must have been true throughout history, too. The same but different.'

Josie had flown out to New York three days after handing over the keys of her mother's house to the young couple who had made her feel inadequate. She was full of excitement, brought on by a dramatically quick decision to take up the sabbatical offered to her by her boss. She had negotiated a week's holiday to find an apartment in New York before starting work there.

It was a momentous time in Josie's life. Who knew what would happen in the future? If New York did not work out or if she did not want to return to her old job at the end of it, so be it. She suddenly felt bold and free. She was fed up with her work and her life. She needed a change, and these recent events had forced her to make a decision. With the money from her mother's estate, she could keep afloat for some time. Now was the opportunity to travel and do something with her life. Suddenly the things she had yearned for – a partner and children – did not seem so important. Unlike her friends who were tied down by family responsibilities for the next twenty years or so, she was still free to do what she fancied.

It was Will's call that had set her thinking about what she should do. On his return to New York, Will had started making enquiries about Blanche Hamilton and her family in Savannah. None of the uncles were of any help but one of the cousins had an old family photograph album which showed a picture of a very young Blanche sitting in front of a young black maid who was doing her hair. Someone had thoughtfully captioned it: 'Blanche and Simmy – the second generation of Chambers to come to us.'

Will had then got hold of the Savannah telephone directory and proceeded to call every Chambers in Savannah to ask if they had a Simmy in the family who had been born around 1900. His diligence paid off with the thirteenth call, when a young woman said that her grandmother was called Simmy, and that she had once been a maid to a white family in Duffy Street.

'I should be a detective,' said Will. 'The frustration of finding a trail go cold is more than made up for when you hit gold.'

'You had it easy, though,' replied Josie. 'It just so happened that the family still lived in Savannah and that the old lady is alive. If she were dead, we wouldn't have anything to go on.'

'You never know,' said Will. 'Families usually have their

own oral histories, handed on down from one generation to the next. If Simmy were dead, we might have discovered that she had told her children or grandchildren information relevant to us.'

'Yes, though the danger is that it's second-hand by that time, so already less reliable than if it's from the person who experienced it.'

Will laughed. 'Even when it's first-hand, it's not necess-arily reliable – any lawyer knows that. That's why they say history depends on who's telling the story. Still, it's better than nothing and may give you some more leads.'

Josie shrugged. 'We also don't know how lucid Simmy is going to be. After all, she was born in 1900, just one year after Blanche. She'll be ninety and she may be completely senile.'

'That's not the impression I got from her granddaughter. And remember that old people have very good long-term memories. They can recall their childhoods better than people of our age can.'

'I'm beginning to feel a bit funny about doing this, Will. Even though Grandma is dead, I feel we're snooping into her private life, into something she wanted kept a secret. Perhaps it's wrong to find out what happened.'

Will turned on his cousin with a look of mock disdain. 'Don't tell me that you've come all this way and you're having cold feet about it? Do you think your grandmother is watching you with disapproval? Do you believe she would think you were doing wrong? Whatever we find out, it can't be that bad. Moral standards have changed so much since your grandmother's day that the birth of an illegitimate child – if indeed that is what she had – is hardly going to make you feel anything but sympathy for her.'

Josie shook her head. 'No, I'm not having cold feet. I'm just afraid that we might discover something I don't like.'

'It can only make her more interesting. And I think she would approve of what you're up to. I think she would have done the same. Blanche was never one to hold back from doing what she wanted.'

The Chambers lived in a small brick house on the outskirts of the city. Josie and Will were welcomed by a tall black woman in her early twenties.

'Hi, I'm Louella Chambers,' she said. 'My grandmother is on the back porch.' She led them out through the house to a wooden porch overlooking a small pretty garden. A wizened old woman sat in an armchair in the corner. She was crooked and bent but her eyes were bright and alert as she shook hands with the visitors.

'You're Miss Blanche's daughter, I hear,' she said, her voice cracking in her throat.

'No, her granddaughter,' corrected Josie.

The old lady nodded. 'I get all the generations mixed up nowadays. I can't keep nobody straight – there are too many of them, too. But my how they've done well! That Louella there is at college, studying to be an accountant, and one of my grandsons is in medical school. Going to be a doctor, he is.' She paused and shook her head in wonderment. 'Everything's changed,' she said. 'Time was us black folk couldn't go to college. My grandparents were slaves. Look how far we've come.' She smacked her lips and pulled them over her toothless gums.

She looked up at Josie. 'You come to ask me about Miss Blanche Hamilton, your grandmother. Well, that's a fine thing. Is she still alive?'

Josie sat in a chair next to Simmy. 'No, she died about

seven years ago, sadly. I was very fond of her. You knew
her a long time ago. Do you remember her?'

'Sure I do. I remember the Hamilton family so well. My
mother was the maid there and then I came too. I was
younger than your grandmother by one year. I remember
thinking that we were so close in age but so far apart in every
other way. But that wasn't the way for a maid to think.

'I was a maid in that house until poor Mrs Hamilton died,
of influenza. Then the brothers sold the house and I had to
find other employment. I went to work for a doctor and his
wife then.'

'What do you remember about Blanche?' Josie asked in
a soft coaxing voice.

'What do I remember? Why, she was a beautiful girl with
hair the colour of copper – it was a very unusual colour. She
had the deepest brown eyes, and the finest figure. She had
all the young men interested in her. And she had a laugh, I
remember that laugh – clear as a bell and loud and genuine.
She loved life, and she let you know it.'

Simmy's face was animated as she remembered her life all
those years ago. 'I was her personal maid, so I did everything
for her. I washed her hair and bathed her, and got her clothes
out and dressed her. She wore the prettiest dresses you can
imagine, and was always careful about what she looked like.
Everyone turned to stare at her wherever she went. I was
very proud of her.'

'Do you remember when she left for Europe on her
trip?'

'Of course I do, for that was when my life changed, not
having Miss Blanche to look after any more. But it had
to be. Things like that don't happen in families like hers.'
She corrected herself. 'Or if they do, they have to be
covered up.'

'Things like what?' Josie's heart was beating fast as she felt she was nearing the truth.

Simmy looked at her and then at Will. She looked back at Josie and cackled. 'She had a child. It seemed like the immaculate conception to me because she was a well-behaved and proper lady and would never have done anything improper. At the time, I was as ignorant as a crayfish. I didn't know myself how babies were made, so I just thought it happened on its own.

'At first I noticed that she was putting flesh on, her dresses were tighter and I had to sew in panels to let them out. She never said anything to me, apart from commenting that her clothes were uncomfortable. Then I mentioned what was happening to my mother, who still worked as Mrs Hamilton's maid. My mother waited a few weeks and then had a good look herself when Miss Blanche was being bathed one evening. She told the mistress, and my, did things happen then. Miss Blanche was sent from here. The story they told everyone was that she had gone to a young ladies' academy to perfect her French before going to Europe. I was still naïve and innocent and I had no idea what was happening. Now I know they had to send her away before the baby was visible to avoid any scandal.

'She was away for four months. When she came back she seemed different, quieter and subdued. Not surprising when you think about it, poor child. She spent hours doing embroidery and making what I thought at the time were doll's clothes. Obviously, they were clothes for the baby. Beautiful they were, too. But at least she'd got her figure back, like you do when you're that young. Your body springs back as if nothing had happened. They left for England soon after she returned, she and Mrs Hamilton. Then she came back a year later for her wedding here – her husband must have been your grandfather. I remember him, and his brother who came out for it. I remember them being shocked that there was no drink. They were complaining at the wedding. It was Prohibition, you see, and there was no liquor for those who wanted it, not in public anyhow. They had their honeymoon here in Savannah, and then they returned to England. And Miss Blanche, she never came back.'

'Your memory is astonishing,' said Josie.

'Well, I remember the past better than the present now I'm so old, but it's in the blood,' the old lady grinned. 'It didn't do me much good but my children and grandchildren all have good memories, too. That's why they've done so well.' She cackled. 'Some of them have visited England, you know.'

'Do you know anything more?' asked Will. Do you know which town Blanche was sent to? Or where she stayed?'

Simmy Chambers screwed up her eyes in thought. 'I did know some of those things but I have to think back. I have to let my mind go back to the things my mammy told me and what I can visualise.'

She seemed to go into a trance, rocking gently backwards and forwards in the chair, her eyes half closed. 'I can't quite see it. I can see letters addressed to her sitting on the hall table waiting for the mail man to collect. She went to live with a preacher and his wife, friends of the family I believe, and she had the baby there. She left the child behind. I don't know what happened but she didn't come back with no baby. I always believed that the preacher adopted that baby, but I can't be sure. For some reason I have that idea stuck in my head, but for the life of me, I can't recall the name of the town.'

As Simmy screwed up her face again in frustration, Josie leaned towards her. This was their only chance. If she could not remember the town, then the trail was dead. 'Can you recall the name of the town?' In her head, Josie was praying, please let Simmy know, please let her remember . . .

Simmy's eyes suddenly opened wide. 'Why yes, Vidalia, that was it!' She smiled broadly, revealing her toothless pink gums. 'Vidalia, that's right, where the onions come from, the sweetest onions in the world.'

Josie sat back, relieved. 'Vidalia,' she whispered, 'Vidalia, Georgia.'

Will leaned forward eagerly. 'Simmy, can you remember when all that happened?'

'Why, it was just before Miss Blanche left for Europe, going up to New York first. But it must have been in the spring of 1919.'

Will looked excited. 'Well, we have quite a lot to go on now. I don't suppose you remember the name of that preacher by any chance?'

Simmy shook her head. 'That's gone, if I ever knew it.'

The old lady looked drained. Josie got up and held out her hand. 'You've been very kind.'

Simmy looked up and squinted at her. 'You going to track down that baby, then?'

'I don't know,' said Josie. 'Maybe, if we can.'

Simmy shook her head. 'You be careful. Don't mess up no lives, now.' Then she sighed dreamily. 'I often wondered what happened to Miss Blanche. I'm pleased to meet you and to hear that she was a good grandmother.' She gestured towards Louella, who was watering the flowers in the garden. 'I hope she thinks the same of me when I'm dead and gone.'

'I'm sure she will,' replied Will. 'And thank you.'

The old lady suddenly put her finger to her lips to hush him. 'It's coming back . . . no, it's gone. No, I can't remember the preacher's name but I think it began with "H".'

Outside the house, Josie pulled a package from her bag. 'Well, I think we may be on the right track,' she said. She held out the yellowing envelope with an excited grin.

Will took the envelope and read the name on it again: 'Mrs James Holbrook'. He laughed. 'I think so, too. Vidalia, here we come!'

The next day Josie and Will travelled fifty miles to Vidalia. There, in the public records office, in a leather-bound volume, they found what they wanted. In April 1919, the registration of a male child born to Blanche Hamilton at 25 Oak Drive, Vidalia. In another bound volume, they found a reference three months after the birth to the christening of Cooper Holbrook, son of Mr and Mrs James Holbrook, of 25 Oak Drive.

Afterwards, Josie and Will sat in a coffee-bar and tried to piece together the information they now had.

'So we know she had a baby. We know that she gave him up for adoption by the Holbrooks and that he was subsequently christened Cooper. But can we ever find out what happened to him?' Josie felt frustrated to have got so far and yet still have so many ends to tie up.

'But where do we go from here?' Josie looked up to find Will staring at her with a seriousness she had never seen before. 'What's wrong?'

Will quickly relaxed. 'Nothing's wrong.'

'Why were you looking at me like that?'

Will shrugged off her question with a sheepish smile. 'Now,' he said, 'we can't stop here. It's amazing to have found out so much already, but I'll tell you what I want to do next . . .'

Back in the library, he strolled over to the librarian and

spoke to her. Moments later he returned with a large leather-bound volume. 'This is the index for the local paper for the 1930s. If the baby was born in 1919, then he will be doing things of note during this time.' He grinned. 'And in small towns like this, the newspapers found everything newsworthy. Provided the Holbrooks didn't move away from Vidalia, there's bound to be some entry for them.'

Indeed there were, hundreds of them.

'It's hopeless. It'll take all day,' murmured Josie, suddenly feeling rather tired of their quest.

'I'll look in the local telephone directory to see if there's a Cooper Holbrook listed.'

The telephone directories were on the far wall. Will flicked through the pages and studied them for a few minutes before returning, shaking his head. 'There's every other Holbrook but no Cooper, not even a C Holbrook.'

He paused. Then his face lit up. 'Hang on a minute, I've had an idea.' He went back over to the librarian and engaged her in conversation. Josie watched as the two of them talked with great enthusiasm for a good ten minutes. The librarian was smiling and nodding her head, and gesticulating. Soon Will came back, grinning.

'There's nothing like a small town to tell you everything. People tend not to move very far away from where they grew up. The librarian is about fifty so I reckoned if she's local, she'll know the name Holbrook, since it's clearly a well-known local name. And she certainly does. It turns out her son was married to a Holbrook, until they got divorced, and she says there are lots of branches of the family still here.'

'What about Cooper Holbrook? Did you ask about him?'

'I did.' Will smirked. 'You're never going to believe this. Cooper Holbrook is a doctor and he lives and works in Savannah. The librarian thought he had probably retired by now as he must be seventy or so. We'll be able to find him in the Savannah telephone book, which is on the shelf over there. You look.'

Josie was trembling with excitement as she picked up the heavy directory and placed it on the table. Opening to the relevant page, she ran her finger down the entries for Holbrook. And there, in block letters, was Cooper Holbrook, MD, and his address was Oglethorpe Avenue.

'We probably walked past his house the other day. We may even have passed him on the street or sat next to him in a coffee shop.'

'Right, back we go to Savannah,' said Josie. 'Perhaps I should tell Dr Holbrook that I've got some property that belongs to him.'

CHAPTER 24

Savannah, Georgia

Dr Cooper Holbrook's house was one of the largest on Oglethorpe Avenue. Josie and Will walked past it several times, peering up at the tall windows with their ornate iron guards. There was a polished copper plate fixed on the delicate iron railings next to the gate engraved with the words: Cooper Holbrook, MD.

'Now what?' Josie stopped and turned back to look at the house. 'What do we do now?' They had discussed their plans the night before but had come to no decision about how to proceed.

'Ring the doorbell and introduce yourself,' Will said. 'I believe in being direct.'

'Introduce myself as what?' Josie grimaced. 'I can't just march in and introduce myself as his niece. You can't do that to people. After all, he might not even know that he's been adopted.'

Will nodded. 'Yeah, you're right. Don't want to give the guy a heart attack. You might get sued.'

As the two of them stood on the street looking up at the house and discussing what to do next, an elderly man walked past them carrying a large brown paper-bag in his arms. He looked at the young couple in the street and then, to Josie's surprise, turned into the path of the house. He looked at her again and stopped. 'Can I help you?' he asked in a soft Southern drawl. 'You look in need of some guidance, ma'am.'

Josie shook her head quickly and blushed. 'Oh, no,' she said, 'we're okay. We're just admiring your house. It's very handsome.'

The man smiled and looked up at his home. 'Yes, ma'am. It's the best in the street,' he said proudly. 'It's always been looked after, this house, unlike many others in this town. And just down the street is the house where our poet laureate, Conrad Aiken, lived. The house next door was where his parents lived. When he was a boy, he witnessed his father shoot his mother and then shoot himself.'

He paused again. 'Say, where're you from? Are you from Canada?'

Josie smiled. 'No, I'm from England, and my cousin here is from New York.'

Cooper Holbrook narrowed his eyes to scrutinise Will carefully. 'A Yankee, eh?'

Will nodded deferentially. 'That's right, sir. Born and bred in New York.'

'Did you go to school there, too?' Cooper eyed him.

'No, I went to school in Cambridge. Harvard Law School.'

The man threw back his head and laughed. 'I'm a Harvard man myself,' he said. 'Harvard medical school. But a long time ago now.'

'Do you go north much?' asked Will.

Cooper shook his head. 'Not as much as I'd like to,' he said. 'We used to go every year to New York and New England. I've always loved it there. But in recent years we've been trying out new places before we get too old to travel far. This year we're going to England.' He looked at

Josie. 'I haven't been to England for about ten years. I love it.
And I just love hearing that accent. It sounds so educated.'

'Do you come from Savannah?' Will wanted to keep the
dialogue going.

Cooper shook his head. 'No, I'm from Vidalia originally
but I've lived in Savannah for some fifty years – all my
adult life.'

He looked at the young pair. 'Hey, how would you like
to come in and have something to drink? My wife made
some lemonade this morning and I'm sure you would like
something to quench your thirst on a hot day like this. And
you're welcome to see around the house, if houses are what
you're interested in.'

He led them up the steps and through the front door into a
cool vaulted entrance hall. This opened into a more spacious
one with marble floors, where, at one side, a mahogany
staircase curved its graceful way to the upper level. Cooper
Holbrook showed them into the room on the left. 'This is
the north parlour,' he said and chuckled. 'Make yourselves
at home and I'll find something to drink.' He disappeared
down the back stairs to the kitchen below.

Josie and Will looked at each other and winked. Josie
could hardly believe that they had found their way there.

A few minutes later Cooper appeared carrying a silver
tray with a glass jug filled with lemonade and three glass
tumblers. 'It's a shame my wife's not here,' he said. 'She
loves to meet new people, and especially people who come
from different places.' He set the tray down on the side-table
and filled each glass with the cloudy liquid.

So Josie spent the afternoon in the company of her uncle,
Cooper Holbrook. He was a delightful old man, full of
stories and anecdotes but also very interested in his young
visitors. He wanted to know all about Josie: where she

was raised, where she had been to school, what she did for a living.

Then he told them about his upbringing, adopted by a preacher and his wife who had had two daughters already but wanted another child. He told them that he and his wife had three children of their own but then adopted two, and he himself had been very involved in the seventies with the campaign to give adopted children the right to search for their birth mothers.

'Did you search for yours?' Josie asked tentatively.

Cooper shook his head. 'No. You know, my dear, I never felt a desire to make contact with my birth mother, whoever she was. My parents were always very good to me. They were kind people and brought me up well. They were also educated and wanted me to be educated as well.

'Of course, that doesn't mean that I didn't wonder about the woman who gave birth to me – and I still do. I wonder about those things, who she was, what she looked like, what her circumstances were, and what she did for the rest of her life after giving me up. Every adopted child has such thoughts and questions. But I never rejected my parents. I always felt they were mine and I was theirs. I guess I was born with a sunny disposition. I am blessed with an optimistic and happy personality. And I've always been more outgoing than my parents.'

He sat back in his chair. 'In that respect I was so different from them. I have always liked to think that my extrovert nature was my mother's gift to me. My natural inclination has always been to be happy, and my parents developed that in me to the full.'

Watching and listening to Cooper talk, Josie suddenly saw her grandmother in his keen brown eyes and his engaging manner. She recognised her grandmother in his face and mannerisms. When he pulled out some photographs of himself as a young man, she saw that he looked even more like her as she appeared in Ivo's paintings. 'You wouldn't know it now,' he said, running his hand over the thick white hair on his head, 'but I had copper-coloured hair when I was a young man. "Copper", I was known as. Yes, all the young ladies liked my hair in those days,' he added with a wink.

Then he paused and looked thoughtfully at Josie as if he were making up his mind about something. 'My mother's main gift was my sunny disposition but I do have something she left for me.'

He pulled himself to his feet and shuffled out of the room. Moments later he was back. He handed a small white cardboard box to Josie and sat down to watch her open it.

Inside, a small ring lay on a soft bed of cotton wool. It had a gold setting and on a bright blue background the classical figure of a woman in ivory.

'It's Wedgwood: English, like you,' chuckled Cooper.

Josie held the ring up in her fingers. As she handed it to Will, he leaned towards her and whispered, 'Are you all right? You've gone very pale.'

Josie blinked and shook her head. 'No, yes, I'm fine, thank you,' she said quickly. 'I'm just a bit hot, that's all. It's a lovely ring, isn't it?'

Cooper nodded. 'My parents gave it to me on my twenty-first birthday. Apparently it was the only item they had that belonged to my mother. They always said that they didn't know her and that she moved out of Georgia after I was born. I often thought that they were not telling me the whole truth. I always had a feeling that they did know who she was or that they certainly knew more than they were prepared to let on.

'When they gave me this ring, I knew that she had been

well-born, since this is an expensive piece of jewellery. But by that time, I was in medical school and too busy thinking of my career to wonder too much about my past. After all, I had spent my life up to then coming to terms with the fact that I was different from most of my friends but had finally accepted the view of my parents that I was somehow special because they had chosen to have me and bring me up as their son. By that time, I was not going to upset them by suddenly trying to find out more about the person who had given me up at birth.

'Anyway, I have kept the ring carefully and occasionally, when I am in a certain mood, I will get it out and hold it while I let my mind run free, when I imagine this person who gave birth to me. I wonder what sort of woman she was, what she looked like and what she did with the rest of her life. And, of course, I wonder about my father, and hope that maybe he and my mother had loved each other, that I was a product of love, and that maybe they had managed to find a life together, away from the forces that compelled her to give up her baby.'

Listening to Cooper talk and watching his intelligent bright brown eyes, just like her grandmother's, Josie longed to tell him the truth, to tell him that she knew something about his unknown mother, who she was, what she did. She longed to tell him that she was a much loved and wonderful person – like him – and that he did inherit that extraordinary zest for life from her. But she knew that she should not.

Cooper tossed his head and sniffed. 'Of course, I know it's all nonsense. By the time you get to my age, you know that the chances of that being the case are slim. My poor mother was probably married off by her family to a respectable man for whom she bore four children and she took her secret with her to her grave. And she never had contact with my father again. End of story.'

He topped up their glasses with the tangy lemonade.

'Ah well,' he sighed. 'We all have to make the most of what we have and not dwell on what we don't have. Would you like to see pictures of my family? As I said, I have five children and now, five grandchildren.' Reaching behind him, he picked up a framed photograph of a family group. 'This was taken last Christmas. We all managed to get together for the first time in years.'

Cooper went over the group in the photograph, pointing to each in turn, giving each person's name and their relation to him. 'And this is my son, Rick. He's a doctor, too. This is his wife, Janey, who's a lawyer. They've got three kids. They live right here in Savannah, but they've just bought a weekend house on Savannah Beach. It's a house I've always had my eye on – right on the end of the creek, overlooking the ocean. It belonged to one family for years – they bought it just after the war in forty-five. It just came on the market last year, and Rick snapped it up immediately.

'You should go out to the Savannah Beach,' he said, looking at Josie. 'It's an interesting place, past Fort Pulaski. That's worth seeing, and you feel you're on the edge of the world there.'

Will nodded in agreement. 'There used to be a family house on Savannah Beach,' he said. 'My cousin Jasper used to tell me about it, and I've seen pictures. It was built by his uncle at the turn of the century, and then passed to him. It was sold after he died. I wonder if it's the same one. I think it was on the edge of a creek.'

'What was your family name? Perhaps it is the same house.'

'Hamilton. He was called Jasper Hamilton, but I don't know how much time he spent there. He had moved up north as a young man.'

Cooper shook his head. 'No, it doesn't mean anything to me. But you have all the more reason to take a trip to the beach.'

He put down his glass and pulled himself to his feet. 'Now, I'm afraid I have to say goodbye to you young things. It's time for my nap. I'm not the man I was and I have to conserve my energy.'

Josie and Will rose to their feet and prepared to leave.

'My wife and I have booked a trip to Europe next month,' Cooper said. 'We're going to London and Paris, on that new train. Perhaps we could give you a call and take you out to a meal in London, if you're there.'

'I'd like that,' said Josie, pulling out a pen and paper. 'Please do.' She liked this intelligent, kind old man. 'I'll give you my phone number, and you must get in touch.'

They left the house and walked down Oglethorpe Avenue. 'Well, that was certainly worth it,' said Josie. 'What a wonderful man.'

'He's your relation and he doesn't know it,' said Will.

'Yes, it's an odd feeling. It's as if we've been spying on him, or as if we've got something on him, which I suppose we have. You know that ring? Well, I'm not certain, but I think I've seen that jewellery before, that exact design.'

'I suppose that wouldn't be surprising, if Blanche gave it to him,' said Will.

'My grandmother had a pair of earrings and a brooch in that same Wedgwood design, I'm sure. It was sky-blue and had a classical woman in ivory. I think she said they were a gift from her mother's cousin, Henrietta, on her sixteenth birthday. Henrietta also had some scandal behind her but I have no idea what it was.'

Will tossed his head casually. 'Perhaps we should try and find out what that was, too.'

'Some chance!' laughed Josie. 'It's amazing that we've got this far.' She felt quite exhilarated. It had been thrilling to have tracked down this relation, to have discovered much of her grandmother's secret history. But at the same time she felt a little uneasy about deceiving her relative – he seemed like such a nice old man. But what could she do? Telling him the truth could do untold damage, upset his life for ever.

Will looked thoughtful. 'Are you sure about that ring? Doesn't most Wedgwood look like that?'

Josie shrugged. 'Maybe, but it is exactly the same as the earrings and brooch my grandmother wore most of the time. My mother sold them after her death but I think I have photographs which show her wearing them.'

Will took her hand and squeezed it. 'I wish you weren't going home,' he said quietly.

Josie looked at him in surprise. He was staring intently at her.

'I really enjoy being with you,' he said. He let go of her hand and stepped back. He looked suddenly sheepish and awkward.

'So, are we going to Savannah Beach?' he said quickly.

Josie looked up at him, excitement shining in her eyes. 'Of course,' she said. 'My grandparents spent their wedding night there.'

The next morning they drove to Savannah Beach, past Fort Pulaski, over the bridge to Tybee Island and up the main drag to the long white beach at the end.

The sun was hot but the warm blustery wind blowing off

the tossing blue water felt cool on their faces. The hot sand forced them to replace the sandals they had kicked off in a hurry. They walked along the beach and down to the end where it turned into the creek. A row of old wooden houses with first-floor balconies looked out across the creek. Here the water was still and safe. Children stood on the sand with buckets and chicken-necks on the end of a line of string. They watched the children dangling the strings in the water, then suddenly yanking them out, often with a blue crab hanging on to the chicken neck. With shrieks of laughter, they held the crab over the bucket and banged it against the side until the fierce crustacean let go to drop into the pile of other angry captives below.

'Catching blue crabs. My grandmother used to do that. She would describe how they did it, often dressed to the nines in spotless white dresses which would get soaked with sea-water.' Josie looked around her, imagining her grandmother as a small child running along this very beach, carrying a bucket full of snapping blue crabs which the cook would boil up for supper.

'That's the place,' she said quietly, pointing to the house at the end of the beach. It was old and weather-beaten, with a certain grand elegance, and surrounded by flowering shrubs. 'My grandparents spent their honeymoon here,' she said. Her thoughts drifted back seventy years as she imagined her grandmother as a young bride with her new English husband. She imagined her in her elegant clothes leaning out over the balcony rail with the evening sun casting a pink light on her face and making her skin glow with passion.

Josie felt a strange surge of feeling, as though she were in some special place, connected with her history, her past, linking her with the generations of people who had come before her, before Blanche and before Blanche's grandmother. It

made her suddenly feel both important and insignificant.
She had a place here. She was more than just a tourist. She
felt she was a part of it. And the house in an extraordinary
coincidence had been bought by Cooper's son to live in.
Cooper's son, who was Blanche's grandchild, just as she
was. He was Josie's own half-cousin. So although they did
not know it, Cooper's family would be walking on the same
floorboards as their own ancestors. There was something
wonderful about that, given the sad chapter of their personal
history.

'What are you thinking? You look sad.'

Will's question made Josie start. 'Oh, I'm not sad,' she
said.

'But you have tears in your eyes.'

Josie shook her head and laughed. 'I just find it so moving
to be here and to think of everybody in the past.'

'Well, now we know what happened to Blanche,' said
Will, 'and what happened to her son. It's a happy ending.
She would have been pleased to know that this child she
gave up had a full and happy life.'

The two turned to look out at the ocean. A ship was passing
by on the horizon. The shallow waves lapped at the white
sand and the sea breeze rustled their hair. It seemed perfectly
natural when Will placed his arm around Josie's shoulders
and pulled her to him. Josie felt her grandmother's spirit in
her veins as she leaned towards her cousin. This relationship
had been building up over the last few days. She had an
intense feeling for Will, which she knew was returned.
'We've found out a lot, haven't we? In three days we've
added a whole chapter to our family history.'

Will placed his finger under her chin and pulled her
face up towards him. 'We've learned other things, too,' he
whispered, placing his dry lips on hers. 'I've always liked

you, Josie, all my life I've liked you. And now I realise I love you. I want you to come and live with me here in America.'

Josie smiled nervously. 'I don't know. It'll be strange to come back to where it all began for my grandmother. But I *will* come and work in New York for a bit. I'd be crazy not to take up the opportunity.' She turned to him and sighed. 'And we'll see how it goes . . .'

They walked along the beach for a while, hand in hand. 'We know some of Blanche's story, but there is still so much we don't know – what really happened. How did she get pregnant? And with whom? These are not the things recorded in newspapers or record offices, and unless the details are reported within the family, they are lost for ever. She never talked about it, so no one can know. Or if they did, they would not be alive now to tell the tale.'

'Or they would tell it wrong, get the facts wrong or exaggerate,' said Will. 'Still, we haven't done badly.'

'No, we haven't,' Josie leaned against Will's strong body. 'I've learned a lot of things, I think, over the past few weeks.'

The seagulls flew around them, giving out their shrill cries, and diving for fish in the deep water. Josie felt a wonderful sense of freedom as she watched the birds in the sky. For all the sadness of her mother's death and the weeks that followed, she now felt that the shackles of her family history had fallen away. She was set free to embark on a voyage for the rest of her days, to seek excitement, to enjoy what the world had to offer. If it worked out with Will, that would be fine, but she was not going to risk losing the great friendship they had. She knew now, as clearly as possible, that what she yearned for and needed was not a man, it was the courage to live her life to the full. And she felt she had at last reached the point when she could do that.

CHAPTER 25

Sussex, 1990

As Josie turned the car off the Midhurst road towards Graffham, she felt a lump rise in her throat. A cocktail of feelings seemed to flood through her – feelings of nostalgia, sadness and loss. As she drove on, they became stronger. The road was astonishingly familiar. She felt she knew every bump and bend, though there were some new houses in Selham, and the big house on the corner had its entire garden exposed where before it had been hidden from the road by a line of trees. No doubt they had been lost in the big storm of 1987, after Josie's grandmother had died, and she no longer had any reason to come down to this part of the world.

She drove on down the long stretch of road and round the bend and on up the hill towards Graffham. At the drive of Avery Hall she stopped the car and got out. She had not planned to do this at all. She had intended to avoid the house but she had found it impossible to stay away.

The air was cool and fresh in her nostrils and a deliciously familiar smell of pine needles and leaf mould tingled her nose. She took a mouthful of this air and breathed out slowly. This had not changed.

She hovered in the driveway, looking up at the big house

at the top of the hill. The place looked different. There was a smart new front door and what looked like a conservatory built on the south side of the house facing the Downs. The garden had been radically changed, with vast areas now paved with York stone and pots full of bright red pelargoniums. All her grandmother's herbaceous borders seemed to have gone. Now it was all lawn – much easier to look after.

Josie felt a sadness dragging her down, and she knew it was time to leave. This was not why she had come. Climbing back into the car, she drove back half a mile and then turned up a small dirt track where a sign pointed to Fox Cottage.

The car shook and rattled over the bumps. There were deep ruts which made it difficult to steer. Not wanting to risk damaging the vehicle, Josie pulled the car over to the side and got out. She would walk the rest of the way.

Frank Knight opened the door moments after she knocked, almost as if he had been waiting behind it. Two large black labradors rushed at her, wagging their tails and wiggling their haunches at her in greeting.

Her father was as she remembered him, but older. His hair was grey but still thick and curly, his eyes dark, almost black.

'Hello,' Josie said cautiously. But she was relieved to see him smiling. He seemed pleased to see her but there was also a look of uncertainty in his face.

'Josie!' He put his arms around her and hugged her. 'I'm so glad you came. Come on in, now. I've got a fire going because it's still rather cold, and it makes the place more friendly.'

He ushered her into the small sitting-room at the back of the house. French windows looked out on to a lawn cleverly landscaped to lead the eye into the mysterious darkness of the woods beyond.

'I'm sure I know this house. I'm sure I've been here before,' she said. 'There's something really familiar about it. Either that or I'm having a strong case of déjà vu.'

'An old man lived here a long time ago, a painter. He died, oh, twenty years ago. The house fell into disrepair and was just a ruin when I bought it,' replied Frank. 'It doesn't take long for nature to take over if left to her own devices.'

Josie's thoughts went back twenty-five years or more. 'The painter. Ivo Barnard. Of course! I used to come here with Grandma,' she murmured, 'but we always walked through the woods, so I never knew how you got to it from the road.'

'Ivo? I didn't know you met him?'

Josie looked up sharply. 'Why should you know? There're lots of things you don't know about me.'

As she said it, she wished she had not. She had not come here to pick a fight, she reminded herself. The contact alone had been a surprise, for she had seen little of her father over the whole of her life. She had learned long ago not to care.

'Can I get you a drink?' He ordered the two excited dogs into their baskets and opened the door of the corner cupboard.

Josie sat in a comfortable armchair and accepted the glass of sherry. Her father sat down opposite her. A fluffy black and white cat walked into the room and leaped gracefully into his lap, where he stroked it gently.

'I'm very pleased you've come,' he said.

Josie stared at the cat purring blissfully on her father's lap, and said nothing.

'I'm glad you responded to my note. I was worried when you didn't return my telephone call, but then I suppose it was silly of me not to write first. I wanted to see you because believe it or not . . .' He paused and then went on, 'I want to try to make up for my failings in the past.'

Josie stared at the floor. Her eyes flicked from the rug to the fireplace and round. Her heart was beating hard as she waited for her father to say more.

'I was a terrible father to you.' He paused. 'I'll correct that. I was never a father to you, and you have every reason to hate me. That's why I'm touched that you've come, because it does suggest that not everything is lost, something remains for me.'

Now Josie looked at him.

Frank shrugged. 'Of course, you might only have come because you felt nothing but hate for me – and you would have reason for that, too . . .' He stopped, then went on, 'I'm seventy years old and I have to make amends. For the past few years I've been living in this house. When I retired from the City firm I worked for, I came here and started doing voluntary work in the local law centre in Chichester. Recently I've begun to realise how selfish I've been. I treated your poor mother like dirt. I grew up an angry and greedy young man and took everything out on her.'

'My mother had a happy marriage in the end,' said Josie, 'she doesn't need your belated regrets now.'

'No, of course not,' said Frank, 'and I'm not trying to excuse or explain myself in any way. I just wanted to say sorry to you.'

Josie did not know what to say. She sipped her sherry and stared out of the window, praying that the tears pricking her eyes were not going to flow.

Her father continued, 'I grew up longing to be rich. My parents were servants, always working for rich people. They accepted their position in life, but I could not. I thought that if you had riches you could be as happy as you chose to be.

My ambition overrode everything. I married your mother, a rich woman, and spent years wanting to make a fortune as fast as I could. When I couldn't get accepted in any barristers' chambers I was so angry because no matter how much money my wife had, it became evident that I simply hadn't come from the right background. I began to gamble and went through much of your mother's money, I'm ashamed to say. Eventually, after your mother and I divorced, I went on to do very well in a City law firm, but I never quite got over that original failure.

'It's the experience of living down here and giving my services free to the law centre that has made me realise how much I've wasted my life. I feel saddled with huge regrets that I did not do this sort of thing earlier. Instead of spending years trying to turn myself into someone I was not, I should have used my talents and skills to help people like my parents – honest hard-working people who never question the world, and then find they haven't the means to fight the establishment when it turns on them. I deserted them to pursue my own interests. I deserted my own parents, too. Soon after I married your mother, they moved away from Avery Hall. I think they found the situation too difficult to cope with, and I had less and less time for them. I'm ashamed to say that I was ashamed of them. They were good, decent people but I rejected them. By the time I was mature enough to see them for what they were, it was too late: they were dead.'

He sighed deeply and was silent for a few moments. Josie saw how old he looked. And tired. She almost felt sorrow for him, but then she reminded herself that his behaviour had deprived her not only of a father but a set of grandparents, too, and her feelings hardened again.

Frank continued. 'You know, Josie, old age changes one.

When you're young all you do is look forward and strive for something new, something you haven't attained. When you get to my age, you look back a lot, whether you like it or not. And the regrets grow.'

Josie looked at her father with steady eyes. 'That must depend a little bit on how much you have to regret.'

The sarcasm was not lost on Frank. He nodded. 'Of course,' he said quietly. 'I can't ask you to forgive me for being such a bad father. Or I can, but I don't think that would be fair on you. What I wanted to say to you is that I am sorry and that I hope that we shall have some contact from now on. You and Jamie are my only family. Jamie will have nothing to do with me, though I think he might if it weren't for that wife of his. I haven't been able to see my grandchildren, which I regret. I deserted my own children and now, when I am mellowed and wishing to act like a grandfather, it's not possible.'

Josie raised her eyebrows. 'Well, I can't help you there,' she said sharply, 'I have no children.'

'No, but you have yourself. We could begin to see each other. I would like to make up in any way I can.'

Josie contained the anger building up inside her. What she was about to say gave her power enough. 'Well, it won't be possible,' she said quietly, 'because I'm moving to the States for a while. I've been offered a sabbatical to work in the American branch of the company I work for, so I'm leaving England for the time being. And who knows about the future?'

Frank looked surprised and then his face almost crumpled with disappointment. But he kept his composure. 'Congratulations,' he said. 'Well, you do have American blood in your veins, so it seems right.'

Josie nodded. 'It does seem right. I have a work visa for a

year, and after that, we'll see . . .' She did not tell him that
Will had urged her to marry him. She wanted to wait, to see
if it all worked out first.

They ate a lunch of cold chicken and salad followed by
cheese. Josie told her father about her recent trip to Savannah
and what she had discovered about Blanche's life before she
came to England.

Frank listened with great interest. After their coffee,
he said, 'Come with me, I have something that might
interest you.'

He led her out across the garden towards an outbuilding.

'I remember this. It was Ivo's studio, where he used to
paint.' Josie's memory was vivid.

'That's right. I use it as my own retreat, with no phone or
anything to distract me. I sit here and read for hours.'

Frank unlocked the door and ushered his daughter into the
bright room which looked out across the field towards the
Downs. There was a small chest of drawers pushed against
the far wall. Frank pulled open the bottom drawer. 'After
your trip to Savannah, I think you should have this.' He
pulled out a large envelope and emptied its contents on the
floor. Josie knelt down to pick her way through a small pile
of photographs. She was amazed. There were photographs of
her mother as a young woman looking into the camera with
bright sparkling eyes, and smiling, and many photographs of
Jamie and Josie herself as babies and young children. There
were photographs of Blanche holding the grandchildren, and
several of Blanche and Augustus in the early years of their
marriage.

'You've kept all of these?' Josie murmured.

'You sound surprised,' said Frank.

Josie bit her lip and nodded. 'Yes, I didn't think you ever
thought about any of us.'

Frank reached out and squeezed Josie's shoulder. She wanted to pull away but she did not.

'Believe me, I did think about you,' said Frank. Then he leaned down and picked out a large mounted photograph at the bottom of the pile. 'It will mean more to you than it does to me, now that you're the family historian.' He handed her the stiff board.

Tears pricked Josie's eyes as she peered down at the faded grey photograph. It was of a large group of people of all ages, posed in a garden with an enormous house in the background. On the bottom there was some writing in faded blue ink: 'Jasper's 50th birthday party. Amagansett, Long Island, 1919'.

'Thank you,' she said.

Frank smiled. 'Now, look at these, too.' He held up a series of photographs of paintings.

'That's Grandma,' she said. 'They're all of her.'

'That's right. All painted ten years apart. The dates have been written on the back. They run from her twenties to her sixties.'

Josie picked one up and turned it round to look on the back. 'July 1939. Just before the war began.'

Frank looked at it and nodded. 'That's how I remember your grandmother, Mrs Champion to me, of course. As a boy, that's what she looked like. Memories from childhood seem to be more vivid than anything else, though obviously I had more dealings with her later, when I married your mother.'

Josie picked up another photograph. 'This must have been the last. She's beginning to show her age there, but she's still looking as if she's got a lot of life in her. Her eyes are so lively.'

'You have the same eyes.'

Josie looked up sharply, surprised by the gentleness in her father's voice. For the first time, she felt a stirring of tenderness nudging its way up through the protective layers of anger. 'Do you think so?'

Frank nodded. 'I do think so. You look very like her. Much more than your mother did. You have the same eyes but also the same shape face and similar physique. Hasn't anyone ever said that to you before?'

Josie shook her head. 'No.'

'Well, perhaps you've grown to look like her over the years. That happens, too.'

They walked out into the garden and down to the gate that led out into the wood. A squirrel was hopping about in the undergrowth. When it heard them, it stopped and listened.

Then a remarkable thing happened. It turned and looked at them. Then it bounded over to Frank and ran up his leg, resting on his hip.

Frank laughed and pulled a nut out of his pocket. 'Hello, there.' He held the nut out for the squirrel, which grabbed it in its mouth and ran down to the ground where it sat nibbling at the nut.

Josie watched in amazement. 'Mum always said that you had an almost magical effect on animals, but I never quite knew what she meant.'

Frank smiled. 'I don't know what it is. Whether it's my smell or manner, something they sense in me. I've always had it. I should have put it to good use in some way. It's been good for me. I have never had any friends, but animals have liked me even if humans haven't.'

Josie looked at her father and felt that perhaps she could form a bond with this man after all. On her terms, she thought it was possible. He had neglected her all her life but now he wanted to be friends. She had a choice. Either she could seethe about the past or she could let it go, pack it into a chest with all her childhood things and put it in the attic. She was fairly sure about what she would do.

She left Sussex with her spirits high. What she had thought was going to be a difficult and confrontational meeting had turned out to be, potentially, an additional dimension to her life.

When she got back to London there was a message on her answer machine from Cooper Holbrook, saying that he and his wife were in London, staying in a hotel in South Kensington, and that he had taken her at her word and called her as she had told him to. They would very much like to come and take her out to dinner.

Josie rang Cooper at his hotel and they arranged to meet later that week.

Tired from her day and her trip to visit her father, Josie poured herself a glass of wine and settled into the rocking-chair. The quiet rocking soon made her relax. She pulled out the photograph her father had given her to have a closer look. It was strange to feel that this photograph had extra value to her. It was of her mother's ancestors but given to her by her father – the only gift she had ever received from him.

Now she could scrutinise the picture closely. Someone had been very diligent and written down the names of everyone in the group, though of course she did not know many of them. She recognised a very young Blanche smiling confidently into the camera. Her thick hair was piled up on her head and she wore a delicate costume in white. Other names were listed: 'Henry, Gilbert, Richard, Ellie, Harriet, Nancy, Rose'.

Rose, Blanche's mother, Josie recognised from other photos that Blanche had had on her dressing-table. John, Jackson, Eugene, Albert, Leonard. Young men, whose names were vaguely familiar. From their ages, they must be Blanche's brothers, or cousins. There were some more uncles – Randolph, Francis, Jasper, Alexander, Hayward.

Josie's eyes flicked past Hayward and then back again. She stared hard at the image. He looked very like Blanche, too, a male version, as Cooper had been. In fact, he looked just like Cooper! Josie squinted at the print again. It was an extraordinary likeness! How familiar he looked! It was very like the photograph Cooper had shown her of himself as a young man in his Army uniform. Blanche's genes had been passed on to Cooper. You cannot escape the genes. They just go on for generation after generation. For all she knew, she herself looked like one of her ancestors living in the fifteenth century or the Middle Ages. It was thrilling to think about it but also so frustrating never to know.

Josie hugged the photo to her chest. How much she wanted to show it to Cooper, just as she wanted to show him the mittens which were rightfully his! He would be fascinated and delighted by the coincidence of his son buying the house that had belonged to her family. But if she showed him the picture, would he recognise the family likeness?

It was an exciting secret, but was it fair to share it? She had come to the end of one period of her life and was about to start another. This was her choice. If she told Cooper the truth, or let him deduce it, it could change his life for ever, and not necessarily for the better. He was an old man who had made a good life for himself and his family. It would be wrong for her to march in and shake it all up.

But she did not put the photograph away. Instead she placed it on the table, against the wall, and sat back in the rocking-chair, staring at it. She would think about it in the morning. The faces of those people frozen in the photographic image spun around in her head. What were they like? What did Blanche think of them? What did they do?

Tomorrow she would have to begin to sort out the flat, which she was letting to a recently divorced friend who needed a place to live. As she thought about having to pack away her life before starting on a new one, she considered how sad it was that she would never know what had really happened to Blanche. She had discovered an enormous amount, and had been unusually lucky in finding leads. But one mystery would always remain – the circumstances that led to the pregnancy. Josie liked to think that it was a wonderfully romantic story involving a passionate affair which ended with a forced parting and exile to Europe. That would be fitting for Blanche, the woman who had always believed in going with your heart. It had to be something like that.

And she would be proud of Josie now for choosing to follow her own heart and move to America. Even if it did not work out with Will, she knew it was the right thing to do, and that she would have had her grandmother's approval.

BLANCHE

CHAPTER 26

❦

Long Island, 1919

Uncle Jasper's summer house in Amagansett was set on the rise of a hill looking out over the Atlantic Ocean. It was enormous, even by Long Island standards. He had had it built fifteen years before just after he had been made a partner in his law firm. Black, white and red, it was built on a Chinese theme, to look like a massive pagoda. With twenty bedrooms and set in three acres of garden, it was the perfect setting for the weekend house parties Jasper liked to hold for his New York friends and colleagues. It was equally perfect to house his entire family for the weekend of his fiftieth birthday.

Twenty-year-old Blanche was loving every minute of her stay. She had arrived in New York earlier in the week with her mother on the ship from Savannah, and then stayed for two nights at the Hotel Pierre in Manhattan, where they shopped at Bloomingdale's and Lord & Taylor and saw a show on Broadway, before taking the train out to East Hampton, where they were met by her Uncle Jasper and various excited young cousins.

Blanche had been to Jasper's house on Long Island a couple of times before, and had enjoyed it each time. The carefully tended garden ran down to the beach, so in order to reach it all one had to do was step through the small wooden

gate at the end. Blanche braved the cold Atlantic Ocean many
times a day, plunging into the water like an enthusiastic seal.
The temperature of the water was several degrees lower than
she was used to in Savannah, but the air was hot and the
huge crashing waves were much more exciting than those
that lapped the Savannah Beach. With her uncles, she could
spend hours body surfing – swimming fast in front of a wave
until it caught up with her and swept her along, throwing her
up like the Little Mermaid on the sandy shore. She learned to
get the timing perfect. A few seconds out and the wave could
come crashing down on top of her, spinning her round and
dragging her down in the undertow to leave her scraped and
mauled by the rough sand and in danger of being pounded
by the next wave.

During the day the beach was full of people enjoying the
heat of the summer, sitting in deckchairs, lying on towels,
dogs chasing balls, children making sandcastles. Then in the
evenings, when the crowds had collected their belongings
and returned to their homes and beach houses, it became
quiet and serene. Seagulls would walk along the sand,
picking up the remains of picnics left behind. Wearing a
wide straw hat to protect her skin, Blanche would wander
along barefoot towards East Hampton, picking up shells and
seaweed, enjoying the sensations of the evening sun on her
skin and the warm sand slipping between her toes.

At other times she would sit on one of the sand-dunes and
look out to sea, watching a steamship in the distance, and
wonder where it was going and what it carried on board.
And sometimes she would look out at the horizon and think
about what was beyond that line between sea and sky. A
whole world unknown to her which, some day, she hoped,
she would reach.

This time, Blanche felt a new emotion which unsettled her.

She felt she was the odd one out at this house party. She was too old to join the children, her nephews and nieces, who were shepherded about by a bossy English nanny, and too young to enjoy the company of the adults. Even her own brothers were too old, with a ten-year difference between her and Gil, the younger one.

The highlight of the weekend was a dinner-dance on the Saturday night. The preparations had been going on all day with servants carrying tables outside on to the terrace, and the cooks in the kitchen working as fast as they could to get ready a meal that would feed the fifty guests expected.

The one person Blanche had been looking forward to seeing was her Uncle Hayward. Her mother's younger brother had always been Blanche's favourite. She saw quite a bit of him when she was a child, for he had continued to live in Savannah then, when his brothers had chosen to move north. He was fond of his sister Rose and used to come regularly for Sunday dinner at the house in Duffy Street. Blanche remembered him as someone who was lots of fun, someone who knew how to talk to children, perhaps because he was still a bit of a child himself. She had vivid memories of herself as a little girl balancing on his shoes while he held her hands, then he lifted his feet and walked around like a lumbering giant. He would tickle her under her arms until she begged for mercy, or lift her high on his shoulders and make her feel like a giant herself. Then, as she grew older he still paid her more attention than any child might expect, and he talked to her and asked her about school and her friends and the books she liked to read. Hayward himself was a poet, and he would read poems he had written and ask her what she thought of them. Sometimes he wrote poems about Blanche, which he would read aloud to her until she blushed to the tip of her nose. He gave her volumes of poetry by English poets – Keats, Wordsworth, Shelley and Elizabeth Barrett Browning. 'Poetry gives a language for people's feelings which they cannot express themselves. It takes us away from the mundane things in life,' Hayward would say to her.

Blanche loved Hayward because he never behaved like a grown-up. He responded to life as he came across it, spontaneously and impulsively, like a child. That was what made him so special, and for years Blanche worshipped him. As she had become older and the poetry she read began to stir adult emotions in her, she would dream of marrying Hayward, of having him sweep her up into his arms and kiss her. He was her secret fantasy.

Then he had gone away, moved up north to New Haven. He hardly came down south at all after that. It was such a long way. Now, apart from at her father's funeral six months before, Blanche had not seen him for at least two years. He had seemed uncharacteristically subdued, but then nobody was feeling in an exuberant mood at such a solemn occasion, and Blanche had not thought too much about him, except to observe that he looked very tired, with dark rings under his eyes.

Hayward arrived at the house at about three in the afternoon. Blanche was emerging from her room when she saw him coming up the stairs, the servant behind him carrying his bags.

'Uncle Hayward!' Blanche ran to greet him.

Hayward stopped at the top of the stairs. 'Why, is it Blanche? My, you've grown into a fine young woman!' He picked up her hand and kissed it.

'I've been waiting for you to come,' she said breathlessly. A tide of childish exuberance ran through her as she almost jumped up and down with joy. 'Come on down to the beach, why, it's been a divine day and the crowds will be going soon.'

Hayward looked distracted. He ran his fingers through his hair. 'Yes, I shall, but first I have to have a word with your Uncle Jasper. I really want to speak to him before the festivities begin.' He continued on down the corridor. 'We'll talk later on. I apologise for the rush but it's important that I see him.'

Blanche watched her uncle's back as he went on towards his bedroom, and felt a sad flatness of feeling. She had been so looking forward to seeing her beloved uncle and now he barely had time for her. She had always fancied that she was his favourite in the family, that he would always find time for her. Surely he knew the strength of their bond, surely he valued that? Pushing back a lump in her throat, she walked down the stairs and went outside for a stroll.

When she came back, she walked past Jasper's study. The door was closed but she could hear male voices, raised and excited, first one and then another. She could not hear what they were saying to each other but she knew from the tone that it was not an amicable conversation. Then there was a female voice, Blanche's mother, joining in, soft and gentle, followed by the sound of an angry rebuff.

For a moment, Blanche hovered outside the door. Then a maid appeared carrying candles that were to be placed outside in the garden for the evening. Not wanting to appear a snoop, Blanche walked on down the hall as though she were aware of nothing. She went into the morning-room where she sat looking at a newspaper, while her ears listened out for interesting sounds from the study. She could hear nothing. But suddenly there was the sound of a door opening, an angry voice and hurried footsteps down the hall and up the stairs. Blanche peered through the gap between the door and the door-frame and saw Hayward's figure disappearing from view.

She felt compelled to find out what was going on. She could not stop herself. She crept back up towards Jasper's study. The door was open and now she could hear the conversation clearly. Her mother and Uncle Jasper were talking.

'He's just impossible,' Jasper was saying. 'How old is the man now? Nearly forty? And still as useless as ever. How dare he ask for more money from me! He squandered the last lot, and now it seems he's been borrowing money from you for all this time. Rose, I wish you'd told me what he was up to. I would have put a stop to it immediately.'

Rose's voice was quiet and despairing. 'I just always wanted him to find his feet. He's so convincing when he comes and tells me why he needs funds. I find it impossible to say no.'

'From now on, you're to give him nothing. The man's nothing but a wastrel. He's squandered his legacies, and he's gone through every cent you and I have lent him. And you know where he's spent all that money, don't you?'

There was a pause, then Rose's worried response. 'No, where?'

'In the casinos, and on women.'

'No!' Rose sounded truly shocked.

'I'm afraid those facts have been confirmed to me more than once.'

'Well, what are we to do? Whatever you say about him, I still feel it's our duty to help him sort himself out. I just wish he would find a nice girl and settle down, I'm sure that would make all the difference.'

Jasper snorted. 'What girl is going to want a man like him? He has no profession, no prospects. He's as full of ridiculous dreams as he was when he was twenty. What he fails to see is that most of us can only realise our private dreams through a lot of damned hard work. Hayward's never worked a day in his life. He sneers at good hard-working folk like the rest of us, but he expects us to bail him out whenever things get tough. I can tell you, I've had enough of it. It's embarrassing enough having him living in Manhattan. Too many people know that he's my brother, and I don't think it's good for business.'

'So what can be done? It never seems to end.'

'I have an idea,' said Jasper. 'I'm going to lend him what he asks for.' He let out a sarcastic snort. 'Lend! The very idea of him paying me back makes me laugh! No, I'm prepared to say goodbye to this money on the condition that he moves away from New York, away from the East and goes somewhere thousands of miles away where nobody knows him, or me.'

'Jasper, it seems that all you care about is your reputation.'

Blanche jumped at the loud slap of a hand on a hard surface. 'Goddamn it, Rose, I'm entitled to be worried about my reputation. I've worked hard all these years and I've built a life for myself and my family that I'm proud of. I'm not going to have my youngest brother messing things up for me, causing a rumpus at my club, telephoning my clients and friends, trying to get them involved in his little scams. You have no idea of the extent of his skulduggery, and I have to get rid of him. This is the only way – to bribe him to get out of my world.'

'It makes me so sad,' Rose said. 'When he was young he was so gifted. It seemed that he could do anything he wanted.'

Jasper's voice sounded harsh. 'Yes, perhaps he could

have. But you know, some people never fulfil their potential. It seems that our little brother is one of them. And he's too old to change now.'

Blanche had heard enough. Her heart was thumping in her chest as she crept away and headed to her room by the back stairs. The words she had just overhead spun in her head and her own voice inside was shouting back at them: 'No, no, none of it's true!' She was shocked to hear these things said of Hayward, her dear uncle, who was always so funny and warm and clever. It was true that he never seemed to have employment and spent much of his time enjoying himself, but he was honest and kind, and good to his family. How could they say these things about him?

Blanche sat in her room looking out to sea. The servants were scurrying about the garden preparing for the evening. Her little nephews and nieces were being brought in by the nanny for their supper. Their excited high voices rose up to her window.

This was indeed a shock to Blanche. For years she had idolised Hayward. He was the perfect model for a man. In her young heart she had secretly thought that one day she would marry a man like Hayward – handsome and tall, and full of life and poetry. Yet here she was hearing that he was unsuitable for any respectable girl. And did he really spend money on women? Blanche was not sure what that actually meant but she knew it was not a good thing to do.

The knock on the door from the maid who had come to draw her bath interrupted her thoughts. As she was undressed and bathed, she felt a strong feeling building up inside her, a feeling of anger at the injustice being done to Hayward, these unfair accusations, these unkind words. Why, they were not giving him a chance to prove himself because they did not understand how different he was from them.

Of course he would find the right occupation one day, it was just a matter of time. Then they would be sorry, or then they would appreciate the sort of man Hayward was, and how very special he was.

A family photograph was taken in the afternoon. It took a long time for the photographer to arrange everyone into the pleasing order he wanted. Children kept wriggling and poking one another, while the grown-ups tried not to yawn or look bored. Once it was over, everyone dashed away, looking forward to the fun to come.

The guests started to arrive in the early evening. The house was filling up. A string quartet played in the ballroom, a magician was performing clever tricks in front of an enraptured audience of small children. Men in dinner-jackets and women in long ball-gowns laughed and chatted and drifted around with elegant ease.

An enormous buffet had been laid out in the dining-room. The tables offered platters of shrimp and crab, hopping John, hush puppies, grits, all Southern specialities cooked by Jasper's black cook, Delilah, who was overjoyed to be given the chance to prepare the dishes of her birthplace.

Couples danced in the ballroom or wandered around the grounds of the house, which were lit up by candles and oil lanterns strategically placed around the gardens to cast an eerie glow across the trees and shrubs. Fortunately, although the air was warm, there was enough of a breeze to keep the worst of the bugs away. It could not have been a more perfect night.

Blanche was dressed in a white satin evening-gown, which emphasised her long waist, and sat delicately on her shoulders, showing off her swan neck and strong chest. Her copper hair was pulled up and piled on top of her head. Long white gloves reached her elbows. This was her first grown-up dinner-dance. In Savannah she was used to parties but they were always for people of her age. This time, it was for an older generation. She felt both nervous and excited about it. She was aware of appreciative eyes looking at her, and compliments murmured to her mother. A few young men asked her to dance, and she was proud to be able to waltz and tango with confidence and ease.

In the early evening Hayward sought her out. 'At last, I have the pleasure of your company.' He was smoking a cigarette and drinking a Martini. 'Would you do me the honour?'

For those ten minutes, Blanche was very happy, dancing with her uncle, showing everyone that she was behind him, whatever anyone thought. She looked up at him as she danced. 'It's so good to see you, Uncle Hayward. I've missed you, down in Savannah. You haven't been home for so long.'

Hayward looked over her shoulder and then down at her. 'You're very kind. Not many people feel that way about me any more.'

Blanche felt a blush run over her. Having overheard the conversation between Jasper and her mother earlier, she could not ask in all innocence what he meant. She continued to dance and at the end of it, Hayward pulled away. 'I must leave you to more worthy dancing partners now. I'll see you later.'

For the next few hours, Blanche was in constant demand on the dance-floor. Every now and then she saw Hayward leaning against the door, drinking another Martini and smoking another cigarette. At one moment she thought she saw Jasper watching him with disapproval from across the room, and once she caught her mother staring thoughtfully at him with great concern in her eyes.

Later in the evening, she watched Hayward sitting at a table on the terrace, nursing another drink. He was beginning to look more and more forlorn.

She watched him get to his feet and walk down the garden path to the gate that led out to the beach. As he disappeared from view, Blanche excused herself from her partner and ran down the path after him.

She found him standing on the edge of the water, where the crashing waves reached up the beach and ended in friendly little laps at his feet. He was silhouetted against the sky.

'Uncle Hayward,' she called. 'It's me, Blanche.'

'What do you want? Go away and leave me alone.'

'I came to see if you were okay. You don't seem to be enjoying the party very much.'

Hayward laughed, a dry mocking laugh. 'Why, that's for sure. How can I possibly enjoy a party celebrating the success of my big brother when that same brother has spent the afternoon telling me I'm a failure?'

'Oh, that's so unfair,' said Blanche quietly. 'You're not a failure at all.'

'By his standards I am,' sniffed Hayward.

He turned and held her hands. She could just make out his features in the light cast from the house. 'You don't think I'm a failure, do you, Blanche? You see hope for me yet, don't you?'

It was strange having a grown man suddenly seem so vulnerable, to be asking her for reassurance and support. It made her feel uncomfortable but at the same time important and valuable, someone with her own power to protect him, this poor misunderstood man. 'I'll always believe in you, Uncle Hayward,' she said. 'I'll always be on your side, whatever anyone says about you.'

They stood on the beach for a while, listening to the sound

of the crashing waves mixed with the music and voices drifting down from the house.

A stronger breeze had begun to blow off the sea. Suddenly, Blanche shivered and hugged herself. 'I have to go in, I'm getting chilled out here,' she said.

Hayward turned back to look out to sea. 'I'll stay here,' he said. 'I can't face all those successful, self-satisfied people in there.'

Feeling heavy-hearted, Blanche returned to the house. She felt so impotent, so useless in the face of Hayward's despair. She longed to be able to put everything right for him and make everyone pleased with him.

The party went on into the early hours, the eating and drinking, the dancing. By all accounts it was a great success, a tribute to Jasper, the guests agreed, as they took their cars and carriages home.

When Blanche finally climbed the stairs to go to bed, she was exhausted from the dancing and ready to fall asleep immediately. As she closed the door to her room, she let out a startled cry. In the corner, slumped in a chair, was Hayward.

'What are you doing here?'

Hayward looked up at her with half-open eyes. His speech was slow and slurred. 'You are the only person who has faith in me.' He looked pathetic. 'You are the only person who thinks I have any reason for living.'

Blanche frowned. 'Uncle Hayward, you shouldn't be in here. It's most improper. What would people think?'

Hayward snorted. 'What would people think? I've stopped wondering what anyone thinks, since they only think badly of me. You're my niece, for goodness sakes, there's nothing improper about our having a civilised conversation . . . You're the only member of this family with any sense of the importance of spiritual things, of pleasures beyond material wealth.'

Blanche was feeling very tired. 'I think you should leave and go to bed. I need to sleep now.'

To her dismay, Hayward suddenly broke down and began to sob into his hands. 'Don't throw me out,' he begged, 'not you, too. Let me stay here in this chair for a little while longer. I feel safe here with you. I've promised Jasper that I'll be gone in the morning. It's not long now. I just need to stay for a bit and then I'll go.'

Blanche hesitated. She felt flattered that this man was begging her to let him stay, but shocked at the sight of a grown man sobbing like a child. She bowed her head. 'All right, if you must,' she said quietly, 'but you must leave before the servants get up.'

Blanche had been asleep for half an hour when she was woken by the presence of someone on her bed. As she surfaced from sleep, she remembered leaving Hayward in the chair. Here he was on her bed. She sat up quickly. 'What are you doing?' she hissed. 'Stop it at once.'

'I just want you to hold me,' Hayward whispered pathetically. 'Please just hold me in your arms, just for a little while.'

This grown man was begging her to be maternal, to place her arms around him as she would a child, and comfort him. She did so, and found herself kissing the top of his head gently. 'Everything will be all right,' she said, drifting off to sleep again.

Her sleep was deep. She dreamed that she was dancing faster and faster around the ballroom. She was dancing close to her partner, and she could feel his body pressed against hers, rubbing against her. She was allowing herself to move in time with his movements. His presence was overpowering. She could feel his chin on her shoulder, his hands on her hips.

Then she knew it was not a dream, that she was not dancing. Hayward was behind her, pushing himself against her, between her legs. She let out a cry and twisted round, pushing Hayward away from her. 'Get away!' she hissed at him. 'What are you doing? Get away from me!'

She kicked him hard with her feet.

Hayward tumbled off her. 'I'm sorry, I'm so sorry,' he wailed. 'I didn't mean to, it just happened. I didn't know what I was doing.'

Blanche glared at him. 'Get out!' Her voice was low and fierce. 'I don't want to see you. Get out.'

With a low sigh, Hayward picked up his clothes and quietly left the room dragging his feet in self-pity.

Blanche lay in the dark trembling. She felt very confused, unsure of what had happened, if anything had happened at all. But what she did know was that Hayward had betrayed her. He had taken advantage of her goodwill and kindness. He had used her.

For all these years she had loved him intensely. In some ways she had even been in love with him. From an early age she had felt that Hayward had qualities that were rare in a man – sensitivity, warmth, a genuine interest in her welfare. Ever since she was a little girl, he had represented the sort of man she might want to marry. But not literally.

For all these years, she had heard the family criticisms of his behaviour. Blanche had listened to her mother and uncles bewailing Hayward's faults and shortcomings, and she had always jumped to his defence, convinced that his critics were wrong and that she, only she, really understood him. She had been his staunchest defender, the greatest believer in his talents and his potential. And now he had betrayed her.

She knew what the truth was. She knew that Hayward had taken advantage of her.

Biting her lip, she shut her eyes tight to squeeze back tears. He had violated her. He had assaulted her, he had raped her.

How could he? How could her beloved uncle have done this to her? Surely he had cared for her? Her fists clenched the sheet so hard that her knuckles turned white.

She could hear the maids moving in the corridors, preparing the house for a new day. Blanche's thoughts were a mass of confusion. Panic merged with anger and bitter sadness and the awful realisation that she had been wrong about him for all this time. All her life she had stayed on his side, defending him. Now this was how he repaid her loyalty, by showing that he had no real feelings for her.

Then, as the weak rays of the morning sun flooded the room, something strange happened as she felt an extraordinary lifting of her spirits. Her fists relaxed; her hands opened. There was a solution to this, she thought. If she could believe that nothing had happened, then perhaps the terrible events of the night would disappear. If she never mentioned it to a soul, no one would know. She could make herself believe it was all simply a bad dream to be blotted out of her memory. She could make herself believe anything if she tried hard enough, she thought, rolling over on to her back with a sigh.